Advance Acclaim for *Crooked Lines*

Crooked Lines was a qu̶a̶r̶t̶ ... mazon
Breakthrough Noveli̶

"*Crooked Lines* builds ... ...ragedy,
spirituality and survival ... ...man heart in the face of cruel
adversity lie at the center of this fascinating and ultimately
uplifting novel."
     — EDITH PARZEFALL, AUTHOR OF THE ADVENTURE
TREK SERIES, *CRUMPLE ZONE*, AND *STRAYS OF RIO* (GLOBAL
EBOOK BRONZE AWARD WINNER IN THE THRILLER CATEGORY
2013), CO-AUTHOR OF THE HIGHER GROUND SERIES.

"A beautiful tapestry of God's weaving, Holly Michael's debut
novel *Crooked Lines* will stay with you long after the last page.
The threads gently intertwine as two souls on opposite sides of
the world reach for faith, hope, and love, but the greatest of
these…is love."
     —CARYL MCADOO, CHRISTIAN AUTHOR OF *VOW
UNBROKEN, HEARTS STOLEN*, AND *LADY LUCK'S A LOSER*.

"Two lives, touched with tragedy and despair, meet with hope
that God isn't finished. A tender, heartfelt, but ultimately faith
affirming story."
     — RACHELLE AYALA, AUTHOR OF *MICHAL'S WINDOW,
BROKEN BUILD, HIDDEN UNDER HER HEART, KNOWING VERA,
TAMING ROMEO*, AND *WHOLE LATTE LOVE*

"Fascinating blend of two cultures and two life paths in a well-
written, inspirational story that puts God in the middle of their
hearts' desires and making Him the ultimate match-maker."

— RICK BYLINA, AUTHOR OF *ONE PROMISE TOO MANY, A MATTER OF FAITH, ALL OF OUR SECRETS,* AND *SHORTS: BATHROOM READING: SHORT STORIES FOR SHORT VISITS* AND *POEMS FOR A PLATYPUS.*

"*Crooked Lines* is a beautifully crafted story spanning two continents."

— RASANA ATREYA, AUTHOR OF AMAZON BESTSELLER *TELL A THOUSAND LIES,* SHORTLISTED FOR THE 2012 TIBOR JONES SOUTH ASIA AWARD.

"From opposite sides of the world, two teens skitter stones over the top of water. When they take their place in the adult world, the author reveals with an amazing understanding how, although the depths of their lives swirl with different challenges, kindred spirits float over the sea of life."

— FRANCENE STANLEY, AUTHOR OF THE FANTASY SERIES: *STILL ROCK WATER & TIDAL SURGE* - SOLSTICE PUBLISHING. CO-AUTHOR OF THE DYSTOPIAN SERIES: *WIND OVER TROUBLED WATERS, KNIGHTS IN DARK LEATHER, GOLDEN SUBMARINE* AND *LONG DOOM CALLING,* RELEASED BY DOUBLE DRAGON PUBLISHING.

Crooked Lines

Holly Michael

Ad Majorem Dei Gloriam Publishing

Published by AMDG Publishing

© 2014 by Holly Michael
First Edition
September 2014
Printed and bound in the United States of America

Cover Art by Kirk Dou Ponce of Dogeared Design, Woodland Park, CO
www.dogeareddesign.com
Interior Book Design by Lee Carver

ISBN-13: 978-0692259894

To contact the author for speaking engagements please visit
www.HollyMichael.com

Dedication

To God who never let me let go of Him, to my mother who gives the best hugs, to my husband, Bishop Leo Michael, for his constant love and never-ending support, and to my children, Jake, Betsy, and Nick. And of course, my many critique partners and fellow writers who encouraged me along the way. I thank you all.

"God Writes Straight Through Crooked Lines."
– Proverb

"And we know that all things work together for good to those who love God, to those who are the called according to His purpose." Romans 8:28 (NKJV)

One

The End of Childhood

"All you need is the plan, the road map,
and the courage to press on to your destination."
~ Earl Nightingale

Rebecca Meyer
White Gull Bay, Wisconsin
Summer 1985

It didn't occur to me at the edge of the pond that I'd broken the sixth commandment, actually committed murder. I was busy working out a deal with God, swearing to Jesus I'd become a nun if He helped me breathe life back into my baby sister's limp body. At the time, it didn't matter that I wasn't Catholic.

Now, a week after the funeral, Mama set me straight while flipping pancakes in the kitchen. "Daddy blames you for Kara's death." She said it like I'd let the milk spoil because I hadn't put it back in the fridge, but the weight of her words cemented my bare feet to the green linoleum.

She reached for a platter and set it under the open window. The morning sun highlighted old stains, batter spills, and cracks on the brown laminate countertop. A cool morning draft rustled the faded yellow gingham curtains. Mama got a deal on that material from Woolworths before Kara was born. Along with curtains, she sewed four sundresses for each of my sisters and me. It wasn't fair that the fabric was still with us, fluttering over the sink, yet Kara came and went as quickly as the wind.

Mama transferred pancakes to the plate.

My plan to breeze through the kitchen and escape the house unnoticed should have succeeded because for a week, I'd been a ghost. None of the people in the house—my parents or any of my brothers and sisters—spoke to me. I'd lived a cloistered existence with my blue notebook and unsettling thoughts.

Now, I only wanted to sit under the maple, read the Kara stories, and wind back time.

I tightened my arms around the notebook, holding it to my heart like a talisman, as if my words of love for my sister could erase the raw sting of truth in Mama's words. Since that day at the pond, I'd been carrying that notebook everywhere, even sleeping with it. In my lake of sadness, in my whirling murky thoughts, those sacred pages had become my life preserver.

Mama snapped the griddle knob off and faced me. "We left her with you that morning. She was only seven." Her words rushed out in a seething whisper. My shoulders fell and hope slid from them and disappeared out the kitchen window.

Only a month ago in my white cotton confirmation dress, I cited the Ten Commandments and professed my faith at St. Andrew's Lutheran Church.

So confident. So holy. Mama baked a cake.

Now, because of me, Kara was dead. I tugged a loose string on the frayed edges of my cut-offs, then looked back up at Mama. Her short blonde hair was a tangled mess. Her red-streaked eyes shot angry darts laced with sadness. C'mon Mama. Don't you get it? The deep muddy waters consumed Kara. She's gone, but I'm here, still drowning.

I ran my big toe over a rip in the linoleum, wanting to bolt, take off and run as far and fast as my long legs would carry me, but Mama's eyes told me she had more to dish out. I sucked in my breath, stuck out my chin, and met her stare, my five-foot eight-inch frame matching hers. I could take it.

But she walked away, left me standing there. Every fiber in my soul told me to run after her, beg forgiveness, and cling to her legs until she hugged me and told me everything would be okay. That's what mothers were supposed to do. But no longer a child, those days were over. I winced when the slam of her bedroom door, like a gavel, sentenced me.

"Becca, bring the pancakes." Tom rose from the dining room chair and waved his fork.

"Hurry up!" Bobby pounded a fist on the oak table. "I'm starved."

At least one thing at home remained the same; after morning barn chores, my brothers only cared about food.

My limbs loosened. With shaking hands, I grabbed the platter, set it on the table, then tore up the stairs—two at a time. I didn't look at my brothers. They probably blamed me, too.

In my bedroom, I kicked a pile of dirty clothes and hit something solid, a tennis shoe. I crouched and peeked under my bed. The other. Good.

I kissed the notebook, then stuck it under my pillow. I'd started writing Kara stories in it a week before she died—the funny and intuitive stuff she'd said and done. I even taped her photos inside the pages. How could I have known to do that right before she died?

Tugging on my shoes, I wondered if the Holy Spirit had prompted me to create the Kara notebook when I was still a child of God. He'd visited me once. I remembered Him, not ghostly and elusive, but someone so real. Someone who loved me.

When I was six, He came to me in the meadow. I danced and sang for Him. I couldn't see Him, but He was there. In my yellow butterfly dress, I laughed and twirled with the dandelion seeds, my blond hair bouncing in the breeze as I basked in His immense love. I stretched my hands high and offered songs of thanks for the creator of the ladybugs, the zippy dragonflies, and the warm summer sun.

God knew me. I knew Him.

But that was then.

I rested my foot on the vanity bench, tied my laces, then looked into the mirror. Eyes dull and ringed by dark circles stared at me, not my bright green ones. Since that day at the pond, I slept in fitful interludes in the hallway in front of the door, me and the notebook with my pillow and a blanket.

I wanted to sleep in my bed, but Kara and I had shared the room since she was born. Every night she left her bed, crossed the room, stood beside me, and called my name until I woke and lifted the covers, inviting her in.

Standing outside the door each night, my fears would grow and shrink me from a teenager into a child, scared Kara's ghost would come knocking.

What if she came to my bedside and called my name? Would her eyes have the same accusing stare as Mama's had? Did she hate me, too?

Chills tickled the back of my neck. I yanked the other shoestring tight, then fled downstairs and out the front door. At the end of the driveway, I turned and ran past the silos toward Lake Michigan. Tears blurred my vision as I ran past fields and farmhouses, cows and cornfields, apple orchards and cherry trees. I ran past evergreens, Indian Paintbrushes, Queen Anne's

Lace, and Black-eyed Susans. Fuzzy cattails poked from marshy lowlands.

Miles later, when grassy ditches turned sandy and the scent of pine replaced the earthy smell of cow manure, I slowed. At Evergreen Lane, I shoved the bad stuff out of my head, leaned against the weathered fence post, and kicked off my shoes.

Summer bungalows loomed over the tops of cedars on both sides of the gravel pathway that allowed public access to the beach. A few silhouettes—like mannequins in store-fronts—faced the lake. Who were they? What did they think? And where would they fly back to before the first flakes of winter fell. Those lucky visitors came to the peninsula of White Gull Bay to escape from places I'd never been, places I'd always longed to run to.

The whoosh and trickle of the whispering waves beckoned me to the shoreline. Gulls screeched and circled around dead glittering minnows. Chilly water rolled over my feet and lapped my ankles.

I scanned the beach for glass stones, bent over and picked up a round flat black one. I tried to skip it, but it sailed straight into a small cresting wave. No luck today.

A long ship crept across the horizon, cutting a path between the cerulean sky and the blue-green lake. Next week, Daddy would be out there sailing on one of those iron-ore freighters. He only came home when November gales churned the icy waters and during spring planting and fall harvest—and for a death.

I watched the vessel disappear until guilt rode on the waves like bobbing driftwood and landed on the shore before me. Daddy would miss Kara sitting on his lap on the John

Deere. I didn't blame him for hating me. I didn't blame Mama. Kara was the baby, the ninth. I was the seventh. Seven wasn't a lucky number.

My legs quivered. I sat, hugging my knees. Tears plopped tiny craters in the sand. I was guilty. A sinner with no hope because it was worse than anyone knew. I couldn't admit to anyone all that had happened at the edge of the pond. How could I say I knew Kara would die that day and I did nothing to stop it? How could I talk about the way I freaked out and ran away when I saw her form in the murky water, even though I knew I'd find her there?

My childhood was over.

"Where do I go from here?" A wave rolled in and nearly swallowed my small voice.

Ignoring the plaintive cries from the screeching gulls, I stood, straightened my shoulders and looked to the horizon. Only two more years of high school. I'd plan. Work hard. I had one thing going for myself. Everyone considered me the smart one because I got good grades and read a gazillion books. Yes, I was smart, smart enough to figure out my escape. I'd find a place of peace, far from White Gull Bay and the awful stuff I'd done.

Then, I'd find someone, somewhere, who'd love me.

Sagai Raj

Sheveroy Hills, Tamil Nadu, South India
Summer 1985

"Sagai, wake up. It's time."

He opened his eyes. His father, kneeling on the dirt floor beside his reed mat, held out a small tin cup. Sagai reached for the milky sweet coffee. In the soft glow of the hurricane lamp, he sat, sipped, and glanced around the room at the curled, sleeping forms.

His father struggled to his feet with a grunt. Limping since last year's bicycle accident at Little Lake, he hobbled toward the door, lifted the metal latch, and disappeared into the predawn darkness. Sagai admired the elder man's quiet noble manners, his wise words, and the kindness he showed toward everyone. Had he caused his worry?

He slid his hand under his mat and pulled out the invitation. After a month at camp, he'd been chosen. He'd been carrying the postcard around for a week, praying his father would give his blessings. Time was running out, school would begin soon, and his destiny did not lie in Sheveroy Hills.

Soft snores from his mother and siblings filled the room. He stepped around them, kissed his fingertips, then touched the Sacred Heart of Jesus picture on the wall by the doorway, as he did every day.

In the small courtyard, the cow mooed and shifted, full with milk. "Don't worry Muttura Madu, you'll be milked soon."

He stepped beside his father, almost shoulder to shoulder now. Appa heaved a deep sigh, then turned and faced him with an outstretched palm.

"Appa?" Sagai rested his hand on top, then his father covered it. An unspoken message of love. Top hand covering and protecting, the bottom holding and supporting.

"You're my seventh child. Seven is a good number, a heavenly number. My hope was that you, the smart one, could become a doctor and help the family—"

"But—"

Appa raised a finger. "—but God has a different plan." His tone sounded peaceful, accepting. "Now, run along."

He let go of the breath he was holding. "I may go? Truly?"

"Yes, son. You may go. You will leave on Saturday."

Sagai bent down and touched Appa's cracked calloused feet. He pressed the postcard to his pounding chest, then returned to the house and tucked it in the edge of the framed picture of Jesus. He rushed outside, said goodbye to his father, and stepped onto the narrow cobblestone road. Unable to hold back any longer, bubbling laughter rose from his chest and escaped into the misty morning air. He raised his arms toward heaven as he ran, thanking God for this true blessing.

For the past eight years, God's love had pulsed through his soul, fueling his zeal as he ran the four miles each way, every morning. God's love came with the morning's rays, His kiss in the whisper of a breeze on hot afternoons, His presence in the mist that settled over the Tamil Nadu hill station at dusk. And as Sagai sloshed through pounding rains during monsoon season on roads reduced to muddy footpaths, the Lord never left his side.

Now, Sagai's smile wrapped around his heart and traveled to his feet, hastening his momentum. The five o'clock Muslim call for prayer reverberated in the hills when the road became packed dirt. The chants, low and monotone, interrupted the lulling crickets and broke the sleepy quietness of the night.

He ran over another hill, then down, leaping over slushy mud holes in low areas.

A cock crowed. Another answered, encouraging dawn to break. They always crowed right before his half-way point—the Hindu shrine. At the base of the huge Banyan tree with its intertwining aerial root vines dwelled a Hindu deity, a huge cobra coiled in a snake pit. A shock of hair tacked to the tree indicated a recent exorcism. Instead of speeding past in fear of the snake striking his legs, Sagai stopped. At age fifteen, about to leave home forever, he shouldn't shake like a small child at this place.

Today, he would defeat his fear. Under the dim streetlamp, he forced his gaze into the ebony eyes of one of the two angry soldier statues that guarded their deity. A tongue sticking out from the huge oblong face challenged him.

Frowning, he looked from one statue to the other. "You two aren't so frightful."

A rustling in the bushes shot a jolt of fear through him that rattled his bones and made his heart nearly thump out of his chest. He tore past the shrine, made the sign of the cross and sent a flying prayer to Jesus. On the way back, in daylight, he'd look those horrible fellows in the eye and tell them he wasn't frightened of them or the snake.

Alongside the old stone fence dripping with purple bougainvillea, he ran. Tamil hymns blasted from homes and out of church doors. *O Jesus you are my all. O what a joy…* Only the Protestants could shower the streets with their hymns like that. The tune stuck in his head all the way to Little Lake, where dawn had painted a pale orange streak over the calm surface.

Fascination and fear of Little Lake slowed his pace. Last month his cousin happened upon a dead body floating in the water. The source of life-giving water lured suicidal villagers as well as recreation seeking Brits and rich Indians who came to Sheveroy Hills for holiday. Their grand bungalows stood like jewels around the lake.

He often wondered what their eyes beheld when they looked out from their fancy homes. Did they see his cousin, the boatman who offered a leisurely ride for two rupees? Did they notice Sagai and his brothers catching fish for Amma's curry? Where did these visitors return to when God breathed His peace into them from this fertile hill station of monasteries, convents, and spirituality centers?

Bells chimed from the tower of the Catholic mission church, alerting Sagai. Six chimes meant he must arrive at the silver Mahatma Gandhi statue in the town center. He ran...one...two...three...faster....four...five...and six. Gandhi came into sight.

He ran past the statue, past Jack fruit trees, past cypress entwined with pepper vines, and orange groves. A grey stone fence, now speckled with tiny blue flowers continued to snake along the curvy pebbly road. At Pullathachimedu, Pregnant Ladies Hill, he sped by the resting stone. No time to rest. The bell at the novitiate gonged. Fifteen minutes to go. The white steeple spiked over the top of the umbrella trees, sliced with morning sunbeams and decorated with bright orange flowers.

Reaching the wicket gate just in time, he witnessed nearly one hundred novices in habits, slightly bowing and silently processing, two by two, into the church. He slipped in after them. Mosaic tiles cooled his tired bare feet. Thanks to

God and his landmarks, he'd made it on time to assist Father Louis at Mass.

In the sacristy, Sagai tightened the cincture rope around the red cassock, then pulled on his white surplice. When a very small boy, he had held mock Mass at home. Amma would pin one towel to his front and one to his back—his chasuble. Circles cut from cardboard served as the host, fruit juice as wine. He'd light two candles and arrange everything on a small table. Vijay, his younger brother, acted as altar server. By age six, he had memorized all of the prayers of the Mass.

Now, ready for the real service, Sagai knelt before the crucifix and promised to stay on his path toward holiness and keep all of God's commandments. He rose when Father Louis arrived to vest, and handed the priest his cincture, stole, and chasuble.

After the service, Sagai shuffled his bare feet in the dirt at the wicket gate, watching the retinue of nuns file into the refectory. Waiting made him feel like a beggar. If he left, Sister Mercy would think her daily offering of a few slices of bread was not appreciated.

Peals of laughter drew his attention across the road. The private school had already begun their quarter. Two enormous lion statues guarded the compound beside the white pillars that shot up to a high arch where St. Alban watched over the village hill station atop a golden dome. Fenced in by black wrought iron, school children—Brits and rich Indians—in suit jackets, ties and long pants, trickled out of the dormitory for breakfast.

Sagai slid his hand inside his shirt where the two buttons were missing, then tugged the frayed edges of his faded shorts, patched in the back. Sometimes after serving at Mass he'd watch the boys put on leg pads and knee guards, and use real bats on their lush green field. At his school, on the other side of the village, they used a flat stick and played cricket barefoot on a rocky uneven patch.

Hoofs tapped the hard packed dirt road. A cow plodded past.

Sagai rubbed his rumbling stomach and returned to the wicket gate. He was tempted to pluck fruit from the guava tree, or at least pick up one of the many that lay on the ground rotting, but that would be stealing. A sin. The cow, not knowing better, could eat the fallen fruit. He should not.

He knelt and picked up a small round stone and rolled it in his hand. Perfect ammunition. Those pesky monkeys, now awake and watchful, were known thieves. Would knocking one of those screeching troublemakers out of a tree be a sin? Before he could ponder further, a young novice approached, smiling.

"For you." She smiled and handed him a package.

"Thank you." An entire loaf of bread. Enough to share with all at home. Sister Mercy must have asked her to give it to him. The novice bowed, nodded, and walked away.

Before he could run, Sister Mercy marched toward him. She eyed the loaf tucked under his arm. Her nostrils flared. Smack. Her palm cracked against his cheek.

"Thief!"

"No, Sister." He pointed, blinking back tears. "That novice gave it to me."

Sister Mercy wagged her finger. "Even so, you know that I usually give you bread. You should not have accepted it." She snatched the loaf from Sagai and thrust her slices at him.

He turned and ran all the way to Little Lake without stopping, horrified he'd be branded a thief. Would his future lie in jeopardy?

On the grass beside the water, he stared at the bread. He never went to church to get free bread. He went to serve. He rubbed his cheek. A monkey eyed him from a rock. Sagai tossed the bread. "Have it. I don't want it."

He wouldn't mention the incident to anyone. He prayed that Sister Mercy wouldn't report it to Father Louis.

A flat black stone caught Sagai's eye. He skipped it on the lake. One, two, three, four times it bounced before sinking. Lucky day. He leapt to his feet and ran toward home. God would make sure his dream came true. He'd been chosen. He would go to seminary and become a priest. His older brothers and sisters dropped out of school by seventh standard, but surely Vijay would do the needful—finish school, and go to college. He must. Someone had to take care of the family. His place was no longer in Sheveroy Hills.

Two

A New Way

Let your heart guide you. It whispers, so listen carefully.
~ Littlefoot's mother, Land Before Time

Rebecca

I ran my fingers through the dust motes floating in the late morning rays, squinting to focus on them instead of the empty cot across the room. Determined to be brave, last night I left the hallway and returned to my bedroom with a little help from The Beatles—cassettes left behind when my older sisters moved away. They sang "Golden Slumbers," telling me to sleep and not cry, promising a lullaby. This morning the Fab Four prophesied that I'd carry my weight for a long time. I could worship them. They knew me.

I pulled my knees to my chest. Couldn't turn back time. I wouldn't spend evenings reading storybooks to Kara until she fell asleep. I wouldn't wake to soft whispers of "Becca," then lift the covers for my little sister to slide in and snuggle. She wouldn't be tapping my arm when the tip of the sun kissed the corn field. What would life be like now?

The Beatles, now hailing the coming sun, didn't know it all. Everything was not alright. I flipped onto my stomach, stretched to shut off the boom box, then stuck my hand under my mattress and pulled out the notebook. I'd begin my days reading a Kara story so I'd never forget her.

I read the skunk story, then closed my eyes, reliving that evening.

I'd just put Kara's pajamas on when Bobby and Tom
hollered and Sparky barked like crazy. I snatched up Kara,
rushed down the stairs, and out the front door.

"What's up?"

Bobby pointed to the open garage door. "Skunk! We
sent Sparky in to get him!"

"Sic em, Sparky," Tom yelled. "Kill that good-for-
nothing critter."

Kara twisted from my arms and ran inside.

A minute later, Sparky ran out of the garage, followed
by the skunk, then Kara.

"Bad Sparky." She shook her small pointer finger.

I grabbed my baby sister and hugged her, grateful she
hadn't been harmed or sprayed. "I thought you went inside
because you were scared. You could have gotten hurt! Did you
go into the garage through the laundry room?"

She nodded. "Poor skunk." Her almond-shaped eyes
glistened, full of pity for the underdog. That extra-chromosome
must have enlarged her heart. She was pure love, and every
living creature, her friend.

That happened last month, a lifetime ago. I leaned back
against my pillows. Now, Kara was gone. Sparky too. She was
supposed to be in heaven and maybe our dog, too, but
embracing the concept of heaven was like believing one of the
floating dust specks was a planet and Kara lived on it with
Cindy Lou Who.

I closed the notebook and tossed off my covers. Not a
sound in the house. Over the years, vacuums and voids in our
farmhouse increased with each sibling's leaving. The day
Mama said she was pregnant again, my oldest sister threw her
fork on the table, swore in front of everyone, then announced

she was leaving and not taking care of any more brats. She fled to San Francisco with her hippie boyfriend before Kara was born. When Mama placed my baby sister in my arms for the first time, all soft and pinky-sweet, I promised God I'd love her, take care of her, and never call her a brat.

The others went their own ways, graduating, getting married, moving. Besides me, only three remained home: Tom, Bobby, and Heather, who was two years younger than me. My older brothers, who both dropped out of school, would be milking cows now. The others had gone back to their lives after the funeral.

A door squeaked in the hallway. I shut off my boom box and found Heather sitting on the top stair, resting her head in her hands. She met my eyes with a pained expression.

I slid beside her and touched her arm. "Are you missing Kara, too?"

She bristled. "Don't want to talk about it."

I shrugged. I rolled my sweatshirt sleeves up, then unrolled them. After several moments of silence, I glanced sideways at Heather, then cleared my throat. "Besides babysitting, I'll be looking for a job next week. Maybe two jobs."

Heather stared at her tennis shoes.

"How 'bout you?"

She sighed.

"You're old enough to work during cherry picking season. If you pick fast enough, you can make good money. I made enough to buy my bike when I was your age."

"No."

"Well, I'm not staying around here forever. I want to go to college, maybe join the Peace Corps—"

"Who cares?" Heather stood abruptly and rushed down the stairs.

My heart should be numb by now, but it wasn't. Silence stabbed. Harsh words, too. I blinked back tears, returned to my room, and hoisted the wooden window frame. Each time I reached out to Heather, she pushed me away.

The front door slammed. I watched her yank her bike from the side of the garage and pedal down the road until I couldn't see her anymore.

Dewy morning air filled my lungs. A lonely cow offered a low bellow from the back pasture. Outside, everything seemed normal, except for the absence of Sparky barking his response to the cow. He went missing the day Kara died. Nobody talked about Kara or Sparky. Nobody talked.

And the silence deepened the empty hole left by Kara's death. How big and deep would the empty hole grow before I caved inside of it?

I reached for the boom box, hoping music might fill the void. The Beatles assured me all I needed was love. They were right. My unconditional source of love was Grandma. If I didn't hang on to love, darkness would destroy the little bit of me that was left. I tossed off my pajamas, pulled on jeans and a t-shirt, and ran next door to the trailer beside our farmhouse.

On the other side of the screen door, Grandma, in her faded flowery housecoat, rocked in her chair.

She lifted her head. "Rebecca?"

Although nearly blind from diabetes, she always knew it was me at the door. If I had a question, from how to tie my shoes to why God lets innocent children die, I'd take it to Grandma. Though she didn't belong to any particular church, she knew stuff. When I was a little kid, she'd always answer

God questions with sensible answers, like, "Yes, you can squish spiders, even though God made them. Some creatures were made for squishing." Then she'd hug me and tell me that I was made for hugging.

I approached her, squeezed her hand, and settled into the comfort of our wordless connection, cross-legged at her feet. After a few minutes I began forming and reforming about twenty questions, a half a dozen different ways, in my head. Finally, I spoke. "That day…when…Kara…when I came here…."

"Spit it out child." Grandma never minced her words.

"Remember when I…I…told you what happened to Kara? You just nodded. You said you knew." I picked up her spotted wrinkled hand, held it in mine, then looked into her glossy, foggy eyes. "How did you know?"

Grandma closed her eyes. "I just knew."

"But no one had come to tell you what had happened yet. How could you know?"

"I just did."

My heart hammered against my chest. I had to tell her more. Had to find out more. Mama always said Grandma had an uncanny sixth sense. She always said I was most like Grandma. Did she, like me, receive a supernatural message that that sunny morning was doomsday?

I twisted a length of my hair and stared at the floor. "I knew too. I mean, even before I found her. Grandma, I knew." My words rolled out in a rush of unbridled emotion. "When I was searching for Kara, I hollered for Sparky, thinking he'd come running and lead me to Kara because he never left her side." I paused to catch a breath. Grandma's eyes brimmed with tears, but I had to confess the rest because only she would believe me and understand.

"Then it happened, Grandma. While I was in the back field, shouting Kara's name, it was kind of like a lightning bolt flew out of the sky, hit me on the head, traveled right through me, and dropped me to my knees in the dirt. But there wasn't any lightning, only a freaky force that zapped through me and left me with a memory of what I was about to see. It was like I'd leapt ahead into the future and knew everything." I dropped my head into her lap and sobbed.

"Shh…shhh…it's okay." Grandma stroked my hair.

"Why?" I looked up. "Why did that happen?"

She sniffed. "Because your eyes see more than what is in front of you."

"But I didn't save Kara." I wanted to tell Grandma about how I went straight to the pond and saw Kara's form in the murky water and how I screamed only no sound came out of my mouth, just like in nightmares. Even though I knew I'd find my little sister there, I couldn't bring myself to pull her out. I didn't dare tell her that I ran away with my legs moving in slow motion, like my feet were stuck in cement. I didn't know how many minutes wasted away before I found Tom by the barn and yelled for him to get Mama and come to the pond. I ran back and forced myself to drag Kara out of that dark water, but by then it was too late. I didn't tell Grandma about her blue face and those eyes, clouded and staring at nothing, almost like the tired old eyes I looked into now.

I lowered my head. I wanted to tell her more about what else had happened earlier that morning, about why it really was my fault that Kara died, but she was all that I had left and she might not love me anymore if she knew the whole story.

Instead, I said, "Sparky is gone. I haven't seen him since that morning."

Sagai

Sagai hoisted himself onto the cement courtyard wall, climbed onto the tin roof of his house and peered over the top of the guava tree, searching the hills for Tiny.

His beloved mutt led the procession each evening. First dog, then goats, next the cow, then Amma, who'd bring the grazing animals home after her long day's work as nurse at the government hospital.

A thousand worries fell on his head. Who would watch and wait for Amma after he was gone? Who would take care of the family? Would Vijay go back to school? Just when the thrill of tomorrow's journey made him feel as though he could soar like the long-winged kite bird, worries about home weighed him down.

A song from the radio inside filtered upward. *Ellaam Yesuve, enakkellam Yesuve, Thollai migu ivvulagil thunai Yesuve.* With hope swelling his heart, Sagai swayed and sang along with the high-pitched melodious Tamil hymn, *"In this troubled world, only you are my friend...to me everything is you, O Jesus."* He offered his cares to the Lord.

The sweet fragrance of jasmine mingled with stench from the cow dung pit and drifted upward on a gentle breeze. Tomorrow his older brother would pluck the tiny white flowers for his wife. His sisters would string them into garland. New brides were required to wear flowers in their hair every day for at least one year. Soon the year would be over and the new bride would be more concerned with the child she now carried. When would he return home to see his new nephew or niece? So many unknowns.

An irritated cluck from a nesting chicken below, a grunt, and a bang on the tin roof interrupted his thoughts.

Vijay's leg appeared first, then his head. "No Amma yet?"

Sagai offered his hand and pulled his brother up. "Not yet."

"Are you still angry, *Anna*?" Vijay touched his shoulder.

The respectful term for "big brother" made him cover his smile with one hand. Vijay felt guilty. Good. His little brother ought to feel shame and change his ways, but he didn't want to leave with an unresolved quarrel between them. "No *Thambi*." He teasingly used the formal term for 'little brother.' Only, I'm concerned for you. School starts soon and you must go and do well in your studies. Racing old cycle tires with a stick all day will not help the family. Do you want to be sixth grade fail?"

Vijay knelt and gathered chilies that were left drying on the roof. He placed them in his cupped T-shirt. "What's the use? I got too far behind last quarter. Appa says it's a miracle I survived typhoid fever. My friend Jai wasn't so lucky."

"I miss Jai, too, but you are healthy now. You should not use that excuse to get Appa and Amma to coddle you like a baby. School starts next week. You must go."

"Don't need school." Vijay stood and rolled the end of his shirt to secure the chilies.

"That's what our older brothers said and now they are earning very little. Don't you want a well-paying job someday? Maybe go to college?"

"You are the one who receives high marks and makes first rank distinction every time. Not me."

"But I'm leaving and cannot help the family." The house was growing crowded, especially with the addition of his brother's wife and a baby on the way. His oldest sister was angry because Appa hadn't yet found a suitable marriage partner. The reason for the delay—lack of sufficient dowry. Where would they find dowry for his other four sisters? They were not wage earners and would all go off to live with husbands' families, if Appa found them alliances.

Vijay's stomach rumbled. "I hope Amma returns soon I won't die."

"You won't die." Sagai shook his head. His brother's stomach ruled him.

A high yapping sounded in the distance.

"Tiny!" Vijay slid off the roof. "Amma's coming. I'll inform the others."

Sagai lowered himself from the rooftop and leapt over drying coffee beans strewn into the street, avoiding the sharp edges that pricked through the rough flesh on his feet. He walked past the trees toward the well. A Brahmin Hindu woman drew water and spoke in a low tone to a Muslim lady. He said hello and nodded.

Beyond the well, Amma and her entourage appeared under the dim light of the street lamp. Her rosary dangled from the crook of her elbow while she struggled with an armload of fodder she'd gathered along the way.

"*Stholthiram* Amma!" He lifted the long grass from her arms. The ladies at the well also greeted her. She had delivered their babies and they respected her.

"Amma, why so late?" Sagai scratched Tiny behind his ears.

"Babies come in their own time." Lines around her eyes crinkled, always happy after delivering a baby.

Many times, a late night shout from outside would rouse his mother and she'd rush off without complaint. The only nurse in the region, she always helped others and never accepted a rupee. She cared for everyone else, but her absence at home was taken advantage of by those like Vijay who would rather play than go to school. But what could he do? He could no longer be his brother's keeper.

Amma led the cow into the shed alongside the house, then tugged the rickety wooden gate shut.

"A baby was giving trouble, like you did." Amma clicked her tongue. "Such a big baby you were."

The moon spilled silver light onto the cobblestones in the courtyard and he caught the wistful glint in her eyes. He waited patiently while she retold his birth story.

"Terrible delivery. Oy-yo. I wondered if either of us would survive. I asked your grandmother for the picture of Our Lady of Perpetual Help, placed it over my stomach and prayed to Mother Mary. 'If this baby is born, I will give him to God,' I said. Then one more push, and out you came."

His name meant "perpetual help." Maybe when the image of Mother Mary rested on mother's abdomen, the desire to serve God imprinted upon his heart. For as long as he could remember, he felt called to serve God.

Amma tousled Sagai's curls and ducked, stepping over the threshold of the dimly lit smoky house, pungent with the smell of fish. Out of hunger and devotion, everyone in the house quickly dropped to their knees before the crucifix. Always prayers before dinner. Amma began. "Hail Mary…"

Somewhere between the fourth and fifth decade of the rosary prayers, Vijay leaned against him.

Sagai elbowed him.

Vijay straightened and whacked the back of his head. Amma, never taking her eyes off the Lord, grabbed a mango from the windowsill and flung it. They both ducked and continued. "Holy Mary, Mother of God, pray for us sinners…."

After dinner, Sagai approached his mother at the bedside of his ill grandmother. Amma squeezed a lime into the curative mixture of betel leaf and areca nut. His *thathi* had no teeth so Amma ground the mixture with pestle and mortar. She stuck the mixture into Thathi's mouth and wiped drips of dark juice with a cloth. "When you were born, your grandfather spit on his finger, stuck it into your mouth and said, 'this child will be like me'."

Thathi pressed her hand over her heart. "Your *thatha,* Balu, God rest his soul, always listened to his heart and gained the wisdom of angels." She made the sign of the cross. "He was a wise, powerful man. Even as coffee estate owner, he'd take off his suit and work in the fields in only his loincloth. Uncle has sold off most of the property and reduced the remainder to weeds." Amma lifted her palms upward, as if Grandfather listened from heaven.

"Once, Thatha dreamt that one of his workers was crushed by a large boulder. The next day he worked close to the man. When a boulder rolled down the hillside toward them, he shoved the man out of the way, saving his life. Dreams are the language of God, you know."

Sagai nodded. "The day Appa met with that accident at Little Lake, a bad feeling had settled in my mind. All day I'd worried something might befall him."

"Did you pray?" She asked in her raspy, rattling voice.

"Yes, Thathi."

She shot Amma a knowing look. "Then you did what God wanted you to do."

"God gave me those bad feelings?"

Amma thumped her fingers on his chest. "Only because He knows you have a heart with deep pockets for loving. He knows you will listen to Him and pray. Your prayers may have kept something far worse from happening."

Sagai smiled and lay down on his mat. He slipped off peacefully, comforted knowing he'd received the same special gift God gave his grandfather.

Morning came soon and all at home woke early to bid Sagai goodbye. Vijay promised he'd go back to school. Kneeling for his grandmother's blessing, he wondered if he'd ever see her again. If he held them all close to his heart, they'd never be too far from him. He'd pray for them every day.

"Whatever is God's will for you, so be it." Amma kissed the top of his head, then turned to climb the long hill to the hospital. When she disappeared around a corner, he wiped a tear.

He and his father walked to the bus stop in silence. Tiny followed close behind. The exciting tug of his new life wrestled with sad goodbyes. He hugged Appa, then stepped onto the awaiting bus and slid into a gray cracked plastic seat closest to the driver. He lifted the corner of his shirt and scrubbed dirt from the window and studied his father's face so he would never forget him. Appa nodded from the street side, forcing the lines of his mouth into his typical slanted grin. Tiny cocked his head.

Sagai pressed his hand to the glass as the bus lurched forward. Street dogs darted from underneath its shade. The driver weaved the bus around cows that plodded at their own pace. A goat, chewing trash, stared from the roadside.

Through the filmy window of the sweltering sweat-stinky crowded bus, he watched the road as the vehicle slowed around hairpin curves and descended toward Salem. The thrill of his future diminished his sadness with each bend in the road. God would be with him on this journey.He would become a priest!

Three

Loneliness

"The most terrible poverty is loneliness, and the feeling of being unloved."
~ Mother Teresa

Rebecca

Grandma got out of hell. That's what I thought after her casket was lowered in the semi-frozen ground beside Kara's plot, dug only eight months earlier.

When I was little, I asked Grandma about hell while helping fold laundry over the dining room table. "Hell is a place where God does not exist." She stacked a t-shirt on a pile.

Sugar was her poison and after Kara died, Grandma consumed it like she wanted to join my little sister. I'd visited every day, brought meals, sat with her, and helped her into bed at night. In the daytime, she rocked, cried, and picked scabs on her flabby old arms, her blind eyes fixed in far-away places. I didn't mourn for her now. She wanted out of hell. I had peace about her passing. Not about Kara's.

At the minister's final words, Heather's bottom lip quivered. I reached for her hand, but she yanked it away. I wrapped my arms around myself and left the gravesite, shivering against the cool spring breeze that cut through my coat. At the station wagon, I opened the back door, climbed into the small seat, and cried for layers of reasons.

A few minutes later, Heather rushed ahead of a small crowd making their way toward the car. She climbed in beside me, not because she liked me, but because she hated Uncle

Gene. Everyone did. Getting stuck sitting beside him meant the
creep would have his paws all over you.

"Everything happens in threes." Heather chewed her
lip. "Someone else will die soon."

"Who makes those stupid rules?"

"I don't know, but that's what Uncle Eugene said."
Heather had real fear in her eyes as she watched the group
make their way to the car.

"Why do you even listen to him? Stay away from him.
He's no good."

Daddy slid in the driver's seat and Mama and Aunt
Linda sat beside him. Bobby and Tom climbed in, in front of
us. Uncle Eugene squeezed next to the boys.

"I hope his plane crashes on his way home to Utah
tomorrow," I whispered in Heather's ear. "Maybe he's the third
one."

I meant it as a joke, kind of, but Heather didn't break a
smile. I studied her face. Her jaw was clenched. Her lips,
pinched.

Sure, life had been rough on both of us since Kara died,
but the difference between us was that my little sister
swallowed everything. When emotions choked me, I cried, got
angry. If Heather would talk or listen, or even cry, I could get
somewhere with her. Was she drowning in toxic feelings? The
walls around her would break my head if I tried to bust through
them.

~~~

One Saturday, a few weeks after Daddy returned to his
job on the ship, I found Mama and Heather looking over old
photographs in the living room. Mama blew her nose into a

handkerchief then stuck it in the back pocket of her stained coveralls.

I picked up one of her wedding pictures. She stood tall, thin and young, her blond short hair curled so cute. She flashed a happy, hopeful smile while hugging Daddy's arm. White dress, white gloves, red lipstick. Stuff now stashed in the back of her bureau drawer.

Mama pointed to the picture of a tiny house in a black and white picture. "This was our first home. I taught school in Milwaukee and Daddy worked at the printing press."

"Why'd you leave?" Heather asked.

"Grandpa got sick and called Daddy back to farm. I knew those happy days wouldn't last. Farming is in your father's blood."

Mama's sigh sounded as lonely as the Mourning Dove's coo. "If someone would've told me I'd have nine kids and run a farm, I would've said they were crazy."

Shoveling cow manure, milking, feeding pigs, and picking field stones obviously wasn't in her blood.

Heather picked up a photo of us in matching skirt and vest outfits—mine red, hers blue. Long pointy collars on our white shirts, long white socks, Mary Jane shoes, and big smiles.

"We look like a couple of dorks." I nudged her.

"Yeah." Heather sounded as sad as Mama.

"Will we ever have happier days?" I whispered.

Our hug-less semi-circle grew uncomfortably silent, then Mama wiped a tear and walked away. Heather followed.

Like Daddy and everyone else in the family, Mama rarely spoke to me. She still blamed me for Kara's death. She would forever. Heather remained a locked diary.

I climbed the stairs. Time for meditation to maintain balance in my body, mind, and consciousness. I'd been reading about Maharishi Mahesh Yogi—guru to the Beatles—and his Transcendental Meditation technique. Hadn't mastered levitation yet, but sometimes just remembering to breathe was enough.

I turned into my bedroom and locked the door. Maybe someday I'd get to India and become a disciple of that giggling guru. Spending last summer babysitting and cleaning cottages and the school year taking care of teachers' kids, I'd socked away a bit of money. Sixteen now, I'd get better jobs this summer. Money would be my ticket out of this dysfunctional family—to go to college, travel.

In the meantime, I did my best to fit in. At school, avoiding the edge of loner nerd land, I wore mostly pink and acid washed jeans. I experimented with make-up, kept my hair big, and taped a Tom Cruise poster onto my closet door and imagined he loved me. I wore colorful high-top Converses and ripped and slashed my clothes like Madonna. I organized my homework in my Trapper-Keeper and carried it along with my chaotic thoughts to school each day. I might have look like a typical teenage girl, but my journals knew the real me.

I closed my bedroom door and pulled notebooks from under my mattress, setting aside the blue Kara one. A few months back I'd dedicated a new notebook to be the keeper of my confused jumbled thoughts. If I could turn my thoughts into spoken words and share them with someone, they'd become real and mean something. Now, they were only lines that could be erased when I didn't feel them anymore or hopeful thoughts that, like shadows, would disappear when the sun went away.

I flipped through months of journal entries, loaded with oversized question marks and dots that poked holes clear through the page. Angry exclamation points slashed the lined pages. I flung the dumb notebook across the room. It hit the wall, then fell near the trash can.

I zipped my Kodak instamatic camera inside my sweatshirt pocket. Outside, my breath made frosty plumes in the crisp March morning air as I ran toward the lake, squinting against the bright sun and sparkling snow.

I slowed at Evergreen Lane, then approached the edge of the lake where gentle waves rolled short of a snow-crusted shoreline. My shoes crunched fresh impressions on the deserted beach.

Icy ripples at the water's edge turned my feet numb and tingly. Maybe I'd catch pneumonia. I didn't care.

A shimmering light caught my eye. I bent down and peered at the spot where waves, slapping against the high snow bank on the shore, had carved out a glistening icicle cave. I gasped. Thousands of icicles hung like a display of diamonds. The sun's rays made everything white, clean and dazzling, reminding me of pictures of the white-marbled and bejeweled Taj Mahal. I couldn't imagine that Shah Jahan had such a mausoleum—a monument of love—built for his beloved dead wife. Who loved another that much?

I lay on the cold ground, peeking into that brilliant icy structure, but soon my frozen wet toes tortured me. I scrambled to my knees, pulled out my camera and snapped the rest of the film roll.

I ran back to the house with a lighter heart. Finding the twinkling icicle-land was like happening upon a new world. I longed to travel, see fascinating places. When Grandma told tales of her childhood in England, I'd sit at her feet enraptured and eat up stories about castles and grand cathedrals. Begging for more, she'd laugh and say, "You are filled with Wanderlust, just like I always was."

Mama used to save the pictures I'd drawn of places I'd dreamt or read about, exotic places. I'd tell her that someday I would go abroad and bring her real pictures. After this year, only one more year of high school, then I could leave home, discover new, happier places, and live out my plans, go to college, maybe join the Peace Corps and visit the one place that I'd been reading about, thinking about, dreaming about—India.

I kicked off my wet shoes inside the doorway and tugged off my damp socks. Heather leaned against the kitchen counter, averting my eyes. Bobby and Tom ate sandwiches in silence in the dining room. They chewed and stared like intrigued cows as I crossed through the room. Something was up.

I ran up the stairs and almost smacked into Mama. She waited with crossed arms. Her eyes were a toxic mix of anger, hate, and pain. Since Kara died, she always looked accusingly at me, but today her eyes were burning mad. She rarely came upstairs, never went into our bedrooms. Oh, please. I prayed she hadn't gone into my room. I wanted to push past her, but she blocked me. I held my breath, wishing I could fly back to the lake and die in that icicle cave.

"Get in there and get rid of everything." Her voice cracked as her pitch rose to a scream.

She stepped aside. I rushed into my room, slammed my bedroom door, leaned against it, and slid to the floor. My heart pounded as Mama thumped down the stairs. No one should have trespassed my sanctuary. I hugged my knees until my breathing slowed, then looked up.

Kermit the Frog, missing one eye, stared at me from Kara's cot. Her pink fuzzy pajamas remained where they'd fallen that morning, nearly a year ago. A blanket spilled from her bed onto the huge half put-together puzzle on the hardwood floor. The toe of a lonely pink tennis shoe peeked from under the dresser. I pressed my face to my knees, finally seeing what had upset my mother. So not normal. I couldn't keep a monument of love for my sister. I should have put this stuff away months ago.

I forced myself to my feet and circled. What did she expect me to do with it all? Couldn't throw it out. I flopped onto my bed, grabbed my pillow, and released a choking sob. I hurt—a pain so deep I thought I'd have a heart attack. I cried until my head ached, wondering if anyone died from crying. I imagined my gravestone. "Cried herself to death at age sixteen."

With slowing sobs, I sat up and grabbed a tissue. My head was so stuffy I couldn't even blow my nose. No more crying.

A burst of anger fueled me down the stairs. In the kitchen, I flung open the pantry and grabbed a handful of large black garbage bags. I shut the door, turned, and faced Mama, her red eyes more sad than angry now.

"Kara's things need to be put away. Can you do it?" She sniffed.

I nodded. With shoulders curled inward like a holocaust victim, Mama wrung her hands. If Kara were here, she'd hug her, then me. Those hugs might have been the glue that held us together.

Mama tugged the zipper up on her coveralls. "I'll be in the barn."

I left the kitchen, stopped at the stairway and sat on the bottom step, breathing deeply. I closed my eyes and thought back to the day my baby sister died. While sweeping the kitchen floor, she stumbled at my feet, tripping over her coat while hugging her red rubber boots. I helped her dress, then sent her outside, watching through the window. She selected a kitten from the litter on the porch and tucked it under her arm like a rag doll. Each time she discovered a new litter mewing in the haymow, she'd adopt the runt and declare it her special kitty. Until a new litter was born, the special kitty lived in the crook of her elbow.

That day, while watching Kara with her furry friends, images popped in my mind. A small casket in a funeral parlor. Relatives offering condolences. I blinked away the images, shook off the awful feelings, and peered outside. Tail-wagging Sparky and two other cats had joined Kara's cadre. While the felines circled her, her big toothless grin revealed a safe, happy girl.

Why'd I dismiss those strange images? Why'd I continue sweeping floors and cleaning toilets, my little sister heading toward her demise? It played out like a movie scene. If I'd been given a special preview, why didn't I tear up the script, refuse it, kick it back to hell or heaven or wherever it came from?

Then there was the weird incident in the field that I'd shared with Grandma. Had that been a leap into the future, a second chance from God to save her? If I had sprinted to the pond and yanked her out, would I be bagging up her stuff now? How could I have ignored the signs?

I ran upstairs and slammed my door. I pulled my hair into a pony tail and took a deep breath. Kara's elephant, with the crinkly ears, stared with lonely sad eyes. I picked him up, spun the ball on his nose, then set him gently into the bag. "Sorry, Elephant. Kara won't be playing with you anymore."

I picked up her small purple sweatshirt, held it to my face, and breathed deeply. Kara used to smell like baby oil and fresh air. Now her clothes lost their scent and had taken on mine—Love's Baby Soft perfume. How long could I hold onto Kara's memory? Would she drift away like perfume or fresh air on clothesline dried laundry?

I continued mindlessly placing Kara's stuff into bags, emptying drawers, cleaning out the closet. I yanked the sheets from her cot and tossed them down the laundry chute in the hallway. Returning to my room, I picked up Kermit. Sorry Mama, Kermit isn't going into the black bag. Kara loved him best. I stashed the green frog under the covers of my unmade bed. Satisfied I'd packed it all, I shoved the bags in the large cubby hole in my room. Except for her empty bed, Kermit and the notebook, every bit of evidence of my sister's existence had been erased.

The door creaked and Heather poked her head inside.

"You told her, didn't you?" I clenched my teeth.

Heather scowled. "Drama queen!"

"Leave me alone!" I screamed and threw a shoe.

Heather slammed the door, and my shoe landed against it with a thud.

I pulled Kermit from under my covers and hugged him. Falling onto my bed, I stared at the cracks in the ceiling, willing them to split and for the entire house to cave in and crash down on me. Meditation wouldn't fix me now.

It's ok Bec. I help you. The voice rolled into my head like a gentle wave. A memory. Those words had floored me once at the hospital. I had documented those days in my Kara Notebook.

I sat up, grabbed the notebook and flipped through pages until I found the story and photo of Kara standing in the hospital crib.

When snowflakes smacked the window in the children's ward, Ma said she had to get back to the farm. I offered to stay. Kara was having tubes put in her ears and her adenoids removed. I was twelve. She was three. I slept in a chair beside her crib.

During the night, she stood, wide-eyed. "Listen," she said. "Babies crying. Get babies." She patted her bed. "I help babies."

How small I felt compared to Kara. She wasn't worried about herself, but the other children. Tears rolled down my face. Kara wiped them with her tiny hand and hugged me. "It's ok Bec. I help you, too."

I had wanted to be brave like her then, so I managed everything those three days, even cradling her small drugged body and handing her to the doctor before surgery. Mama picked us up when Kara was released. I remembered that I didn't feel twelve anymore when I climbed into our rusty green Ford pick-up and held Kara on my lap.

I grabbed the other notebook and as fast as the thoughts came, I wrote, page after page. Finally, I set down my pen and re-read my last sentence. "Don't let me let go of you."

I flipped through pages, re-reading from the beginning to the end. My words, scribbled and tear-stained, began as a letter to Kara, but ended like a prayer.

I gathered my notebooks, pressed them tight against my chest, and closed my eyes. I hadn't listened to God the day Kara died. And at the pond, he didn't listen to me. Would He hear me now?

"Don't let me let go of You," I whispered.

Sagai

In the early hours of the morning, Brother Lawrence clapped, and Sagai bolted from his reed mat. Even if tired or sick, when the clap sounded, he'd better scramble or Brother Lawrence's sandal would meet his backside.

Twilight cast weak rays through the barred windows that nearly reached the high dormitory ceiling in the Junior Seminary in Vellore. Dust motes raced and swirled with the swift rolling up of mats. Sagai glanced at Arjun, still curled up. He rolled his bedding and slid his small suitcase—their partition at night—against the yellow concrete wall.

"Arjun." He nudged his friend. "Get up."

The boy didn't move. Sagai stood faced the crucifix, as was expected. "Arjun?"

"Let us bless the Lord," Brother Lawrence bellowed.

"Thanks be to God." A choir of voices chanted their first words of the day. Sagai hoped Brother Lawrence didn't catch him trying to rouse his friend. Last night, when Sagai asked Arjun why he was crying, Brother Lawrence shouted, "Mind your own duties."

The throng of boys rushed toward the door for their morning run. Sagai joined them. Running. Chores. Angry

Brothers. Math. Where was the priestly training in a holy location? The Junior Seminary—the two-storied, three-sided gray concrete building, with a veranda all the way around— was high school, only they couldn't step beyond the compound wall, and friendships were not permitted.

The morning sun made him squint. While still in the state of Tamil Nadu, this place was not like home. Spring in Sheveroy Hills was never this hot, but at least the flat agricultural landscape inside the grounds made running easier, compared to his village's hilly terrain. Running allowed him time to think, even to silently mourn. If a tear escaped, he could blame it on the sun or the wind.

Last week he received a telegram from Appa. Thathi passed away. He'd dreamt about her the evening of her passing. She came to him and kissed his forehead.

He couldn't go home for the funeral because of exams. Another letter carried news that his older brother's wife had a baby girl. In unsupervised moments, he'd scribble his thoughts in the memo section of his school calendar. At home, he hadn't needed to pen his thoughts. Someone had always been there to listen.

"Slow down Sagai." Victor huffed as he drew close to Sagai on the pathway between the wall and the rice paddy field. Sagai relaxed his pace so they could talk out of Brother Lawrence's earshot.

"What happened to Arjun?" Victor sucked air again. "Why isn't he running?"

"Cried all night." Sagai raised his eyes. Brother Lawrence was far ahead, almost to the sugar cane field.

"Still whining?"

"I don't know what's troubling that fellow." Sagai wiped his forehead. "He's fair, pretty, and favored among the brothers. He even gets private time with the rector, yet he cries at night."

"He's not black like me." Victor smiled. "He should be happy."

Sagai had come to understand that everything mattered at the junior seminary—from fairness of skin to how smart you were, to how well you kicked the football. And though fairer than Victor, he wasn't as light-skinned as Arjun. "Perhaps his marks are low."

"He's a baby. He should go home."

"Only we will miss him on the football field."

"True. He is our best player, better than you." Victor playfully shoved him.

Brother Lawrence slowed, now almost beside them. "Keep quiet," he ordered. "Focus on the path ahead or you'll stumble."

Sagai quickened his pace and shot ahead. Aspirants were scrutinized every few months and any small infraction would end up in their file. They were warned that the contents of their file stuck with them forever and would impact their future, even when priested. He'd do his best never to get a bad mark in his file.

Sagai ran on in silence, past coconut trees and a small mango grove until they circled back to the refectory. *Sambar*— spices and onions blended with lentils—made his mouth water. Breakfast! The rector leaned against the cement pillar in his white cassock with folded arms resting on his rotund belly.

"Good morning, Father Rector," the aspirants chorused.

Victor lined up behind Sagai. The two always sat together at meals and during prayers and Mass in the chapel. But he must be careful. Every time he spoke to Victor, even put his arm around him in the corridor, his superior's critical eyes became arrows seeking a target.

At night, when Arjun's whimpering woke him, Sagai would turn and listen to Victor's soft snoring. Maybe the boy was still determining his calling. Not Sagai. He refused to whine or misbehave or stumble in any way. He never doubted his calling, even when chores meant toilet duty or when he was dogged-tired from clearing stones, helping dig the new well, or hauling rice from the paddy field. Even if it took a long time and hard work, he would become a priest. Life in Vellore was all about fitting in and learning the system, and a first step toward priesthood.

Sagai and Victor, along with nearly one hundred boys from ninth to twelfth standard, found seats at the long tables. Each boy had been chosen. Last year, Brother Lawrence and Brother Michael had walked the streets of Sheveroy Hills, blowing whistles. Like mice, Sagai and his neighbors scurried out of their doorways and followed them to the oratory alongside Little Lake. A few times a year, the brothers sought out boys for Catechism stories, a football match, and maybe for the priesthood.

Brother Lawrence coached that match, more than a year ago. Sagai bungled it. He stubbed his toe on a stone and missed the ball, but fared better during the Catechism session on the grass by the lake, led by Brother Michael. Though only priests or brothers were allowed to read the Bible, having served at Mass every day, Sagai knew the entire Holy Book.

That day, seeing Brother Michael in his white cassock, standing near the water's edge, must have been how John the Baptist at the Jordan River felt seeing the Lord. Though a dove didn't descend upon Brother Michael, Sagai knew he was the one, the brother who would see to it that God's will for his life was carried out.

He'd forgotten the throbbing pain in his bruised and bloody toe because he could hardly contain the words that had been bottled up for so long.

He marched up to Brother Michael. "I want to become a priest." For the first time he didn't look away when speaking to an adult other than his parents.

Out of fifty kids, he'd been the only boy chosen for the next step. Brother Michael had recommended him for Vocations Camp in Vellore. Two hundred kids throughout the state of Tamil Nadu attended that camp for one month. Only thirty were sent acceptance postcards.

He was blessed. He'd made it to the junior seminary, where Brother Michael now knelt beside a table and spoke gently to a tearful aspirant. That kind brother, in charge of the tenth standard batch, had not spoken to Sagai since that day at the oratory, but his smiles carried affection. It was enough. He would be indebted to Brother Michael for life.

Victor elbowed in the ribs. "Arjun is not eating with us."

Sagai circled his hand around, on his banana leaf plate, mixing rice into his runny sambar. "Arjun has elite duties this week. He's probably serving the superiors in their dining room."

"Lucky fellow will be eating the food they get, thick sambar or maybe *dosa* with meat curry." Victor rubbed his stomach. "He told me he ate lamb curry when that priest from Rome visited."

Sagai raised his head. "Shh!" Father Rector! He was not in his dining room with the other priests. The rector circled the table, then lingered near them. Sagai rapidly scooped curry and rice into his mouth.

"Sagai, come." The rector walked away.

He swallowed.

Victor ducked his head.

Sagai followed the white cassock down the long corridor toward the office, feeling feverish. Had Brother Lawrence read his notes? Was speaking to Victor his sin?

Standing inside the doorway, Sagai held his sticky unwashed hands behind his back. His knees felt watery weak.

The priest drummed his fingers on the desk. "You and Victor sit together at each meal? He's your friend, is it?"

"Yes, Father Rector." The words came out a croak.

"You've been here for nearly a year. By now you should fully understand that particular friendships are not allowed. Do you understand?" The rector folded his hands and pressed his pointer fingers together.

"Yes, Father Rector." Questions built in his mind, but he replaced them with his mantra. Follow orders. Learn the system. Discipline. Respect. Work hard. Study well. Obey and Go. Never question authority. He bit hard on his tongue to keep from speaking.

"Go." The rector snapped. "Join the class." The priest made a shooing motion with his hand, put on his glasses, and scribbled in the file.

Sagai bowed and left with a heavy heart. He'd tried to avoid trouble. He'd failed. But at least he didn't have to spend

the afternoon kneeling in the gravel in prayer, like Hari when
he giggled out of place in the science lab yesterday. Yet, the
rector wrote in his file. Maybe Hari got the better punishment.

At supper, Victor sat in silence alongside a cleric.

Later in the evening, Sagai and dozens of undressed
boys stood shivering under shower heads, waiting. Brother
Lawrence clapped. Brother Solomon cranked the knob to
release the trickle of cold water and counted to ten.

Clap.

The water stopped.

"Soap," shouted Brother Lawrence.

Ten seconds to apply soap. The next clap.

"Rinse!" Brother Lawrence ordered and Brother
Solomon began another rapid count to ten.

Final clap.

Today Sagai got the soap rinsed before the water was
cut. He was learning. Managing tasks quickly paid off.

"The brothers are so concerned about saving water."
Naveen, not as fast as Sagai, grabbed his towel and wiped soap
from his eyes.

"Or concerned about saving us from the occasion of
sin," Dominic mumbled.

"What sin?" Naveen asked.

Dominic laughed. "The same sin that keeps the light of
Brother Solomon's torch on you all night."

Naveen scowled at his taunter as Brother Solomon
shouted to get moving. It dawned upon Sagai what sin Dominic
meant.

At night prayers in the chapel, Sagai searched out
Victor. He wasn't in his usual place. Flanked by two brothers,

they guarded and protected Victor like Sagai was a leper or a devil.

Compline ended with an "amen" and the aspirants followed Brother Lawrence to sleeping quarters. Tomorrow they'd return for early morning matins, then six o'clock Mass, lauds at mid-morning and vespers before dinner.

In the dormitory, Albert dragged his suitcase to Arjun's spot. Sagai turned to the other side to find another aspirant in the spot where Victor had slept for the last seven months. He drew his knees to his chest. He wished he could talk to Appa about his thoughts, about the changes in his body, and the shameful feelings that followed. He wished he could sit with Thathi and Amma and absorb their wisdom. He wished he could perch on the rooftop with his brothers and listen to the radio. At a time when streams of questions surged through his mind he was forced mute.

Someone passed gas, and it set off a series of giggles. A light snapped on above Brother Lawrence's corner. Brother threw back the curtain and rushed about with his torch, shining it on each boy, earnestly seeking the gas leak and the identity of the chucklers.

Sagai maintained a serious face. If Brother Lawrence detected a smile, he'd sleep alone on the cold veranda. Sagai reached his hand under his cot, touching his diary. Only God and those pages knew his worries. He closed his eyes and prayed.

Brother Lawrence's light fell on him. "What's under your mat?"

Sagai retracted his hand. His heart sank. A short squeak of breaking wind sounded a few rows away, followed by more giggles.

Saved!

Brother Lawrence moved on. Sagai let go of the breath he was holding. Better he only share his thoughts with God.

Four

Springtime Awakening

"The Rose does not preen herself to catch my eye. She blooms because she blooms.
A saint is a saint until he knows he is one."
~ Anthony de Mello

Rebecca

While unloading the dishwasher, I spied a small yellow ceramic vase, tipped over on a corner shelf. RM3L was etched on the bottom. Rebecca Meyer. Third Grade. Mrs. Liston.

I remembered when I stepped off the bus with that vase. I plucked a dandelion, stuck it in my new creation, then handed it to Mama. She oohed and aahed, then placed it on the windowsill. She once marveled at my artwork, my poems, my photos, my gifts of flowers.

Each spring, throughout the summer and into fall, I'd fill the tiny container with violets or little white bellflowers or even a sprig of mustard. During winter the vase was a symbol of hope, a reminder that I'd pick flowers again. The vase had always rested on the windowsill, but I hadn't seen it since before Kara died, almost two years ago.

Another spring had arrived and I was looking forward to freedom, graduation, and college. I'd never found a niche in high school where I belonged. I could've made cheer team in our small school, but when I watched the girls all giggly at try-outs, I didn't want to fake it. I liked acting, too, but when it came to auditions, who wanted to deal with drama queens who insisted lead roles were created for them?

Writing and photography interested me mostly, but Tammy and Kathy, editor and co-editor of the school newspaper and yearbook, claimed that territory. And though I could run fast, because I worked so much—housework, babysitting, my job at the drive-in—sports wasn't an option. Neither was dating.

"Sacrifices," Mama said. "Sometimes you have to make sacrifices." That was her mantra.

I set the broken vase on the windowsill. Life shouldn't be all about sadness, sacrifices, and work.

I ran to my bedroom, gathered my notebooks, a pen, and my camera and tossed it all in a satchel. For the first time since Kara died, I prepared to visit the woods.

On the mossy carpet, we'd discover four-leaf clovers, and I'd make up stories about a fair forlorn princess whose dark handsome prince would rescue her. In our woodsy haven, time had no measure and gentle breezes, crickets, and the bubbling brook created symphonies that never escaped Kara's ears.

"Shh! Bec, listen." Kara would alert me to croaking frogs or buzzing honey bees. "Look!" she'd say, and point out a ladybug on a leaf.

I stepped outside. The grass had tossed its blanket of white and the tulips and daffodils were popping out all over the place. I felt like Rip Van Winkle, waking to a world that kept changing though I'd ignored it. The forest floor would be filled with milky white trilliums and yellow Dutchman's breeches by now.

I knew many flower names, thanks to Kara. When the bookmobile parked at Sawyer's corner, I'd pedal her on the back of my bike, and we'd fill my basket and satchel with books, always a flower book. She'd point at the pictures and ask me the names.

I walked past the barns, toward the field, pleasant memories filling my head. I stepped over chunky clumps of dark earth. At the edge of the woods, I stopped at the sitting stone. I ran my hand over the gently curving rock-bowl, wondering if generations of girls—Daddy's sisters, Grandma and maybe even her mother—had worn the concave place in the stone.

I sat and opened the Kara notebook to an entry I wrote the summer I'd volunteered at Sunshine School. I'd brought in a tape recording of her. The teachers acted surprised at how well I could get her to enunciate words.

I was Kara's teacher, her record keeper. I'd kept her words on paper, her voice on a tape, her image in photos, her memories in my mind, but I didn't keep her alive. I closed the notebook and opened the one where I recorded my thoughts. My last entry was a poem.

Red rosy cheeks
Sun bleached hair
Tiny fingers holding flowers, crayons and kittens
And little feet so precious charged
Running through fields
The sound of your voice—laughter, a small cry, soft
*   breathing at night*
No longer are your cheeks red
Your hair, now, untouched by the sun
Your precious hands, immobile
And the grass grows long, no longer trampled by your
*   feet*
And I lie here listening for you
But hearing only—the wind

I closed the notebook, looking toward the pond. The morbid constantly tugged at me. I should be living, figuring out what I was good at and where I wanted to go with my life. But maybe I needed to face the past, get over my fears.

I pressed my hands on the cold gray stone. Making it to the rock—a safe happy place—proved no great achievement. I had to go farther.

I shoved the notebooks into my satchel and proceeded toward the pond like that little train in the book Mama used to read to us…I think I can….I think I can. I paced the words with my heartbeat until they couldn't keep up with the pounding inside my chest.

Listen. Look. Kara's voice? I heard it like a whisper in my mind.

I shook my head, rejecting chilling memories. Oh God, my head ached. I didn't want to remember. Didn't want to see. The last time I looked into the water and saw Kara in there, I panicked. Ran.

Foul play. The paramedic's words ran through my mind. Bump on her forehead. Bruises on her arm. I'd forgotten. Maybe she slipped on a rock and fell into the water, someone had said then. Not sure who said it. Everyone but Heather had gathered at the pond by then.

Memories replayed like scenes from a horror movie that stayed in my head long after the film ended. I didn't want to stay at the pond one second longer.

I ran through the woods. "Don't think. Don't think. Don't think." I crossed the field, ran past the barns, into the house, and up the stairs. I fell on my bed and stared up at the ceiling, slowing my breathing. Why did I want to relive that horrible day? Not a good plan.

After a couple of minutes, the stairs creaked, then a soft rap sounded.

"It's me." The door opened and my brother Eddie walked in, looking like a hippie with his long dark hair and bangs sweeping over his right eye. He tossed me some Bubble Yum.

"Thanks." I caught the gum with one hand.

"You all right? I was in the barn, talking with Mama, and saw you running into the house. You looked upset. Mama asked me to talk to you."

I sat up and pretended everything was normal, that I could actually breathe. Eddie left home and joined the Army before Kara was born, then went to college in Chicago. He'd never paid much attention to me. I never had a real conversation with him. "I...I...didn't know you were home. Thought you were in school."

"I quit." Eddie blew a large bubble that popped and smacked against the tip of his nose and stuck. His eyes went crossways, looking down. "I meant to do that." He pulled the gum from his nose.

"But the Army was paying for college. Why would you leave?" If I wasn't opposed to war, I might join the armed services for scholarship money.

Eddie shook his bangs from his eyes. "Needed a break. I'm moving into Grandpa's old farmhouse. Going to fix it up. Maybe help out on the farm."

"It'll need a lot of fixing up. Nobody's lived there in years."

Eddie blew a more sensible bubble, shrugged, then popped it. "So where were you just now?"

I hesitated, worried he'd think I was weird.

"It's okay. Talk to me. I don't have cooties."

I blew out a deep breath. "I went to the woods, then the pond...you know...where Kara..."

"Sheesh. Why go there? "Eddie moved to the edge of my bed.

"I dunno. Sometimes I feel like Kara's lost and I need to find her. Sometimes I feel like I'm lost and the only way I can find myself is by..." The words got jammed in the back of my throat. "It's been hard, you know, living without her." With shaking hands, I unwrapped the gum.

Eddie sighed. "Listen Becca, I know you loved her and cared for her, but you gotta let go and trust she's with God."

"God wasn't there that day." I didn't feel I had a friend in Jesus, like the lines to the song I'd learned long ago in Sunday school. Though we were never regular church-goers, we hadn't gone since Kara died.

Eddie raked his fingers through his hair. "Look, I'm no expert on God or Bible stuff, but...I had a...well, um...a spiritual experience recently...and—"

"Yeah, I heard." I squished the pink square between my thumb and finger.

His eyes narrowed. "What'd you hear?"

"I heard you met Jesus while smoking dope."

"Who said that?"

"At the dinner table, Mama was talking about some Jesus experience you had and Bobby said you'd been smoking a lot of weed lately. Now they're really worried you're going to become a Jesus freak." I popped the gum in my mouth.

"Which would be way worse than a pothead, right?"

I put my hand over my mouth and stifled an unnatural giggle. My brother, for the first time in my life was sitting on my bed, actually listening to me. We were Joni and Richie from Happy Days and I wanted to pour out my heart. "It's horrible around here since Kara died. Mama still cries a lot. Daddy won't even look at me when he's home. Not that he ever did, but still. The boys act like I don't exist. Heather hates me. Nobody else comes home. Kara was my entire world. I loved her. She loved me."

I shoved the Kara notebook at him. "It's all in there. Proof! Look, if you want. I wrote all the stories about her and me, all a week before she died. Can you believe it?"

Eddie's intense brown eyes had drawn out words I'd only written, never spoken. I stared at my hands. "Everything changed when she died. It's like I don't even exist." I leaned against my pillow and sighed.

"Do you have friends? Do you talk to them?"

"Yeah, sure, but I can't talk about this stuff. And I never hang out with anyone outside of school."

"I'm sorry." He folded his hands. "So what are your plans after graduation?"

"I'm looking into colleges, but I'd love to travel, too. My dream is…" I bit my lip.

"What?"

"To go to India."

Eddie drew back. "India? Why?"

"I don't know." I fiddled with the drawstrings on my hooded shirt.

"You can tell me."

I shrugged. "India fascinates me. I can't explain it, but I've always wanted to go there, read every book in the library about India, and sometimes I wake from dreams, so vivid, it's like I've been there." I looked up at Eddie, amazed he was still listening and not laughing.

He rubbed his nose. "Do I have gum on my nose?"

"No. I'm just surprised I have a brother who wants to hear about my dreams." I shook my head. "It's kinda weird. Basically, Bobby and Tom just grunt."

Eddie chuckled. "Back to India. So what about the dreams?"

I straightened. "I had one recently, then woke up and wrote down all of the details."

"Go on."

"There were colorful birds in the dream, monkeys, too. Palm trees. And I was searching for someone…um…like a prince." My face flushed. I lowered my head and mumbled, "That's so corny. Can't believe I just said that."

Eddie didn't laugh or call me stupid. He never looked away. "What else?"

"I kept searching, crossing a desert, then a green field with long grass. I met dark-skinned people—women in colorful clothes, men in turbans—and asked about the prince."

The corners of Eddie's mouth turned up. "Do you find your prince?"

I nodded. "I found him at the sea, and then…." I stopped and squeezed back tears.

"You fall in love with an Indian prince and live happily ever after?"

I shook my head, my lip quivering. "We save children who are drowning." Tears avalanched onto my cheeks. "But sometimes I can't reach some of them…and…" I broke down, sobbing.

Eddie pressed his hand on my shoulder. "I don't know what that all means, but maybe you need to focus on your future, who you are and who you want to be. Let go of the past. Kara is with God. We can't bring her back."

I nodded and sniffed.

The phone rang downstairs. It quit after one ring, then Heather yelled, "Eddie! It's a girl. Says her name is Diane."

"Diane?" I grabbed a tissues from the night stand. "Your old girlfriend from high school?"

Eddie shot me a Fonzie smile and walked toward the door. "One more thing—" He turned. "Now that I'm home, I'm going to throw some parties. Let's do a graduation bash."

I wiped away tears, smiled, and gave him a thumbs-up.

He tipped his finger toward me and made a clicking sound. "Catch ya later."

Eddie was my new guru. He was right. I had to let go of sadness, get my life back on track, and have some fun.

Sagai

The artist set the mosaic tiles, piece by piece, into the plastered pattern inside the chapel, bringing the Risen Christ to life with brilliant color and captivating depth.

For the past two years at Vellore, Sagai and the other aspirants had hauled mortar in a metal basket on their heads helping to build the house of the Lord.

Foundations were being laid for the new chapel and for their formation. That's what the Brothers said. Free time was an offering for the building of God's church. Now, it was nearly complete, down to the art and Sagai's time as an aspirant drew to a close.

A hand pressed his shoulder. "*Magnifico,* is it not?" Father Costello's eye wrinkles multiplied.

"So many tiny pieces, Father."

"And yet each *tesserae,* when placed together becomes *bella arte.*" Father Costello tugged his beard that dropped past his ribs. "*Opus* is Latin for work, and it also means the way in which the *tesserae* are positioned."

The old priest always used conversations to teach, ever since his arrival three months back to oversee the completion of the art. The bicycling priest pedaled around the campus in his white cassock and with an ethereal grace, he'd often stop and divulge sacred bits of wisdom to the aspirants.

Father Costello patted his shoulder. "You did *meraviglioso* with your Italian last week, reading the welcome speech for the visiting bishop from Rome."

"Only because of your help with the language, Father." Sagai fidgeted, rubbed his toe in the dust on the cool pearlescent marble. How could he thank this great teacher? He'd been the only person on campus who'd listened to his thoughts, dreams, and hopes. Brother Michael had spoken kindly to him a few times, but he left after the first year.

"God willing, you will soon leave here and enter the novitiate, a place of spiritual discerning, where you'll live like a monk." Father Costello raised his eyes to the Risen Christ. "It's time to consider your *opus,* and think about what way the Lord can use you in His *magnum opus,* His *grande opera.* You must search inward for your real contribution to God's Kingdom, your vocation within your vocation."

The bell sounded. "Run along," he said, waving. *"Vai alla tua classe.* Go to your class. We will chat later."

"Thank you, Father." Sagai bowed.

Opus and *opera.* How he admired wise old Father Costello. For the past two years, sameness had been the status quo. Same haircut, cut by the same brother, in no particular style. Same uniform. Sameness in all things. Father Costello's talk always sounded fresh and exciting. Like the pieces of tile, every aspirant was different.

Sagai circled behind the chapel and passed under the shady palms, considering his contributions to God's *"Grande opera."* As lead trumpet in the school band, he'd performed solos and often won prizes. Recently the band performed, "Hava Nagila," a Hebrew folk song with different movements and rhythms. Each person had their own part, but what a lovely symphony when they played together. On stage, for drama class, making people laugh or cry became a catharsis for restricted emotions.

He could sit with Father Costello talk about God, life, and Italy all day. Now that he could speak Italian, perhaps someday they'd meet in Rome someday. He hustled to the classroom, questions running through his head. When would he be made a priest? What would the power of God feel like when it came through his hands at the time of consecration? Where would he go for his novitiate? He wondered about his gifts, his vocation within his vocation. He wondered if Vijay stayed in school.

Sagai slid into his desk moments after the second bell rang, catching a frown from the priest. Tardiness ought to be forgiven in the last week of school, especially since he'd given up his lunch hour offering food to the poor at the compound gate. Superiors said that good works mattered to God and towards his priestly advancement, but he didn't do it for rewards. Chatting with locals meant staying connected to others and the world outside the gates.

After classes and dinner, night prayers closed the day. Before dawn the next morning, Brother Lawrence's claps woke Sagai from a dream where no one at home understood him because he spoke English. His mind—his thoughts and dreams—had now switched to English.

"Let us bless the Lord." Brother Lawrence's shout echoed in the dormitory.

Everyone hustled. Today was Senior Cycle Picnic Day. After morning prayers and a quick breakfast, Sagai and forty others began their three hour journey to the Krishnagiri Dam on rented bicycles.

It should be a happy day, but while pedaling, an ominous feeling settled in his mind like a ribbon of fog. Sunshine, cool breezes and laughter couldn't lighten his mood. He knew this feeling and prayed God would protect those whom he loved.

The bicyclers ahead of Sagai stopped at a rice paddy field where an irrigation pump shot fresh water from the well. Superiors and classmates cupped water in their hands, and drank from the stream. Sagai dunked his face into the gushing flow, the water cooling his face and quenching his parched throat. Victor nudged him out of the way and followed suit.

Back on the road again, nearing the dam site, Victor whizzed past. "Pedal faster!"

Under constant scrutiny, Sagai had avoided his dear friend. But secret looks, smiles, and affirming pats on the back kept them connected in a friendship that didn't require words.

Sagai sped up. Finally at the site, he rested his bike near his friend's then pitched in to set up day camp.

During the Tambola game, Victor sat cross-legged on the grass across from him as brothers called off numbers. Sagai placed a numbered button onto a corresponding square on the board, then glanced up.

"Ohhhhh!" Victor clutched his side, and toppled over.

Sagai rushed to his side as Victor writhed in pain.

"Back! Back!" Brother Lawrence knelt beside Victor.

"Clear the bullock cart!" a brother shouted.

"Jesus, have mercy." Sagai repeated his prayers over and over while helping unload supplies off the cart. Others joined in, then the brothers lifted his friend on the back. Brother Lawrence shook the reins and urged the bullocks onward. Sagai covered his trembling lips, watching the cart until it turned the corner.

With Victor's fate unknown, there could be no celebration. Wiping tears, Sagai helped pack up camp, and a brother led the group back to Vellore. With the afternoon sun pressing on their backs, recalling the words from his grandmother and mother, Sagai continued with vigilant supplications until they arrived at the seminary. He fell asleep that evening praying the rosary for Victor. His first petition of the morning was for him, too.

After morning Mass, Sagai asked Brother Timothy if he'd received news. The brother dismissed his question with a warning. "Mind your own matters."

Later, in the dormitory, twenty-five boys from Sagai's group silently packed, preparing to go home for a break before their novitiate. Thirty-seven hopeful candidates for priesthood had arrived in his batch. When the boys left, no mention was made of them.

Deva tossed a stinky undershirt at him. "It's yours. I borrowed it last week."

"Keep it. I like you, but not enough to carry your sweat with me."

Albert, who'd slept beside Sagai after Arjun left, sniffled while packing. Had he heard news of Victor?

"Albert? What is it? Tell me!"

Albert scanned the room. "I'm not supposed to say, but I won't become a priest. I didn't pass assessment." He glanced past Sagai, then lowered his head.

Brother Lawrence approached.

"Father Rector will see you now."

"What has happened to Victor?"

The brother crossed his arms. "Never mind Victor. Father is waiting for you. Hurry! Go."

With fists balled, he walked the long tiled hallway toward the rector's office. He should be told about Victor. The entire campus, busy with assessments and leaving, had forgotten their classmate. He would not.

Beginning last week, one by one, the rector summoned the students. Unlike Albert, Victor had passed his assessment. His friend's grin after his scrutiny, the day before the picnic, gave it away. He hoped, if he was okay, they'd be assigned to the same novitiate. Maybe in the training institute, friendships would be allowed.

At the rector's door, Sagai rapped a bit too loud.

"Enter." The deep voice sounded harsh and irritated.

He unclenched his fists and opened the door. "Good morning, Father."

The rector picked up the file and leaned back. Each year he'd been assessed and had always passed, in spite of his file's bad marks for small things that shouldn't have mattered. No telling how those marks would affect his future as a priest, though. The rector flipped through papers.

Sagai bit his tongue until he could no longer keep quiet. His file might grow fatter, but he had to speak. "Father, what happened to Victor?"

The priest's thick brows merged into a bushy furrow.

"He is my friend. I want to know what has become of him. We never come to know what happens to our classmates. It's not right."

The rector drew back. His lips puckered into tight wrinkles. "You are telling me what is not right?"

"I only want to know about Victor."

"He is not your concern."

"But—"

The rector thrust his palm upward. Their eyes locked. Sagai quickly lowered his head, not out of submission, but to hide his angry eyes.

The rector snatched his pen and crossed and scribbled. "After your break at home, in one month you will report to the novitiate in Nashik."

"Naaa…?" Sagai raised his head.

"Nashik. It's five-hundred miles north, towards Bombay."

"Thank you, Father." Thank you meant he accepted the assignment. He had no choice. He'd go to the moon if that's where they sent him.

Returning to the dorm, he discovered a few classmates had already left. From the chatter and happy faces, he gathered they were all going to Tamil Nadu training institutes. No one mentioned Nashik. But he couldn't worry about that now. He had to find out about Victor.

He grabbed his suitcase and ran toward the new church. Father Costello's bicycle rested against the wall. Inside, he found the priest staring at the Risen Christ. He rushed into the sanctuary, slid onto his knees and crossed himself before the mosaic Jesus. He turned toward Father Costello, raised his clasped hands, and begged. "Please, Father! Can you tell me what has happened to Victor?"

"He is in Krishnagiri, in the hospital."

"Grazie, Father." He leapt to his feet, shoved his hand in his pocket and felt the coins. Enough for bus fare to Krishnagiri and back home before his journey to Nashik. Suitcase in hand, he ran past the rice paddy field. When he looked back, Father Costello waved from the church. Sagai hoped he'd see the kindly priest again.

"*Arrivederci*, Father!"

A peacock shrilled from the field. Bad sign. Shivers ran down his arms. Sagai crossed himself, said a prayer, and ran toward the bus stop. This act of defiance could have consequences, but it didn't matter. God would be with him.

Five

Rebellion

Emancipate yourselves from mental slavery;
none but ourselves can free our minds.
~ Bob Marley

Rebecca

Siren wailing, tires squealing, the police car sped into the driveway at Grandpa's old place. Tires crunched and flung gravel as the car slammed to a stop. Deputy Holder bolted from the car as smoky flames licked the night sky in a crescendo of cracks and pops. The stench of burning rubber saturated the night air.

"Help!" Eddie screamed. My brother ran to the cop with flailing arms then pointed toward the blazing barn. "Some guy drove through the yard and slammed into the barn. Must have hit a propane tank. He's still in there!"

The deputy's eyes widened and darted from Eddie to the fire. The barn, car, and assorted old tires blazed in a noxious tower of smoke. The cop reached for the mike on his car radio.

I backed up and ducked behind the tall grass surrounding the old gray farmhouse and watched the crowd.

A few low chuckles erupted. A couple of knee-slappers rose from their fold-up chairs and howled with laughter.

"Eddie M--Meyer, you're full of sh..sh…"

Deputy Holder, a stutterer, must have noticed the keg.

"I c-c-could haul you off to jail right now on several counts."

Whoops and hollers increased. "Soo-eee," echoed from the shadows.

"Whose c-c-car is in there? And...and...that k-keg...over there...you...you got minors here? I want to see I.D.s."

I should've hid in the house when I heard the siren, but the few sips of Pabst Blue Ribbon had given me courage.

Though blood might be thicker than water, beer bonded our family. Tragedy and sadness had unraveled the thin threads of our relationships, but in front of a bonfire with a buzz on, my brothers noticed me and thought I was someone. Parties would end, but the stories were everlasting.

While the cop shouted at Eddie, I tugged the old screen door and slipped inside. Eddie's girlfriend peeked out the kitchen window.

"If I were you..." Diane nodded toward the hallway. "...I'd high-tail it to the back bedroom, climb under the covers and pretend you're asleep." She placed her hands on her hips. "I suppose I'll have to make up some story, tell the deputy the fire was accidental, not purposely lit by your brother, then called in *anonymously*." Diane shook her head. "I can't believe they pushed that old car inside to add drama."

"Think the cop will come in?"

Diane pulled back the new apple-print curtains and peeked out. "Nah. Never mind. Looks like he's leaving. He's probably too embarrassed to be a real cop with everybody laughing at him. Your brother's been teasing Andy Holder since he peed his pants in kindergarten. Eddie needs to respect authority. The army should have taught him that."

Diane might have been right, but in my last hurrah of high school, being Eddie's sister made me cooler than the cheerleaders. His parties and antics were known from one side of the county to the other. Who knew cutting loose could be such a confidence booster?

With the deputy gone, I returned to the bonfire. Eddie put his arm around me and shouted to his friends standing around the keg under the cherry tree. "Get her another beer, fellas. She'll drink you guys under the table."

Eddie's friend handed me a red Solo cup, foam spilling over the top, then nudged me. "Promise you'll call me when ya turn legal."

There wasn't enough alcohol at this party for me to make deals like that, legal or not. I had bigger plans. Though I'd dated a few guys, not much time for dating with work. Besides, they didn't hang around when they realized I wasn't easy and didn't worship them or their cool truck.

Eddie tightened his grip around my shoulder and pulled me a step back from his friend. Bobby and Tom doubled over near the fire, wiping tears of laughter. While my other brothers weren't as hilarious, gregarious, and philosophical as Eddie, they loosened up after a few drinks.

A few weeks back, when I got way too loaded at one of Eddie's barn parties, Tom's hands reached into my spinning world, guided me outside and held my head while I threw up in the weeds. Then he took me home and never said a word to Mama. I learned a few lessons from Eddie's parties—while beer bonded us, best not drink too much. No fun cleaning toilets at work with a splitting headache and weak stomach.

Meatloaf's "Bat out of Hell" blasted from the porch speaker and Eddie gave me a sideways hug. "Do you know what I like about you?"

"That I can chug as fast as you?"

"Well, yeah, but also that you bugged the hell out of Mama until she signed for you to get a passport. So, where ya going? India?"

The heat from the fire added to the warmth on my face. A big dream, maybe too big, especially for a poor farm girl, but I'd been working for years and saved every penny. "The big non-denominational church in town has a group going on a mission trip at the end of the summer. I don't know if I can come up with enough money for that and college, but am seriously considering."

Even if I didn't go, I now had a passport. I could pull it out any time and tell myself, Hey Rebecca Meyer, that's your face on that passport and you're going places.

I smiled at Eddie. "Maybe I'll study abroad one semester. Maybe I'll spend a summer in Paris. Maybe I'll meet a hot Italian exchange student at college and move to Italy. The possibilities are endless."

In the light from the fire, Eddie's jaw tightened. He saluted the wheat fields and his beer sloshed over the edge of the cup and spilled onto the Sperry Topsiders I'd bought at Goodwill. "I've got to get out of here, too. Mama and the old man may not get it, but I wasn't born to be a farmer."

"Really?" Daddy bought more cows and they were counting on Eddie settling down with Diane, fixing up Grandpa's house, and farming.

"Don't tell Mama or even Diane yet, but you inspired me with your talk about India. I'm thinking about taking off for a few months to backpack around Europe."

"My lips are sealed." No way was I going to tell anyone that I'd influenced Eddie to escape White Gull Bay and go abroad. "Maybe I'll join you. Cheers! Here's to going places!"

I lifted my plastic cup to my brother's and downed my beer. He flashed me a loopy grin, looked into his empty cup, then joined Rick at the keg.

The elemental power of fire and water mesmerized me. I'd put everything that happened at the pond behind me. In my relationship class at school, for our final grade we had to write a paper entitled, "My Personal Philosophy of Life." I got an "A" with three pluses after it.

A small book inspired most of those twenty pages. "The Gift of Acabar." The story told of a boy who lost his parents and built a big kite to bring a star from the sky to survive a long cold winter. It helped me realize that choices alone form, and with determination, one can do anything.

Staring into the fire kindled thoughts of my future. What would it bring? Where would I go? Who would I marry? School was over and after summer, I'd be so gone.

My Mickey Mouse watch showed it was nearing midnight. Before my job cleaning cottages in the morning, I had an interview at Lake Shore Resort, a favorite place for rich Chicago vacationers. Once the tourist season began, I'd earn big bucks to add to my college/travel funds.

I returned to the house to ask Diane, the only sober one, for a ride home. Two miles later, I said goodbye, thanked her for the ride, and slammed the door of the old pickup. Upstairs, I climbed in bed, opened the Kara notebook, and read the Grasshopper story, one of my favorites: *I stepped off the bus in a bad mood and found Kara lying on the grass laughing. With a toothless grin, she smiled, pointed. "Look Bec, hoppers." Then she threw back her head and giggled when they jumped. I spent hours with Kara laughing and searching for hoppers.*

I closed the notebook, remembering that day, one of my happiest, and for no other reason than Kara's contagious laughter and grasshoppers.

Before I climbed into bed, I read the Desiderata poem I'd copied by hand and pasted on my mirror. The last line summed it all up "...*with all its shame, drudgery, and broken dreams, it is still a beautiful world. Be cheerful. Strive to be happy.*"

Amen. That was the plan. My acceptance letter from the University of Wisconsin remained safely tucked in my notebook. If I worked hard all summer and got financial aid, I might have money enough for that mission trip before college. I closed my eyes. Soon I'd be gone, gone gone. The Meatloaf song from the party still echoed in my head.

~~~

In the morning, I met Mama in the kitchen, frying bacon. Heather, seated at the small round table, snapped a piece in half.

I opened the fridge, poured creamy milk into a glass. "I'll need the Pinto. I have an interview before work."

Ma pushed the eggs in another pan. "Car is at the police station."

I gulped a drink, then almost spit it out. "What?"

Heather giggled. "Police chase last night. Tom and Bobby abandoned the pinto and hid in a corn field."

"Thankfully they didn't get caught." Mama flipped bacon.

Bobby stepped into the kitchen, bleary-eyed, and rubbing his temples. He pulled up a chair. "Hey, Bec. Call the police station and report it stolen. Tell them you had it and when you woke up at Eddie's, it was gone."

"No way!"

"If I claim it, they'll arrest me!"

"And what about me?"

Mama raised her eyebrows and said, "Well, maybe Rebecca—"

"No!" Somewhere inside that woman at the stove was the mother of a daughter who needed her to at least pretend she was her child. I wanted to shake that mother out of her.

"Just a thought." Mama shrugged and set a platter of eggs and a pile of bacon before Bobby.

My brother stuck his fork in the eggs. "Forget it. It's a junker anyway. Never starts. Let 'em keep it."

I fell in the chair, threw my head back, and stared at the ceiling. "How could you guys have been so stupid?"

"Don't call names, Rebecca. Boys will be boys. They've worked hard, sacrificed a lot, and need to blow off steam once in a while."

"How am I supposed to get to work?" I stole a piece of bacon off Bobby's plate.

"Hey!"

"What about the pick-up?"

Mama shook her head. "Tom needs it for repairing fences."

I leaned forward and scrunched up fistfuls of hair. I was so done with looking at life through the eyes of beer-drinking cheese-heads. I wanted to go on that mission trip and look through the eyes of someone from a different culture and see what they saw. I wanted to meet people who didn't crush the can of what they just drank on their forehead. But I'd never come up with enough money for that trip or for college without wheels.

With a mouthful of eggs, Bobby said, "I fixed up my old motorcycle to sell. Two hundred bucks and it's yours. Sell it at the end of the summer for the same amount. It's a deal you can't refuse."

"I'm not sure I can handle a motorcycle."

"Keys are in it. Go learn."

"Fine. I'll buy it. I'll pay you after I make sure it works."

I pushed away from the table, ran outside, and hopped on the motorcycle. Small enough bike. Should be easy to manage. Bobby came outside, showed me how to start it, and gave tips and pointers. After a few rough starts and stops, I gained confidence and ventured onto the road.

A mile later, at a bend, a small yapping dog shot from a driveway and headed straight toward me. A car too close behind. "Ahhhh!" Stupid dog. A rumble under my wheel, a yelp. The dog limped off. Tried to straighten. "Oh no!" The ditch! A tree! I tilted the bike. My head grazed the tree and the bike landed on my leg. Oh, the pain! My leg! Stupid dog!

A car door slammed.

"Are you okay?" A man with blue eyes and blond hair stood over me.

Sagai

Sagai had watered the dead stick in the pot outside his novice master's office every day since he'd arrived in Nashik last month. He was fairly certain it wouldn't miraculously bud forth a blossom, but he didn't want to kill Father Antony's hope. Today it dawned that Father Antony wasn't looking for a miracle. This was a test in obedience.

So be it. He'd water the dead stick for the entire year, an easy task, given obedience was the most troubling obstacle on his path toward priesthood.

He'd committed an act of disobedience even before arriving at the novitiate training institute when he defiantly hopped on a bus, found the hospital and waded through rows of cots in the long ward, searching for Victor. He ran to him, knelt and wept. His companion had survived a burst appendix.

While disobedience remained wrong, it was somewhat liberating.

He set the watering can on the cement corridor that wrapped the courtyard. If he admitted what he'd done before arriving in Nashik, they'd kick him out. For simply inquiring about Victor, he'd been banished to the state of Maharashtra more than six hundred miles from his classmates at a South India, Tamil Nadu novitiate.

Sagai picked up the clippers.

"If my rose garden is not abundantly blooming, you will be held accountable." The booming voice belonged to Father Antony, standing outside of his office door in his white cassock, arms crossed over his chest. "Everything matters here, from how well the roses flourish, to how clean you scrub the kitchen floor, to your studies. Be vigilant! Your scrutiny is more critical here than in Vellore."

"Yes, Father."

Father Antony proceeded toward the priest's quarters as Sagai eyed the bush. If he snipped a bud before it bloomed, would it be noted in his file as a grave offense? Could a dead rose keep him from his next step, earning his degree in philosophy?

"Hai, Sagai." Binny D'Souza strolled toward him in his slow easy gait, coming from kitchen duties. His bellbottoms swayed and the breeze lifted his long hair. He claimed the wide-legged jean pants were the latest fashion in nearby Goa, his home at the Arabian Sea where Bollywood movies were made. Binny withdrew clippers from the bucket and approached, humming an unfamiliar upbeat tune.

"What is that song?"

"'Mohabbat ye Mohabbat' from "Hero." Haven't you seen it?"

Sagai knew enough Hindi to understand that mohabbat meant love, but the only movies he'd ever seen were sixteen millimeter Tamil devotional films, shown once a year, projected onto a classroom wall in Sheveroy Hills. He shook his head, then cringed when Binny haphazardly snipped off a rosebud.

"What's it about?" He squinted into the late morning sun.

"A criminal who wants to settle scores."

"He's the villain?" Sagai raised the clippers to a dead rosebud.

"Yes, but under the influence of love, he transforms." Binny pulled a rose to his face and sniffed it. "I had a girlfriend who did that to me." He shook his finger. "Ouch. Roses are like women. They're lovely, but prickly and can wound a man."

Sagai lowered his clippers. Back in Vellore he was not allowed one genuine friend. Here, fellows talked of girlfriends and of love. When his parents had found a suitable spouse for his older brother, the couple only had fifteen supervised minutes during the bride viewing to make up their minds. He wasn't certain what, exactly, Binny meant by girlfriend.

Sagai glanced toward the offices, then whispered, "You really had a girlfriend?"

"Like the film hero, I had many lovers, until I met the love of my life, then everything changed."

"What happened?" Sagai's closed his slack-jaw.

"She rejected me for someone else. That's when I sought God and turned my life around, realizing my true path. I've given it all up, Sagai, even Goa's nude beaches."

Sagai drew back. "What is it you're talking? What sort of beaches?"

"Beaches where people are nude."

The clippers slipped from Sagai's hand. He jumped to prevent the sharp tip from stabbing his sandaled foot. "They wear nothing?" He remembered again to shut his dropped jaw.

Binny laughed. "You're shocked, Sagai?"

"Such a thing cannot be true. You are playing the fool with me." He knelt to pick up the clippers.

"Friend, I have lived a scandalous life. I've been the worst kind of a scoundrel, but no more. I came into the novitiate a sinner seeking forgiveness. You, on the other hand, are the Immaculate Conception, grabbed straight from the womb and dropped here."

Binny gave him a playful shove. "What a shocked face you have. Maybe I'm wrong, and you left behind a love in Tamil Nadu? Hmm? Is that why you've been sent so far from home?"

"Never." Sagai bristled. "Nothing like that."

"Whatever it is, relax my friend. Move on. Forget and let go."

He'd kept quiet about his trip to see Victor on his short visit home before his arrival at the novitiate. If he'd told his Tamil Nadu friends that he had disobeyed his superiors, he could imagine their reproaches. They'd wag their heads and click their tongues. "Drastic mistake!" Binny didn't care what he'd done. Forget it and let go, the fellow said.

The older boy set his clippers in the grass and pretended to roll something in his hand. Then he put his fingers to his lips, holding an imaginary cigarette. He stumbled and reached out his pinched fingers. "You want some, bubba? It'll loosen you up."

"You're acting drunk!"

"That's how people take dope." Binny threw his head back and laughed. "You're so naïve, Sagai." He waved his hand and picked up the shears. "It's fun to play with you."

The lunch bell interrupted the boy's odd behavior. Sagai shook his head. Mad fellow.

"Chef is preparing Vindaloo." His friend turned. "Come along."

Hot spicy Vindaloo. Bell bottom jeans. Long hair. Girlfriends. Nude beaches. Dope. Sagai was only used to white rice and chapattis, wearing school uniforms and being serious about life. He'd never thought about a girlfriend. Never imagined a nude beach. He shook the thoughts out of his head. These cheerful fellows from the north had been telling incredible stories about things he'd never heard of, eaten foods he'd never tasted, and done things he'd never imagined. He was thrilled as well as troubled.

That afternoon, he fidgeted in class, finding it difficult to concentrate during the canons and constitutions class. Was C&C class meant to be so boring? Learning rules of the order must be, so that novitiates could make their temporary profession of faith—poverty, chastity, and obedience—at the end of the year. Still years before he'd get priested. And if not careful, he could be kicked out any time.

As the father droned on about church mandates, Sagai forced sinful thoughts of nude beaches out of his mind to focus on canons and constitutions. Losing concentration again, he thought about his last visit home. Vijay had broken his promise and quit school. Amma had retired from nursing and cried over the loss of her ancestral property. Grandfather Balu's small coffee estate had fallen to ruin under her brother's care and he'd sold off all but one small parcel bequeathed to Amma, to the Brothers of Mercy Monastery.

Appa tried to keep up the plot, but weeds gained on the plants and now water buffalo and monkeys made it their home. One sister married and lived with her husband's family in another village. His older brother's family, now numbering five, crowded in the little house. His other sisters demanded Appa find spouses for them, but he didn't know where to go for money. His uncle, who had three boys and only one girl, said the family was cursed with so many daughters. Sagai witnessed a rare streak of anger cross his gentle father's face as he had ordered his brother-in-law out of the house. He could do nothing to help them.

The bell sounded an end to C&C class. He and the other novitiates proceeded in the courtyard for the Novice Master's spirituality class.

In the midst of the sweet aroma of roses, jasmine bushes, and fresh cut spring grass, Father Antony began his lecture. "This is the springtime of your lives. Time to meditate, pray and discern your future."

He was a disciple of Father De Mello, a Jesuit priest from Bombay who ran the Sadhana Spirituality Center. Father Antony explained how Sadhana—a discipline practiced to achieve a spiritual goal—would bring them to a deeper awareness of God, where they could discover the "divine in all things, and all things in the divine" along their sacred Christian path.

Sagai leaned forward, placed his elbows on his knees, and rested his chin in his hands to listen to the Sufi story that told a joke and taught a moral and a little extra which always deepened his consciousness.

Father Antony smiled. "One hot day, Nasruddin was resting in the shade of a walnut tree. He eyed huge pumpkins growing on vines and small walnuts growing on a majestic tree. 'Sometimes I just can't understand the ways of God,' he mused. 'Just fancy letting tiny walnuts grow on so majestic a tree and huge pumpkins on delicate vines.' Just then a walnut snapped off and fell smack on Mullah Nasruddin's bald head. He rose at once and lifting his hands and face to heavens in supplication, he said, 'Oh, my God! Forgive my questioning your ways! You are all-wise. Where would I have been now if pumpkins grew on trees?'"

Neither could Sagai question or understand the ways of God.

"Wake up!"

He jumped as Father Antony clapped again.

"Open your eyes and see what is real, both inside and outside of yourselves." The priest raised his hands to the sky. "The greatest human gift is to be in touch with one's body, mind, feelings, thoughts and sensations."

An awakening washed over him, a thawing—a springtime in his soul—in this new environment with his colorful classmates, their liberal thinking, and carefree attitudes. Sexual feelings were discussed, especially during lessons on sublimation, where instructions in the act of purifying and refining primitive instincts taught diverting and channeling sexual energy into acceptable, honorable, activities of divine love, like praying or meditating.

Before Binny's talk about nude beaches, sexual desires never rose to any problem. Women were not even allowed on campus. His only sought healthy friendships.

Throughout the following months, in the pleasant climate at the compound, surrounded by vineyards and flower and vegetable gardens, he embraced his entry into monastic life. Conflicts and worries about home, his future, and his past evaporated with the novice master's teaching of consciousness of perspective versus measurement.

Measurement of religion offered a few explanations to his questions, but perception went beyond, taking him deeper into his spirituality. Meditating in the grotto garden one day on a lesson about the immeasurable length, depth, and breadth of spirituality and perception, he looked toward heaven and shouted, "Ah-ha."

Guilt about his impulsive hospital visit to Victor no longer tormented him. He let go of his anger and frustrations with superiors. He released every worry about his family to God.

Perspective.

Now he understood. Though his superior's perspective to teach him obedience held value, so also his perspective to love his friend. God helped them all, even his family. He only needed to cherish the divine present moment.

Months passed and a few novitiates left, either discerning or having it determined for them that monastic life would not suit them well. He carried on, determined to become a priest.

~~~

Nearing the end of Sagai's year at Nashik, a large red-headed Czech priest joined the staff. Father Danek's wild fiery brows and his hot breath on Sagai's neck inspired terror.

One afternoon, while scrubbing the floor during kitchen duty, the priest's shoes appeared under Sagai's eyes. He looked up. Father Danek pointed to a missed spot and left.

After the evening meal as Sagai wiped the sink. Bruno, a novice, entered the kitchen.

"Father Danek wants you."

Sagai's stomach churned. Something was wrong. He hung the cloth and crossed the courtyard to his superior's office. Fear built with each step. He reminded himself to breathe and rapped on the door. Ordered to enter, he found Father Danek at his desk with a large knife in his fist. His bushy red brows furrowed in anger.

Father Danek raised the knife. "Why was this in the trash?"

"I...I...don't know." Sagai searched his mind. He'd washed the cake knife earlier. "Father, I recollect putting it in the drawer."

He slammed his fist and the knife bottom clanked on the metal desk top. "Silence! That is a lie! You've been negligent. This instance will be duly noted in your file. This grave error will have consequences." He thrust the knife forward. "Take this and go! Put it in its rightful place."

Sagai walked toward the kitchen with his head low. Bruno and Thakur leaned against a column snickering.

"You're not so perfect, Sagai." Bruno lifted his chin in perceived arrogance. "Your file is bad and this means you're finished."

"I am not finished." Sagai stomped toward the boys and jutted his chin forward and peered into Bruno's dark narrow eyes. "I am phoenix and will rise from the ashes." He raised his fist, forgetting the knife in his hand.

Fear filled Bruno's eyes. Suddenly, Sagai realized the magnitude of his actions. The moment contradicted his training and his peaceful nature. If a superior appeared, consequences would be terrific. Horrible. He lowered the knife, took a calming breath, and turned away.

Those two were never serious about their calling, but no secret they hadn't been kicked out of the novitiate. At school, they called them *kolmoottis*—informers. Superiors loved this type. The scoundrels had probably tossed the knife into the trash to get him into trouble. Didn't matter. He couldn't argue his case.

He returned to the kitchen, washed the knife, and put it back in the drawer while wondering what consequences Father Danek meant. He prayed Bruno and Thakur wouldn't tell that he'd raised a knife against them. He'd be kicked out. Done. Finished!

With no further mention of the incident, Sagai accepted extra hours cleaning toilets, and scrubbing floors. At Christmas break all novices were sent home. Sagai was not. His orders were to travel north to serve thirty days in Wadala, a slum in Bombay.

The path to priesthood proved a rocky one. So be it. Sagai grabbed his suitcase.

Six

Defining Moments and Undesirable Places

Still round the corner there may wait,
a new road or a secret gate.
~ J. R. R. Tolkien

Rebecca

In a booth at the fast food joint near campus where I worked and ate for practically nothing, I stared into the blue eyes of the tall, broad, out-of-towner who rescued me from the ditch last summer. Nate had taken me to the hospital and held my hand in the emergency room as the doctor stitched my gashes and wrapped plaster around my leg.

The handsome college graduate, seven years older than me, was spending the summer with a friend. He showed up at the farm the next day with pink roses. Big and strong as he was, he carried me in his arms, lifting me in and out of his truck. He became my north star, guiding me out of what could have been a spiral into despair. Couldn't go to India with a broken leg. Couldn't work. Even college became questionable.

Nate showed up the next day, and the next, followed by months of Nate and me.

I smiled at my boyfriend and bit into my cheeseburger. At the end of the summer when my cast came off we drove west, almost to the Minnesota border and I enrolled in the small college near his hometown.

Not exactly living my dream like Eddie, who still, as Mama said, gallivanted in Europe, but when your path gets wiped out due to unforeseen circumstances, you have to hop on a new road. It came down to Nate, standing at a bend in the road, inviting me to walk with him. That, and the college closest to his hometown was the least expensive in the state.

Now, almost finished with my freshman year, I considered my major before fall course sign-up. "I'm thinking journalism or photography, but I love philosophy, psychology, and especially English. So many choices."

"None of those degrees will pay well in terms of a job, especially around here."

I let his "around here" comment pass. Though he had a job as area supervisor at a local plant, I wasn't planning on sticking "around here" forever.

"I want to do something to help others, working with people. What about Elementary Education? I could see being a teacher. I'm good with kids."

"Why would you want a degree where you have to deal with children? Wasn't it your fault your little sister died?" Nate bit into his burger.

A sting rose through my nostrils, forcing tears. How could he chow his cheeseburger after saying that? I blinked back awful memories of what happened at the pond. I'd never told Nate it was my fault. In an awkward moment of mentioning Kara, I'd only said that my parents had blamed me. Why was he bringing it up now?

I set my burger on the tray. Reality flicked me like a pine branch would, following someone too closely in the woods. I shouldn't have come to this tiny agricultural college where prairie winds shake cornstalks into fits of mocking laughter. I should be stepping to a quicker pulse of life, bathed in city lights. I shouldn't have let Nate talk me out of that dream. I could have managed on loans and grants.

Mama warned me. Huge mistake, she said. Don't change your college choice and follow a guy you hardly know.

Run and don't look back. The silent voice sounded so loud, it obliterated every other thought and made me wonder who said it—maybe some remnant of me before my head hit the tree and knocked out my sensibilities.

My leg twitched. I saw myself shove away from the table, tear past the Piggly Wiggly and the Ford dealership and sprint down the sidewalk that led back to campus. I imagined myself yanking my duffel bag from under my cot, stuffing in whatever fit, and telling Stacy, my roommate, she could have the rest. I'd take the next bus to Milwaukee. This wasn't the first time Nate's stinging criticism slapped me, but this one carried a message: Defining moment!

Like zombies climbing out of a grave, a barrage of negative thoughts pummeled me. I'd done bad things. Running landed me in trouble before, when I left Kara submerged in that muddy water. Don't run now.

My sensible side agreed. Nate was there for me when I was injured. He told me he loved me, charmed me all summer, got me away from White Gull Bay.

I lifted my head and our eyes met again. Could he see my pain? Did he love me?

"Probably shouldn't have said that." Nate's blank look turned to concern. He must have realized the impact of his words, yet it didn't make it right.

"Sorry." He crammed a fistful of fries into his mouth. "You done?" He wiped his face then tossed his napkin on the tray. "Let's go." Nate walked toward the door, confident I'd follow.

My hesitation was like a breeze, nearly closing my defining moment door. But guilt was a gale that slammed it shut. I swore I heard the click of a lock. But Nate was right. Like Mama, he spoke the truth. My fault Kara died. I tossed my uneaten food into the trash and followed him.

At the dorm, Nate put the pick-up in park. I wanted to talk, but cotton filled my mouth and screws cemented it shut.

"What's wrong?" His voice carried an irritated edge.

"What you said…at the table…"

"C'mon Bec. You're always too sensitive. Forget it."

"But…"

He grabbed me, pulled me close, and smothered my words in his big bear hug. "I'll call you."

Later that evening, I gripped my backpack and followed the sidewalk toward the library. What if I hadn't gotten injured last summer? Would India be stamped in my passport? Was life just a matter of tumbling through days and following whoever said, come? Was there a secret passageway that led to my true destiny? Had I missed it?

I climbed the wide concrete stairs, walked between tall pillars, and entered the library. Somewhere I'd read a quote from Mother Theresa that the greatest disease in the west was feeling unwanted, unloved, and uncared for. She said we could cure physical diseases with medicine, but only love cured loneliness, despair, and hopelessness. I knew myself well enough to understand that since Kara died, I danced on ledges of loneliness and despair. Was this love? If so, it tasted like bitter medicine.

At a quiet table in the corner, I set aside my questions, and studied for exams. Cocooned by rows of books, I dropped my head. My hair fell around sensible words *Dualism. Reason.*

I breathed deeply, inhaling the inky fresh new textbook smell. Like Mentholatum for a cold, the scent cleared my head, comforted me. I could be whatever I wanted to be. Photojournalist. Teacher.

I lost myself in more definitions. *Assimilation. Cognitive Therapy.*

Maybe Nate was right. Maybe I should consider a major that didn't have anything to do with children. Maybe I was unfit, even to be a mother someday. I shook away tears that threatened to spill all over Pavlov's dogs. I was those dogs. I was a rat in a Skinner box. I was conditioned and trapped because of what had happened at the pond.

Later in bed, images flashed in my mind's eye. I immediately burned them into my memory.

My roommate yawned from the cot across the narrow space between our beds. "You're awake?"

"Wasn't sleeping yet." Stacy rolled over. "We just said goodnight like five seconds ago."

"I had a dream."

"How can you dream that fast?"

"You're going to think it weird, but it was more like an image that popped into my head."

"Like a vision?" Stacy flipped on the reading light.

"I don't know."

I closed my eyes and recalled the scene, similar to the reoccurring dreams from a few years ago. "I was in a foreign country, taking photos of children. I stood beside this dark, handsome man, and—"

"A man?" Stacy say up. What happened?"

"He turned to me and though it was only a flash of a moment, and oh my goodness, his eyes."

"What about his eyes?"

"They were so full of compassion, love. Hard to explain, but I saw so much in those deep brown eyes."

"Maybe the vision was a peek into your future. Was it India?" She glanced above my cot at the map pinned on my bulletin board. I didn't get to go to India, but got the map.

"Maybe."

Stacy switched off the light. "Cool. Maybe he's your soul mate."

"Think he could be?"

"Who knows? Now close your eyes and have a vision about me."

I grabbed a teddy bear from the shelf and threw it at her. "I'm not a psychic and besides, we both know your future is with Blake."

She tossed the stuffed animal back. "And I'm going to sleep and dream about my wedding."

I could hear Stacy's smile, happily engaged to the man of her dreams. I flipped onto my stomach. Who was the real man of my dreams? Was my destiny to be a photojournalist? Travel to India? It'd be an incredible dream come true.

I flipped onto my back and recalled those eyes, so deep and caring. Were they looking at me, or at someone else? Nate never looked at me like that.

I rolled onto my stomach and adjusted my pillow. There had to be life beyond America's Dairyland. I'd wanted freedom, but had moved from one side of Wisconsin to the other and the state line was a barbed wire fence, holding me in like a dumb cow. The past summer was heavenly, but during the school year Nate worked long hours at the plant. School and work consumed all of my time. No time to really consider our relationship.

I glanced toward Stacy's bed. "You asleep?"

"Not anymore."

"How do you know Blake is the one?"

"Are you asking because you're wondering about your relationship or are you wondering about mine?"

"Both."

She spoke softly in the dark. "I can't think of a future without him. Blake's my best friend."

"So marriage will make you happy?"

"Well, duh!"

"I want marriage, too, but I also want to live out my true destiny."

"Blake is my destiny. We'll be there for each other, every step of the way, whatever we decide, wherever we go." Stacy grew quiet for a moment. "What is it with you and Nate? Are you two friends or more than that? This is personal, but have you and Nate—"

"I'm not ready to give myself to anyone in that way."

"Why not? You're practically twenty, have a smoking body, and he's a red-blooded male. I totally don't get how it doesn't happen. You know how guys are."

I didn't get it either, but figured he was a good guy not to push me before I was ready.

"You don't talk much about your past, but I'm guessing someone hurt you and now you're afraid."

"Okay, Doctor Stacy." My psychology major roommate hit too close to home, only she didn't get it exactly right. It wasn't a guy who'd hurt me. Life hurt me.

"Sometimes people who've been hurt are afraid to love. They put up walls."

I wasn't afraid. I only wanted to give myself to the right person.

"Becca? Did you fall asleep?"

"I'm thinking."

"I'm here if you want to talk."

"Thanks, Stacy."

Silent moments passed. "So what will you do this summer? Are you going back to White Gull Bay? Staying with Nate?"

"Haven't figured it out."

"Maybe your dreams are calling you somewhere else."

"Maybe. Goodnight."

Stacy's breathing slowed to a soft peaceful snore. Almost one year of college behind me and I wasn't sure of anything—my major, my summer plans, or my boyfriend. I'd worked all year, saved all I could, and got grants and loans. A mission trip to India could be a possibility at the end of summer. Was India calling? Would I discover my true purpose there? I closed my eyes, and though it felt like cheating, I surrendered to a fantasy of kissing a dark-haired man with dark brown compassionate eyes.

Sagai

In the corner of the cell, Sagai glanced in the cracked mirror above the basin. He washed travel dirt from his face, then raked his hand through his unruly hair. The shared space was a narrow cinder block room with two cots on opposite sides. One cot for him, the other for Brother Cyril, a middle-aged monk who assisted Father Alvin, the elderly scraggly-bearded parish priest.

The knife incident changed his course. He should've returned to Tamil Nadu with his classmates. While Sagai hadn't expected to go to the slums of Bombay, he would serve the oppressed with a glad heart. Jesus would.

"Your duty is to be among the people and prepare them for the birthday of Christ," Father Alvin explained as soon as he had arrived, hours earlier.

The next morning, he followed Brother Cyril through a filthy maze of slushy, narrow streets lined with shacks that blocked any air flow. The stench of feces and urine rose up from overflowing gutters, grabbed his throat, and threatened to choke him. He waved off swarms of flies. Rats, as big as cats, scurried fearlessly in the light of day as children—equally fearless—whacked them with sticks.

The monk occasionally paused in an alley to speak with people. Sagai followed bits of conversations, paying attention to the words and pitching a phrase here or there.

How could he prepare anyone for the birth of Christ when he couldn't even breathe in this place, let alone speak the language? He'd have to learn Hindi quickly and add it to the Tamil, English, Italian, and Nepali that danced in his head and sometimes rolled out entangled.

"There is one parish family whom you will be interested in meeting." Brother Cyril motioned. "Come."

Sagai followed him through more crowded corridors, past rag-pickers—the children sorting through trash for recycling. He and the cleric dodged mucky potholes and beggars with bony outstretched hands. Women wearing faded *sarees* cooked in dinged up vessels outside their homes. Shimmery sewage meandered in swills and streams around and into tiny shanties patched together with sticks, sheets of tin and pieces of bamboo mats.

"Be watchful." Brother Cyril wagged his head. "Crime is rampant. People come in search of jobs because of the proximity of the Arabian Sea docks. That makes it a haven for smugglers. Here, slum lords reign."

How could a nineteen-year-old make a difference in this place in a month's time? He trailed after the brother, down more chaotic mazes and alleys. The monk stopped at a doorway covered by a cloth, its colors and pattern nearly erased by sunshine and grime.

"Hullo. Hullo. Brother Cyril from St. Joseph's Parish here."

"*Alo. Vaanga, Vaanga*," answered a voice.

Sagai smiled. It'd been long since he'd heard a welcome in his mother tongue.

Brother Cyril lowered his voice. "This family has been coming for the English Mass. They are prominent in this community." He pointed upward to a crisscrossed wire apparatus rigged on the tin roof.

Into the dim, modest room, he followed Brother Cyril. A glow illuminated nearly a dozen faces. TV. Sagai had never seen one before, though aspirants and novices from wealthier homes had talked about the box that could change their world.

Brother Cyril spoke English to a middle-aged man inside the doorway. Women knelt over a small low table before the TV, one rolling balls of dough and the other tossing flour and flattening dough to make chapattis.

An elderly man rose from the cot against the wall and approached him, shuffling through the crowd.

"*Vanakkam.*" Sagai placed his palms together and bowed.

"Ah." The old toothless man grinned and clapped his hands. Instantly, the room buzzed with Tamil.

Brother Cyril tapped Sagai on the shoulder. "I'll take leave. You will find your way back to the parish?"

"We will see that he gets back," Grandfather Antonysamy said.

Sagai spent the day with the family, enjoying a familiar lunch of chapattis and sambar. He'd landed in the midst of a Tamil colony from South India who struggled to maintain their culture in the Northwest. He could relate.

"The children are growing in poverty," Grandfather Antonysamy said. "Here in this cosmopolitan city, they have nothing." He waved his hand toward the TV. "That box is a curse and a blessing. News and cricket matches, the blessing. A curse because it holds the children hostage. Makes them lazy."

Family and neighbors remained glued to the intriguing box for most of the day. Sagai cut his stare when the stories began to mesmerize him. No point getting caught up in a love story. Love wasn't in his future.

Before nightfall, the oldest son guided him back to the parish.

The next day, he dodged sudden sheets of rain, rats and mud puddles and found the mother sweeping sewage slush from the doorway with a broom made from the stem of a coconut leaf.

"*Thosthiram* Ma," he said, pressing his hands together.

"*Vanga,* Sagai," she answered. "Come."

Sagai followed her, stepping over the threshold. His heart ached for the Tamils. They yearned for a better future. He couldn't give them anything politically or financially, but last night while lying on his cot, an obvious idea struck him. In the morning he shared it with Father Alvin. The priest agreed. He would translate the Sunday sermon and parts of the English Mass into Tamil. Holding onto their culture meant holding onto their language and using it in social settings.

Grandfather Antonysamy clapped when Sagai shared the news. "Sunday Mass will be filled with Tamils."

He studied the children, entranced by this entertainment box. Perhaps he could break into their world. He sat near the twelve-year-old girl. "What is this you are watching?"

"Doordarshan TV." She tucked her chin low. "The show is called 'Hum Log'."

"And who is that pretty lady?" He pointed at the screen.

"That's Badki, the eldest daughter. She is a social worker, helps people."

"She wants to be Badki." Her brother nudged her shoulder.

A younger girl scooted closer. "I want to be Majhli. She is going to be an actress and me, too."

The older brother laughed. "And when you're rich and famous, do not forget me." He leaned forward and pointed. "That's Lallu. He's just come home after searching for a job. Can't find one. Our older brother is like him."

Sagai visited the home every day. The Tamil community, in the heart of the Mumbai, searched for themselves in the TV personalities and spoke of the characters like beloved relatives.

Like Lallu on the show, many locals, unable to find work, took to drinking. The oldest Antonysamy son was discouraged, not finding work. Grandfather expressed his fears about Tamil youth falling into bad situations, selling contraband or drugs.

That afternoon, as Sagai headed back to the parish and smacked into the elder Antonysamy son, breathless and dripping wet. He grabbed him by the shoulders and yanked him into an alley.

"What's going on?"

Fear flashed in his eyes. "Follow me!"

Sagai ran after him, down another alley, and another until the doorway of the Antonsamy home. The two ducked inside.

He doubled over, catching his breath. The TV group rushed to his side.

"The police truck hosed down a group of boys," the older brother said. "I heard them shouting, 'Thief!' I was lucky not to be caught up with them. I saw our friend running straight into their path." The whites of his eyes grew huge as he faced Sagai. "You don't know how close you came."

Sagai thanked him for the rescue. An arrest would have been horrible. He'd be kicked out of the priesthood, and who knew what could happen in jail?

"Did they apprehend the boys?" Grandfather Antonysamy wrung his hands.

The older boy nodded. "After they took them, the police continued hosing everyone on the street."

"Ay-yo!" Grandfather shook his head. "The police will beat those boys bloody. Their families may never see them again." He threw his hands up. "Probably because a starving child slipped a mango off a cart. Such is life here."

Wagging heads, sighs, and clicking tongues ceased when the TV drama returned after a commercial break.

Sagai sat on the floor, forced out a deep breath. One wrong turn could have changed the course of his life, and through no choice of his own, yet God spared him.

The past few days, he'd been listening to the Tamil families and praying with them. These deeply spiritual people trusted God above all else, but lived in hopelessness. What could he do to prepare them for the hope of a coming Savior?

Then Sagai heard angels singing. He approached the TV crowd. The youth sang along with the operatic TV voices in a harmonious delight. He had an idea.

The next day he arrived in the Tamil home with sheet music that had been chosen for midnight Mass at Christmas. He'd found a guitar at the parish. He'd practiced with lesson books in Vellore, and with a little help from Brother Cyril, quickly managed the chords. The Tamil youth would sing during Christmas Mass.

Singing lessons soon grew too large to hold in the Antonysamy home. Sagai invited his youth choir— Antonysamy family and friends—to the parish for practice, catechism lessons and help building and decorating the Christmas crèche. Maybe he wasn't fixing anything in their lives, but the group was busy and anticipating Jesus' birthday.

Christmas Eve arrived. Before Mass, the concert— under his direction—ended with a collective sigh of bliss from attendees.

Then Sagai stepped to the pulpit for the first time to read the sermon he'd translated into Tamil. A holy chill hopped on his arms and walked all the way up his shoulders. He felt like Moses at the burning bush. This was holy Ground. Here, God's Word went forth to hungry souls starved for spiritual nourishment. He lowered his head. He didn't feel worthy.

He prayed. Jesus, I'm not a priest yet, but someday I will give my own reflections, my own thoughts from my heart about You and Your love for humanity. For now, may the words of my mouth and this meditation be pleasing in your sight, O Lord, my Rock and my Redeemer.

Sagai cleared his throat, straightened, and lowered his voice. "How beautiful are the feet of them that bring glad tidings of good things. Two thousand years ago, angels told shepherds in the fields the good news of the birth of our Lord, Jesus Christ."

Tonight he was the bearer of good news to a sea of Tamils packed in the church, kneeling in the back and in aisles. Tonight they'd hear the Gospel of the coming of the Lord in their native language, listen to the sermon, sing carols, and receive in faith, the body and blood of Christ. These were the rich in faith.

He continued reading. "In his letter to the first century Christian community, John begins by saying, 'How great is the love the Father has lavished on us, that we should be called children of God! And that is what we are'!"

"We cannot have any hope of establishing a relationship with God on our own merits, but through the powerful hope of Christmas, God has declared the depth of our worth by the extent of His love. A love that brought Jesus to Earth and hope to a hopeless world. Jesus chose the lowly, the outcasts, the poor to receive this great news, the greatest news the world has ever known…"

After the Amen, Sagai scanned the congregation. He blinked and looked again. He'd seen the faces of the Tamils in the glow of the TV screen. Now, the faces, turned toward heaven, appeared illuminated. Though he could never determine or measure a heart changed by God's Word, maybe for just one night or maybe for good, something had happened within the hearts of the Tamils. What joy to be God's instrument!

Sagai descended from the simple wooden pulpit. Indeed a holy night. He didn't feel like leaving the slums of Wadala, but in the morning, he'd return to Nashik for his next assignment.

Where would the path to priesthood lead him next?

Seven

Temporary Vows

It is important to expect nothing, to take every experience, including the negative ones, as merely steps on the path, and to proceed.
~ Ram Dass

Rebecca

At a quiet corner table, candle light flickered over the menu's double-digit priced meals. I crossed my legs and adjusted the flower print dress I'd borrowed from Stacy, unable to make up my mind about what to eat or what to do about my future.

Nate, seated across from me, tugged at his tie, then met my eyes. "Hurry up and decide."

I lowered my head. For weeks, decisions hung in the air like summer mosquitos in the Wisconsin woods. The semester nearly over, and I didn't have a clue about my next step. Nate agreed to meet and discuss plans, even surprised me with an invitation to an expensive dinner out.

Through the past week, I couldn't concentrate on homework. My passion for adventure, like a hibernating bear, stirred with spring's urgings. The summer I met Nate, I was wounded and weak, craving love. My life since had revolved around classes, studying, working, and sometimes spending rare free time with him. India still haunted my dreams and my passport, sadly, hadn't been stamped.

I placed my order for shrimp. Nate ordered steak. After the waitress left, he clasped his hands on the table and grinned like he'd swallowed a big secret.

"I had a long talk with Mother." Nate shook his napkin and rested it in his lap. "Then we went shopping."

Shopping with his mom? He hated shopping.

He scanned the room. "She made the reservations here." He reached into his coat pocket, pulled out a small box, and set it on the table. It wasn't my birthday. Wasn't Valentine's Day. Movie scenes ran through my mind. When guys did this, it meant one thing. Oh please, let it not be.

He picked up the box, flipped the lid, and pushed it toward me. Good God! A diamond!

"It's not very big, but Mother said it was good enough for you."

An insult? A proposal should not begin with an insult. I swallowed. "I'm not even twenty." I gulped. "I have to finish college."

Nate shrugged. "It doesn't mean we have to get married right away. I just want to know I'm not wasting time."

Wasting time? Was I wasting time? He was pushing me away. Then I stared at the ring. The diamond spoke of things like desire, love, need, cherish. I shook my head to clear out the sparkles. "But I want to finish college, travel…and so much more. I plan to take a mission trip. I don't think I'm ready for this."

"You can still do what you want. The ring can be like a promise to make a promise." Nate beamed. "It doesn't have to mean any more than that for now."

"Really? It just means we're committed to being engaged someday?"

He clapped his hands and rubbed them. "Yep. Sounds perfect. I'm in no hurry, but I think we need the commitment at this point."

I shook my head. "I don't want to settle down here."

With a crestfallen face, he reached for my hand. "I'm not married to the plant and don't have to stay in my hometown."

Maybe my doubts were unfounded. Maybe it was time to love someone for real, like Stacy had suggested. Maybe I was afraid. It made sense to move into a more committed phase of the relationship.

Nate picked up the ring, reached for my hand, and slid it onto my finger. He smiled with satisfaction, then downed his Jack Daniels on the rocks, icicles clinking in the glass.

That was it? Was this a temporary or a real engagement? What'd I just do?

Sagai

"Before God, I, Sagai, make this vow, temporarily, to be poor, chaste and obedient." In Nashik, with his back to a congregation of peers, he knelt at the altar in his new short-sleeved button-up shirt and trousers. He'd grown out of his old clothes and Appa had sent new ones for the profession of temporary vows.

With shoulders back and chin high, Sagai returned to the pews. The smug look that passed between Bruno and Thakur couldn't erase his smile. They'd caused him enough grief this past year, but God remained on his side. What kind of priests would Bruno and Thakur make? He stopped the thought from going further. Only God could judge. These fellows did one thing right. They'd mastered the vow of obedience and knew how to curry favor with superiors.

He knelt in the pew. Formal vows waited years away, but he thanked God for bringing him one step closer to priesthood.

After the ceremony, he stood before Father Antony and Father Danek in the office, anxious to learn where he'd go for his Philosophate. Father Antony had explained that a degree in Philosophy was meant to help seminarians better understand Theology, the next degree on the ladder to Holy Orders.

As Father Antony shuffled papers, Sagai hoped he'd study in Tamil Nadu with Victor and some of his old companions from Vellore. Or maybe he'd go to Goa with Binny. The rose bushes were flourishing, and he'd served well in Wadala.

"Darjeeling." Father Danek shoved papers toward him.

"Travel instructions." Father Antony clasped his hands. "A forty hour journey from here. There, you'll earn your philosophy degree along with a Bachelor's in Literature."

"Two degrees?" Sagai swallowed. "In Darjeeling?"

Father Danek glared.

"Thank you." He accepted the traveling money and papers, bowed to his superiors, and returned to the dormitory for the last time. He'd travel alone on the four day journey on buses and trains almost to the Chinese border.

The empty dormitory echoed. He opened his suitcase and set the constitutions and cannons book on top—his graduation gift from the institution. The book contained the rules of the church to which he'd just professed obedience.

He placed his Bible beside it, considering the places in the sacred text where Jesus criticized the Pharisees for putting laws before the greatest commandment to love one another. Some priests, like Father Antony, swung toward love. Father Danek, law.

This move might very well be punishment. A second late for class and Superiors would grab pens and rush into a scribbling frenzy. Didn't matter if he was feeding the poor. Good deeds were often overlooked while his file grew fatter with tallies that wrongly branded him. Every explanation, question, or plead of innocence was noted as an act of disobedience or a challenge to authority—the greatest sin. A catalogue of unfair charges dogged his heels like a screeching monkey after his lunch.

He was twenty, a college student, not the naïve boy who left Sheveroy Hills four years ago. Rearranging his suitcase, he found a t-shirt he got during a recent visit home. Vijay said shirts with saying on them were the latest style and offered to buy him one. Sagai chose a shirt that read, "Somebody Somewhere Loves Me."

Cheeky to wear it back to the novitiate, but he did anyway. Immediately teachers ordered him to get back into his plain button-up shirt. Vows should not be a problem. He'd been love-starved and friendship-starved. That was true poverty. He closed his shabby brown suitcase.

"Congratulations."

Sagai turned to an old familiar face. "Father Michael!"

The brother responsible for his entry into the junior seminary reached out his hand, and Sagai grasped it with both of his. "Congratulations on being priested."

Father Michael took a step back, looked him over, and smiled. "You've grown into a tall, handsome young man."

He lowered his head, not used to compliments.

"Ready for your journey?"

"I've never been to Darjeeling. It's quite far north."

"And I've never been to America, but I'll be leaving in a few weeks to mission preach in Wisconsin, a northern state. Sometimes the longest journeys can be the most rewarding."

"Will you return to India?"

Father Michael laughed. "Yes, of course. My move is only temporary. I know where you'll be, and I'll write from America."

Sagai smiled. "Letters from America would be very special indeed."

"Better not miss your bus."

Sagai knelt at Father Michael's feet. "Please bless me before I take leave."

The kindly priest blessed him, then made the sign of the cross on his forehead.

"Pray for me, Father."

"I've been praying for you every day since I met you and I will continue to do so."

"Really?" Sagai could hardly believe it. Father Michael thought of him, prayed for him every day? He smiled. With the priest's prayers and fatherly love, even from across the world, everything would be okay. He bid him goodbye and ran to the bus station with a lighter heart, eager to begin his journey to Darjeeling.

Eight

Navigating Uncharted Territory

*Have no fear of moving into the unknown. Simply step
out fearlessly knowing that I am with you, therefore
no harm can befall you; all is very, very well. Do this
in complete faith and confidence.*
~ Pope John Paul II

Rebecca

"Oh. My. Gosh!" Tammy, from down the hall, fanned her face. The glitter from my left hand, as small as it was, caught her eye during an attempt to sneak into my dorm room.

"Tell me the story!"

Romantic proposal stories were the coolest happenings in the dorms. After a weekend, if you came back with a ring, you were queen at least until Wednesday. I lowered my head. I didn't have a good story. Stories mattered. I wasn't going to make a good queen.

The door opened. Stacy's eyes darted to my hand, then back to me. Her fingers flew to her parted lips. "She'll tell you later."

My roommate shut the door and rested her hand on her hip. "What'd your mom and dad say?"

"Didn't tell them." I pushed past her to my desk and shuffled papers.

Stacy sat on the end of my bed. "Becca, do you love him?'

"I think so." I stared at my ring. "This, by the way, isn't...I don't think...an official engagement ring. Not a promise ring either, I don't think." I twisted a strand of hair.

"What! You accepted a pretend engagement ring?" Stacy sat on her bed. "Give me a moment. I'm trying to understand." She crossed her arms. "So, instead of breaking up you get sort-of engaged."

"Something like that, but you kind of had to be there."

"Whatever. I have never heard you talk about Nate like you're crazy about him. Your relationship with your family is almost non-existent. Is this a daddy issue?"

"Quit analyzing me. Do that with your patients when you get your degree. I don't know anything for sure. That's the point of being young. We are allowed to venture into unknowns with complete unsureness. We leap and trust the net will appear." I pressed my forehead to the desk and banged my head. "Oh, what if there's no net? I think I made a big mistake. What should I do?"

"Take at least one night off waitressing this weekend and spend it with Nate's family. See how he treats his mom. Hang out. Then come back and tell me why you want to marry him, and I'll tell you if you should."

I took Stacy's advice. On Saturday, while Nate watched TV with his dad, I helped his mom set the dinner table for our formal "almost" engagement party.

Diamonds and colorful stones decorated Harriet's manicured hands and clinked against wine glasses. She wore a navy dress with a white collar. Her blond hair poofed high, hair-sprayed to perfection. From the bureau, she pulled out weighty silverware and real china, actually from China. I'd checked the back of the plate when I set it on the table.

She handed me cloth napkins, then asked me to light candles. We never had dinners like this at home. She talked about her work downtown as a bank president secretary and the grocery store her husband owned.

By the time the table was set, Nate's older sister arrived with her husband. She had long fingernails painted blood red and wore a shoulder-padded dress, heels, and panty-hose.

I didn't own panty hose. With my chewed off nails and wearing jeans and a cable sweater and sneakers, I was slumming it with the ladies of Dynasty.

During the dinner, unsure which utensils to use and where to put the napkin, I watched and followed.

I wanted to be in this picture, but not in this place. I liked their polite and proper ways compared to how things were on the farm. Nate's hometown was quaint, but a panicky fear hung onto each breath. I didn't want the western edge of Wisconsin to be the end of my road.

After dishes, Nate's father retired to the recliner in the living room and his son mixed drinks with fancy names and poured them in fancy crystal glasses. I asked for a beer, but he plunked an olive stuck with a tiny sword in a drink, then handed it to me.

Melodious clinks and eloquent toasts to our engagement rang festively in the kitchen, but when Nate dealt the cards, the evening took an interesting turn.

Raunchy jokes made me blush. Mama would have slapped us if we used words like that. I set my glass down after two sips. The more they drank, the louder they got, the nastier the language became, and all the more I felt like an outsider. I excused myself to the living room where Nate's dad snored from a recliner.

I literally backed up when Harriet cooed. "I'm sooo happy you're settling down." She pinched Nate's cheeks and made chirping noises like to a baby. "My sweet child."

Through a mirror over the bureau in the hallway, I watched the activity in the kitchen like Alice in Wonderland, looking into an odd land, trying to figure out the players.

Harriet downed her drink. "If you don't get that promotion to plant manager, join your father at the store. After all, it'll be yours one day."

She had her claws deep in her son. I sat on the couch and twirled the ring as Nathanial's snore rose over the sound of the late night news.

When the party wound down, I returned to the kitchen. Nate's brother-in-law pressed too tightly against me when he hugged goodbye and the thrill he got from it was obvious. The hug took me back to Uncle Eugene's unwelcomed touches.

Nate shut the front door.

"I don't like him. He hugged me in a perverted way."

"You're just not used to a normal, close family."

The word normal and a large question mark waltzed in my head. I crossed my arms.

"He's harmless." Nate waved his hand, chasing away my concerns.

I grabbed my worries back. "Your mom wants you to live here, stay here and settle down."

"I'm going downtown for a drink," Nate slurred.

He didn't invite me, didn't say goodnight, just turned and walked out the front door. I retired to the guest bedroom and locked the door. Why didn't I open my mouth and say what I thought. When it would come to the obedient part of the vows, I'd have no problem. That thought unnerved me.

I hardly slept, but never heard Nate come home. Sunday morning, his mom morphed back to stoic matronly

Harriet and insisted we all go to Mass. He rolled out of his bedroom bleary-eyed.

We all walked two blocks to the Catholic Church. They loved their little church because Father Stan could have them in and out in less than thirty minutes. Best kept secret in the county, Nate's dad said.

"Who's that foreign priest with Father Stan?" Nate asked no one in particular, as the bell rang.

A collective fidgety nervousness filled our pew during the procession. At announcements, Father Stan introduced his guest priest, Father Michael from India, an average built, thirtyish looking man with twinkly, smiling eyes.

"Way cool!" I whispered.

Father Stan announced Father Michael was doing mission preaching and would speak in lieu of the sermon. I clapped. I was the lone clapper. Nate nudged me. Harriet frowned and shook her head. Clapping wasn't appropriate in the Catholic Church.

During the sermon, I hung onto every word from Father Michael as if God were speaking. Nate's family repeatedly checked their watches. Father Michael talked about Tamil Nadu. Thanks to my India map, I knew Tamil Nadu was a state in South India. When he talked about the orphanage where he served, I almost scaled the pews, fell at his feet, and asked him to sign me up for missions work. I prayed he'd ask for volunteers, but today he only wanted funds. I emptied my wallet into the second collection plate.

"Twenty-five dollars is way too much." Nate tossed in fifty-five cents.

After Mass, I bounced on my toes as we filed out of the pew. Nate grabbed my hand after greeting Father Michael at the doorway, but I pulled back. "I want to talk to him. I'll meet you at home in a few minutes."

He rolled his eyes and left with his family. After Mass, I waited until everyone cleared the church entry way, then introduced myself to the Indian priest. In a rush, I shared my dream of coming to India. "I already have a passport."

"You are most welcome." Father Michael clasped his hands together and emphasized the word, "most." I loved his whispery, kind, sing-song voice. "You will stay at the convent and we will take very good care of you."

I loved how he said, will, like it was destiny, like it was going to happen for sure, like he'd landed from India just to rescue me.

"Even if I'm not a Catholic?"

"*Vanakkam.*"

"Pardon?"

That means 'welcome,' in Tamil." His head bobbed slightly, from side to side.

I wanted to hug him and almost did, but he kept his palms together in front of his chest in proper Indian manner. I gave Father Michael my name, address in White Gull Bay, and my parent's phone number and took his card.

"We will be pen pals."

I pressed my clasped hands to my chest. "Fantastic! I'll let you know when I'm coming."

I twirled and danced on air, all the way back to Nate's house. By the time I reached the front door, I had my plan. With a place to stay, I only needed air fare, so I could apply for a visa and work all summer and probably earn enough to visit India before next semester.

I rushed, breathless, into Nate's house, and twirled into the kitchen. "Guess what?"

Nate looked up from the kitchen table. His mother shut the refrigerator and stared.

"I'm going to India." I stretched out my arms.

He took a bite of his sandwich, unfazed. Had they not heard me? I moved beside Nate, searching his eyes.

Harriet tied the bread bag, put it in a drawer, then sat between me and her son. Her eyes zeroed in on the ring. "That's a big decision. I'm sure you and Nate will talk it over." She patted my left hand, stood, and nodded at Nate.

I felt the weight of the ring deep in my heart. The diamond tied me to Nate and his family. Did it mean I had to do whatever they said? Let go of dreams?

Harriet set a BLT before me. "If you're looking for summer work, a friend of mine owns a darling boutique in town and needs help. I've already spoken about you, and I'm certain she'll hire you."

"But where will I stay?"

"The spare bedroom is yours."

"But—"

"You'll get a discount on clothes." Harriet looked over the top of her bifocals. "Stylish, decent outfits." She rose. "You don't need to thank me."

That evening, while Nate watched a Dirty Harry Movie, I broached the subject. "I really want to go to India. Don't you feel there's so much out there besides Wisconsin? Don't you want to—"

"Hush." His tone sounded mean around the edges. "I'm watching the movie."

A red flag slapped my face and made me burn with anger. I recalled another red flag a few weeks earlier. Nate called me a loser because I wouldn't drink or smoke pot at a party. I didn't like the way drinking made me feel. Couldn't believe it. I'd avoided drugs in high school, only to get pressured by my fiancé?

I kept all these things in my heart as the blood flowed on the TV screen. I thought about what I wanted in a relationship and what ours lacked. I never saw expressions of love between my parents. Did my married brothers and sisters love their spouses with passion at the center of their relationships or were they settling? Would I settle and give up everything if I married Nate?

On Monday morning, he took a personal day and drove me to college, hardly speaking a word. Before he turned into the parking lot, I knew what to do. I'd call Father Michael and plan my India trip. I'd turn down Harriet's job offer and work in White Gull Bay over the summer. I'd earn more at the resorts. Then, at the end of the summer, I'd go to India. Finally!

Distance would help decide if Nate and I were meant to be. I twisted the ring, considering giving it back while silently rehearsing my leaving talk. Nate pulled into a parking spot. My heart raced. I didn't want to hurt him.

I opened my mouth to explain and Nate turned toward me. "I got a job offer in Southern California."

I snapped my mouth shut, rearranged my words and processed these new ones. "What? When did you apply?"

He parked and faced me. "I didn't want to talk about it until I got the offer. Just found out this morning. I haven't even told Mother."

"But—"

"I'll make three times my salary. You've been complaining about living in Wisconsin and about how much you want to travel."

"You want me to come with you?"

"I start in two weeks, but I could push it a few days later so you can finish the semester. I don't want to go without you."

Think. Think. Think before you speak. I tried to keep this mantra going in my head because I was too capricious for my own good, always letting words fire impulsively, even agreeing with others just to please them. Mama would freak if I went to California with Nate, especially not married.

I pressed my hand over my pounding heart. "What about India?"

"We'll take a mission trip once we get settled in California. I get a paid vacation in the first year."

"But Nate, I…"

"Becky, I'll do anything for you. If I have any flaws, anything you don't like, tell me. I'll change. I need you."

I need you. Those three words tugged my heart. Nate also needed rescuing from his mother. California dangled like a carrot before me and I hopped right on that. India would be a life-changing experience for both of us. Maybe it was our destiny to marry, then go together. I took a deep breath and a blind leap of shaky faith. "Okay."

Sagai

Sagai shut his suitcase, left the novitiate, boarded a bus in Nashik, then at Bombay's Victoria Station he caught the train to Calcutta.

Hours later, he woke hungry, missing South India trains with canteens and smells of frying oil and spices. This train didn't serve food and smelled sour, like sweat.

In the early hours of the morning, Sagai arrived at Calcutta's Howrah Junction. He waited on the platform—as per instructions—for a priest to meet him.

On the sides of endless rows of tracks, porters scurried nearly as fast as the rats, offering to carry baggage. Corporate business travelers in white shirts intermingled with men in long white *kurtas* and young men wearing t-shirts and bellbottoms.

Sagai searched for a white cassock in the midst of saffron robes and turbaned Sikhs with bushy mustaches. A rainbow of *sarees* flowed by in a rush of color. College girls milled about, wearing their modern *salwar kameez* and even shorter styles of *ghagra skirts* and *cholis.*

Over the speaker, a female voice announced incoming and outgoing trains in three languages: English, Hindi and what he thought must be Bengali. Families slept, huddled on mats or blankets in groups on the station floor.

A young clean-shaven tall man in a white cassock walked toward him. "Sagai?"

"Yes, Father."

"Come."

He followed the priest outside the station, then glanced back at the grandiose red brick building trimmed in white, probably built by the Brits when they'd colonized India. A magnificent bridge stretched over a large river.

"The holy Ganges?" He hustled to keep up.

"The Hooghli River. It's an arm of the Ganges, and that's the Howrah Bridge running across it."

He took one look back at the long suspension bridge with high looming steel chords of trusses. He hurried after the priest through endless hordes of travelers, beggars, street vendors, cows, and goats. Horns blasted a cacophony of pitches. Men shouted, naming their goods. Pungent petrol fumes hung low in the thick air.

The priest climbed into a rickshaw. Sagai hesitated. In Tamil Nadu and in the state of Maharashtra, he'd only known bicycle rickshaws.

"Come."

"Father, please. I can run alongside." He could not let a barefooted human pull him in a cart, not after taking a vow of poverty.

"Tsk, tsk. Come."

Obedience ranked higher than doing the right thing. He wouldn't become a priest unless he learned to be obedient. He cringed and climbed into the seat.

The hunch-backed old man with bowed, bony legs poking like sticks from his *lungi* pulled them through a chaotic cluster of trams, buses, camels, horses, lorries, autos and rickshaws and bent-over walkers lugging all sorts of materials on their backs. Traffic policemen in blue uniforms attempted, but failed, to put sense and order to it all. Smells of sweat, petrol, and cow dung plumed upward with the dust on the road.

After a meal and a good night's sleep at the monastery, Sagai insisted on walking to the station to continue the next phase of his journey to Darjeeling.

After another day and a night on the train, he arrived in Siliguri with the rising sun and a cacophony of strange words. A brother from the college would meet him on the platform.

He recognized a bit of the local language, but it didn't sound like Bengali nor Hindi. The word "chow" repeated often. A Nepali greeting?

A small bus pulled up to the platform. Sagai spun, searching for the brother. The sweaty crowd filed into the tiny bus, cramming into every seat and filling each possible place to stand. Some balanced on one leg like chickens. When not one more could sandwich into that horde of bodies, passengers climbed onto the roof, clutching their baggage. How would they manage through the hairpin curves and narrow roads, where in some places, plummeting drop-offs met the edge of the road?

A young man about his age ran toward the bus.

The brother?

He slid into the driver's seat and called, "To Darjeeling!" He met Sagai's eyes and motioned him to board. The boy could not be old enough to drive.

Sagai stepped back in sheer terror and waved off the bus. As it pulled out of the station, he whispered a prayer, especially for those on the roof.

While pacing on the cement platform, worry built. A few passengers and some vendors mulled about. Maybe another bus, not so crowded would come soon.

He approached a cart vendor. "Will there be another bus?"

The man offered an odd piece of fruit. Misunderstood, Sagai held out a palm full of rupees and studied the fruit. The merry-eyed vendor took the coins and grabbed the fruit. He peeled the prickly pink-red rind to expose a layer of white flesh. "Lychee." He handed it back.

As Sagai wiped juice from his mouth, a young man in a cassock, about his age, but taller and more dark-skinned, rushed toward him.

"Sagai?"

"Yes, that's me."

"I'm Mondal."

"We missed the bus." He popped the last bite in his mouth.

"Thank God! A fellow could die on that damn thing."

A couple of short whistles sounded and Mondal pointed. "Look."

A tiny train, only a few feet wide, chugged into the station.

"The Darjeeling Toy Train. Come along."

The train wasn't in his travel instructions. He hesitated.

"Don't worry. I'll get your fare."

He peeked into the open front engine where a man stoked coal into an engine, then boarded into a narrow wooden bench alongside Mondal.

Piney scents, carried on the mountain breezes, entered the open window. Mondal pointed out the Mahanadi River that flowed from the Himalayan foothills. The train passed through manicured rolling fields dotted with small bushes.

"Tea gardens," Mondal said.

"Wish I had a camera." He'd never seen these endless fields of brushy shrubs, and forests. The immense valleys opened up like large mouths and high majestic mountainous jutted like spikes into the sky.

Locals with slanted eyes and fair skin waved. People ambled alongside the train tracks with huge loads on their backs: lumpy burlap bags, too many sticks, sacks of potatoes, and sometimes children in baskets. One man stooped over low, carried a large door on his back.

"Tibetan prayer flags." Mondal pointed to long strings of small colorful squares tied to trees, flapping in the wind. Flags with an unknown script written on them also waved from posts in front of homes.

The train wound through the piney mountains, passing shops that clung onto the mountainside, so close Sagai could have reached from the train and grabbed a snack from the shelves. Roses, magnolias, rhododendrons, and poinsettias lit up the ditches. Northeast India was beautiful indeed.

As the train whistled and chugged into a station, a sign read: Ghoom 7407 feet.

"The highest point of our journey," Mondal explained. "Second highest train station in the world. Next we descend to Darjeeling. Mother Teresa realized her calling on this train when she left the Loretto convent to begin the Missionaries of Charity." Mondal stood. "Watch, Sagai."

As the train pulled away, the brother leapt off and disappeared. Sagai held his breath until he hopped back on the train at the other side of a large loop.

"You gave me a fright." Sagai removed his hand from his heart. "I thought you were leaving me for good."

"Not yet my friend. Just having fun."

Majestic snowy peaks of the Himalayas appeared. Sagai felt pangs of guilt that he'd considered this place punishment. Maybe his file contained good things or perhaps God was fond of him to send him to the top of the world, an incredible place he'd call home for the next four years.

Monkeys darted across the twisty turning tracks and peered curiously at them from rocks. Sagai stretched his legs, folded his hands, and smiled. Soon the train slowed, nearing their destination. Mondal put his hand on Sagai's shoulder. With serious, unblinking eyes, he said, "I don't want to frighten you, but you could encounter difficulties at the seminary."

"What are you saying?"

"Be on guard. Keep to yourself."

Nine

Vows and Predicaments

Commitment is an act, not a word.
~ Jean-Paul Sartre

Rebecca

I stood in the driveway, holding my wedding dress in one hand and my suitcase in the other. The sound of gravel crunching under tires gave way to the rev of an engine when my in-law's Cadillac turned onto the road and sped away. Tears fell on white satin, or polyester, or whatever my cheap dress was made of. When all I could hear was the faint rumble of a John Deere in the corn field, I looked toward the front door of my parent's house.

I didn't want to go in. Mama would say, "I told you so."

The day before, I'd walked down the aisle in a small country non-denominational church, married by a pastor who was willing to do the job on short notice. Today, I was alone.

Mama's face appeared in the window. I willed myself to move toward her. She met me on the porch. Her eyes searched mine. Oh, how I needed her now.

The strength to hold her gaze drained away and I flung myself at her, wrapping my arms around her neck. The feeling of my cheek against her shoulder drew all my sorrow to the surface until it welled out in ragged sobs and tears. I don't know how long she held me there, rocking me slowly, shushing in my ear, but I never wanted to let go. This was the hug I needed years ago and what I desperately needed now.

"He's gone." I blew my nose in the ugly dress. "And I'm so stupid."

Mama put her hands on my shoulders and stepped back, her forehead wrinkled, her eyebrows furrowed. "Come inside."

I followed her to the couch.

"Anyone home?" I didn't want to see Heather and worried the boys would laugh at me for such an idiotic move.

"Heather's working, and the boys and Daddy are picking stones in the back forty." She took my hand, led me to the couch and searched my eyes. "What happened?"

I recalled my waking moment as a new bride. "Bright and early, I opened my eyes, nothing covering me but a sheet, and there was my mother-in-law. I didn't know his parents had the room next to ours. Never heard her knock, but Nate did and let her in."

"Tsk, tsk." Mama shook her head. "That's odd." She placed her hand over mine.

"I pulled the covers around me and she waltzed right up to the bed and insisted she was taking Nate home so he could spend the week with family."

"My goodness! What did Nate say?"

"Nothing. He also said nothing when she accused me of forcing her baby to move to California. She said he was hers for the rest of the week. I hate her."

"Don't say that." She tapped my hand.

He shouldn't dump me for a week, the day after we get married. I burst into a loud wail. "I made a huge mistake."

Mama's lips tightened. "Yes, you did. You shouldn't have rushed into marriage."

"But you insisted we marry before leaving for California. You said we shouldn't live in sin."

"That much is true, but I warned you, even that morning, I said it wasn't too late."

"I should have ran! But, I did mean the vows I spoke. Before God, I'd given myself to him wholeheartedly. I assumed he would love and cherish me, like he said. I assumed, once we got married, he'd at least want to be with me. You know what he said when I reminded him of that?"

"What?"

"When you assume, you make an ass out of you and me." I tossed the stupid dress on the floor, rose to get a tissue, and blew my nose.

"He's no good." She shook her head. "He was acting strange at the wedding. Why was he late?"

"Hung over."

I sat down, and Mama patted my hand. "Horrible."

The way we bonded over hating Nate eased my pain. "He said the wedding was a joke because we had a protestant minister. He said it was stupid to get married here and that the reception on the front lawn was lame. He said your brats and beans sucked."

She raised her eyebrows. "Really?"

"I think his mom bought the ring and made him propose so he'd settle down, only that didn't go as she planned. And now he's happy because he gets to party in his hometown without me for the week." I pounded my fist on the couch cushion. "She might even talk him out of going to California."

Mama narrowed her eyes and shook her head. "There was nothing wrong with my brats and beans."

"No kidding. What kind of a loser doesn't like your brats and beans?" I slumped into the couch. "The night didn't get better. I wanted to be the bride and wear the dress a little longer, even though it was a blue-light special at the bridal shop. I asked to go dancing at The Well. He made me change into jeans, then he danced with Heather more than me." I grabbed Mama's hands. "Tell me what to do now!"

She closed her eyes for a few moments, as if she had wisdom printed on the back of her eyelids. "Sleep on it. Tomorrow is a new day."

Her "Gone with The Wind" attitude wasn't helping. Something outside caught her eye. I followed her gaze. Daddy approached the house from the barn. "You took vows. You made a commitment before God."

I understood commitment, but I wanted a happy relationship, not a cold marriage like hers. When I was in grade school, at the dinner table Mama offered an opinion on something Daddy was ranting about. He narrowed his eyes at her. "You don't know what you're talking about. You're stupid. Shut yer trap."

Mama had clutched her chest then, as if she'd been stabbed. Did Daddy know those sharp daggers cut all the way through her and landed in my heart? I'd hoped for so much more for myself.

My father opened the door, raised an eyebrow when he saw me, but didn't say a word.

I didn't feel better the next day. I sulked in my pajamas in the recliner in front of the TV, watching a Gilligan's Island rerun, wishing for a marriage like Mr. and Mrs. Howells. For the first time, I noticed that Mr. Howell was really into Lovey. He adored the woman. Lucky Lovey. Mama shut off the television just when they were about to get off the island.

"Mama!"

"I think you know how it's going to end." She handed me a bus ticket, and reminded me of my vows before God.

"But...but...I don't know if I want to go back to Nate."

"You made your bed, now lie in it. Sometimes you have to suffer. That's life." Her jaw trembled. I wasn't sure if sadness for me or regrets in her marriage caused the quiver.

I went to the window and stared outside. Mama loved me yesterday, for a moment. Now, she hated me again. A familiar ache of loneliness and abandonment made me feel like running, but where? Who could help me now? And India? It drifted out of sight like the clouds outside, blowing eastward. Bus ticket in hand, I embraced my fate.

The next morning, Nate and I sat with his mother at her kitchen table. I found it awkward to make eye contact with Harriet, let alone converse. She'd seen me naked.

And the master-at-diminishing-his wrongs-and-turning-me-into-the-crazy-one wasn't into discussing feelings. So I stared at the wood grains, following curves and circles with my finger.

Harriet cleared her throat. "I spoke with Father Stan earlier. Given that your flight leaves in the morning, he's willing to work with us. He'll bless your marriage this afternoon, making it valid in the church."

"What? You mean it's not valid, um, like God doesn't acknowledge it happened?" Holy cow! This could be my loophole. No way was I meeting Father Stan. I bit my lip and silently ruminated on what a horrible husband Nate had been so my transparent face wouldn't give away my delight about this gold nugget of information. I wasn't even sure we consummated the marriage. For my first time, it was a rather disappointing thirty seconds.

I faked a yawn to hide my smile. "Is Father Michael, by chance, still there?" A fantasy played out in my head. I'd say I was going to confession, then ask Father Michael to hide me out, maybe in the confessional booth, and then I'd fly back to India with him. Problems solved. I'd go to the convent and live with the nuns. Maybe even join Mother Teresa's order. That blue-trimmed cotton habit would be prettier than my wedding dress. Oh, what a wonderful fantasy I allowed myself to escape into, new bride and all.

Harriet shook her head. "He returned to India."

"Oh." Bad news, but I still had the invalid marriage thing going, or did I? Mama considered the marriage valid. And then there was law versus church, and even then, one church would claim it happened for real, even if the Catholic Church claimed it didn't.

While I pondered which church God would side with, Harriet cleared her throat. "I'll call Father and let him know you'll both be at the church at three o'clock?"

Under the table, I pinched Nate's leg. "We'll discuss it." I wasn't doing it, but Harriet frightened me. I'd make Nate tell her the bride was going to be a no-show at the afternoon wedding.

After breakfast, I insisted on a ride in the country to settle a few matters.

On a road to nowhere, I stuck out my chin. "I am not getting married again. If our vows in the protestant church meant nothing to you, why repeat them? Makes no sense."

"Aw Rebecca, c'mon. You're acting childish. Do it for Mother. She's really upset with our leaving."

I crossed my arms, not giving a flip about his mother.

"I took the California job for you."

My arms relaxed and I folded my hands in my lap.

"You know I love you. You got bent out of shape for nothing just because I wanted to spend time with friends and family before moving away."

"You've had your entire life to do that. I'm supposed to be your family now. You could've brought me with you." I inched toward the door.

Nate groaned.

"I'm not in the mood to repeat vows, and I don't want to go to California with you."

He stopped the car and shifted into park. Hedged in by acres of cornfields on that lonely road, we sat in silence. I'd taken a risk. He could kill me and throw me into the field. No one would ever find my body. It would decompose. The farmer would combine me into cow feed and eventually I'd be deposited back to the earth. A long process, but at least I'd have served some purpose in life.

After spewing a few cuss words and pounding the steering wheel, Nate spoke quietly through gritted teeth. "Don't do this to me. It's not fair."

I hated and loved Nate in equal measure. When I first met him, he was kind and caring. His pendulum swung a wide path between sweetness and anti-Christ tendencies.

I sighed. I was stuck in a situation far worse than being eaten by cows then pooped out. But I had no choice. Time for lying in the bed I'd made. "You deal with your mother. Tell her we're not going to the church today and I'll go to California with you tomorrow."

"Whatever." He shifted the car to drive and slammed his foot on the gas. From the rear view mirror, I watched the black marks he laid on the road disappear.

I didn't know what he told Harriet, but the next day, after tearful goodbyes—not on my part—we boarded a plane. Looking out through the small oval window, the world below grew tiny as the possibilities ahead appeared immense. Leaving worries behind, my hope soared when the plane zoomed through fogs of clouds. A thrill of excitement, that had nothing to do with Nate, brought a smile to my face. Marriage might be a challenge, but I'd make the most of my new life. I wiggled in my seat. I was on a plane heading to sunny California. I'd finally escaped out of Wisconsin.

Sagai

The rector pulled the white cassock over Sagai's head and blessed it. "Don this robe and know that you are now a religious, a brother, no longer of the secular world."

At Sagai's first Sunday Mass in Darjeeling Christian College, having already professed temporary vows in Nashik, he completed the next step: The Investiture Ceremony. The rector's deep voice echoed through the high vaulted chapel and reverberated through his heart, the words and their tone, impacting Sagai with the weight of this new phase of his life.

"As a Brother, you will keep your vows and wear your cassock, a sign of purity, wherever you go so that you will witness to your commitment to God."

That evening Sagai stood before his cot and fidgeted with the buttons on his cassock.

"Go ahead." Mondal patted him on the back and laughed. A few other classmates chuckled. "Most of us slept in our cassocks the first night." His new friend nudged him and pointed across the dorm at another classmate. "That fellow slept in his cassock for one month."

Sagai's Northeast Indian classmates had already celebrated their ceremony at the end of their novitiates. He removed his sandals and climbed into his cot. Arms wrapped around the cotton cassock, he considered the stricter moral code he must now follow. There would be limits to what he could and could not do. He couldn't go out to a hotel to eat and socialize with friends. He couldn't be around girls in casual situations or go to a movie theater dressed in his cassock.

Vijay had taken him to a movie in Salem during one of the breaks, and he'd enjoyed it. Perhaps he could watch a movie if he removed his cassock. That seemed wrong. He resolved never to disgrace the habit. He would set aside the secular world. This lifestyle meant sacrifices, but all for the glory of God. He had surrendered his free will to God and to his superiors. He prayed his superiors would be men of God.

In the large, white-columned, three-storied institution tucked in a forest in the Himalayan foothills, Sagai welcomed a routine of studies, prayers, Mass, and activities. He couldn't imagine what difficulties Mondal meant during their train ride.

He met his first real difficulty in the refectory. Noodles! What a challenge. Instead of his usual staple of rice and watery curry eaten with hands, he had to match this unwieldy pasta with the varied utensils on the table. It would have been sensible to grab the noodles in his hands and slurp them in one fell swoop, but no one else had discovered that. He waited and watched as others picked up the tined utensil and skillfully hooked the noodles. He followed their lead.

~~~

"There's been another suicide," Father Ambrose announced during an afternoon lecture.

Sagai gasped and leaned forward.

"A boy from a nearby village where one of the brothers has been doing Sunday ministry failed his final exam, then threw himself over a cliff. Bollywood movies teach the youth if they fail, they are doomed and suicide is the answer. Themes of destiny and fatalism are prevalent in the movies."

Father Ambrose delved into different local religious viewpoints of destiny versus free will. The priest strolled through the aisles and stopped at Sagai's desk. "This Sunday the first year students will find a village to adopt with help from senior students. Your mission will be to organize a youth group and combat this fatalistic thinking by empowering the youth, building them up, and teaching that God gives free will to make good life choices."

Sagai pressed his hand on his bouncing knee, anxious to begin youth ministry.

After class, he and other first year students sought out seniors to help them find a village. Sagai discovered Mondal in the stone-walled grotto, seated on the bench with his face buried in his hands. The peaceful grotto, nestled in the midst of thick leafy ferns, was modeled after Lourdes, where Bernadette witnessed the vision of the Virgin Mary.

A trickling brook chorused with chirping birds, offering an overture of peace. Mother Mary, nestled in the rocks, gazed serenely toward Heaven. Sagai asked her to pray for Mondal, then took a deep slow breath, allowing earthy bouquets to fill his lungs.

At his exhale, Mondal turned. "Sagai, I didn't know you were there."

He sat beside his classmate. "Any problem?"

"Pray for me."

"What's troubling you, friend?"

A long sigh.

Sagai placed his hand on his friend's shoulder. "Could you help me?"

Mondal perked up. "Certainly."

"I want to find the most neglected, far-away village to adopt for my youth ministry."

"Simply take a close-by village. It'd be easier."

"I seek a tough situation for the glory of God."

"You don't have to go far for that, but come along with me, and I'll show you tough. My village is almost a four-hour hike. You can go further if you wish."

The next morning, after six o'clock Mass, Mondal and Sagai left the hillside campus and set off toward the village carrying a lunch sack of noodles. They hiked through rolling hills of tea gardens where workers sang and rhythmically plucked tea leaves from the short flat bushes, then tossed them in huge bamboo baskets strapped to their backs.

Villagers washed clothes, bathed, and drank from the little river that accompanied them along their trail. Tribal folks with slanted eyes and flat noses nodded as they passed, raising their heads while balancing fantastic heights of sticks on their backs. What a glorious place.

Through ridgeline trails and sharp inclines that tripped their toes, Sagai hiked with his friend. He passed through foggy lowlands then rose up bends to see ghosts of hills emerge.

Sometimes the road became a packed-mud passage carved through a high bank.

With the sun straight up in the sky, they stopped in a secluded piney grove. On a large stone, covered in ancient lichen, Mondal opened the sack of noodles.

A pheasant, blue with a white breast and a red patch over his eye, strutted out of the bushes and crossed the road.

"Only us and nature." Sagai inhaled the smell of evergreens. "What a beautiful place."

A rustling sound. Tall bamboo bushes parted and the face of a wrinkled old woman appeared. She leapt out, cackled, then thrust out her open palm.

Mondal and Sagai jumped to their feet, spilling noodles in the dirt. They sprinted until they were breathless, then stopped under a fir tree. Sagai leaned over, gasping, his side aching. "I thought that old woman was a ghost."

"I thought she was a witch."

Sagai gently shoved Mondal. "You're white now! He leaned his hand against the tree and burst into a raucous laughter that rang through the hills. Tears spilled from his eyes.

Mondal crossed his arms. "While I enjoy your contagious laughter, that old woman cost us our lunch."

"Why are you always so serious? It's really funny. We got so frightened."

Mondal forced away the beginning of a smile. "Let's keep moving."

Ignoring his hunger pains, Sagai hummed as they continued their walk.

Stopping where the road turned and curved upward. Mondal rested his hands on his hips. "It's the end of the road."

"What's down there?" Sagai peered over an embankment.

"No-man's land."

"Look!" Sagai pointed. "Something's happening."

A small party climbed the hill, hauling a sort of a stretcher.

"They must be coming from Bansghari. It's a tiny Hindu village at least an hour's walk straight down that ravine. There's no road from here to there."

The two watched the troupe struggle up the rocky gradient.

"Go and see, if you wish." Mondal waved his hand. "I'm going to my village. Shall we meet along the road at the *Dhukan Dara* before the sun is down?"

"The roadside shop?"

"The only one along the way."

He agreed, then snaked downward, toward the activity. "Namaste!" He introduced himself in his best Nepali.

Two men carried a pregnant woman on a sheet, stretched and tied at both ends to sticks. Three women and a teenage girl wearing dresses and boots followed behind.

Sagai understood enough Nepali and grasped the situation. The men were carrying the woman to the hospital. She had complications beyond the local midwife's expertise.

He insisted on taking the front end of what they called the *tonga*. The teenage girl, walking beside him, introduced herself as Geeta Tamang. She encouraged the woman in the *tonga* and as they continued their ascent. The girl explained in Nepali-English mix, that the village headman had a Jeep, but it couldn't manage the vertical terrain.

The woman's wails diminished to the sound of a mewling kitten. They climbed on. Sagai's sandal strap tore against a stone. He kicked both sandals off and picked up his pace, watching for rocks and snakes. The moans ceased by the time they arrived at the hospital. Sagai continued to pray, but feared the worst.

He waited and prayed, seated on a stone bench under a rhododendron tree. A little while later, Geeta emerged from the hospital wiping her eyes with her shawl. He rushed to her side.

"The baby girl survived. My sister did not." Understanding her tears and her Nepali, he led her toward the bench.

"I'm so sorry." Hand on her shoulder, Sagai allowed her to empty herself with expressions of grief.

"She didn't want to get married." Geeta buried her face in her shawl and wept. "We both dreamed of going to college. Her life is over. Now, I will marry a boy my father has chosen for me and help raise her baby."

She lifted her head, sobbed, and turned toward him. "My mother died giving birth to me. Was this my sister's destiny?" She raised her hands and shouted at the sky. "Is it mine? Is this fate written on our forehead?"

He opened his palm toward her, and she rested her hand in his. He placed his other hand on top—one hand supporting hers, the other covering, reassuring, like Appa always did.

Sagai continued to hold her gaze. "I'm sorry. God is with her and with you, even in this sad moment. He will comfort you and will always take care of you, come what may."

He offered a short prayer for God's mercy and healing for Geeta and her family. He sat with the girl until the rest of the group exited the hospital with the dead woman wrapped in a white sheet on the *tonga*. Another woman held the wailing newborn. He imagined the trail of tears they would leave on the way home.

With more condolences and prayers, he bid them good-bye then returned to the road to meet Mondal at the shop.

The walk home was a silent one. That evening, Sagai fell into his cot and crossed his arms over his chest. His sighs declared his sadness, and his prayers expressed his hope for Geeta, her family, and for the entire village. Women had a tough life. He thought of Amma. She ministered to ladies after they gave birth to babies that did not survive. He considered his sisters who married and went to live in their husband's homes, caring for his family. How tough to be a woman. With a deeper respect, he vowed to cherish and always hold women in high esteem.

Ten

Challenges in New Locations

The difficulties you meet will resolve themselves as you advance. Proceed, and light will dawn, and shine with increasing clearness on your path.
~ Jim Rohn

Rebecca

If my life was measured by my postcard snippets and exclamation points, it'd be an awesome picture. Found an adorable apartment near the beach! Getting a terrific tan! Chillin' on a lounge chair beside our aqua-blue pool! Love the white sandy beaches, the salty sea air, and the huge waves! The ocean floats me like driftwood! Love it! Stepped through a portal of fantabulous fun at Disney Land! Palm trees at Christmastime? Sweet! Working part-time at a flower shop! Be back in college next semester! Wish you were here!

Though not a drinker, alcohol became the best bonding agent in my marriage, times we laughed more, talked more. Most of the red flags of the past flew away in the California breeze. Our biggest difficulties lie in finding commonalities.

"Close your eyes," Nate said one evening as he burst into our apartment, all smiles. He grabbed my hand.

You realize how much or how little you trust someone when they lead you with your eyes closed. I peeked.

"Come on." He pulled me along. "It's a surprise."

The front door opened, and a warm December breeze brushed my face.

"Now look."

Two matching red motorcycles with knobby tires sat parked on a trailer.

"Mother said we should share a hobby, you know, do something we both like. They're on/off road bikes, so we can even take them in the desert."

"But I wrecked a motorcycle the first time I got on one." The thought was sweet. I should focus on his thoughtfulness and generosity, but I was genuinely scared.

The grin on his face faded. "Maybe it's time to face your fears."

I agreed and next Saturday, in the desert, I rubbed sweaty palms against my jeans and exhaled. Nate stuffed the helmet on my head and gave it a sound pound.

"Ouch! That hurt."

He laughed and pulled on his helmet.

Maybe he was right. I shouldn't be afraid. After he unloaded the motorcycles, I started the bike, gave it too much gas and the back wheel slid sideways. I jumped off. "I can't ride. I don't want to ride. This is not my idea of fun."

That was it. Nate packed up everything and didn't talk to me all the way home.

A few weeks later, I grabbed my book on the way out the door.

He raised the tackle box. "We're going to the lake, not the library."

I tucked the book under my arm. "Just in case the fish aren't biting."

The fish were biting, but the whole thing grossed me out. He wanted me to put a worm on the hook, but when I touched the metal hook to the yucky wiggly worm, I screamed.

"For crying out loud." He yanked the pole from my hands. "Give me that."

A tug on my pole changed the mood. A thrill of excitement had me gripping the handle and nearly dancing in the boat. The fun ended when I reeled in my catch. I grimaced when Nate twisted the hook from its mouth.

"Hold it while I take a picture."

The slippery unwieldy thing slid from my hands and landed at my feet the moment he snapped the picture. I screamed and jumped on the seat as it flipped and flopped on the bottom of the boat.

"Don't freak out!" Nate yelled. "You'll scare the other fish away. You'll flip the boat. Knock it off. Stupid girl! You're such a loser."

Stung by his words, I rested my chin in my hands, and watched that fish open and close his mouth with nothing coming out. I was that creature; a fish out of my element trying hard to breathe in this marriage. I wanted to toss it back into the lake. Go! Be free! Breathe again!

"I don't want to fish anymore." I pulled my book from under the seat cushion.

A few minutes later, I raised my eyes to Nate staring across the water, his jaw firm. I set my book down. "I'm sorry. I'm happy sitting in the boat with you, but I don't like fishing. Is that good enough?"

"We have nothing in common."

"We like the beach."

"I sunburn quicker than you."

"We like hiking."

"I only like hiking in the woods if I'm carrying a gun. And I'll never again take you with me."

"I did not cough on purpose." I lied. I'd joined Nate on a hunting excursion in the mountains. He had a ten-point buck in his gun sight and was about to pull the trigger when that beautiful creature raised its head and blinked innocent eyes. I had to do something before he killed Bambi's daddy. Was I supposed to pretend to like things I didn't like? Smile, when he murdered a sweet animal?

I returned to my novel. Maybe when I got back to college in the spring, everything would be okay. I longed to get my hands on new textbooks, breathe in the fresh inky smell, and hear the crackle of the spine when it's spread for the first time.

I hadn't forgotten about India, either. A recent letter from Father Michael showed him in the state of Karnataka, in the city of Bangalore, the silicon valley of India, he'd written. Bangalore was called Garden City, a city full of flowering trees. It almost sounded like Santa Barbara. I researched each place Father Michael sent letters from, getting to know India well.

I looked up at Nate. "Maybe we could go on that mission trip to India during my spring break, after I return to college."

He cast his pole. "Forget college. Forget India. We can't afford either."

The tips of my ears must have lit up and it wasn't from sunburn. I'd saved money for years for India, until Nate made me dump it in an account that he now managed.

"But you said…"

Nate yanked his fishing pole. "I thought you'd be happy in California. Don't be a nag." He huffed, reeled in his bait, and packed up his gear. "I'm done fishing. This is not relaxing."

He gave me the silent treatment all the way home, then left the apartment without mentioning where he was going.

I opened the door to the back patio, sat on a plastic chair, and stared at the fence slats for hours. I rubbed my breast bone with the palm of my hand as if I could somehow massage out the deep cutting pain. I was willing to settle into life not feeling loved by my husband, but how could I manage life without a purpose, a goal. When Kara was alive, I felt loved. I had a purpose. I was her caretaker. I'd been wandering ever since, going nowhere. Forced to let go of my dream of going to India, now college was out of the picture, too.

I closed my eyes and raised my face to the sun. Tears, as salty as the ocean, landed on my lips. "What am I going to do now?"

Then a picture flashed before my eyes, like how it did when Kara died, and again in my dorm room with my roommate. This time I saw a hand. A big, muscular, tight-fisted hand with veins pulsing blood. A hand of power and might. The fist pumped toward me, holding a pen tilted in my direction.

God's hand?

Amazing. I didn't get pity from the Almighty. I got a challenge.

"I take your challenge," I told The Hand. The pain in my chest dissolved. For years, I'd figured God forgot about me or was mad at me, or maybe I was mad at Him after He wouldn't save Kara. Then I remembered a prayer I'd written, then prayed years ago. I hadn't been holding onto Him, but signs over the years proved He wasn't letting me let go of Him.

God cared. I thanked Him through happy tears. Hope returned. No matter my circumstances, I would rise to this holy challenge. I knew exactly what to do. I'd write Kara's story. Maybe God would be enough.

Sagai

The misty monsoon season gave way to a pleasant warm autumn as Sagai settled into his philosophy and literature studies. He appreciated Robert Frost's poetry, especially the way he used nature and imagery to reflect human emotion. In analyzing the poem about two roads diverging in a yellow wood, the author was sorry he could not travel both, Sagai considered his pathway that had led him thus far.

Though God had called him down a twisting and often stony road, he'd reached a brilliant mountaintop in West Bengal, on the border of Nepal, Bhutan, and Tibet. Here, he imagined he'd gone abroad. He'd only known the Nepalese people in Tamil Nadu as the tribal Gorkhas, a serious able-bodied part of the British Regiment who carried large knives and guarded huge mansions. His affable gentle Nepalese classmates were nothing like that.

The hot individual showers, heated by a coal burner, proved heavenly. No more ten-second claps and cold water. He smiled just thinking about the ease of stepping into a hot shower at the end of a long day, especially Thursdays.

On Work Day Thursday, Sagai and the Brothers split and hauled wood and carried loads of provisions on their backs. He avoided staring at his biceps and flexing them, as some of his classmates did, but he could feel muscles pressing against his cassock sleeves. He sent a letter to Appa requesting a new shirt, pants, and sandals.

After Sunday Mass, he and Mondal visited the villages for youth ministry. Subba, the village headman from Sagai's adopted village— nearly three hundred small mud houses in the midst of orange groves—welcomed him in their midst. To his delight, the college-educated, middle-aged Hindu spoke English.

During their long Sunday walks, Sagai and Mondal engaged in pleasant conversations about life on campus to animated discussion about philosophers. His friend often grew reserved when the conversations became personal, but nevertheless, he'd gained a friendship he hadn't had since Sheveroy Hills.

One morning, his friend gave him a warning. "There's a Hindu majority government now, and they've imposed the anti-conversion bill. We could be prosecuted for evangelizing if we aren't careful."

"Subba, the headman, is very open to my ministry." Sagai pushed forward on the trail "And I'm not forcing conversion. Bansghari is secluded from the rest of the world, bereft of government aid." He kicked a small stone into the bushes. "I'm more troubled that they don't have access to the main road."

"Have they tried to build one?"

"They build, but Subba said the river washes away every path during monsoon season." He thought of Geeta and her sister. "The people need easier access to the hospital and to market with their orange crop."

"There is something called, Food for Work Program. It's through the United States if the villagers are willing to help."

"How does it work?" Any help, especially from abroad, would be great.

Mondal explained that locals got paid in bulgur wheat for building roads and such work and sometimes visitors from America pitched in to help. "Speak to Subba and the rector."

Sagai approached the headman and he readily agreed. The rector also concurred and promised to follow-through with the plan.

Each Sunday, Sagai returned to his village, often carrying a ball for a game on a makeshift field. He also taught moral lessons, using parables from Scripture. He played guitar and sang with the children in their native language. *Prabhu mero ghotalu ho—The Lord is my Shepherd* was a favorite. The children helped Sagai with his Nepali and in turn, he taught them English.

He also met with families, including Geeta's and ministered to them. This close knit Bansghari community mourned, laughed, and worked together, their lives intertwined with one another. The Hindu people sought guidance from their gods in every aspect of their lives, when to plant, when to cultivate, and they gave thanks both in sunshine and rain. After spending about five hours in the village each Sunday, with the sun lowering over the tips of the highest firs, he would bid goodbye to meet Mondal at the *Dhukan Dara*.

One morning on the way to the village, Sagai grabbed his friend's arm and stopped. Ahead, at the *Dhukan Dara,* a beautiful girl with shiny dark hair falling around her shoulders stood on the road. His heartbeat quickened. Her elegant silk *saree* set her apart from the local women who worked in the tea gardens in their faded tops and dull wrap-around skirts. Neither was she like the Buddhist women who wore the more earthy-toned *chupas* wrapped around and tied at the middle.

"Hello, brothers!" Her eyes twinkled like sparkling half-moons. "I'm Bindu Thapa. Where are you journeying?"

He hadn't seen a girl for a long time, but she was the most beautiful female he'd ever come across. His mouth went dry and he tugged on the collar of his cassock. "Um...to..."

His friend nudged him. "I'm Mondal and this tongue-tied brother is Sagai. We are college students on our way to our village ministry."

"I'm attending St. Joseph's Christian college, on break now. Please, come into my father's shop."

"Thank you." Sagai got a couple of his words back.

Inside, an old stoic man approached the counter from a side room.

"Father was offering his *puja* in the shrine." She leaned closer, giggled, and whispered, "Don't be frightened. He is very nice." She went to her father and clasped her hands around his arm. His eyes narrowed to slits and darted from Mondal to Sagai.

Sagai introduced himself and Mondal followed.

The old man nodded.

"Father, these Brothers have come from the college to do ministry in local villages. May I offer them tea?"

He nodded again. Bindu went behind the counter and into a back room. Sagai avoided the old man's discerning eyes until she reappeared with two steaming cups.

"This is from our spring flush."

"How kind of you to offer." Sagai sipped tea with his friend, while Bindu inquired about their studies and ministry. The tea must have loosened his tongue because he talked up a storm and laughed with Bindu until Mondal tapped his arm, interrupting their conversation. "Shall we take leave?"

She smiled. "Yes, Sagai has a long way to go. Bansghari is still a few hours walk from here."

The next Sunday, while traveling home with the sun lowering over the mountains, Sagai waved and quickened his pace seeing Bindu waiting with Mondal outside the shop.

Each week, he'd arrive with his friend at the shop, dog-tired. Tea, sweets, food and friendship refueled him. Bindu, bubbly and talkative but always respectful, engaged him in the most delightful conversations. Though she spoke perfect English, she'd end her sentences with "la," which meant yes or ok in Nepali. The lilt at the end of her sentences and her constant, "la las", made Sagai smile all the more.

"I like Jesus," Bindu admitted one day during their late morning tea. She leaned close. "I shouldn't tell this, but at college, when I had to deliver the holy bread to the priest, I snuck one piece in my pocket and ate it later, but I didn't feel anything happen to me." Mondal didn't look amused, but Sagai didn't hide his smile.

"We should take leave now." Mondal stood and cut the conversation short. "It's time."

Sagai caught a look passing between the two that he didn't understand.

Something was up with his friend. He was quiet during tea. Along the pathway he only answered in short clips and appeared jittery, often looking from left to right. Where their paths separated, Sagai bid him good-bye and turned toward Bansghari.

"Wait!" Mondal reached out and grabbed Sagai's arm. Then he took a step back, pulled off his cassock and walked toward the edge of the cliff.

"What are you doing, man? Mondal! My God!" Sagai rushed to the side of the road and peered over the edge, into the Balasun River.

His friend's cassock fell like an injured white dove, spiraling downward.

"I'm leaving."

"What are you saying?" Sagai searched his eyes. "Have you gone mad?"

"I'm getting married."

Thousands of thoughts ran through Sagai's mind and one led straight to the Dhukan Dara. "Bindu?"

Mondal found a grassy spot and sat, cross-legged. "No. I am eloping with Hasita. She is from the village where I have been doing my ministry."

"But you have nearly completed your Philosophate. You want to leave now?" Sagai pressed his palms to his forehead.

Under the shade of a fir tree, Sagai knelt beside him. Perhaps he could talk him out of this drastic move. His professor had discussed these types of relationships that had become the spirit of Bollywood movies. Boy falls in love with a girl from another caste. Delusional portrayals, the professor had said. No one can run away and sing and dance their way into a happy ending.

"Do you remember when I met you for the first time in Siliguri?"

He nodded.

"I was returning from a visit with Father Superior about a problem with a priest at the parish near the college."

"What problem?"

"The priest was bad."

"That is not shocking news." An uneasy laugh erupted from Sagai's mouth. "While most priests are good, some are bad. I have had my share of troubles with some, but—"

"Listen to me. Mondal clenched his jaw. "I'm talking about a priest who spoiled boys."

"What?" Sagai's voice caught in his throat. He knew what it meant to spoil a girl, but a boy? A priest? "That cannot happen." He repeatedly shook his head, not wanting to allow awful images to enter his mind.

Mondal pulled his knees to his chest, wrapped his arms around them, and lowered his voice. "When I met you in Siliguri, I'd just told Father Superior about that priest. I know too much, Sagai. I saw too much. I wanted to leave the congregation. Father Superior convinced me to stay."

He clutched his cassock, bunching up the material near his chest. "It's horrible and unnatural."

"He deserves the worst kind of death."

The wind carried Mondal's whispered words away, and Sagai prayed they would land as a curse upon that priest. He trusted priests, put his will, life in their hands. This news was too much. "This priest...is...is he there? Still?"

Mondal shook his head. "They finally sent him away."

Sagai let out a deep breath. "Stay in the congregation. The culprit is gone."

"It's too late. I have come out of my valley of decision. God gave me free will and my fate will not lie in the hands of these so-called holy men. Mondal spat on the ground then looked up to the sky. "I fell in love with Hasita after returning from Siliguri." At his mention of her name, his jaw relaxed. He smiled. "Friend, this is my day of freedom. I will be out and away from politics and nonsense where obedience is ranked highest among all virtues. I have been waiting my whole life for this day, for the right time. It is time."

"The village is Hindu." Sagai touched Mondal's arm. "And friend, you are Christian."

Mondal swept his hand before him. "Those who toil in these tea gardens doing honest labor are holier than some who preach the word of God in churches. What does it mean to be a Christian if you do evil things?"

"But what about the girl's parents? Won't they beat you for taking their daughter? In Tamil Nadu eloping is a serious crime."

"Hasita and I have spoken to her parents. They have given permission. Since I am a brother and an outsider, we cannot marry the traditional way. For the sake of their custom, we will sneak off today and hide in the forest. Before nightfall we will flee to her cousin's house in a neighboring village." Mondal chuckled. "Her parents will wait and pretend they don't know where she is. Some will suggest she was dragged off by a wild beast into the forest."

"Is that so?"

Mondal nodded. "Hasita and her family have explained the process to me. It's all very complicated and quite entertaining." He plucked a nearby flower and tugged the petals. "Next, a search party will be called. Someone will say they saw us together, then tongues will wag left and right. After a while, late in the night, when the drama is at its peak, the cousin will send a messenger to tell the family that we arrived at his house."

"And no one will be angry with you?"

"They will pretend to be. The news of our elopement will send the village into an uproar. The parents and headman will rally a search party, and they will come to the cousin's house. They will bring us back to the village and perform the wedding in the morning. First they will cry and lament, then we will all celebrate." Mondal tossed the flower stem and leapt to his feet.

Sagai rose, walked to the edge of the cliff, and looked into the bubbly river, settling this news in his mind. Mondal's white cassock was caught on bramble, waving. The sight of it cut deep into his heart. "And you won't regret not becoming a priest?"

He moved beside him and clicked his tongue. "The brothers wanted that for me. The congregation took me in as an orphan. I am grateful, but they don't own my heart and soul." He touched his heart. "I belong to Hasita now."

"I will miss you." Sagai turned to him and sighed. "You have been my dear friend."

"If you love me, help me. When you return this evening, they will ask where I am."

"What shall I say?"

"Simply tell them you did not meet me and that you do not know where I am. Can I trust you to remain my loyal friend and not betray me?"

For his friend, he would do it.

His eyes darted toward the road ahead, then Mondal looked back to Sagai. "Jesus sends us as sheep in the midst of wolves, and then says, 'Be ye therefore wise as serpents and as harmless as doves.' You are a dove, Sagai. You've mastered meekness. Now please, be wise as the serpent and do not allow a religious institution to destroy you."

He blinked hard. "It will not. Many priests are good, holy men."

"Not all are good." Mondal placed his hands on Sagai's shoulders. "Your naiveté will never gain you a crown. My friend, it would be better for you to elope with Bindu. She loves you and you are blind."

"What are you talking?" He took a step backward.

"Hasita goes to the store for supplies. Girls talk. She says you have very good energy and she likes you. She will be inside the shop tonight, and if you wish to settle with her, enter the shop and tell her you spoke with me."

"She's my friend only. I cannot!"

"I thought you would say as much." The muscles in Mondal's arms tightened as he leaned forward. Like a deer, he was ready to dart into the forest, happy and at peace. He wasn't afraid. He was ready to go home.

All he could offer his friend was a handshake. Mondal grabbed his hand, pulled him close, and hugged tight. He clapped his hands on Sagai's shoulder, smiled, then sprinted down the road and disappeared around the bend.

Under a noon sun, Sagai continued toward Bansghari. He had put his all into caring for the villagers, but the place could never be home. Neither did his life path end at the Dhukaan Dara with Bindu.

Entering the village, Sagai measured time in terms of what Mondal would be doing. By the time he gathered the youth from their homes, his friend would have met his love. During Sagai's confidence building singing exercise, the couple might be walking into the forest, out of view of others, giggling, holding hands. Perhaps his superiors were wrong and there were Bollywood endings in real life.

"Brother, we scored!" shouted one of the children during the football match.

Sagai didn't notice the white ball had shot straight between the two small pine tree trunks he'd posted in the ground for goals. He clapped his hands to cheer and also to alert himself to the present.

After moral lessons, Sagai stood near the well and spoke some Nepali, some English, while Subba translated unclear parts. He talked about the importance of formal education and the benefits to families and their village if they would send their youth to college.

On his return walk, repugnant thoughts coursed through him in nauseous waves about the priest who spoiled boys. Could godly men do such things? Scripture taught that more is required from those to whom much is given. This priest would be harshly judged by God.

As he approached the Dhukaan Dara, his heart raced. Had he misled Bindu? Had he disgraced the cassock by sitting with her at tea? He'd been told that the habit does not make the monk, but the integrity of the person mattered. Had he maintained integrity? He'd hoped to hold onto her friendship and his vows, but that did not seem possible now. He walked past the shop and continued alone on the dark crooked pathway toward the college.

That evening, the campus buzzed about Mondal's disappearance. He shrugged off questions from classmates. The rector summoned him. He clasped his shaking hands and sat before his superiors for the interrogation.

Horrible! Hard accusing eyes. Fevered scribbles in his file. Raised voices.

"Why didn't you report him missing as soon as you returned?"

"I'm sorry, Father." Sagai's rubbed sweaty palms on his cassock.

"What if he's fallen over a cliff?

"I…I didn't think…"

"Was there an argument? Did the two of you fight?"

"No, Father! My Lord, No!"

"Did you ever see him in the presence of a girl?"

"No, Father."

"Were you in the presence of a girl?"

Sagai shook his head. He could not implicate Bindu.

"Did he tell you of plans to leave the congregation?"

"No, Father."

The superiors fired questions like bullets. What an inquisition! His arm muscles quivered walking back to the dormitory, his legs threatened to fail. That night, on his knees in the chapel, he begged God to forgive him for the lies he told for his friend.

He'd lost Mondal and most likely Bindu. Sagai sighed. He missed them both. He missed Victor, whom he'd loved as a brother in Vellore. He missed his family.

After night prayers, Sagai removed his cassock and draped it over his arms. He climbed the staircase to the dormitory and stopped halfway. The huge painting above of the Sacred Heart of Jesus looked upon him from the high stairwell wall.

"Is this how it will be, Lord? Will I continue to be led to unknown places and meet new faces that will come and go? Can I not keep one friend for myself?"

Sagai stared into the deep eyes of Christ, then lowered his head. "I will keep you, Lord," he whispered. "I will follow wherever you lead me. I will become your priest, even if it means a life of loneliness."

Tears fell on his cassock. He walked upstairs and gently hung the cassock on the wall hook near his cot. He vowed to fit the mold of what his superiors wanted in a priest and also what God wanted. If he never saw Victor, Mondal, or Bindu again, so be it.

Sagai climbed into his cot. The weather was turning cold in the mountains again. Mondal was right. There were difficulties in this beautiful place. A chill of loneliness settled into his bones. Could Jesus really be enough?

Eleven

Christmas Surprises

*"Our worst days are never so bad that you are beyond
the reach of God's grace. And your best days are
never so good that you are beyond the need of God's
grace."*
~ Jerry Bridges

Rebecca

Working full time at a florist shop, I spent nights writing Kara's story, *Lessons of Love*. Father Michael and I stayed in touch. I opened up to him, shared more about my life. Letter writing became therapy. Sometimes I'd wonder if he'd stop writing after I unloaded all of my craziness, but he was a priest. I supposed he heard it all. His return letters always offered nuggets of sage wisdom.

Wherever his letters were postmarked, I'd stick a tack on the map above my computer in the spare bedroom, then research the locale. Presently, he served at a parish in Sheveroy Hills, a hill station in the South Indian state of Tamil Nadu. He'd written about the twenty-two hair-pin curves winding up a hill, monkeys on the roadside, and a cool mist that settled over the mountaintop each evening. The British had settled the hill station, built up monasteries and convents, and used it as a vacation spot until India got its independence

Father Michael assured me I'd come to India someday, but it seemed an impossible dream. He also told me about a young man my age from Sheveroy Hills whom he'd mentored and sent to the junior seminary, Sagai Raj. He'd asked me to pray for him. Though not faithful and constant with prayers, I made a promise to a priest and had been praying for Sagai Raj every day. By doing so, I became more engaged in conversations with God.

One Friday night, after finishing a chapter in *Lessons of Love*, Nate arrived home late from work and reminded me of his co-worker's Christmas party. I'd forgotten. I pulled on a red mini-dress and did a quick hair fix and was ready to go within minutes.

Greg's apartment twinkled with shiny mini-skirts, flashy tight leather pants and colorful chunky heels. The beat of Jingle Bell Rock pulsed through the speakers. Nate handed me a Long Island Iced Tea, a delightful California style drink with a tiny umbrella in it. I reminded myself to sip because I'd already discovered they were quite strong.

He rolled tension from his shoulders, then eyed the crowd gathering around the glass coffee table. Greg spilled some white powder on the surface. My husband moved in that direction and when I tugged on his arm, he shooed me away like an insect had landed on him. I followed him to the table where Greg took a razor blade and cut into cocaine.

I mouthed the words, "I want to go."

"Come on." He raised his eyebrows and smiled. "Try some."

"I don't think so." I stepped onto the balcony, hoping he would follow. I took a few long sips and a flash of dizziness hit me. Whoa. That was quick.

I leaned over the rail, looking at the deep blue colors in the pool below. Was I a stuffy do-gooder? What did I care if others did drugs? It wasn't like Nate was a drug addict. And I certainly would never touch the stuff.

Nate suddenly appeared beside me and grabbed my arm. "Come inside. Everyone's having a great time. If you're not having fun in ten minutes, we'll leave. Deal?"

"Ten minutes? Really?"

"Ten minutes." He smiled, more charming than usual, put his arm around my shoulder, and led me to the living room.

Greg winked, giving me the same feeling when a sudden dark cloud would settle over Lake Michigan, burst open, and pock the calm waters. We'd run like the wind. My leg twitched. Ten minutes seemed like a year away. I turned to my husband, but he was gone.

Why'd I feel so dizzy? I knew my limits, never drank too much. I set my glass on the coffee table and slouched into the sofa. Greg sat beside me. His grinning face blurred, moved closer, then farther.

I caught a glimpse of Nate in a chair across the room. His look didn't make sense. Wanted to form a sentence, but it wouldn't come out right or I kept forgetting the thought I had. What did I want to say?

Leather Pants Dude sat on the arm of the chair alongside my husband. He squeezed Nate's knee. The hand didn't look right there. I wanted to get up and slap it away. My legs didn't work. Greg's face. Why was it so large? So close? Lips on mine. I pulled back or he pulled back.

"Okay?"

Okay what? Was he asking if I was okay? Okay if he kissed me? His voice was like silk, smooth, nice.

"It's okay, Baby." Greg stroked my cheek. Nate never called me Baby.

Nate! I looked up. Still in the chair, he threw his head back and his chest shook with a deep throaty laughter at something Leather Pants Dude said. Didn't Nate see Greg kiss me? His hand on my thigh, lips on mine. Warm. I liked it. Was I in love with Greg and not Nate?

I woke the next morning alone in a strange bedroom, wearing nothing but a sheet and a thick fog of confusion. Clock on the nightstand said it was almost noon. How'd I sleep so long? What happened last night? Where were my clothes? I got up quickly then had a momentary black-out from the sudden movement. I felt like someone had stoned me in the night, while I slept. I ached all over.

I planted my feet on the carpet, gathered my dress from the floor, and pulled it over my head. Did I drink too much? Greg? Oh God! What'd I do with Greg? No way!

An ache between my thighs and the images in my head lurched up bile from my gut into my throat. I stumbled to the master bathroom and vomited. I couldn't have…wouldn't have. Never had I been so drunk I didn't remember stuff. Everything was fuzzy. Did I cheat on my husband? No! He slept with me last night, not Greg. Yeah. It was Nate.

I found mouthwash in the cabinet, gargled and spit. I ran my fingers through my hair, stared at myself in the mirror and cringed. Who was that awful person? I crumpled to the floor and sobbed. I'd wandered too far from who I was supposed to be. Oh, God. Why did you let this happen to me? This is not how my life should be.

I stood. Gotta get out of here. Sobbing, I splashed water on my face, then brushed away tears. I took a deep breath and opened the bedroom door.

In the living room, my husband rested in a lazy-boy with the remote in his hand. Greg knelt in front of an open cupboard in the kitchen, shuffling pots and pans. Nate's hair was a mess, his eyes blurry. A sick guilty feeling roiled in my gut. I stopped, thinking I needed to run to the toilet again, but the feeling passed.

Nate patted the arm of the chair. I released a slow easy breath, sat and clasped my shaking hands. He either didn't know I kissed Greg—or whatever I'd done—or he forgave me. Maybe nothing happened. I didn't remember going to the bedroom. Couldn't remember much.

I exhaled. If he didn't ask, I'd never talk about it. Merry California Christmas to me.

Sagai

Freezing temperatures in Darjeeling and the threat of landslides forced even the locals to safer, warmer plains. With college closing for the winter, Father Superior sent orders for Sagai to return to tropical Tamil Nadu and assist a parish priest in the village of Polur.

He hoped this assignment to Tamil Nadu would include a family visit. Polur was only a few hours bus ride from Sheveroy Hills. But asking would be tantamount to questioning authority. The superiors were already angry about the circumstances surrounding Mondal's leaving.

Lying, inappropriate behavior with a girl, and questioning authority were a few of the charges listed at his assessment, put in his file, and copied to Father Superior at Superior House. He accepted it without argument. The worst scrutiny he'd ever experienced and it would surely return to haunt him. He was surprised they didn't kick him out. He wrote to Father Michael, sharing everything in confidence, and the wise mentor, now back from America, had encouraged him to stay strong. His letters always contained good advice. The priest also asked Sagai to pray for an American his age, Rebecca. Not knowing her troubles, he added her to his daily prayers, remembering her always to the Lord.

Sagai stared from the window of the train leaving Darjeeling. The morning mist hid the mountains and chilled his bones. A fog over campus also clouded his superior's brains. He shrunk lower into his seat. Jesus knew his heart, and that was enough.

After days of bumping, jostling, and elbows jabbed into his ribs on buses and trains, Sagai arrived at the station to a buzz of traffic jammed up and pressed against a lowered train gate. Petrol and diesel fumes left an acrid taste in his mouth. Women on backs of motorcycles raised the corners of their *sarees* to their mouths.

An impatient fellow stepped off his motorcycle and pushed it through traffic, nearly knocking over a bicycle that carried a large tin milk can strapped to the back with ropes. The man approached the gate, tipped the motorcycle, then dragged it under the barrier. Others followed his lead, until the moment the train passed.

Sagai walked from the station toward the heart of the village where massive old tamarind trees formed umbrellas over small assemblages. Under their branches, cart vendors— with *veshtis* wrapped around their waists—sold fruits and snacks.

Men sipped coffee and tea from small steel tumblers. Barefoot kids in school uniforms adjusted heavy satchels while digging coins from their pockets. Sagai passed cows and goats mingling among the folks. Large brown tamarind pods fell at the feet of old men reading newspapers under bright green feathery foliage.

The women paid no attention to any of it. Friday was an auspicious day for Hindus, and the women focused on *Kolam*, their folk art decorations to welcome their deities. Ladies in bright new sarees bent low, shuffling their broad behinds, as they swept swirling dust piles away from their doorways with coconut stick brooms.

Others ahead of the sweepers sprinkled cow dung water onto the streets to prepare a spot for decorations. A few women must have woken earlier than the others and were already spreading their colorful rice flour powders in front of their homes, creating intricate geometric and flower shaped patterns. Very good to be back in South India among familiar sights and sounds.

A woman cried from the side of the street, "*mokku mavu, mokku mavu.*" She was selling flour for the artful doodles—*kolam*—to adorn the doorways of homes. Another called from the other side, "*malli, kadhambam.*" Her sweet-smelling basket held white jasmine and orange flowers along with strands of garland—a medley of yellow mums, green *tulsi* and violet *marikolundu.*

Sagai breathed in the pleasing potpourri and the mingling of earthy smells, coffee, teas, spices and frying oil.

He left the shade for the shops. Mosquitoes circled and buzzed around stagnant water in the gutter near the buildings. The *Suprabatham* Hindu chants blasted from All India Radio from a receiver wired onto the small tea shop's outside wall. He stopped, mesmerized by the melodic chant and the whoosh whoosh of the tea shop owner's skillful cooling and mixing of the steamy coffee. The man raised one cup high, held one low, then switched the other hand high, the other low. A long line of frothy coffee masterfully streamed from one tumbler to the other. The rhythm of life in Tamil Nadu.

Sagai handed a rupee to a vendor. The man plucked a tender coconut from a large bunch on his bicycle cart, chopped the top off with a large knife, dug a hole with the tip of the blade and inserted a straw. Sagai drained the coconut water then handed the shell back to the man. The vendor whacked it in half, took one piece, dug around the sides then did the same with the other before he returned both halves. Sagai scooped and ate the loosened pulp.

A high white steeple loomed over the top of the tamarind trees. A villager affirmed it was Our Lady of Perpetual Succor. He spotted Father Jansen, the Dutch rector, offering rice and sambar on banana leaves to beggars on the church steps. As Sagai came closer, he tossed the empty coconut shell and realized these weren't ordinary beggars.

Curved, bandaged appendages reached for the green leaves. Taking in their distorted faces, he stifled a gasp. Some lacked noses, their flesh eaten away. Others hobbled on crutches, bandages dragging in the dirt. Lepers. He'd never seen lepers this close before.

He shook off repulsion and the shame that followed. A priest should never recoil from these people.

"Good evening, Father." Sagai pressed his palms together. "I am Sagai."

"Welcome, Sagai. *Aandavarukku sevai seyya ennodu va pa.*" Father Jansen nudged him and smiled. He'd said, come with me to serve the Lord. "My Tamil is improving, but don't tell Father Superior, or he won't send me any more Tamil clerics."

He followed the father to a gathering of teenagers in the parish hall. "What's going on here?"

"We're recreating Holy Land for our Christmas project." A teenage boy stopped his work. "We've been germinating grass for the fields for a few months."

Small buildings and houses and even sign posts were already in the works. "Very nice." He patted the boy on the back.

As Christmas drew close, Sagai and the youth carried on with festive activities—building of the crèche during the day and caroling in the evening, led with his guitar.

Almost daily, the parade of lepers appeared at the church steps with outstretched hands and each day, he wrestled with feelings of disgust. The horrible odor from their sores nauseated him.

"When you serve these souls, you are serving the Lord," Father Jansen said one afternoon as Sagai handed out plates.

The next morning after Mass, the priest invited Sagai for a walk.

"Where are we going, Father?" His sandaled feet kicked up dust on the street that led out of town.

"To see saints."

They walked for miles, past rice paddy fields and coconut trees until laughter reached his ears. Barefoot children played cricket with three sticks stuck into the road, a ball, and a plywood bat. They dodged cows and chickens on their makeshift field.

Just off the road, a row of small single room concrete homes stood like matchboxes. Sagai followed Father Jansen into the community. He turned toward the sound of a creaking brass pulley as a woman drew water from the well. Sagai watched her struggle to hold the rope and pull up the bucket with her maimed hands.

A leper colony.

He took the rope from the woman at the well and pulled up the bucket. She nodded and offered a toothless grin then filled her plastic water pot.

"This colony is ostracized by the village. When they come to the church for food, the villagers cross to the other side of the road." Father Jansen waved his hand toward the tiny homes. "These structures were mud huts a few years ago. I had them razed. Last year, we dug that well."

A woman with a young boy in tow approached them. She held her palms together before her face. She had no fingers, only short filthy blackened stubs at the ends of her knuckles. "Father, please my son needs your help. She nudged the boy. "Speak to Father, Seenu. Tell him."

The boy hid his face in his mother's *saree*.

"What is it Seenu?" Father Squatted to the boy's level. "Speak child."

"He is shy and embarrassed." Her voice cracked as she spoke. "Classmates tease him because his parents are lepers. Horrible names they shout at him." With her nubby hands, the woman pushed her torn tail end of her *saree* to her face and wiped tears. "He will not return to school. He is a bright child, Father. Can you get him admittance in the boarding school where he can wear a uniform, and no one will know his mother looks like this." She touched her hands to her chest as the boy hid his face.

Father Jansen nodded. "Bring him to the parish after Christmas."

Sagai's attitude had been no better than the boys who had wounded Seenu's heart and driven him away from school. He dragged his feet in the dust and followed Father Jansen to another concrete structure.

"You'll discover more saints in here." The priest pushed the creaking wooden door. Inside several lepers sat on long benches—the blind, the lame, and those with various deformities. A nurse shooed away a buzzing fly, then applied ointment to a man's infected foot. Another kind woman wrapped a fresh bandage on a lady's leg.

Father approached the nurses, quoting scripture. "For God is not unjust so as to forget your work and the love which you have shown toward His name, in having ministered and in still ministering to the saints."

These were the saints of God and he had a long way to go before becoming a good priest.

After the tour of the colony, he and his superior returned to the parish in contemplative silence. The youth were adding final touches on Holy Land, adding hay to the manger. Christmas Eve Mass was only hours away.

Immediately after service at Our Lady of Perpetual Succor, he and the priest climbed into a jeep. Through the moonlit night, he helped celebrate Mass at fourteen substations around Polur. Some were small rooms in mud huts with thatched roofs, others dark cinder-block buildings. From place to place, over bumpy roads, he traveled with the cleric. At each stop, congregations met them with claps, beaming faces, and shouts of "Happy Christmas."

Sagai did whatever Father Jansen asked—read Scripture, offer Holy Communion, sing and strum carols on the guitar, set up the Altar, read the homily.

At each stop, angelic faces illuminated by the soft glow of candles sang praises and offered prayers to the Lord. They'd waited through the dark hours to celebrate the birth of Christ and to receive His body and blood on this most holy of nights.

When the Jeep halted at their last stop, the leper colony, Sagai rubbed sleep from his eyes. The sun would be up in an hour. Here, the bandaged, ostracized, weak and crippled folks had kept vigil through the night.

Sagai wished he was more like Father Jansen and challenged himself to overcome his weakness and love these souls wholeheartedly. They had nothing. Not health, wealth nor love or acceptance from others, yet they loved God. Sagai prayed. "Jesus, help me to see these rejected outcasts through your eyes. Let me look into their hearts and see what you see."

While Sagai helped the priest offer Communion, one of the lepers knelt and murmured the words, "If you are willing, you can heal me."

Two thousand years ago, a leper cried those very same words to Jesus, begging for His healing touch. Sagai prayed and placed the host on the man's tongue. "Body of Christ." He continued down the line, no longer seeing deformities, but deep faith on faces surrounded by halos in the candlelight. Sagai drew succor from these most deprived, yet most trusting in God.

Elated and exhausted, he climbed into the Jeep with Father Jansen. He gazed out his window into the early morning sky. Two thousand years ago, one star shone brightly. His heart was full, his cup filled with grace when he returned to Our Lady of Perpetual Succor in time for morning Mass.

Twelve

Pressing On

"It is the Lord who goes before you. He will be with you; he will not leave you or forsake you. Do not fear or be dismayed."
~ Deuteronomy 31:8

Rebecca

Holding the phone in one hand and wiping the toothpaste out of the sink with the other, I decided to only tell Ma the good stuff. "Still working at the florist shop and writing…" I hesitated, then said, "…a story about Kara." Other than my Indian pen pal, now in Chennai, I hadn't yet told anyone about *Lessons of Love*. "It's a story about the incredible love and wisdom of a Down syndrome child."

"Her story is worth telling." Ma's voice cracked. "When you were seven, you said you wanted to be a writer." I could hear the growing smile in her voice. "You stapled papers, made a little book and wrote a sweet little story for me. I still have it."

I pulled back the Windex container. Ma approved? She also kept my writings? Amazing. Obviously the bond of love never fully tore at Kara's death. Our relationship was like a cancer in remission. The disease had done its damage, scars existed, and although I hoped for true healing, I understood that toxic emotions could return any time.

"How's Nate?"

"He's fine. Everything's great." Only good stuff, I told myself. Just like at the florist shop, I sniffed the roses, avoided the thorns, and got rid of the damaged blossoms.

Nate gave up on the idea of shared hobbies—hunting, fishing, shooting, visiting porn shops. Fine with me.

Sometimes, when he stayed out late with friends, he'd call and tell me he wasn't coming home. Sometimes he didn't. Didn't matter. If you're alone with someone, you can't be lonely without them. On the scale of love to hate, I tipped toward tolerable dislike. Him too, probably. Nevertheless, I kept busy writing and with my work at Angelo's Flowers.

When the jingling bell alerted Angelo to my arrival one morning, he raised his deep brown eyes from the arrangement—fiery orange tulips mixed with rich red hypericum berries, our hottest selling autumn arrangement—and his smile bloomed into a bubbling "ah." Kind, sweet Angelo, always happy to see me.

"I have wonderful news." He fanned his fingers toward me then curled them back. "Come. Come."

I stepped around the counter and grabbed my green apron.

"You're work here is exceptional," Angelo said in his sweet Italian accent. "You're great with customers, responsible with every task—learning the cash register, taking orders. You have an artistic eye for arrangements, too. It's time to take your responsibilities one step further."

I tied my apron, intrigued by what "one step further" could mean.

"I want to train you to manage this shop, so I can take time off or perhaps open a second shop across town." Angelo shook his long dark bangs from his eyes.

"Really?" Managing a flower shop wasn't my plan, but I kept an open mind.

"The Society of American Florists is having a conference next month in Marina Del Ray, and I'd like you to join me. Would your husband allow me to steal you away to the beach for a few days?" He winked.

"I'm sure he won't mind." I let Angelo think his flirtation went over my head. He flirted a lot, but he was Italian. If it weren't for his dreamy brown eyes and lovely locks, I'd have considered him a pervert and quit.

That evening, I told Nate about Angelo's confidence in me and the upcoming conference. He grunted a response that didn't register as feelings. His brooding, as he flipped channels from his recliner, revealed something slightly more decipherable. Disapproval? Jealousy?

Finally, during a commercial break, I said, "Are you worried about me going with Angelo?"

"I don't care where you go. I just think you could find a job that pays more. The guy's a loser. It's a flower shop. It's not like you're management material for a big corporation. He's giving you more responsibility while you work for nothing. Ask him to give you a raise."

"How do you expect me to get a high-powered, high-paying job with no college degree?" I pushed off the couch, retreated to the spare bedroom, and fired up the computer. I closed my eyes and hoped for a flash of wisdom, but nothing happened. My flashes never appeared on demand.

I had a glimpse into the future when Kara died. Since then, images or scenes popped up randomly in my head, like when I was looking in the fridge or putting up laundry. They appeared most times at the edge of sleep as if someone switched on a TV then shut it off, like the one in college about the dark man in the foreign country.

The flashes often left me baffled about their meaning—unknown faces, unseen places. Other times they were direct and clear, like the last one. I wrote to Father Michael, asking him about these moments, and he said it was God's way of talking to me.

Even if I didn't know what God was saying, the holy flashes always left me with hope. Pooling the bad stuff with the good was like mixing hot and cold water together. It wouldn't burn or freeze me.

As conference time drew closer, Angelo flirted less, but lingered and chatted more about ideas for the second shop. His dark liquid-center eyes mesmerized me, listening to him like relaxing to sounds of classical music, even if he was just complaining about his wife not having time for him.

Angelo and I were becoming good friends, and I didn't like it one bit. I felt more comfortable with his flirting, like a clinking glass of ice water at poolside in the heat of the day. If I took one sip, I'd want to empty the entire glass, and I wasn't ready for that long cool Italian drink or the consequences that would follow. Good thing I was forced to go home in the evenings.

One night at dinner, either too honest or too stupid, I spoke with Nate about Angelo, hoping to incite a smidgen of jealousy. At least then, I'd know that he cared. "Remember when I told you that Angelo flirts a bit..."

Nate nodded and took a bite of my meatloaf, his favorite dish. "This is really good."

"...well, I don't think Angelo would make any moves, but I think he likes me, you know, as a friend, but maybe more than that."

He took another bite.

"Doesn't it bother you that I'm going out of town with him? He's not gay, you know."

He shrugged. "I trust you."

The next day, when Angelo turned onto Highway 1 toward Marina Del Ray, he said, "Carla was worried this morning. But she said she trusts you more than she trusts me."

Humbling and scary how much everyone trusted me.

He glanced over. "Was Nate okay with your leaving?"

"He was fine."

Angelo looked over his left shoulder and pulled onto the fast lane. "I've been asking Carla to go away for a few days without our daughters, but she won't. The girls and work come first. Me? I'm at the bottom of the list, if I'm even on the list."

I leaned back in the passenger seat and watched the busy highway. "At least she cares."

Angelo raised one eyebrow. I shut my mouth and during the three hour drive, I let Angelo vent about his marital woes. If I talked about my marriage, it'd be like opening a sealed Tupperware container of green stuff. I'd have to deal with it. Maybe throw it away.

By the time we reached the convention center, people milled about, laughing and greeting each other. The agenda listed talks and sessions, exchanging of ideas with top retailers, wholesalers and growers, and a peek at the year's finest foliage and blooms. Angelo said he'd pick a few relevant sessions.

That afternoon we attended a break-out seminar about the do's and don'ts of phone orders. We were cracking jokes about putting condolence cards on wedding orders, when a woman sitting next to him spoke up. "You two are such a cute couple. How long have you been married?"

Angelo and I exchanged surprised looks. "We're not," I said. "He's my boss."

The woman apologized as Angelo flashed a dazzling smile.

That evening, he met me at my motel door, and we strolled along the palm-lined boardwalk to an oyster bar. I had never tasted an oyster, but with a little bit of coaxing, I decided to go for it. It was icky and gritty.

Angelo laughed. "You should see your face." His face grew serious and he leaned over the high table near the bar, his bangs falling to the edges of his high cheekbones. "Funny what that lady said today, you know, about us being married."

"It was."

"Rebecca, I really like you."

"I…I like you, too." I slowly released my breath. "You've been really sweet." A lame understatement, granted, but I meant it. I enjoyed his uncomplicated, undemanding companionship. I wanted the kind of marriage I imagined I could have with him.

The waitress arrived and set margaritas between us, interrupting our gaze. As the evening hours flew by, we moved closer and laughed louder. I could see the night playing out, and I grew worried. I wasn't sure I wanted to douse long-buried happy, tingly feelings.

Later, we walked under the palms back to the motel. His body, so close to mine, made my heart race. I had to remind myself to breathe. He rested his hand on my back at the door, under the light, and I wondered if Marina Del Ray was having an earthquake. My knees went weak. When had I ever felt like this? Maybe never before with a guy, not even Nate.

I lifted my face. He leaned close. I held my breath, my lips burning to meet his, but knowing we'd never stop at one kiss, and for sure that would be a sin.

I pulled back, remembering that party when I'd kissed Nate's friend. I was not a good person. I looked down, dug into my purse for the key, found it and opened the door. I turned back to Angelo. He moved close again and I knew exactly what to do—yield to temptation. Then I heard the ringing.

I broke away, pushed open the door and ran to the phone. Nate. He said he'd been calling all evening. I tried to sound normal, like I hadn't almost committed adultery. I looked to the open door. Angelo lowered his head and walked away. Dang. Thank God.

During the ride home from the convention, I wondered if his feelings mirrored mine; relieved, yet sad. He wasn't a cheater. I wasn't a home-wrecker. But I still had strong feelings for him. If he pulled over, I'd be tempted to hop in the back seat with him.

His dark thick brows furrowed as his hands gripped the wheel.

"Oh boy," I said, to break the silent tension. "I don't know about you but I think I had one too many oysters last night. Maybe we need to avoid them. What do you think?"

The dimple on his right cheek deepened. "Oysters." He turned to me. "Hmmm…Is that what it was?"

"Could be," I said. "Yeah, I think so. I warned you I'd never eaten them before."

Angelo kept his eyes on the road and drummed a rhythmic beat on the steering wheel while nodding to La Bamba.

"*Para bailar la bamba,*" I belted out.

"*Para bailar la bamba,*" he chorused with me.

We finished off with a Ba....ba....bamba and a bunch of raucous laughter. We were still friends and hadn't crossed any barriers.

Yet.

That Sunday, Nate took off to the lake with a friend. I stayed home. My emotions were shooting all over the place. I'd thrown a match in my box of fireworks. Red hot feelings of passion erupted for Angelo. Sad blue feelings of loyalty sprang up for Nate. Uncontrollable tears burst from my eyes about the sad state of my marriage. Fits of anger that I'd married someone who didn't love me left me feeling exhausted.

At work Angelo and I didn't talk about Marina Del Ray or the near affair. He didn't flirt either. I caught myself staring at him often, watching his hands as he arranged the flowers and thinking thoughts a married woman should not think about a married man's hands and what I wished he'd do with them.

I came home one afternoon to Nate waiting at the door, smiling. "Got some great news!"

"What is it?" I stepped into the living room, kicked off my shoes and sank into the couch.

Nate's eyes went to my shoes, and his smile faded.

"Sorry." I rose and put them in the closet.

Nate clapped, and his happy face returned. "I got a promotion today."

"Great!"

"And a raise."

"Super!"

"But it means a move to Tennessee."

"Tennessee?" I sat back on the couch and rubbed my temples. "What about my job?"

"You have a loser job. You can make minimum wage anywhere." He moved beside me on the couch. His shoulders dropped. "I gotta get out of California. I hate California."

"I like California."

"Please Becky. It'll be a good move for us."

His desperate pleas rushed like cold water over my angry wall, but I crossed my arms, holding firm. He sat beside me and placed a hand upon mine. The cracks in my fortress spider-webbed into deep fissures and my shoulders dropped. Like a loyal dog, I would go wherever he yanked me. That's just the way it was.

Covering my face, I wept for reasons I couldn't express to my husband. I'd been praying more and more lately. Now, I prayed God wouldn't abandon me.

Sagai

Sagai stepped off the bus in Sheveroy Hills as the sun chased the mist from the hillside. His family should have received his telegram from Polur. He'd been granted a short break before his journey back to Darjeeling.

"Sagai! Sagai!" A loud familiar voice filled him with a rush of joy.

Appa! His father hurriedly limped across the street, waving his hand.

"Brother Sagai is home!"

He embraced his father. "Appa! All of Sheveroy Hills will hear you."

"Let them hear. No other boy from this village is in the seminary." Appa rested his hand on his shoulder. "Ahh, good to see you after so long."

Walking toward home, his father slowed, stole a glance, then shook his head. "Look at you in your cassock. And you have grown much taller than me." He squeezed Sagai's arms. "And strong too!"

He realized what he had missed during his years away—his father's constant love. But if he did not sacrifice this secure and safe love of his earthly father, he could not have responded to his calling to do the work of his Heavenly Father.

Appa read his mind. "I have missed you, but look how far you have come toward your priesthood. It won't be long now?"

"I'm a brother only. I must finish my degrees at Darjeeling, then four years to earn a degree in Theology even before I can be ordained a deacon. Priesthood will follow."

Sagai eased into a slower stride as his father limped along. "Father Michael came home a few months back and asked about you. He was here at St. Agnes, but he's since moved on."

"He wrote to me from America and has been writing to me since his return."

"Yes, he told me. Good fortune for you. Father's been good to us. Found a good alliance for your sister, even helped with expenses."

He continued on. Friends and neighbors smiled, nodded hello, and offered congratulations. Nearing home, his dog ran up the road and leapt on him.

Sagai scratched his ears. "Tiny, I must greet Amma first."

At the threshold of his doorway, Sagai dropped to his knees for the traditional blessing. Amma made the sign of the cross on his forehead and kissed the top of his head. "Ah, my son. So good to see you."

Family, friends, and neighbors stopped by the house to greet him and ask advice. How easily they changed their perception, turning him from a small shy boy into a man whom they respected. Was it because of the cassock, or did they see something they never saw before?

Sitting on a cot in the corner of the dim room, he mixed curry with rice on the metal plate and listened to his older brother's woes.

"I'm making so less as a hotel server," his brother said. "Could you get me a loan to buy an auto rickshaw? Then I could make money. Maybe you could approach a generous parishioner?" He gnawed the chicken off the bone. "Mmm. Amma added chicken today for your sake."

Sagai shook his head. "I am no one to ask anyone for a loan. Only rectors have control over funds."

The woeful stories continued until after dark. Vijay fared no better. He was out of a job and would look for work in Bangalore where cousins lived. The help from Father Michael had been a Godsend, but there were more sisters. Appa pawned Amma's gold chain and bangles for dowry. Shame for an Indian woman not to wear gold, no matter how poor.

Sagai listened to the plight of others, He could only offer a listening ear and prayers.

Too soon, he had to return to Darjeeling. His sister-in-law handed him his cassock, folded and pressed. "I stitched a loose button, Father."

"Thank you Sentamil." He accepted the garment. "But please don't call me father yet."

"Father, why should you thank me? And why should you say please? You should never speak like this to family. Father, it is my duty to do these things."

Sagai pulled the cassock over his head. "But I am grateful."

"You were always different from your brothers. Not like Indian men. Now you are even more strange."

"How so?" He lifted his chin and buttoned the top button of his cassock.

"Always thanking."

"But I'm only…"

"Oh, come now." She poked his chest. "Attempting to take your plate to the kitchen. Helping me carry in vegetables from market. Asking questions about what we women think and feel. No man is like that. What are they teaching you in the seminary?" She touched the sleeve of his cassock, and drew close.

"Sentamil!" Amma shouted from the kitchen. Sentamil jumped and hustled out of the room.

He shrugged at her strange behavior, closed his battered leather suitcase, and stood before the photograph of his grandfather. "Amma, what is happening with Orange Valley now?"

"All that remains from Grandfather's property is a small section in the middle of the coffee estate. Only money and sweat can make it prosperous again." Amma lowered head and wiped tears with the edge of her *saree*. "We have sweat, but no money."

"If I came home and settled here, I could help."

"Shush, son. This is not your worry. God will help us."
Amma returned her gaze to the photograph and began to speak
of days past. "We lived happily, like prince and princess on the
estate. Your appa, all fancy in his suit and round brimmed hat,
arrived from Karnataka and found us so well off. He came to
the estate bringing cheese and biscuits."

Sagai looked up at the sound of a low chuckle from the
doorway.

"And your appa would chase me away every time I
came to visit. 'Don't you come near my daughter and try to
impress her with your appearance,' he would say."

"But my prince persisted."

The show of love between his parents warmed his heart,
two distant relatives who had broken tradition by falling in love
before marriage.

"Brother Sagai, are you ready? It is time." Appa picked
up his suitcase, exposing daylight through the cracks in the
wall behind it. With his parents retired and aging, how would
his family survive?

He said a silent prayer for them, then knelt for the
departing blessing.

On his return to Darjeeling, at the stop-gap in Calcutta,
six of his classmates met him to travel the next leg. In the
morning, Father Prior of the religious house announced
permission from Father Superior to stay an extra day to visit
Mother Teresa at her Home for the Dying and Destitute.

At Mother Teresa's *Nirmal Hriday*—Pure Heart—in
Calcutta, wails from within grew louder when a sister opened
the metal door. She greeted them with palms pressed together,
wearing her white *saree* with blue trim—the simple dress

Mother Superior had chosen as the religious habit for all her
Missionaries of Charity.

"Welcome Father, brothers." She nodded and lowered
her head. "Come. Mother will see you shortly."

Men and women wandered about like wailing hungry
toddlers. Some banged their heads against trees. Along with
Father Prior, the brothers and Sagai followed the nun into a
cinder block building. In long rows of cots, the dying, brought
in from the streets, were cared for by the Missionaries of
Charity.

The stench of feces and antiseptic tightened his throat.

One sister cleaned an invalid who had smeared his
excretions on his body, his cot, and whatever area of wall he
could reach. Another sister, with bucket in hand, scrubbed the
wall while a wrinkled faced man with sunken eyes tugged her
arm and moaned unintelligibly into her face.

"Sister, can I help you?" Sagai asked.

"Oh no, Brother." The man continued to lament. "You
are a guest. This is my duty."

One of the brothers held a hand over his mouth while
Sagai attempted to conceal his own expressions of horror.

"Don't worry." The sister glanced at Sagai and the
brothers. "The poor man is confused. Just yesterday his family
left him here."

Sagai had seen people like this in the street of Wadala
and had been around the lepers in Polur, but here, in one place,
so many extreme cases.

The mentally deranged bashed themselves against walls
and cots, obviously having no grasp of their actions.
Arguments erupted between people who didn't understand

what the other was saying. Nuns dutifully waded through the ward, managing the bedlam.

"These nuns make sure that each soul in their care can die with dignity and in peace with God." Father Prior shook his head.

Sagai pressed his hand to his heavy heart and breathed deeply. What problems could he have that could be so bad? The face of real suffering and real humanity was before him. "Father, how do these nuns manage?"

"By the grace of God."

As he and his group walked the hall, Sagai battled with feelings of repugnancy. Could he do what these sisters did— serve people in this state, day in and day out, maintaining a pleasant countenance? Perhaps their strong faith in God saw them through.

He closed his eyes and prayed the Psalms silently. *You have searched me, Lord, and you know me. You know when I sit and when I rise; you perceive my thoughts from afar.* Lord, you know my weak faith needs to grow so I can also do whatever you ask of me. He then searched the room for the face of the one who initiated this work of compassion.

A few years earlier, Mother Theresa received the Nobel Peace Prize for her humanitarian efforts. Sagai imagined her place of high honor here. He followed Father Prior and the brothers into an open space in the corner of the building where several nuns wrenched their *sarees* over buckets of water.

"They only have two sets of clothes," Father Prior said. "One they wear and one they wash."

One of the elderly nuns rose and wiped her hands on her *saree*. It was her! Mother Teresa! The wrinkles around her eyes deepened as she bowed and pressed her hands together.

"Good morning, Father."

"Good morning, Mother. These brothers are seminarians from Darjeeling."

"Good morning, brothers."

Sagai couldn't believe he stood before a living saint. He and the others pressed their hands together and bowed.

Mother Teresa thanked Father Prior for the care given to her congregation, then turned to the brothers. "Become good priests and take care of the sisters and all of God's children."

"Yes, Mother." Sagai, along with the others bowed.

Then, as suddenly as she arose to greet them, she returned to her washing.

The brothers followed Father Prior out of the compound. Sagai replayed everything in his head, memorizing the moment; the way she sat on her haunches washing her *saree*, her words, the deep wrinkles in her face, the joy in her peaceful countenance in this harsh environment.

When he arrived in Darjeeling, he left his cloud when summoned to the rector's office. The usual dread made him pause at the door.

A pleasant smile on his superior's face surprised him. "Good news! Come. Everything is in place for the Food-For-Work program. Next week, forty students will join you and the Bansghari villagers in building the road. The students will camp in the village and work straight until completion."

Good news, indeed!

That week the college community loaded supplies on a bullock cart and hiked to Bansghari. Subba and Sagai had already discussed the engineering of the road, so for the next three weeks they dug holes, dragged rocks from the mountain and laid them, stone upon stone, up the hill to the main road.

More than fifty villagers had taken off work and accepted bulgur for wages. Back-breaking work, but everyone did their part.

Subba worked mostly beside Sagai. They'd become close friends.

"Tell me about your Jesus," Subba said one day. "What is it about Him that makes your faith so special?"

Sagai leaned against his shovel. "Christ is my Divine Friend, to whom I can take everything—loneliness, frustration and sadness as well as joy. My life has a here and now and a future because of Jesus."

Subba tilted his head and squinted against the sun, listening.

"God had a son and placed Him on this earth. Through His death and resurrection, I, a sinner with no hope, have gained eternal life."

"Because of you, I want to learn more about your faith."

Sagai smiled and stuck his shovel in a pile of dirt. "Come to the church, my friend. We can show you the way." He returned to his work with a happy hum. Since he began his journey toward priesthood, God took every challenge and turned it into a blessing. God had not abandoned him, even in his darkest days.

Thirteen

Carrying One Another's Burden

No one is useless in this world who lightens the burden of it to anyone else.
~ Charles Dickens

Rebecca

Nate's huge salary as Plant Manager and an outrageously high loan approval took us from the California apartment to a large three-bedroom, brick ranch house on a cul-de-sac called Magnolia Circle, in a Knoxville, Tennessee subdivision.

Two weeks after I unpacked the house, I hopped on I-65 and headed straight north. I'd earnestly vowed to make the most of my marriage. I committed to love Nate and make him love me back, a daunting task that included making his favorite meals, buying lingerie that would turn any husband's eye, and obediently catering to his every wish and command.

The first strike against the plan was when Nate refused me access to our bank accounts. The second strike was his strike. He might have blackened my eye if I hadn't ducked left. I rubbed my sore, bruised shoulder. Never argue with someone who thinks they do no wrong and turns what is right into black and blue.

There would be no third strike.

His apologies were filled with promises—baby promises, college promises, and promises he'd take me to India. Meaningless promises. He also said he loved me, but love didn't come balled up as a fist and smack you in the upper shoulder. I didn't get the marriage. I didn't understand why he didn't want a divorce. Did he think our relationship was normal?

Throughout the entire five years, I was the kid someone's mom was forcing them to play with. But I was done playing and on my way home.

I reached to the passenger seat and grabbed the scribbled directions to my second oldest sister's home. Michelle had recently moved from Baltimore to Chicago with her husband and new baby. When I informed her I was coming through Chicago on my way home, she asked if she and baby Emma could catch a ride home.

That's all she asked. Nothing more.

Since Kara died, my contact with her had been minimal. Like Heather, she kept the dregs of our childhood buried deep. Birthday cards were one-liners. Michelle dished up her annual Christmas letters as straightforward as pot roast. I, on the other hand, served mine salted with half-truths and peppered with exaggerations. I had to lie. The truth would disgrace the holy image on the other side of the Christmas card.

Getting closer to the end of a long trip—exhausted by thoughts that led to questions that had no answers—I turned into the driveway of a tall Tudor home in a North Chicago suburb.

"Emma is beautiful!" I met my sister on her front steps, bee-lined it to the infant, and breathed in sweet baby oil scented skin. I brushed my cheek against her soft tuft of auburn hair. Baby scent was healing aromatherapy. They ought to bottle it.

"You look great." Michelle looked angelically granola-ish with her soft blond curls, loose bib overalls, flower-stenciled t-shirt, and Birkenstocks.

Her husband greeted me politely and we loaded her suitcases, car seat, and baby gear in my car. After the family hugged and said good-byes, we hit the highway.

During the five hour drive, Michelle answered my basic catching up questions in short, reserved clips. I responded in the same manner, always halting at edges of emotional cliffs. I only admitted that I needed to get away for a little while. How could I explain that domestic abuse was the least of my marriage issues?

I asked about Heather and the conversation piqued.

"I was home last month, grocery shopping with Mama, and we saw this girl in high heels and a tight hot-pink, vinyl mini-skirt. I didn't recognize her until she turned."

I cringed. "Heather?"

"Yes."

Our younger sister's provocative dressing became a bonding opportunity.

"Last I heard she had a Canadian boyfriend."

"He got deported after a drug crime. She's staying in the chicken coop at Mama and Daddy's new place now."

"Chicken coop?" That didn't sound good. I had hoped my parents had bought a decent retirement home after they moved off the farm.

"That's what they call it. It might have been a chicken coop at one time, but they fixed it up. Heather's their first guest."

"Is she working?"

"At The Well. I've heard stories. She's quite popular with the menfolk around town."

I cringed as Michelle talked about our sister's escapades, some of which I wasn't sure were legal in White Gull Bay.

We stopped for gas and I waited for her to finish nursing Emma in the back seat. Back on the road, while the baby slept, I spoke about my Kara story that I'd been pitching to agents.

"No bites yet, but I did get a small essay published in a nature magazine, sort of a childhood reminiscent story about the woods."

"Way to go." Michelle smiled.

Soon we reached White Gull Bay. I slowed as we passed our childhood home.

"Eddie moved in with his family after Mama and Daddy moved out."

"I heard that."

My brother shocked everyone by returning home from Europe with a beautiful British wife and her eight-year-old daughter, Elizabeth.

"How do you like his wife?"

"Barb? Love her. She's so British and sweet as a Cadbury Egg. She's pregnant. And get this, Eddie's studying to be a priest."

"No way! A priest? What's he going to do with his family?"

"He's Anglican now. They can marry."

Michelle and Eddie seemed to have gotten the entire happiness pie. I hoped for a small crumb.

My sister pointed as we drove past grandpa's old house that Eddie once moved into. "Tom and Sally live there now.

Their daughter is one month older than Emma. Bobby and Beth are in Grandma's trailer by the farm. Brian is almost two."

I nodded. Most of this I'd heard. Nate and I had come home for Michelle's and Bobby's wedding a few years back, but hadn't returned since. I'd missed so much.

"How much further to the new place?"

"Just ahead about two miles." In a short time, she pointed to a long driveway that led to a beautiful cedar ranch house, nestled in a pine grove.

"This is it?"

"You'll be surprised at the changes."

Michelle carried Emma in her car seat across the redwood wrap-around porch. I hustled ahead to open the French doors. Streams of sunshine highlighted the cherry wood floors of the high-vaulted living room.

"Nice place," I whispered.

Heather rose from the dark leather couch that faced a stone fireplace stacked with chunks of unlit wood.

Michelle looked over her shoulder, rolled her eyes, and mouthed, "Daisy Duke."

I snickered then coughed to disguise my amusement at Heather's tiny red flannel shirt, buttoned low and tied below her overflowing chest and her super short blue-jean skirt and heels. While we Meyer sisters shared the same physical genes, our styles were uniquely our own. If Heather was Daisy Duke, Michelle was Mother Earth and I was preppy in my t-shirt, blazer, jeans and penny loafers. Our oldest sister, Lisa, would be "hippy-girl," but she refused to talk to anyone in the family.

"Hey, Heather."

"Hey, Rebecca. 'bout time you come home."

Before we got to the awkward stage of deciding if we should hug or not, Mama emerged from the hallway wearing a white cable sweater and dark blue dress pants. Sans her overalls, she looked great. She wrapped her arms around me. "You're home!"

Michelle wasn't kidding about the changes. Mama-love overflowed from this woman. She grasped my hand and led me through her new home, explaining that the round earthy hued stones in the fireplace had probably tumbled through centuries, after the ice age.

From the bedroom window, she pointed to a trickling brook that meandered through the woods where she'd sit and sketch. Mama had retired from farm work and signed up for watercolor classes. Daddy had retired from his ship job and spent his days working with his sons on the farm.

I followed her to the bright airy kitchen with its modern appliances and cupboards and joined Michelle and Heather at the bar that opened to the living room. Emma slept in her car seat on the floor.

Mama set out plates of Rueben and grilled-cheese sandwiches, glasses full of cold milk and a large platter of homemade snickerdoodles, my favorite cookies. Comfort food. I took a deep satisfied breath. The new place already felt like home.

As my mother chatted about family news, I realized that, for the first time in my life, Heather and I shared something in common. While everyone else was busy farming, gaining assets, and spawning genius children, Heather and I were penniless and homeless, serving no greater purpose in life and seeking shelter in our parent's chicken coop.

I shoved another cookie in my mouth. The only difference between Heather and me was that she was looking for a husband, and I wanted to get rid of one.

I lifted the plate to Michelle. "Sandwiches are awesome."

Mama raised her eyebrows in displeasure. "She's given up meat."

While my sister attempted to explain her meatless sin, the front door flew open and Emma wailed. Daddy, in his typical blue and white Key overalls, filled the door frame. A cool spring breeze rustled his thick shock of gray hair. Known for his Paul Newman looks, John Wayne attitude, and Paul Bunyan strength, Daddy made a person feel like a lowly private when a five-star general entered the room.

We all stood.

My sisters stared at the floor.

"Hi," I croaked. Daddy responded with a hello, then announced he was going to shower. We were strangers. Hello was a start.

Michelle picked up Emma. Mama glanced down the hallway. I shivered. Something besides Daddy's sovereign aura and the cool spring breeze had lowered the temperature of the room.

She invited us all to sit in the living room. Michelle sank on the couch, put Emma to her breast, then draped a blanket over her shoulder. I sat on the other end of the couch and Heather took a spot on the fireplace's stone ledge.

Mama eased into a pale floral armchair, folded her hands, and sighed. "With Rebecca here, I might as well tell you girls the news." Her eyes shifted from Heather to Michelle then rested on me. "Daddy has cancer."

Heather pressed her hand to her parted lips. Michelle blinked. I swallowed hard. Daddy was only in his early sixties. Cancer really dared to take him on?

"He'll start chemo next week."

Heather sobbed. One of us should have moved, consoled one another with a hug, but we stuck to old childhood ingrained ways. I needed a moment to sort through my emotions. I used to write poems and draw pictures for my father when I was little. When Kara died, I'd given up trying to get him to love me. A stranger had cancer.

"Daddy can beat this." Mama folded her hands in her lap. "Remember when the barn door fell on him. He was in the hospital, in traction, and he unhooked himself and walked the three miles home. I almost fainted when he showed up at the front door."

"But cancer is different." Michelle put Emma over her shoulder and patted her back.

"He's going to be okay." Mama smiled assuredly. "Last week, sitting in this chair, I had a long cry. I closed my eyes felt a brush on my cheek. A voice whispered, 'It's okay.' It was Kara. I felt her presence, heard her too."

It's okay, Bec. I'd heard that voice many times from Kara and after she died, those words echoed in my head at times when I wanted to give up. But I never wanted Kara to come to me like she came to Mama. I was afraid she'd hated me.

Doors opened and shut in the hallway.

Mama stood. "I'd better get his dinner. You girls catch-up in the chicken coop." She went into the kitchen.

I'd been cheated. My mother showed a tender intuitive side that could have opened the door for real conversation, then closed it.

But I understood the dynamics. Daddy didn't eat if we were around. I never could figure out if he was uncomfortable in our presence because he didn't care to talk with us or if he was annoyed that we never talked to him.

"Goodnight, I'll see you in the morning."

"Daddy leaves early for milking." That meant we were welcome back after he left. Maybe if I stayed home, I could work on breaking the vicious circle of non-communication and build family relationships, even try to gain my father's love before it was too late.

Michelle, Heather, and I walked across the driveway and opened the door to the guesthouse. I couldn't imagine the darling little cottage had been a chicken coop.

"I've claimed the loft," Heather announced, stepping into the kitchen area that opened to carpeted living room. "Back bedroom has a twin bed and the couch is a sleeper. You guys figure out your sleeping arrangements."

I got comfortable on the carpet with Michelle and her baby. My sister pulled toys from the bag and waved them. The sweetie giggled and flailed her hands. After a few minutes, Heather came downstairs in her pajamas and settled into a chair across from us.

I held the baby's tiny fingers as she babbled and balanced herself. "She's so cute, Michelle."

"She'll be nine months old next week, and this is the first time you've seen her." Michelle didn't disguise the hurt in her voice.

"I'm sorry. I should've come home when she was born, but I was so far away."

"Yeah, you've been far away." The double meaning in Michelle's words hung heavy in the air. I would've flown home, but Nate always refused to buy me a ticket. How could I explain to either of them that I'd basically been held prisoner for the last few years.

Emma plunked onto her diapered butt and reached for a plastic donut.

A sniffle broke the uncomfortable silence. Heather buried her face in her hands. Normal sisters would rush to comfort each other. Michelle and I were like soldiers not wanting to deal with the weak link in the foxhole. Every tick of the clock expressed more of the truth, these women as strangers, not sisters.

"There's a lot of cancer in the family." Michelle blew out a deep breath. "Aunt Linda has breast cancer. And you heard Uncle Eugene died last month, right?"

I nodded, glad some words filled the gaps of silence and not saddened at the reminder of my uncle's death. The last time I saw him at Kara's funeral, I hoped to never set eyes on him again.

"I hated him." Michelle spat out the words, then pulled Emma close. She looked up, her eyes damp and darkened with pain. "He attacked me once."

"What happened?" I leaned in close, afraid she wouldn't continue and worried she would.

She bit her lip, breathed deeply, then exhaled. "I was standing in the kitchen when he snuck up from behind and grabbed my breasts. Then Lisa came into the room and cracked him over the head with a broomstick. She threatened to kill him if he ever touched me again."

"Did you tell Mama?"

She nodded. "She just warned to stay away from him. Daddy wasn't home. Lisa was so mad at her for not handling it." Michelle's voice grew quiet. "Lisa had an abortion in high school, but never said who the father was."

"An abortion?" My weak stomach clenched.

"I shouldn't have said that. She swore me to secrecy before she left."

"No wonder." It made sense that she never came home, not even for Kara's funeral.

Heather gasped.

I turned to find her sobbing, shaking. My eyes leaked tears that stung. "Oh, God. Heather, he didn't!"

Heather tucked her knees to her chest, slung her arms around them and buried her face. "My big sister didn't protect me."

"I...I didn't know." I rushed to her side and hugged her. She shook like crazy. "I'm so sorry." Michelle was crying too. I sat on the edge of my little sister's chair, pulled her close and stroked her hair. Could I be made to feel more rotten? I'd failed everyone. "When did it happen?"

"Around the time Kara died."

Had he raped her, too? How could I have not known?

Heather spoke between sobs. "Nobody cared. And now, at least you both have husbands. I have no one."

Had I been so caught up in my own grief that I couldn't have reached out to her? But I had tried, many times. "Do you want to talk about it? About what happened?"

Heather shook her head. Michelle leaned over Emma and pressed her lips on her fingers.

Bile rose from my gut to my throat. "I never knew. I'm so sorry."

Heather breathed slower and closed her eyes. "It's okay."

Given what Michelle had said about her, I didn't think it was okay. No wonder she drank, hooked up with bad boys, and looked for love in one-night stands. But was this my fault?

The baby cried and Michelle picked her up and rocked back and forth. "Becca, did he ever come after you?"

"He tried, but I knew how to run like the wind." I stood and reached out my arms toward my little sister. "Heather, come here." She joined Michelle and me, and for the first time in our lives, we sisters stood in a circle and hugged.

Exhausted, I suggested we all get sleep. Heather slept upstairs, Michelle with her baby in a portable crib in the back bedroom, and me on the pull-out couch. I fell asleep thinking Heather would require a whole lot more help that I could give her. In the morning, I'd suggest she see a counselor.

In the morning Mama kept the baby and my sisters and I drove down to Evergreen Lane.

On the Lake Michigan shoreline, no one talked about Daddy's cancer or last night's revelations. We took off our shoes and socks, rolled up our jeans, and only spoke of pleasant childhood memories as tiny waves tumbled then trickled to meet our toes. Cool water lapped the shore and flowed over our feet like a ritualistic cleansing, washing away the debris of our past and baptizing us into new relationships, true sisters.

Heather stooped and picked up a round stone and turned it over in her hands. "Remember when we all slept on the beach before Kara was born?"

I nodded. "We watched for shooting stars until we fell asleep."

"Remember when we were little and Mama would sit on a big blanket and watch us swim?" Michelle smiled.

"And we all yelled, 'Look at me!'" I picked up a flat stone and skipped it over the water. "Three times. Lucky day."

We continued to Evergreen Lane where I'd parked the car. I winced when I opened the door. My shoulder still smarted, but with Heather's trauma and the news about Daddy, my problems seemed almost insignificant.

Michelle looked sideways at me. "You okay?"

"I'm fine."

Before going back to Mama's house, we visited Eddie and his family, a happy reunion. Barb and her daughter were as wonderful as Michelle said.

Back at our parent's house, Heather retreated to the coop while I walked alongside Michelle into the main house.

She stopped on the deck and tugged my boat neck collar, noticing my bruise. "What's that?"

"It's why I came home."

"Oh, Rebecca. Nate?"

I nodded.

Michelle's jaw tightened. "I knew it. Are you going to leave him?"

"Think I should?"

"Divorce him. I never liked him."

I locked my arm in hers. "Where have you been all these years?"

"Where've you been?" She gave my arm a squeeze.

I opened the door to Mama, standing in the kitchen with the phone in her hand and a frown on her face. "You just missed another call."

"Nate?"

"His mother this time. She said you've deserted him. She thinks you're having an affair."

"She's crazy."

"Nate's been calling, too."

"He's crazier."

Michelle scooped Emma from the playpen and sat on the couch. I moved beside them.

Mama followed us into the living room, hands planted on hips. "Rebecca, what's going on?"

Like ten years old again and caught stealing a marshmallow before dinner, I stuttered. "I…I thought maybe I could stay here for a little while."

She was interrupting my fantasy plan, already taking shape. Get a quick, decent divorce settlement, be Heather's roomie in the chicken coop, and with my one publishing credit I could travel to India, write about the experience, and pitch it to magazines. I planned to call Father Michael as soon as I got a calling card. I just knew he'd say, "*Vanakkam.*"

"What about your marriage?"

Michelle nudged me and lifted her eyes toward Mama. She wanted me to tell the whole story. "Nate's not a good person." It was all that would come out of my mouth.

She crossed her arms. "I told you not to marry him."

There it was. Delayed by a few years, but she got to say it.

"But you went ahead. I told you, even on your wedding day that it wasn't too late."

I watched a bird flutter outside at the feeder, then fly off. "And I should've ran."

"Well, you can't run now. You've made your bed, now lie in it." She spoke calmly, slowly, with her eyes glued on me. If she would've slapped me, it would've stung less.

Tears filled my eyes. "I have zero self-worth left. You have no idea how my marriage has been. I just need a little help."

Michelle shrugged and raised her eyebrows. My stomach churned. None of us had mastered the art of arguing with Mama. She returned to the kitchen and stabbed a tomato.

"I need air." I left Michelle and her baby and flew to the coop.

Shower steam, escaping from the louvered bathroom door, clouded the windows. No telling when Heather would be out.

I sat on the couch, opened my purse and re-read a letter from Father Michael. He had been assigned to Sagai's home parish and arranged a marriage for the cleric's sister. If I had Father Michael to arrange my marriage, I might be happily married now. The letter told of Sagai's good works in Darjeeling, building a road while he attended college. I'd been faithfully praying for him every day, as promised. He was finishing his degree in Philosophy. I should be in college, finishing my degree or building roads that lead somewhere.

I closed my eyes and leaned back, thinking of the pictures I'd seen in books of Darjeeling, the tea gardens, the mountains. Someday I'd get there.

The front door opened and Michelle walked in with the baby. She placed her on the carpet with toys and stretched on the floor, her body protectively cradling.

I reclined on the couch, exhausted. Must have been the walk on the beach, the fresh lake air, the emotional stuff.

"So what will you do?"

I stuck a pillow behind my head and stared at the ceiling. "I don't know. I don't want to go back. It's not like Nate and I let our love grow cold, and we need to rekindle it. We aren't friends, don't have a real marriage. We don't even…" I raised my eyes, not wanting to even admit how ridiculous my life was.

"Never?"

"Hardly ever." I rested the back of my hand on my forehead. "Honestly, I don't know him. Sometimes I think I love him, and other times I believe he's evil incarnate. This last straw was over a money issue."

Another wave of nausea forced me to sitting.

"My stomach's been upset lately. I don't know what's wrong."

"Since you and Nate don't sleep together, you can't be pregnant."

Another wave of nausea made my mouth water. "Although, before he hit me…"

Michelle raised her eyebrows as the shower stopped. "Have you missed?"

I began to calculate, then put my hand over my mouth and ran to the bathroom, banging on the door for Heather to let me in.

Sagai

Subba, the village headman, traveled the newly built Bansghari road often to attend Catechism classes at the parish. Sagai continued his studies, duties, and Sunday ministry through the summer and into the autumn. He never saw Bindu. When the misty mountain air whistled cool through the evergreens once again, he took his last winter break before graduation, journeying the four day route from Northeast India to South India. His orders were to serve in an orphanage in Andimadam, a small Tamil Nadu village.

He caught the train from Chennai to Virudachalem, the last leg of his journey. From there he should have boarded a bus to Andimadam, but the last bus had left.

His shadow stretched long on the platform. What to do? He'd have to wait until morning. It didn't seem right to sleep on the cement in his cassock, but if he removed it, the police might grab him, thinking he was a runaway.

He sat on the bench and stared at the stained platform ceiling, recalling those he'd promised prayers. He stopped on the name Rebecca. He wondered about her, what she looked like. He prayed for her daily, as he'd promised Father Michael. What problems could a young woman in America, the land of plenty, have? Maybe problems of the heart. "Lord, whatever her troubles, grant her your grace and mercy."

Smells of *garam masala* spice and frying onions tugged him to his feet. He hadn't eaten since breakfast. A clink-clankety tune charmed him to a shop where thousands of tiny sparks danced from an open street-side stove. In a swift metallic rhythm, a vendor tapped his metal utensil against the aluminum cooking vessels, banged it against the iron griddle, then rolled the dough in concentric circles for the *kothu paratha*.

As Sagai reached in his pockets for money, cowbells jingled. A bare-chested man driving a bullock cart headed toward the sign pointing to Andimadam. Sagai looked from the vendor to the departing bullock cart and groaned. He shoved the rupee note deep into his pocket and chased the cart.

"Hello! Sir!" He caught up to the cart. "Going to Andimadam?"

The driver nodded, yanked the reins, and halted. He wound the towel from his head and shoed away mosquitoes.

Sagai held out his money. "Can you take me?"

"Where to?" The driver rubbed his bushy moustache.

"The orphanage."

"Erikko. Hop in." The man took the bill, stuffed it in his shirt pocket and nodded back toward the cart.

He slid his suitcase onto the cart and climbed in. Perhaps Mother Mary was looking out for him tonight. He'd prayed the rosary on the bus, asking for her intercession to reach his destination and do his work well in this assignment. He reached in his pocket for the rosary and grasped it. The cart bumped, the suitcase thumped under his head, and bells jingled along the road toward Andimadam.

After a few hours, the motion ceased. Sounds of singing, flutes, and drumming whirled in the night air along with aromatic holy ash, incense, and burning oil. Sagai scooted the suitcase behind his back and sat up. An elephant blessed children with its trunk. This wasn't the Christian orphanage, but a Hindu temple entrance.

He rose to his knees. At the other entrance, a shop front displayed bowls of red powder and garlands, offerings to the deity.

Over the din, he yelled. "Why did we stop?"

"Road block."

He stood on the back of the cart, curious about the crowd beside the temple. Gaslights propped on pillars cast a glow over a musical troupe. Actors and actresses in dramatic make-up and elaborate colorful costumes watched the musicians.

The folklore tradition—*Theru Koothu*—was a street play performed in a junction, in open air, to teach a moral lesson to the community.

When the musical interlude ended, musicians retreated to a wooden bench. Actors and actresses took center stage and the bullock driver leaned back and crossed his arms.

A man dressed in king's finery sat on a gold painted throne in the middle of the street.

"Lord Rama, we do not want you to take a soiled wife." One of the actors bowed before the makeshift throne.

A scene from Uttara Ramayana! He knew this play very well, already half over. When Rama returned to Ayodhya after killing the demon king Ravana and rescuing his wife, Sita, he was crowned king. However, Rama's subjects rejected Sita as their queen because she was no longer pure.

"But as king, I must perform many rituals and in all of them, the presence of a wife is required." Lord Rama raised his hand under the gas lamp glow.

The street scene ended with a compromise. A golden effigy of Sita was placed next to Rama as he performed necessary rituals.

After the scene, a clown ran into the street, a custom to digress from the religious theme to a present village issue. It seemed the headman had some moral issues of his own. The clown lampooned him for taking advantage of certain village women.

The driver, not so interested in the moral lesson, clicked his tongue and snapped the ropes. The bullocks headed down a new road. So, not a road block after all, but an entertainment break. Sagai leaned back and stared up into the night sky, wondering what lay ahead for him in Andimadam.

An hour or so later, long past dinner time, the cart stopped again.

"Orphanage!"

"He's here!" A small boy, filled with so much zeal he couldn't stay in one place, danced around the cart, circled it twice, then ran into the building. Sagai thanked the driver and leapt off the cart.

Within seconds, nearly thirty more boys burst from the doorway and swarmed him. He gathered as many as he could in his arms.

A salt-and-pepper haired priest with his cassock stretched tight around his belly met Sagai in the doorway. "Go on!" He shooed the boys with a wave of his hand, then smiled.

"Welcome, Brother Sagai. I'm Father Joachim."

After a firm handshake, he followed the priest through the banged up metal door of the paint-chipped cinder block building. The boys lingered nearby, dark sad eyes peeking from shadows like ghosts in purgatory waiting to be called to heaven.

A lone bulb hanging from the ceiling in the office shed enough light to expose the many cracks in the faded blue wall.

Stray dogs with ducked heads poked their noses in the office before Father Joachim shooed them, in the same manner he'd dismissed the boys. "The orphanage is in chaos."

Sagai couldn't agree more.

"For the past three months the boys have been managing on their own, older boys running the place, in charge of the younger ones, the kitchen, and chores. I come when I can, but I've many duties with the school and parish."

Sagai's stomach rumbled. "Have the boys had dinner?"

The rector called one of the boys "Dai! Had your dinner?"

"No, Father." The boy scurried into the office and stared at his dirty feet. His clothes were ragged, filthy, and much too small. "Kitchen's empty."

Father Joachim reached under his cassock, into his pocket and handed the boy a few rupees. "Go. Run. Get *idlis* from the closest shop."

Steamed rice cakes would ease his hunger, but how many nights had the boys gone hungry?

Father Joachim stood and motioned for Sagai. When the priest switched on the light in the refectory, rats and cockroaches scurried toward their hideaways, most likely taking with them the last crumbs from the pantry.

They returned to the small dormitory where moonlight shone through the small corner window, revealing piles of trash and mats strewn haphazardly about the room. Sagai shook his head in frustration.

"Shambles." Father Joachim motioned a wide arc. "And there's no discipline. The boys are not following a timetable. Some come to the school for meals, but don't stay for classes.

I've been asking Father Superior to send someone since that last cleric ran off with a local girl."

That evening Sagai swept the dormitory floor, dusted off a mat, said night prayers with the boys, and sometime in the early hours of the morning he fell asleep and dreamt of wolves chasing orphans through a forest.

The next morning, he and the boys began cleaning. He established routines, helped with homework, and put in an order with the parish for food and supplies. The orphans constantly clamored at his side, eager to help, learn, or do whatever he asked.

After Catechism lessons one day, little Dominic grasped his hands and looked into his eyes. "Will you leave us, too, Brother Sagai?"

He sighed, wishing he could tell the boy otherwise, but this was only his winter break assignment. The boys, like lambs without a shepherd, were coming to terms with the brother who had abandoned them.

He knelt beside Dominic and met his eyes. "I'll be here for a little while, but God will send someone else when I leave. No matter who comes and goes in your life, Jesus is a friend who never leaves you."

In the mornings, he walked with the boys to the parish, a mile down the dirt road, past mud homes and concrete dwellings and shops that comprised the small village of Andimadam. They'd sing hymns until they reached the tall wide belfry of the yellow concrete church built years ago by Portuguese missionaries. The boys school, a newer structure that kept Father Joachim so busy, stood alongside the church.

After Mass, Sagai insisted the orphans stay in school all day while he taught English classes. They ate meals at the school, and he received supplies for weekend rations.

He gathered them at the end of each day for short evening talks in the dormitory, complimenting them for the good things they'd done, like helping each other up after a fall or for studying well and earning a good mark. While Sagai lay on his mat at night, waiting for their whispers to settle into quiet breathing, he'd pray that the Lord would send someone to love and care for them after he left. His paternal love for children had greatly increased since his arrival.

A couple of weeks later, during lunch in the refectory, Father Joachim motioned him away from little ears. "Some of the boys from Nedodai, a nearby village, have dropped out of our school." The priest lowered his voice. "I'm growing old and cannot tackle this problem."

"Have you talked to the parents?"

He thumped his chest. "They are asking me for help."

"What is the problem exactly?" Sagai tried to mask his frustration. Father Joachim wasn't so worried when the orphans didn't attend school. The priest had a lot of work at the parish, school, and orphanage, but he should at least handle school issues. Getting the orphanage back to a functioning, orderly institution and teaching kept him running from sun up to well past sundown.

"Nedodai is a low caste village, where the church has a substation. In fact, there is a sense of elitism here in Andimadam, and this poverty and caste distinction does not help, given the recent uprisings. I am teaching through sermons, but my efforts are being overtaken."

"Overtaken? By whom?"

"Communists!" He wagged his head. "They come into villages to fire up the youth in the name of social conscientization, engaging them in their ideologies and propaganda. These outsiders use the popular street theatre to inject their motive of social protest, only they don't use costumes or props."

"One moment, Father." Sagai rushed to help a boy whose food had gotten knocked to the group, served him a new plate, then returned to the old priest.

"I'm sorry, Father. You were talking about the communists."

"Yes, they gather on the street and start opining, talking about Karl Marx's ideology of religion being the opium of people." Father Joachim splayed his fingers in the air with a twist to emphasize his point. "They aggravate tension between the villagers and their religious beliefs, exposing all the problems of the village. Neither the Hindu temple nor the church can handle this problem."

"What can I do?" Sagai worried about the students becoming like the Naxalites, a militant group in Northeast India that attacked the rich and distributed money to the poor.

"I want these boys back in school. I want you to rescue them from the hands of these radicals." Father Joachim touched his chest. "I am old. You are young. Help me, for the sake of these lost boys."

"Yes, Father. I will do my best."

Sagai took the orphans out for a game of football, pondering on the dilemma. There simply wasn't enough staff to handle all the work. The boys needed constant care and attention. No wonder the orphanage was neglected.

After assisting at evening Mass in Nedodai, Sagai walked the village streets. He found a boy who had served at Mass, playing with friends. His older brother was one of those who had dropped out of school. "Raju, where are your brother and his friends?"

"I cannot say." The child stared at his bare feet.

Sagai knelt in the dirt, grasped Raju's shoulders and looked him in the eye. "Raju, do you love your brother?"

"Yes, Brother Sagai."

"Then take me to him."

The boy folded his hands across his chest and jutted out his chin.

Sagai spoke in his kindest voice. "Raju, your brother is in trouble. Together we can help him."

He pointed northward and ran. Sagai followed down streets and alleys away from the lights of the village. Near a lone mud hut on the edge of town, the boy stopped and pointed.

"You've got to fight," came a voice from inside. "Resist the government."

Sagai took a deep breath, made the sign of the cross and offered a prayer, then pushed open the door. Kerosene lamps flickered from the corners. Two young men stood before a group of teenagers seated on the dirt floor. The men stared, eyes wide with surprise. The boys turned around. Raju stuck his head from behind his cassock.

"Raju!" said one of the teenagers.

Sagai took a deep breath, stuck out his chest, and spoke in his deepest, most authoritative voice. "Balu, come. It is urgent. Bring your friends and follow me. Now!" He took Raju's hand and walked out, praying the boys would follow and the men wouldn't. The boys didn't know him, but they'd see he was a religious and hopefully they'd respect the cassock.

Sagai's quick pace matched his rapid heartbeat. A scurry of footfalls sounded close behind him. He continued to the village limits without looking back.

"Father, what is it?" Balu asked when Sagai stopped at a tea shop.

"Let's have a meal, then we'll talk. Come." The teenage boys followed him into the shop.

"Why have you called us?" Balu crossed his arms over his chest. "Why do you have Raju?"

"You should not be in that place with those people. Your parents are worried. Father Joachim is worried."

Balu, just a few years younger than Sagai, stood inches from his face. "We've been asked to become secret members of this cell. We are helping to bring about social justice." His friends nodded.

"Even through violence?"

"If need be." Balu lifted his chin.

Sagai took the *dosas* from the counter and brought them to a table. He blessed the food. "I do not doubt the problems in the village, but why respond through violence?" He touched Balu's arm. "Like Mahatma Gandhi, you can make a change using peaceful means. You can better yourself through education, become a leader, then help the village."

The boys listened. Sagai hadn't touched his food, but continued to talk to the young men. *Please give me your words, Lord. I cannot do this alone. These kids should be studying, going to school, and not getting bombarded with ideologies of outsiders.*

By the end of the meal, he had convinced Balu and his friends to join him at the school in the evenings for meals and a youth meet.

Day after day, Sagai worked with the teens and cared for the orphans, teaching lessons on self-worth. He reasoned with them that solutions to change their social situations could come, but only through intelligent, thoughtful, and prayerful means. He met with the boys, befriended them, and visited their homes, taught in the youth group.

The end of Sagai's break approached with Holy Week. The parish buzzed about a unique village tradition in a neighboring Christian village: A narrative drama of the passion of Christ in verse and song called *Vasagapa*. From Maundy Thursday to Easter morning, the passion would be played out and narrated by actors who engaged the villagers and even the children.

On Maundy Thursday, as the church bell struck twelve, Sagai and his youth group stood on the parish steps. Residents from surrounding villages, Christians and Hindus alike, arrived as the scene opened in the Garden of Gethsemane. A few boys gasped and grabbed onto Sagai's arm when the frightening Roman soldiers arrived to arrest Jesus, taking him to the Sanhedrin to Pontius Pilate.

When they tied Jesus to the pillar, Balu wiped his eyes. The brutality, so well performed, ripped through Sagai's heart as if he were the one being flogged. Feeling each lash, he held back tears, as his body flinched. The women and children didn't control their emotions. Gasps, sobs and wails penetrated the solemn night.

At dawn, Sagai and the boys entered the chapel to sit in silent adoration before the Blessed Sacrament—the Body of

Christ. At noon, the way of the cross began. A few who'd been fasting, swooned in the street as they followed Christ's last steps on earth. Sagai also felt weary, but bore his discomfort as penance for the heavy weight of his own sins, especially his struggle with blind obedience and his occasional revulsion against superiors.

Along the way, villagers served water and buttermilk from clay pots. By the fifth station, Jesus grew weary and fell. Impatient, the soldiers pulled Simon of Cyrene out of the crowd and ordered him to help carry the cross. Sagai kept his eyes on Jesus, how he suffered, yet continued on towards his death—for a purpose.

He breathed a prayer. *Jesus, let me also help carry your cross by carrying the crosses of others. Let me be Simon. Make me strong, Lord. This path toward priesthood is long and difficult.*

Soldiers pressed Jesus' arms onto the large wooden cross, and holding down his hands, seemed to press nails into His flesh. A heavy hammer fell with a clang. Metal on metal. Metal into flesh and wood. Children held their hands over their mouths and over their hearts, women and men gasped and cried out loudly. Many fell to the dirt, wailing.

The fourteenth station, where Jesus was laid in the tomb, brought everyone back to the church. Sagai stood with the boys, staring at the stripped bare altar. In complete silence, they surrounded the cross as though sitting around a coffin.

During the meditation on the last seven words of Christ from the cross, one the orphans tugged on Sagai's arm. "Did my sin cause Jesus' death?"

"All of our sins did."

Balu and his friends lowered their heads as the boy lay prostrate before the cross and wept. "Oh, Jesus. I am so sorry."

Most fell to their knees crying as if they'd lost a loved one.

The Passion narrative continued. Like a typical funeral procession, the body—a life size statue of Jesus, encased in a glass box, was carried to his burial place. Women fell in the street, struck their chests and cried out loud. He could not be a stoic participant any longer. Emotions bubbled up, choked in his throat, and along with the boys he wept openly.

Sagai and his group returned to the village Saturday night for the liturgy of the Paschal Vigil and the joyful celebration of the Resurrection. The sad faces of the previous days were filled with peace and joy. Dancing and shouts of hallelujah filled the streets.

In his last days in Andimadam, Sagai wrote his appraisal, entreating Father Superior to send help. He'd return to Darjeeling and finish college. Then, if his superiors determined him fit for the next step, he'd enter into three years of practical training, his practicum. He'd again endeared himself to new faces and places, only to leave.

Perhaps his time in Andimadam was a foretaste of what lay ahead in his priesthood.

Fourteen

Rock Bottoms and Mountaintops

But with every up and down you learn lessons that make you strong.
~ Charlie Brown, Peanuts

Rebecca

In my Tennessee kitchen, I took a fickle half-step toward Nate. He pulled me into a bear hug. His hugs were rare, but comforting and I needed rest in the fortress of someone's strong arms. A true miracle-believing optimist, I had to think the good guy in him would emerge to become the husband I needed him to be. I exhaled, then melted like butter on steamy corn on the cob, every molecule of my being dissolving into what I believed to be his love.

Maybe this baby would give us the fresh start we needed. Maybe his kindness now, was a foretaste of our family life to come. Maybe I was exhausted, desperate, and hormonally wacked out of my mind.

"Sorry." Nate stroked my head, resting on his chest. "Sorry for everything. A baby is good, right? Just think, if it's a boy, I'll get a fishing buddy."

I pulled away, the fairytale fading as I considered the flip-side of what he thought he'd get if the baby was a girl.

Acting as if his lame apology settled everything, Nate grabbed the remote from the table and flipped channels in the living room.

Shuffling through a pile of mail on the kitchen table, I snatched a letter from Father Michael. Carrying my wounds clenched in a tight fist around my heart, unwilling to unfurl my insanity at anyone, the priest had become the nearest I had to a best girlfriend. His wonderful, encouraging letters—arriving like a message in bottle to a shipwrecked soul—were welcomed advice and peeks at the place of my dreams.

I filled a glass with water, got comfortable on the patio, and read Father Michael's news beginning with word on his latest assignment; a counseling center in Pannur, a village outside of the huge city of Chennai, in the state of Tamil Nadu.

For a few months, while I worked at a temp receptionist job, Nate and I settled into a semi-peaceful existence. Then, his class reunion came and that crushed peaceful like the peanuts shells he smashed on the bar top in his hometown.

"Can we go now?"

"I'm having a good time for a change." His slurred words indicated he'd had a few too many.

While a high-school buddy bragged about an epic football play, Debbie—with over-permed big hair she'd forgotten to return to the eighties—was all over my husband.

I was like an intruder at their prom.

According to his buddy, back in the day, when Nate had hair and was a big football stud, all the girls wanted him. For a ride back to his parent's house, I'd gladly give him to whoever still wanted him. Right now, it looked like Debbie might be the go-to-gal.

She pushed away from the bar, winked at Nate, and slid off the stool. Prom queen put her arm around me. "What's wrong?"

"I'm tired, pregnant, and I want to go home."

She fanned her hand before her face. "Oh…my…gawd! I thought you were just fat.

Fat? I'd never been involved in a cat fight in a bar, but I mentally prepared for a smack-down.

"Nate, you didn't tell me your wife was pregnant."

I didn't like the way she said wife or the angry look she shot Nate. I rubbed my temples. I had to get out of here. Oh, why couldn't this hick town have taxi service?

"Excuse me." I slipped off the stool, ran to the ladies room, kicked the stall open, then sat on a toilet and cried.

Pregnant, and bawling in a bathroom stall. Could I go any lower? "Dear God, this is not the place I need to be in this world. I need help."

That moment, someone rapped on the stall. I yanked toilet paper off the roll and blew my nose.

"Becky? It's Debbie. You in there?"

"Really God? Debbie?" I leaned forward and pushed open the door.

"Do you want a ride home?"

I dabbed toilet paper to my eyes and stood. "Can I be the designated driver?"

"Nobody drives my truck but me." She jingled her keys.

"Let's go." I tried not to think about how pathetic it was that Debbie became my savior and that the best thing happening in my world was a ride from a drunken home-wrecker to my in-law's house.

My husband followed the sorry woman's butt to her monster truck in the parking lot. I brought up the rear of the sick parade. Inside, she squeezed his thigh and shifted into gear.

Thankfully, no one else was on the road when we crossed the center line and nearly careened into the ditch before she snorted and straightened the wheel.

Not soon enough, the tramp turned onto my in-law's street. The truck slammed to a stop and jumped the curb. I quickly unhooked my seatbelt and escaped. Nate didn't move.

"Are you coming?" I shouted from the sidewalk.

"Going back to the reunion. We were having a good time."

"Are you kidding me?" I had no one to blame in this ridiculous scenario but myself. I deserved a Nobel Peace Prize for my pacifistic nature. And if awards were given in reverse, I'd earn a Purple Heart for cowardliness and a Pulitzer for stupidity. "I'm going to wake up your mother, you moron." I screamed loud enough for neighbor's lights to switch on. "I'll tell her you're dumping your pregnant wife to party with your girlfriend."

"Sorry, Nate." Debbie waved her hand. "I tried. Wifey wants you."

I could take them both. Even pregnant. I could climb into that truck. With some quick moves, a punch, maybe a swift kick strategically placed, I could do some damage. Or not. Neither was worth it.

Then Nate rolled out of the truck and landed face first in the street. Good. One down.

Debbie drove off, and I hoped she'd run him over.

She didn't.

My best hope was that she'd hit the ditch on the way home and then someone would come along and run Nate over later. I went into the house, into the bedroom, and locked the door.

The next morning, while I packed, Nate didn't move from the couch. I tried to talk to his parents, explain how he got road rash on his face, but it didn't do any good. They supported the prince and progenitor of a potential son who would carry on the family name. I prayed for a girl.

Desperate for someone to talk to, I longed to connect with my family, but Mama's suck-it-up-and-suffer attitude didn't help. Michelle was ticked off because we drove past her house coming and going, and didn't stop. She didn't understand that I had zero choices in my life and no voice in where Nate dragged me, even if to the pits of hell.

Sagai

From Tiger Hills, Sagai watched and waited, shivering in the frigid cold. Then he heard applause from the crowd and searched the sky. Like the transforming hand of God, the sun appeared over the Kanchenjunga—the highest peak of the Himalayas—turning the white snow-capped mountains into gold.

Sagai and his class had left Darjeeling in the middle of the night to reach Tiger Hills. Though they'd been climbing all night, exhilaration charged him with heightened anticipation. Eight thousand feet was the best place to view the sunrise over the majestic Kanchenjunga, the rector said. This would be their last hike before graduating.

He stood in silence as the sun continued its ascent. In his four years of studying great philosophers and works of literature, he'd searched for the deeply spiritual and the deeply human in all situations. Father Costello in Vellore had spoken of a vocation within a vocation. Now it was clear. While so much had been decided for him, he had choices. Those who stood on this mountaintop had chosen to stay. Mondal and others chose to leave.

On the ridge overlooking Kanchenjunga, Sagai made another choice and a commitment. Wherever he was sent, whatever his future studies, he would immerse himself into the pulse of humankind and be one with the people. He'd follow in the footsteps of Mother Teresa, taking the path of helping others as Jesus taught; to feed the hungry, give the thirsty something to drink, take in the stranger, clothe the naked, look after the sick, and visit the prisoner. In his order, focused on educating children, many would take the academic route to achieve the highest education. He would embrace people first, like Father Jansen who helped the lepers.

Sagai spread his palms out and closed his eyes, lifting his face to the sun. With each breath of crisp mountain air, his soul rose to new heights, ready to begin the practicum, the practical training part of his journey and give his all to God and humanity.

~~~

In the early hours of the morning, Sagai collapsed onto his cot after wiping vomit.

Practical Training.

Before his eyes closed, wails from another boy roused him. He carried Ravi to the toilet and patted his back while the poor child moaned and emptied his stomach of last night's curry.

For the past few months, teaching and caring for more than sixty Anglo-Indian orphans was the easy part. More troublesome was finishing his practicum at Superior House where privileges, power, and politics were posed as pathways that led to the new Father Superior.

The old reign ended and a new dominion began. Days for the religious to make good impressions.

Sagai gave up on sleep and stood before the window. Fresh sea air breezed into the orphanage near Chennai's pristine Marina Beach. He stared out at the white caps on the Bay of Bengal, wishing he could bring back the peace from Tiger Hills, watching the sun rise over the Kanchenjunga. Sweltering Chennai—the Superior House of his community— was stifling thick with white cassocks.

The tall alabaster spires of the Gothic style Santhome Basilica juxtaposed against the cerulean sky and aquamarine sea stood out like whitewashed sepulchers. The remains of Saint Thomas, Apostle of Jesus Christ, rested under the Basilica's altar. Sagai had taken the orphans on an educational tour ten miles from the Cathedral to Saint Thomas Mount, the hill where the saint who brought Christianity to India had been martyred.

While escorting the boys to the Cathedral for choir practice one morning, a young cleric rushed from the school office and sped past Sagai. Could it be? "Hello!" his heartbeat quickened. "Victor?"

The man stopped and spun around. "Sagai! How are you?"

"I am well." Laughter bubbled up in his voice. The boys formed a line behind him. "You've recovered since I last saw you in the hospital so many years ago." He leaned in for a hug, but his friend stuck out his hand, signaling him to halt. Sagai drew back at the awkward moment.

Victor cocked his head. "You are looking...hmm...different. You're thin and you look...well...very tired." Then he glanced at his watch and tapped it. "I must run. I have an important position. I'm secretary to the rector at the Cathedral and we're very busy since we got the news."

"What news?"

"You don't know whose coming?" His jaw dropped like Sagai had missed the blast of trumpets heralding the coming of Christ.

"The pope is coming to Chennai!" Victor thumped his chest. "And I am very happy to be assisting Father Superior with preparations. I'll see you around, man." He took off across the courtyard with a curt wave.

Heading toward the Cathedral, while the boys whispered about the news of the pope, Sagai readjusted to the new Victor. During formative years, cherished friends and sacred moments cling to the soul, became a part of you. Off kilter now, he wondered if he'd just met the same kind-hearted soul mate of his youth who ran with him alongside the rice paddy fields in Vellore. What happened to the Victor who whispered from his mat in the dormitory, who searched out his eyes to exchange a wordless message in the classroom? Now that they could speak openly, the big man dismissed his affections. He had important duties. He'd risked so much to visit his friend in the hospital, and he'd never quit loving him. Had Victor ever thought about him?

The next morning, Sagai looked into the mirror while shaving, recalling the comments about his thin tired face. He ran his hands through his dark hair, still wild and thick in his mid-twenties. Circles rimmed his deep set sleep-deprived brown eyes.

Different from any other orphanage, when boys arrived, they received crisp uniforms and shiny shoes to blend with the wealthy day students—the crème of the society, actors' and politicians' children who were chauffeured to school.

The day students boldly entered classrooms with new small radios called Walkmans. Wearing watches and hanging onto interesting gadgets, they played hand-held games and had attitudes and pocket money for ice-cream.

Sometimes they gave old radios and games to the orphans. At night Sagai policed the dormitory for these devices, hidden under blankets. No wonder he looked tired. He splashed cold water on his face.

During a morning cricket game, a hefty boy's pants burst open at the seams. He ran for a towel, covered the boy, and disciplined those who ridiculed the poor lad. Not ten minutes later, a squabble broke out during outdoor lunch time when a cricket ball landed on the plate of another boy and knocked his food into the dirt.

It was hard work, but his paternal love drove him to get to know each boy's needs, ambitions, and strengths so he could help them reach full potential.

As the months rolled on, the campus became a hubbub of clergy rushing, running, ordering, and preparing for the pope's arrival. Gardeners trimmed rose bushes, clipped hedges around the courtyard, and hauled in new flowering trees and plants.

At Annual Picnic Day, Sagai and another cleric loaded up the children to take a bus to the beach, close to

Mahabalipuram, the place of ancient monolithic stones of kings.

"Sagai!" Father Michael waved from across the courtyard as the boys stepped onto the bus. "How are you?"

"Very busy, Father." Sagai grasped his hand with a firm shake and smiled. "Good to see you. Where are you posted?

"I'm at a counseling center in Pannur. I meet with Father Superior today, then after the pope leaves, I'm traveling to America for missions preaching again."

He squinted as the sun rose over the basilica. "Where to this time?"

"In the south, not far from where my pen pal lives now."

"Yes, Rebecca. I pray for her daily. Please give her my regards." His attention was drawn to the bus. "Johnny! Do not hang out the window! Sorry, Father. That one is a handful."

"I'll take leave then. Good to see you. Take care of the boys and youngest. I think of you and pray for you always." His long-held gaze explored a deeper place in Sagai's soul and spoke a thousand words of love.

"Thank you for caring, Father. Enjoy your time in America."

At the beach, the sea roared then spilled onto the shore and grabbed and swallowed small shells, old pieces of ropes and netting and debris. Sagai looked warily at the ocean as the boys clamored around him.

"Brother Sagai, can we go into the sea?" One of the boys clasped his hands as in prayer. Another tugged his sleeve. "Please, Brother Sagai."

He glanced at the cleric. He nodded, and Sagai grabbed the flying shirts. "The tide is high." He raised his voice above the sea and whoops and hollers. "Keep close to the shore. Stay in knee deep water only." A foreboding shiver sent a chill through him. He whispered a prayer and did not take his eyes off the boys.

He called the boys for lunch. One by one, shirts disappeared from the neat pile. One remained. He stared at the shirt.

No. Lord, please, no. He pressed his hand to his chest as horror flooded in. He trembled, darting among the boys, searching for a bare chest or back. Oh God, let someone be without a shirt. All were dressed. Who was missing?

Johnny! He dashed to the ocean's edge and scanned the rough sea. "Oh Lord, Please, let nothing have happened to this dear boy."

He alerted Brother Cecil and instructed two boys to check the bus. They returned with their palms held outward. "He's not there."

"I'll check the stones!" Sagai shouted to Brother Cecil. Gripping Johnny's shirt, he sprinted to the stones with eyes scanning and arms pumping as if the devil were on his heels.

"Johnny!" He checked behind each stone, shouting his name again and again, running like a mad man from the rocks to the sea, praying. Finally, he dropped to the sand, pounded his hands on the beach and groaned in helplessness.

The boy's father consumed poison when hit-men were on their way to beat him for unpaid debts. The mother followed suit that night, and the ruffians claimed their house. Sagai and the child's grandmother hoped for a better life for Johnny.

In his anguish, a sudden thought came to check the bus again. Sagai raced to the bus and peered under each seat. Under the last one, he found his shirtless orphan curled into a ball. The boys had missed him. He closed his eyes and thanked God.

He rejoiced with every cell of his being. "I found him! I found him! Everyone, he's here." Sagai's shouts woke the startled the ten-year-old. He pulled him close, tears splashing on the boy's bare back. "I thought the sea had taken you. Thanks be to God you are okay."

On the bus ride home Sagai opened his Bible. "If a man has a hundred sheep, and one of them goes astray, does he not leave the ninety-nine and go to the mountains to seek the one that is straying? And if he should find it, assuredly, I say to you, he rejoices more over that sheep than over the ninety-nine that did not go astray. Even so it is not the will of your Father who is in heaven that one of these little ones should perish."

Sagai walked the aisle and tousled the missing boy's hair. "How much I rejoiced to find Johnny. When we found him, we all rejoiced, did we not?"

Many heads nodded.

"This is how our Father in Heaven feels when we go away from him. We must always stay close to the Lord and never allow our sin to take us away from Him. And Johnny, do not ever stray like that again."

Back at the orphanage, Sagai carried on with his duties. Occasionally, he saw Victor running across the courtyard, sometimes offering a quick wave. Once he rushed by with a package close to his chest and made a sign with his thumb and closed fist as if drinking. No surprise. A few times in the night, through the open third story window of the dormitory, the rector and other priests' loud laughter rode on the breeze. He couldn't imagine what it would be like to have time to drink and play cards.

Toward the end of his last week at school, a scream penetrated Sagai's dreams. He bolted upright and scrambled toward the source of the sound, stumbling through rows of cots to find Prabhu curled and clutching his stomach.

"What is it?" He knelt beside the poor moaning boy and pressed his hand to his face. It was hot. Oh Jesus! A fever! Appendicitis?

"Okay, okay." He gathered the child in his arms and made haste to the priests' block, banging on the first door. He asked one priest to take charge of the boys under his care and asked another to get the auto-rickshaw.

Hours later, in the waiting area outside the operation theater, the doctor met Sagai. The Prabhu's appendix had burst, and they were lucky to have saved him. This same thing had happened to Victor, so many years ago.

In the morning, with his young charge recovering in the ward, Sagai caught a bus back to Superior House for his scheduled assessment. With no place to sit on the crowded bus, he stood in the aisle and held onto the overhead bar. He rocked in and out of sleep, nearly missing his stop.

"Wait," he shouted to the driver before the bus could take off. He pushed through the crowd, got off the bus, then sprinted to the rector's office.

Sagai knocked on the rector's door, too tired to care that he was late. He'd done his duties, worked hard, spent every moment giving his all to the boys, taught in the classrooms, and his prayer life was commendable. He'd never left the compound for entertainment.

Once assessment was over, in a few weeks, he'd finish his practicum then get back to college to earn his degree in

Theology, after which he'd be ordained a deacon and at the end of four years, finally a priest.

A throng of clergy presided at his assessment—the rector, administrator, the dean in charge of studies, the principal, and another priest. Sagai apologized for his lateness, greeted them, and sat in the empty chair across.

The rector cleared his throat and handed him the form where one year of his life had been judged. He scanned the page and stopped, stunned by a series of poor marks. "Why was I given a poor evaluation?"

"There have been some problems." The rector raised his bushy eyebrows.

"What problems?"

One priest stared at his shoes, another stretched his legs.

"You are not with the boys." The principal cleaned his nails with the edge of a paper.

"Where am I, then?" Sagai laughed at the ludicrous statement. As quick as the sarcastic chuckle escaped his lips, anger flamed. He pointed at the clergy. "None of you are at the orphanage. How in the world do you know what's going on? How can you sit in judgment?"

The fathers straightened their backs. The principal dropped his jaw. The dean leaned forward and held up his finger. "Now—"

"I barely have time to eat." Sagai shook his fist. "I'm with the boys night and day. I spent the whole of last night at the hospital with a child. What are you basing your scrutiny on? Tell me?" He held eye contact with his superior.

"What is written, is written." The rector slapped his palm against the table.

Sagai stood. The acrid bitterness that he'd been forced to swallow for too many years wouldn't go down. It burned his throat. Years of hushing his voice, bowing and saying thank you when he wanted to argue an injustice boiled like a volcanic core of wrath.

"While I'm cleaning vomit, I hear you from across the street boozing it up. I will not sign this. I do not accept it. Keep it!" He flung the paperwork across the table.

The shock on his superiors' faces did not quell his wrath. "You are all out of touch with reality. You have no idea what you are talking. I'll sign my assessment when it accurately reflects my work. Summon me then. Until then, I've got work."

Sagai walked out. Waves of anger and fear collided with satisfaction of having finally spoken his mind.

A few days later, a white Ambassador pulled up to the orphanage while Sagai coached a cricket game. Victor and Bruno, his rival from the Practicum, raced across the courtyard toward the car. Victor opened the door after elbowing Bruno.

Father Superior stepped out and straightened his cassock and the cortege approached the cricket field. Sagai had heard there would be final inspections before the pope arrived. He hustled to welcome him.

Before he bowed, he caught Victor whispering to Father Superior. Sagai dropped to one knee then lifted his head and looked into the angry face of his ultimate superior, a portly short man with slicked back black hair and a long pointed nose. "You're Sagai?"

"Yes, Father."

"Go! You're finished! Get out!" Father Superior's orders echoed across the courtyard like the hourly gong of church bells.

"But, Father, my ministry...the boys..."

"Bruno will take care. Leave!"

Sagai dropped to his knees on the sidewalk. "Please, Father. God has called me to the priesthood."

The heat on his face, the hot sidewalk, and the Chennai sun conspired to melt the spot where he knelt and draw him down to hell. Sagai lowered his head and touched Father Superior's shiny black shoes, the ultimate expression of submission and respect. He silently repeated, Lord have mercy. Christ have mercy.

Sagai looked up. Father Superior could spit on me now, he thought. Please God. Don't let him spit on me, not with the boys looking on. Victor and Bruno witnessed him groveling like a worm. How could he have come to this low state? But for his priesthood, he had to beg. "Please, Father. Have mercy."

Father Superior crossed his arms over his chest. "I will give you two days to find a senior priest to discern if you have a calling. Return with a letter. Two days. That's it. Leave!"

Fifteen

Humbling Moments

God Writes Straight With Crooked Lines
~ Portuguese Bishop in the 16th Century

Rebecca

"You can't leave." Nate stood in the doorway of the nursery/my new bedroom. "I don't want to divorce. Financially, it'd be a really bad time for that."

I set the last of my clothes in the dresser and shut the drawer. Obviously, worried my next step might be out the front door, he spoke about a possible divorce like deciding whether to buy a car. Like, maybe we'll get into that vehicle in a few months, when we've saved for it, or when we can get a good deal on one of those divorcements.

I held my hand over my belly, as round and hard as a watermelon. "We need marriage counseling." Check-list words so later if anyone asked, I, the martyred saint, could nod serenely and say, "Yes, I did suggest that. I did my best, tried everything."

Nate bunched up his face like a spoiled two-year old. "It'll be about everything I do wrong. Not doing it."

No surprise. He also wasn't doing Lamaze classes.

I consoled myself with thoughts that something new and beautiful, something far better than anything my marriage could offer, had been growing within me. I prayed my baby would be nothing like her father.

Once in a while, baby kicks spiked Nate's interest and allowed for a few giddy expectant parent moments where I'd wonder if we could pull off the family thing. Pretending was one way of survival.

When contractions began, I waited as long as I could before going to the hospital. Everyone said not to go right away, and I mean everyone—Mama, Michelle, the doctor, the nurse, the receptionist at the doctor's office, even the fed-ex guy making a delivery at the doctor's office, so by the time I got there, contractions were one right after the other.

Nate stopped at the lounge and said he'd wait like his dad did when he was born.

"Can you just do this one thing for me?" I shook my fist in the air. "Just stay with me through this, then you can do what you want after I have this baby."

The nurse crossed her arms and gave the bum a killer one-eyebrow-up stare that guilt-tripped him off the couch.

After a few low bellows—not from me, but rather a cow mooing outside the hospital window—and a few pushes that popped out all the veins in my face and tore me in places unmentionable, the doctor placed a baby girl on my chest. White-faced Nate declined the offer to cut the cord.

While he made phone calls in the hallway, I unwrapped my new gift. "Oh my." I looked over my daughter for the first time. For a second, she met my gaze, and I swear I saw a sparkle of heaven left over from the journey.

She looked nothing like her father, nor could I see myself in her. She had dark hair and the tiniest upturned button nose. The worth of my soul reflected in her eyes. I was born to be a mother. "You are beautiful." I stroked her cheek. "You are here, and it's gone." The empty hollow place inside me—that maternal compartment I was born with and filled with dolls as a child, then with Kara—was full again. And me? Complete.

"Baby, what have you done to me? I have someone to love with all of my heart. I'll never be the same. Your name is Grace."

With the confidence of a warrior having won a battle, standing on a mountaintop, holding my flag, I knew exactly what to do. As soon as discharged, I'd file for divorce and leave. Surely, Mama would take me in when she saw this angel. I was so done with Nate that the thought of leaving made me laugh out loud with pure joy.

I pressed my face to Grace's soft head and breathed in her new baby smell. "Thank you for letting me be your Mama. You are mine, and I won't let anyone hurt you or me. Our new life is about to begin. It will be all about you, my sweet baby."

Food trays clattered in the hallway as my nurse entered the room. "I know you don't want to let go of that baby, but you need care, too." She stretched her dark wrinkled hands towards Grace, and I yielded to the elderly woman's nurturing kindness. My baby emitted a high-pitched squeak when the nurse lifted her from my arms.

"She's a beauty." The nurse placed her in the bassinette, then wrapped a blood pressure cuff around my arm. "There's a special dinner tonight for parents. Where's Daddy?" She pumped the little bulb and the pressure increased.

"Who knows? He went to work ten minutes after she was born and I haven't seen him since." I looked into the woman's kind hazel eyes and in my, I'm-so-done-with-Nate attitude, I said, "We don't need him anyway. I'm going to leave him."

She showed no reaction, but separated the Velcro sections of the cuff with a rip, clicked her pen, and recorded numbers on the chart. "In my thirty-five years of nursing, I've seen every reaction under the sun from new fathers. Some take to it like they were born to be daddies and some are scared and as useless as a sore thumb. That doesn't mean they can't grow into the role. Sometimes, a baby changes everything." She patted my hand and walked out.

She was wrong. If he hadn't grown into the marriage role, he wouldn't grow into the fatherhood role.

Later that evening, Nate returned with a bouquet of red roses, a new infant car seat, and a 35 mm Canon camera for me. The camera was awesome. I hoped the roses would last longer than his intentions.

After I assured Nate he wouldn't break Grace, I handed her over to prove to know-it-all nurse that no magic pixie dust would fall from the sky and transform Nate.

The corners of his mouth turned up. Was it happening? There was love in that gaze. I looked up for the pixie dust.

"She's really cute."

Then the corners of Grace's mouth turned down, and she let out a strong angry wail. He passed her to me like she was a hot potato, or like she pooped a hot potato, or like he wanted to eat a hot potato. Who knew what was in this man's mind, and it was pointless to ask. He'd just give the standard "nothing" response, which was probably what would show up on a brain scan.

Yep, I was done.

Later, still embracing a liberated, conquer the world, baby strapped to my back Sacajawea style attitude, Mama set me straight. "You can't leave!"

I winced and held the bedside hospital phone away from my ear. I'd been floating on an endorphin cloud of maternal hormones, resting on an ethereal oxytocin pillow of mama love and she just blew my house down.

"You haven't even left the hospital yet. Your hormones have messed up your sensibilities. You don't quit on marriage just because you get some cockamamie idea to divorce hardly a day after you've had a baby."

With Grace cradled in my left arm, I held the phone to my ear with my right hand and begged. "I should have left long ago. Please. Can't we stay in the coop with Heather? I can get in the car and be home as soon as we're released. Mama? Are you there?"

One ear heard silence. The other heard a female intercom voice calling out a code.

"Mama?"

"Set aside those fancy notions right now." Her voice was slow and deliberate.

I breathed in deeply, inhaling a trace of bleach from the crisp white sheets.

"It's not all about you. You have a child now. Daddy and I have gone through difficult years, but we toughed it out, and all for the good. Marriage is for life. Divorce is a sin."

"But you don't understand—"

"Enough is enough. Your father will never agree. Besides, we're dealing with chemo treatments. It's all I can do to take care of him. I can't add you and a baby to that mix. Case closed."

Her words smacked me like a wooden spoon against my backside. Right about one thing, though, this wasn't about me, but Grace. I had to protect her. I was naïve years ago, not understanding that Nate had probably drugged me at that party before our marriage, slipped something in that Long Island

Iced Tea. He probably offered me to his friend like a loaner book.

If I told my mother that, would she change her mind? This marriage was not good for me. Better Grace had no father.

But Mama closed the case.

I wanted to hang up, but held the phone, controlling my breathing as my right arm brushed the cold metal bed rails. Why couldn't she be there for me, just this one time? I held the line, waiting for that miracle.

"Life is full of suffering."

Through clenched teeth, I said, "I'm done with suffering." I leaned toward the nightstand and slammed the phone in its cradle.

Michelle called an hour later. Mama was the ultimate authority. My sister wouldn't cross her. She'd deserted me, too. Heather hadn't called in months. It was like our bonding time never happened.

Sagai

Sagai crossed the threshold of the Basilica, walked down the tall nave of stark white arches, and slid into a pew. The stained glass depicted the divine moment of St. Thomas's meeting with the resurrected Christ loomed above him. He was to find a senior priest to write a letter on his behalf, but he'd ostracized himself from everyone in the compound during his scrutiny.

Any other local priests would be cronies to those fellows. It'd require more than two days travel to reach someone else to vouch for him. "Lord, whom do I turn to now?"

Father Michael immediately came into his mind. He should be at his counseling center. Sagai remembered he was going to America, but was fairly sure he meant after the pope left. He ran to the bus stop.

Breathless, he scanned the schedule. The bus to Pannur wouldn't arrive for three hours. On a platform bench, he tapped his heel against the concrete and pressed his hands to his knees to control the rapid bouncing.

How could Father Superior order him to get out? Was a man more powerful than God that he could interfere with his calling, even question it?

"Good afternoon, Father." An elderly woman smiled and nodded. Others gathered on the platform, waiting for the next bus. Travelers nodded and smiled, reminding him of who he was and what was at stake. Did others see an angry young man or a holy man of God?

He sat, closed his eyes and recalled the Psalmist's words: *God is our refuge and strength, an ever present help in trouble.*

Finally the bus arrived and Sagai let others ahead of him until only standing room remained. He gripped the bar above his head as the bus lurched toward his only hope.

Nearing midnight, he rapped on the counseling center door. If Father Michael was home, he might not receive him at such a late hour. If he'd had change, he would have found a phone booth and called.

No answer. No lights. He pounded louder, then leaned against the building, sank to the ground, banged his head against the door and groaned. He had nowhere else to turn.

Then he heard keys jingling. He leapt to his feet and pressed his hand against his heart. Thank you, Jesus.

"Who's there?" Father Michael cracked the door.

"Father Michael!" He choked back a sob. "It's me, Sagai. I...I need to talk to you. It's urgent. Please, I need help." His chest tightened, and he thought he might swoon.

"Come in."

He followed him to the kitchen, taking deep breaths.

"Sit. Sit." Father Michael, dressed in his cassock, prepared coffee as Sagai dropped into a chair. "I have left over *korma* and *chapattis*. I'll heat it on the stove."

The thought of this priest waking in the middle of the night and preparing food for him loosed a new wave of emotions. He wept, holding his forehead in his hands. When he looked up, his own father's kind face shone in this man. He breathed deeply.

"Father Superior told me to get out. I've worked so hard. No time to eat. Very little sleep. I don't mind the hard work, but these fellows gave a scrutiny that could keep me from priesthood. I lost my temper when I could no longer endure the injustice."

Father Michael set the plate of food on the table.

Sagai pressed his hand to his chest. "Father, you are too kind."

"Eat, then sleep." The priest patted his arm. "We'll talk in the morning."

He blessed the food and ate, fell into bed, then slept until light bathed the small room. In the morning, his mentor met him at the table with a cup of steaming coffee and a *dosa*.

After breakfast, the priest invited him to the chapel to talk. There, Sagai reviewed his life—growing up, his calling, his assignments all over India, his college years, the difficulties he had with blind obedience to these infallible superiors who could not be questioned. Father Michael listened, often nodding. When he'd had exhausted his words, he leaned back.

"Do one thing." Father Michael's voice emulated his gentle nature. "Write a letter of apology to the superior."

"But that would be a lie. I am right. I cannot say sorry."

"That may be true, but if you care for your vocation you should do it." Father Michael leaned forward in the chair. "Take the day to yourself. Spend a few hours in prayer. Walk along the beach and let the cleansing saltwater wash away your worries. Perhaps Father Superior was having troubles of his own."

"But—"

"The pope is coming. Perhaps he was in a bad mood, feeling stressed from the preparations. By writing a letter of apology, you won't lose much. Your apology will bring down his defenses and then he will begin to reason. I'm not telling you to lie, but only to say you are sorry for what has happened."

"Father, do you believe I have a calling?"

"Absolutely! Why else would I have recommended you for junior seminary?"

Sagai spent time in meditation in the chapel, then walked to the beach. There, he kicked pebbles, still conflicted. Appa had written that their second cow died. More babies were on the way. More mouths to feed. He hated to think about the condition of the home. If he left his order and went home, with his degree, he could teach and help his family.

If he wrote the letter of apology, it would forever remain in his file—an admission of guilt. Along with his poor assessment, he might not reach priesthood anyway. He questioned his humility, then reasoned that it was not a matter of humility, but of truth. How could he admit he'd done wrong when he hadn't?

A bright full moon lit up the beach, catching the whitecaps on the Bay of Bengal and casting a lustrous hue on the beach. Sagai knelt to see a tiny crab struggling against the current. With each forward movement, the sea would pull him back. The crab tried to climb over a piece of bark. That too got pulled back with the current.

The poor creature continued on, making little progress. Sagai watched the crab and considered his journey so far, from the days he ran every day to the church to serve God, his leaving home at a young age, and how far he'd come. Like the tiny crab, so much had come against him. Just then the crab escaped the pull of the current, hustled, then burrowed into its sandy sanctuary.

He made up his mind.

Back at the counseling center, he sat in the chapel, wrote his letter, then said the serenity prayer.

The next morning at the kitchen table, Father Michael read Sagai's letter. He folded it, and gave him his own letter addressed to Father Superior. He prayed, "Lord, when Father Superior reads these letters, let his heart be softened toward Sagai and since this child of yours is an earthen vessel, let your power shine through his weakness and in his afflictions, let him never be crushed by the system. In the name of the Father, the Son, and the Holy Spirit."

Father Michael rose and picked up another letter from the counter. "On your way back, please post this letter."

"Addressed to America. A letter to your pen pal?"

The priest nodded. "Rebecca's struggles mirror yours. Like you, she seeks peace in a tumultuous life. For her, India has always been a symbol of peace, an ultimate fulfillment of a dream, but now that dream seems far away and her life is in disarray. The advice I gave her also applies to you. Peace is not a place. It's in your heart. Peace is when you are living the life God intended you to live."

"I want peace, Father, but others make it so difficult, especially at the Superior House. I only want to serve God as His priest."

"Sometimes the path to our goals is not a straight one, but don't worry. God writes straight through crooked lines. Stay on the path. You and my friend, Rebecca, will both find your way."

The next morning, at Marina Beach, hundreds of thousands had gathered for the papal Mass. Papal flags and banners waved all over the area. Sagai caught a glimpse of Pope John Paul II on stage. Here, before him, the Vicar of Christ. What an honor to hear him preach about God's love toward India.

He wanted that same heart for love, for helping others, for giving hope. He wanted to be a servant of Christ more than anything. Sagai thanked God for the day and for all that had happened to him, the good as well as the bad on his path to priesthood. He offered a prayer for Rebecca, that she also would find her true peace and reach her goals.

After the pope's visit, Father Superior summoned Sagai for his assessment—either a pass to the Theologate or a dismissal. He entered the doorway, ready to accept God's will.

Sixteen

Coping in Serpent Mode and Cutting Loose

Life is not what it's supposed to be. It's what it is. The way you cope with it is what makes the difference.
~ Virginia Satir

Rebecca

The in-laws entered through my front door and I prepared to accept my fate, whatever it might be.

Nate's father—quiet as usual—baby-talked at Grace, but didn't ask to hold her. Harriet snatched her from my arms. I thought about the scene when Mowgli goes to Wolf Mama. Harriet might eat her or embrace her as her own. Either way, a dicey situation.

I almost cheered when Grace cried and reached for me. I insisted she needed to be nursed.

"Time to get her used to a bottle." Harriet frowned and handed Grace back. "She should have been on formula since birth. You've spoiled her to the point that no one else can care for her, not even her father."

Satisfied, I'd done the right thing, I retreated to the room I shared with Grace—my bed on one side, her crib on the other.

After nursing, I placed her in the crib and returned to the living room. Nathaniel the elder dozed in the recliner. Harriet ordered me on the couch, but I heard a wail.

My mother-in-law put her hand on my shoulder. "Sit," she ordered. "She's only been crying for five seconds."

"I know. I feel awful. I usually get to her before three seconds pass."

Harriet's brows, plucked then drawn in with a pencil, came to a v-shape over her nose. "Sit. Grace can cry it out."

"Cry it out?" I remained standing. No way.

"Yes way. It's something all babies should learn to do. That's what the experts say." Harriet applied pressure to my shoulder.

"Are the experts men?" As Grace's wail increased in intensity, so did the tug on my heart and my courage not to yield to Harriet.

Harriet nodded. "You and Nate will get more sleep and get your lives back if you teach her to cry herself to sleep."

I might have to take Harriet down and erase her eyebrows if she didn't release her claws from my shoulder.

"She needs to learn to be independent."

Nate crossed his arms. "She only cares about the baby, not about me."

"She's a baby. She needs to know she can depend on at least one parent." I jerked my shoulder out of Harriet's death grip. If dislocated, I was suing. Nate and his mother were acting like Grace was the adult and Nate, the baby.

Harriet huffed. "Come back. We need to have a discussion."

"I'll be back," I yelled from the hallway. Where in the world could I go? I picked my baby up and held her close. Little red splotches had popped out on her porcelain skin. "Mean old Grandma." I kissed the crown of her head. "I'm sorry. This will not happen again."

With nowhere to run, I returned to the living room and sat on the couch with Grace peaceful in my arms.

Harriet commanded her son to sit beside me. She picked up her large black purse and pulled out a small red booklet. Standing before us, she pinched her brightly painted lips together and narrowed her eyes, looking from Mama's boy to me. My heart thumped so loud, it sounded like as Indian beating on a tom-tom in there.

"I know what's going on. I'm not stupid." She wagged her finger from me to Nate. "I know you two have issues, and this marriage isn't what either of you wants." Then like the Grinch who stole Christmas, the wrinkles around the corner of her eyes and mouth multiplied, and she smiled. "I have a plan."

Harriet shoved a booklet at me. "So You Married a Catholic. What Now?"

My eyeballs rolled to the back of my head and fell out of the same hole my brains fell out when I married Nate. What now? Um…pray to the patron saint of morons to turn him into a normal man? Find a nun to beat him with a super-sized crucifix? Ask a priest to perform an exorcism?

"I've talked to Father Stan." Harriet paced before the couch like an attorney in front of a jury. "He will baptize Grace, bless your marriage, and convert Rebecca to Catholicism during Easter Mass." She wagged her finger at me. "Study that book. You have six months to prepare. Since you can't attend regular classes with Father Stan, he's agreed to bend the rules and bypass the formal process. He'll have a review session with you the Saturday before Easter."

I understood what a prisoner running for life must feel like when the dogs landed on their back. Though I hadn't escaped from my prison—yet—I thought I'd at least arrived at a temporary safe harbor. "But, I've already been baptized and confirmed in the Lutheran Church."

Harriet gave me her you're-an-idiot look. "It's not valid in the Catholic church. Just read the book, and at Easter Mass, he'll receive you into the Catholic faith. You're lucky you don't have to do the entire one-year program. Converts these days know more than the priests. It's a little too much if you ask me."

"But, I'm Lutheran."

Nate's mother narrowed her eyes. "And when did you last attend your Lutheran Church?"

"Um…" Not since my confirmation in the eighth grade, but I didn't want to tell her that.

"Um tells me enough. Since you've been attending the Catholic Church regularly, it makes sense to take the next step."

"We're not attending church."

Nate shook his head in quick warning jerks.

"Is this true?" His mom raised her head and moved like a cobra in his direction.

"What Rebecca means is that we don't go every Sunday." He repositioned his seat like the cushions burned his butt. "She's been sick and pregnant and—"

"Nathaniel James, since Rebecca will be doing her part, you'll do yours. You're a family now. You two can't go on in your heathen ways forever." She raised her hands to heaven. "This is why you two are sleeping in separate rooms, on the verge of divorce."

I quietly muttered, "I'm not a heathen."

Nate's mom raised one eyebrow then slithered to me. "What if something should happen to that baby?"

I tightened my arms around Grace.

"I had my babies baptized the Sunday after my discharge from the hospital. You wouldn't want her to die and land in purgatory, do you?"

"What!"

Harriet sighed. "I'll put this in a nice way. Since the church doesn't recognize your marriage, that baby is illegitimate."

This could not be true. I put my hands over Grace's ears.

Harriet turned on her heels, bent over her black bag and pulled out a small packet. Your lives need to be set right before God. She handed me the packet. "It's a glow in the dark rosary with instructions. Use it."

Nate's dad snorted then blew out a whistling breath. Harriet shook her head, then continued. "If you don't bring God into your marriage, it won't last. At least appreciate what I'm trying to do. You should've been married in the church years ago. Having the same faith and going to Mass every Sunday will set everything right."

Holy fear glistened in Nate's eyes. Finally, we had one thing in common. We were both scared of his mom.

Sunday arrived and Nate rose early and asked me to get ready. At church, he put the truck in park. "Wait here."

He returned a few minutes later.

"Aren't we going in?"

"No. I just picked this up." He waved a church bulletin. "I'll mail it to Mother as proof that we were here. If she asks if we went to church, we won't be lying when we say yes."

I held my tongue, not saying that God would know the truth.

Later, I read the book from Father Stan. It surprised me how readily I accepted most of Catholicism. I'd admired the faith of high school Catholic friends and liked that they felt a sense of protection wearing blessed holy medallions. I liked the idea of appreciating saints and angels and being a part of that bigger heavenly family. Having angels and saints on my side couldn't be a bad thing.

While I wasn't completely sold on the idea of confessing to a priest, I felt okay with devotions to Mother Mary. A mother figure in heaven comforted me given my relationship with my earthly mother.

I even read the rosary instructions and discovered that meditating on the mysteries was steeped in tradition and familiar to other religions, too. Hindus and Buddhists used strings of beads to stay focused during prayerful meditation as they repeated mantras. The rosary had a deeper meaning for Christians, with the beads being points to meditate on the life and passion of Christ.

I also wanted Grace baptized, not because I thought she'd die and float around in a Cimmerian purgatory, but that she deserved to be presented and offered ceremoniously as a Christian, making her a part of God's family. Mama cared enough to do that for me.

According to the booklet, upon Grace's confirmation, years later, she could declare her faith her own. I could buy into Harriet's holy package with the exception of remarrying her son. I agreed to go in hopes of working out a compromising situation with Father Stan.

The Saturday before Easter marked confession day, also the day of my assessment and discussion with Father Stan about Sunday's events.

"Nervous?" Nate's mom hugged onto my arm on the walk to the church.

"You have no idea." I white-knuckled Grace's stroller, pushing forward.

"First confessions can be scary." Harriet patted my arm.

Sunday frightened me more than the imminent confession. I was open to commit any sin the red guy holding a pitchfork on my shoulder suggested to escape the marriage vows.

Harriet raised her face to the sun. "Confession is like a counseling session with a perk. Sins committed during the week get erased on Saturday."

Why hadn't I become Catholic sooner?

I knelt in the church pew. Grace slept in the stroller parked in the aisle. Everyone entered the confessional, one at a time, exited, made the sign of the cross on the red cushioned kneelers, mumbled Our Fathers and Hail Mary's, then left. Green light. Red light. Sins forgiven.

Nate went first. Harriet, the last confessor, finished her Hail Mary, then slid into the pew beside me. The green light on top of the dark wooden confessional booth glowed in the musty cold church.

"I'll take Grace home. Go ahead."

"I'll keep her with me." Grace was mine. Not hers.

"Suit yourself." She shook her head, made the sign of the cross, and left.

I shivered and turned toward the rear of the church. The confessional door opened. I squeezed my eyes tight and offered a prayer for Jesus to save me—really save me from this predicament.

Footfalls sounded on the tile floor. My heart thumped with each approaching step. A hand pressed my shoulder.

Father Stan, probably around sixty, short and round, with salt and pepper hair, had the face of one of those cherubic angels on Valentine's Day cards.

"We don't have to sit in there." He nodded at the confessional booth, then chuckled impishly. "If you like, we'll sit face-to-face in the office for reconciliation, then we'll review what you've learned and discuss tomorrow's program."

Grace still asleep in the stroller, I pushed it behind Father Stan as stained-glass saints peered down at me.

In his office, I did a short form confession of minor sins; random thoughts of poisoning my husband, cursing my mother-in-law behind her back—no heavy stuff—then switched gears, moving on to what worried me more than my transgressions.

I leaned forward. "I like Catholicism. I'm all for Jesus being present in the Holy Communion host. Better the real deal than to pretend He's there. I'm good to go with the confession stuff, too. I mean, what's not to like about having the attention of someone while you talk about yourself, even if you have to admit you did things you shouldn't have done? And we get forgiveness, too. Double blessing!"

I clasped my hands. "I know God forgives, but hearing the words from a priest is a nice little bonus. So all that works for me."

The cherub smiled. "You've learned a lot. It's all Biblical, too. Jesus said, 'Unless you eat the flesh of the son of man and drink his blood, you will not have life in you.' Also, after his resurrection, He told the apostles, 'As the Father has sent me, even so I send you.'" He folded his hands. "'If you forgive the sins of any, they are forgiven; if you retain the sins of any, they are retained'."

I smiled in agreement like a good student. "And I want Grace baptized, but…" I bit my lip and looked at Christ on the crucifix above Father Stan's head. Jesus knew suffering, pain, but did he want me to suffer like Mama wanted me to? Did Father Stan? Father Michael encouraged me to find my peace. There was only one pathway to peace and that one led out of my marriage. "You have this remarriage thingy arranged with Harriet, right?"

Father Stan nodded. "The rectification of marriage."

"Yeah, that." I wished I knew what side this priest was on. Mine or the enemy's. Time for a leap of faith. "I don't want to marry Nate again. Can we work out a deal? The church gets me, but Nate doesn't." I met his eyes with trepidation.

Father Stan shook his head. "I can't officially receive you in the church and give you communion without rectifying your marriage."

"Really?" My palms fell open in the chair.

Father Stan shrugged. "The rules."

I glanced at Grace, still asleep. This was not going well. "But, I do understand."

"Because you just heard Nate's confession, right?"

"I cannot reveal confession secrets. They die with the priest."

I shook my head and fanned the air. "Oh, I don't want to know anything. Trust me. I already know too much." I folded my hands as if in prayer. "Father, please think about Nate's confession. I want out of this marriage, and I'm guessing he does, too."

"The church does not approve of divorce."

"The church doesn't think we're married. Why would it care?" I rubbed my temples. This stuff was so confusing.

Father Stan lowered his head. Was he confused, too? Praying? After a minute, he looked up at the ceiling, or at God, or a fly on a light bulb. Then he sighed. "I can't, before God, tell you to stay in your marriage."

Yay! The priest was on my side. I rubbed my hands together. "Okay, so what's the plan?"

"Confession is over." Father Stan said the final prayers, absolved me of my sins, then did the craziest thing. He took off his stole, pulled out his white collar tab and leaned forward, which wasn't easy, given he had a Buddha belly. "This is me talking, not the church. Life is a game and you should play it well."

Father Stan had my attention.

"Try to stay married, but if divorce happens, be smart. Don't be a victim. You have a child to think about. Plan well and when the time is right, make like the Israelites and leave. Although I think Nate is more stupid and well…unfaithful…than he is dangerous, if you're in a threatening situation, get out right away. There are shelters everywhere."

While I wondered if Father Stan meant unfaithful in terms of marriage or church, he put his collar back in and said, "Jesus says be wise as a serpent and meek as a dove. You've been a dove long enough. Go into serpent mode."

"Thank you Father. I'll take your advice, but I'm scared of Harriet."

Father Stan giggled nervously. "So am I."

"She'll be expecting the whole shebang tomorrow."

"I'll take care of that." Father Stan winked.

"What about the baptism ceremony?"

"Are you willing to raise Grace Catholic?"

"Not a problem, but I can't become Catholic and Nate only comes to the Catholic Church when he's here and Harriet makes him."

"As long as you accept the Catholic faith, I'll baptize Grace."

While I wondered if you could tell a priest you loved them, Grace woke and smiled.

"What a good baby." Father Stan made the sign of the cross. "Go in peace."

"What about my penance?"

"You're already doing it." He patted my shoulder. "Now don't forget. Serpent mode." He lifted his hand over his head and made a sign like a snake.

I laughed.

Father shuffled papers on his desk. "With all the Easter preparations, I nearly forgot to tell you something. Father Michael called. He's here in the States—in Louisville, Kentucky.

"Really?"

"He said he wrote to you, but wasn't sure if you got his letter. He asked for your phone number, but I didn't have your new one. I told him I'd give you his contact information." He handed me a sticky note. "He'll be here for a few more weeks."

Father Michael in Louisville! About a three-hour drive from Knoxville. I'd call as soon as I got back to Tennessee.

On Sunday, Grace was baptized. Father Stan skipped the confirmation and the marriage vows. After the service, I ran out the side door as Nate's mom bee-lined it to Father Stan near the front doors of the church.

Nate shrugged when Harriet interrogated him after the service. I did the same, adding that I didn't know what happened. I'd confess that lie later. Maybe Harriet didn't have a chance to talk to Father Stan, given the big crowd.

We packed quickly, ignoring threats that she'd meet Father and get to the bottom of things. I hated leaving Wisconsin and not seeing family, but Nate refused to go to White Gull Bay.

The next weekend, when Nate left for another fishing trip with work buddies, I packed up Grace and drove to Louisville to meet another wonderful priest. In spite of the difficulties in my life, God blessed me with priests as my best allies.

Even though it wasn't customary for Indians to hug, with Grace balanced on my hip, I hugged Father Michael at the rectory door.

"Beautiful child." He stretched out the word beautiful in his lilting voice. "With that dark hair, she almost looks like an Indian baby."

"My dad had dark hair before it went gay."

Father smiled and made the sign of the cross over Grace's forehead. She reached for his hand and smiled.

At the restaurant, I set my baby in a high-chair and spilled cheerios on the tray. Father Michael ran his hands through his thick grayish hair. "Twelve dollars for a haircut in America. I'll wait until next week when I'm back in India. Calculated in rupees, the same amount would feed a family for a month."

"I still want to go to India someday."

"You will." He smiled. "How is your husband?"

"He's fine, but nothing has changed."

"In India, divorce is almost unheard of. Even in the worst cases of abuse, women must stay in the marriage.

Something nice about America is that women can have some freedom, even in marriage."

"Sure, I have some freedom, but what's the point if you don't have love. I've tried, Father." I lowered my head. "But this marriage is doomed."

"I pray everything will be fine for you." Father Michael leaned forward. "How's your writing?"

"I finished my book and have queried agents."

"You'll get one."

I smiled. "You're so sure. Makes me feel like everything will work out. "

Father Michael folded his hands on the table. "It will."

"How's Sagai? I'm still praying for him."

"And he prays for you. He, like you is struggling—"

The waitress interrupted out conversation to take our orders. I ordered a cheeseburger. Father Michael, the same.

After she left, I asked, "My life is so twisted. Do you think I'll ever get it all straightened out?"

"One saint said, 'God writes straight through crooked lines.' However life gets entangled, entwined, God straightens the lines because He loves us. We only see it all clearly, looking back at the path we have traveled on. I told Sagai the same thing back in India."

I shared my reason for not becoming Catholic and he nodded in understanding.

"I do need a church, though. My brother is studying to become an Anglican priest. He says they are very Catholic."

"Yes, Anglicans are very close to us. I know of a Roman Catholic priest from India who came to America, married, and is now an Anglican priest here."

"Maybe I can find an Anglican church."

"You'll find your way."

Father Michael shared stories about his work in India and I hung onto every word until Grace got fussy, signaling time to leave. We said our goodbyes and promised to keep in touch.

At home, I pulled up to the mailbox, then tore open a letter from one of the agents I'd queried. She wanted my full manuscript!

"Grace, Father Michael was right." I kissed the letter and thanked God just as a SUV pulled up alongside my car.

I lowered my window. Two of my neighbors, in spandex work-out clothes, waved from the front seats of an SUV. The driver, Tammy from across the road, fanned her red face. "We're a mess. Just worked out at 'Bodies for Christ'."

Sarah, her passenger, smiled "It's a new gym where we sweat for Jesus."

"I'm sure He appreciates that."

Tammy leaned forward. "A few of the ladies of Magnolia Circle are getting together for a Bible study on Tuesday afternoons at my house. Bring Grace. We'd love for y'all to come."

I thanked them, then on Tuesday, with our children playing at our feet, I became a witness to real southern prejudice. It wasn't about the color of skin or faith differences amongst the ladies. A deep chasm divided the neighborhood—stay-at-home moms versus working moms. I received instruction on how to deal with unsaved moms from the working side. It was acceptable to wave and smile when we encountered them on the sidewalk.

"After all," as one woman put it, "they might see how charitable we are, and a door may open for conversion."

Sarah pulled out her notes. "Today we begin our first session: 'God-Centered Marriages'."

I glanced at the door, wondering if anyone would think it weird if I grabbed Grace and ran.

"First, a quiz. Who comes first in our lives?"

"The Lord." The women chorused.

"Good! And second?"

"Spouses." Few responded.

"Third?"

"Children." Most chimed.

Before I could disagree with that popular Christian ideal, Tammy leaned forward with a smirk on her face. "Ladies, y'all know that if our children were hangin' off a cliff-side branch with our dear husbands, we'd stomp our spouse's fingers to get to our babies." Tammy slouched into the couch and crossed her arms. "Y'all aren't being honest. The dang dog comes before Glenn in my house."

"Amen." I agreed wholeheartedly. A few eyebrows cranked a notch.

"That's why we all need this study." Sarah offered a weak smile and tucked a lock behind her ear. "Our husbands *should* come first."

Half-way through the hour, with Sarah quoting Scripture to prove God could make our marriages perfect, I offered a concept. "God can't fix every marriage."

Knowing smiles, glances, and a collective leaning forward told me I was road-kill.

"We're not stupid." Tammy handed her fussy preschooler a juice cup. "We know y'all have serious issues in your marriage."

Did they know I didn't sleep with my husband? Were they peeking in my windows after dark?

A shadow of guilt passed over Sarah's face and enlightenment fell upon me. They planned this session for me. A bible study formed to address my messed up marriage. The ladies of Magnolia Circle figured out I had a bad marriage without me saying a word. They were good. I'd become a documented case study. Years later, they'd say, "Rebecca? Oh yeah, that damned-to-hell girl with the most unbelievable, ungodly, problematic marriage in history. Well, this was what we did."

Tammy set her child on the carpet of toys. "If it weren't for seeing Nate pull in and out of the driveway occasionally, I'd swear you were a single mom."

"God forbid." I picked up Grace and bounced her on my knee. "I might have to go to work, then."

"Offer it up." Tammy leaned forward. "It's cheaper to talk here than pay a shrink."

I stifled a sarcastic laugh. The Ladies of Magnolia Circle had no idea what they were asking me to offer up.

"Are y'all even going to church?" Tammy reached down and picked up the tipped over juice cup.

"I'm looking for a church. Nate's Catholic."

Sarah clapped her hands and wiggled in her chair. "So why don't you become Catholic? I'm Catholic. Your family can come to my church."

I sighed. "Unless you're name is Harriet, you won't get Nate into the parking lot of a church." I put Grace back on the carpet. "And my situation is complicated. It's not possible for me to become Catholic."

"Have you tried marriage counseling?" Tammy asked. "We have a great program at my church."

"My husband won't go. He doesn't want to change. I can't change him. I doubt God can change him. I'm filing for a divorce as soon as I get my financial…"

The D-word caused hands to fly to mouths, crossed legs to uncross, and heads to shake.

"God hates divorce," one woman said.

"We'll all commit to daily prayers for your marriage."

Sarah, though sweet, was a naïve one. "Won't we, ladies?" She pleaded with the crowd.

They nodded like bobble-heads.

"And for Nate to get saved." Tammy wiped crumbs from her child's face.

It's not that I doubted God. But He gave us free will, and Nate was all about free will. I'd been preparing for the divorce, writing amounts over the grocery bill, stashing extra allowance from Nate, taking clothes to consignment stores, and working out a plan. Prayers or not, I wasn't budging from Father Stan's sanctioned serpent mode. "I've really got to go."

By the time I gathered my purse and Grace, the ladies were discussing Nancy, a working mom with an excess number of beer bottles in her recycle bin.

"Bless her heart," Tammy said.

In the south, a gossip session could be called a Bible Study, if you blessed someone's heart at the end of every sentence. In any situation, as long as a heart got blessed, you could say anything.

A few weeks later, I heard from the agent. She accepted Kara's story and would submit it to editors and publishers.

Page 273   Holly Michael

So, while I waited for good stuff to happen, I set aside
my marriage woes and fell in love with motherhood. When
Nate honored us with his presence—between long working
hours, business trips, and fishing trips—we functioned in a
semi-peaceful polite existence. He didn't attempt to bond with
Grace and that worked for me. If he didn't love her, he
wouldn't care about custody; an odd, but tolerable existence.

Six months later, my agent had a taker on *Lessons of
Love*. While the ladies of Magnolia Circle prayed, I remained
in serpent mode, one happy step closer to my goal.

Sagai

In the heart of the campus, Sagai sat on a carpet of
purple blossoms under the canopy of the Jacaranda tree and
examined the envelope. Tampered with again. Superiors still
censored his mail, even as a seminarian nearing the end of his
twenties.

He breathed in aromatic scents in a courtyard lush with
flowering trees and rose bushes. The campus—a white washed
three-storied building surrounded by coconut trees—was its
own garden city within Garden City of Bangalore.

Father Michael had written from America. He'd be
arriving home soon. His advice was to chill and if necessary go
into serpent mode. Odd advice from the priest. Had his
American friend introduced those words?

A small tubular flower landed on the page. Sagai
brushed it aside and folded the letter. He'd reply later. Studying
for his Theology major, leading youth group, organizing music

programs, assisting the rector at the English Mass, and helping another local priest with a Tamil congregation, free time remained a rarity.

The next week, permission granted, he traveled to Sheveroy Hills to attend his brother's wedding. He arrived as sunlight outlined the hills and tree tops. That same evening, as the mist fell in waves of opalescent vapors, he would have to leave to take college exams.

In the church where Sagai served as an altar boy, his brother stood stiff and nervous. Sweet perfume from flowers and incense satiated the sanctuary. Handsome Vijay—suited and booted and his hair slicked back with coconut oil—stood at the altar beside beautiful jeweled and veiled Vasanthi, wearing a brilliant red silk *saree*.

The couple exchanged garlands and expressed vows of devotion and lifelong love. During the blessing of the *thali*—the yellow string that signified their togetherness—the couple's eyes met, then lowered. Timid new love.

Vijay tied the *thali* in three knots around his bride's neck. In the Hindu tradition, the three knots stood for the gods, Brahma, Vishnu and Rudhra, but Christians claimed the symbolism to mean The Father, Son, and Holy Spirit. Earlier, Vasanthi would have attached a gold locket embossed with a cross onto the *thali*. The *thali* would always remain around Vasanthi's neck, even if something should happen to Vijay. To avoid evil spirits, elderly relatives threw colorful rice grains in all directions after the service.

During the reception in the church hall, after a meal of rice and *sambar* with curd served on a damp green banana leaf, Sagai bid his family goodbye and waved to the newlyweds accepting gifts on the stage. He could only offer prayers.

As the bus descended around twenty-two hairpin curves, he looked into a black nothingness and battled pangs of loneliness. He thought of Rebecca in America, whom he prayed for daily. He wondered what she looked like and what she thought of this man across the world whose name crossed her lips each night, according to Father Michael.

Never time for thoughts of women, tonight he allowed his mind wandered to what it'd be like to have a woman look at him the way Vasanthi looked at Vijay. He took a deep breath. Using the sublimation techniques he'd learned, he prayed the Psalms.

Returning to campus before dawn, he had just settled into his cot when laughter outside his corner window drew him to peek out.

"What fun we had in Mysore." Joseph patted Savio on the back.

"Everyone will think we were on weekend ministry." Savio chuckled. "Now all we have to do is sleep for a couple of hours and show up for breakfast."

Whistling sounded in the hallway. He rushed across the cell to his door. The rector, always up early for his walk, headed toward the courtyard stairs. His friends! He stepped onto the veranda and shouted, "Good morning, Father Santosh!"

Too late! The rector intercepted Joseph and Savio climbing the stairs to their private cells. "Brothers, where have you been?"

Sagai met the group. "They are waiting for me to join them for our early morning jog."

Father Santosh smiled. "Ah! Good! Such health-conscious seminarians."

"Yes, Father," Joseph stretched his leg on the stairs. Savio circled his arms.

Stronger bonds of friendship between the three brothers increased as the months progressed toward the end of the academic year.

On the morning of Community Day, the day all of India celebrated *Holi*—the festival of colors—the sound of running water and familiar laughter rose to Sagai's open window. He stepped onto the veranda and peeked toward the back of the building. Joseph and Savio dumped buckets of water in the ditch beside the coconut trees.

When Savio returned to the outdoor faucet to refill his bucket, he glanced up. "Come down. It's time to settle scores."

Sagai curiously approached his friends.

"We don't have colors to toss for *Holi*, so we're tossing mud." Joseph stirred the mud with a stick. "Join us in some fun."

"Why not?" Sagai flung his arms wide open. "Better we're camouflaged. Hit me."

Joseph flung a bucketful of mud. Sagai wiped sludge from his eyes, and the three waited at the edge of the building. A few unsuspecting students on their way to breakfast became victims as the three doused them with muddy water.

The fun was on!

A few minutes later, Joseph rushed to the side of the building. "Savio. Sagai. Hurry. The staff!"

As the sludge slinging continued behind the building, Savio, Sagai, and Joseph filled their buckets and hid behind an outside wall as professors descended the inside courtyard stairs.

"Father Simon is mine." Joseph raised his bucket. "Since he's come back from Rome, he's been too snobbish. He needs a mud bath."

"Father Santosh gave me an unfair mark." Sagai readied his bucket.

The two priests descended the stairs.

"You should not get mud on God's holy man." Father Simon, realizing what was about to happen, wagged his finger.

Savio and Sagai looked at each other, tossed the mud on the two, then ran back to a ditch full of students, grown men, acting like little boys. The three friends fell into the pit roaring in laughter.

For days, Sagai worried about repercussions, though never a mention, and serious days of study and examinations followed.

During August, the community celebrated Independence Day. In high noon heat, Sagai stepped onto the outdoor stage for the flag-hoisting ceremony and delivered his speech.

Ascending the stage to raise the flag, Savio winked. "Now, watch the fun."

Sagai hustled down the steps and joined Joseph in the front row. "What is he up to?"

His friend's eyes twinkled with mischief. The gathering stood for the national anthem. As Savio saluted the raised flag, Joseph fell from his chair, landing at Sagai's feet.

"Oh my God!" Savio leapt off the stage. "Joseph has fainted. Heat exhaustion!" He lifted his tall friend in his arms.

"Savio, are you squirting out real tears?" Sagai rose to his feet. "What fine actors."

The crowd of nearly one hundred students and guests pressed around the drama as one friend, carrying the other, ran to a shade tree. Savio dropped Joseph in the grass.

Under the tree, Joseph's acting skills waned as he smiled and opened one eye to the face of an angry rector. Sagai stood near them, biting his bottom lip to hold in the laughter.

"This is outrageous and disrespect to the national flag!" Father Santosh shook his fist. "Because of this and your Community Day antics, you two…" He glanced at Sagai. "…and you, will have a delayed ordination."

He had waited this long. Three months more didn't matter.

After his classmate's ordination to the diaconate, Sagai and his friends, seated in the courtyard, took charge of Community Day. At age thirty—fifteen years since he began his journey toward priesthood—this Community Day would be his last.

"Let's have a bar." Savio, always the prankster, drew a picture of a bar in the notepad on the courtyard table. "We'll offer beer and wine."

"We need more excitement," Joseph said.

"We can dress as characters and tend the bar," Sagai suggested. "But what kind of characters?"

"We'll dress as nuns." Savio sketched a nun in a habit, behind the bar.

"Like the *hijras*, dressing as ladies?" Sagai crossed his arms.

"Just for one night." Savio laughed. "Don't worry, holy man. "It won't become a way of life for any of us." He shot a solemn look across the table. "Well, maybe for Joseph."

Joseph kicked him under the table.

"Ouch." Savio rubbed his knee.

The next day, he and his cohorts borrowed religious garbs from a nearby convent. They gathered coconut shells, two each.

On their way home, Savio patted Sagai on the back. "I think Sagai should be Mother Superior, The Bar Maid."

Joseph kicked a stone across the dusty road. "We'll call him Mother Kamadhenu, the divine cow of plenty, mother of all. What do you think, man?"

Sagai had been willing to go along with the antics so far, but now his friends were putting him in the lead role. "Um...what will I need to do?"

"Learn dance moves." Joseph did the moonwalk in the road. "I have a Michael Jackson CD and some others from one of the Bombay guys."

On Community Day, in the campus hall, Sagai adjusted his veil for the opening act, as the other two adjusted their coconut shells. A natural dancer with an ear for music, he'd learned the moves and was ready. The friends, dressed as nuns, moon-walked across the dance floor to Michael Jackson's, Billie Jean. The seminarians roared with laughter. Even the rector smiled, though Sagai doubted he understood the lyrics.

Savio picked up the mike after the dance. "The bar is open, let the party begin." A psychedelic light show heralded the climax of the evening. *Para bailar la bamba*, blasted from the CD. Then, Savio winked at Sagai. "Mother Kamadhenu, the divine cow of plenty, will now dance with the one and only rector, Father Santosh."

Sagai slapped his forehead. "Don't do this to me."

"No! No!" The rector waved his hand and backed against the wall.

Savio shoved Sagai onto the dance floor. "Father Santosh must not decline Mother Kamadhenu's advances. It would not be good karma. Everyone, let's encourage Father Santosh."

"Dance! Dance! Dance!" The crowd chorused Savio's shouts.

Savio forwarded the song to Celine Dion's, *Because You Loved Me*.

"I'm in this deep, might as well give my all." Sagai/Mother Kamadhenu grabbed Father Santosh's hand, guided it around his waist, and waltzed with the protesting priest. A seminarian with a camera slid onto the dance floor and Mother Kamadhenu took the moment to lift his dress and show a little hairy thigh.

The next day Savio had the photo developed, blown up, and copied a thousand times. The students posted it all over the campus, on pillars, bulletin boards, and classroom doors.

"I want all copies destroyed!" Father Santosh ripped copies from pillars during lunch hour in the courtyard.

Joseph nudged Sagai. "I've got more copies. As soon as he leaves, I'll put them up."

After Community Day, on the Feast of St. Joseph in March, Sagai and his friends entered the church to be ordained deacons. Sagai's parents and most of his family sat in the reserved front pew of the crowded church.

After the Liturgy of the Word, the rector cued the candidates. "Let all who are to become deacons come forward."

Sagai and his classmates stepped before the seated bishop.

"In the presence of God and the Church, are you resolved, as a sign of your interior dedication to Christ, to remain celibate for the sake of the kingdom and in lifelong service to God and mankind?"

The ordinands answered, "I am." Sagai's voice echoed from the walls of the church with conviction.

Next, His Excellency examined the candidates, then each took their turn kneeling, promising obedience. The laying on of hands came next. Sagai took slow easy breaths, praying for the Holy Spirit to fill him.

After the assistant rector draped the stole around Sagai during the investiture, he and the others turned to be presented to the church. He caught sight of his parents' proud smiles.

The deacons recessed from the church, following the bishop and the priests. Sagai smiled at his family and released a happy sigh. Academics finished, he'd taken another step closer to his goal. Six months of Diaconate Field Experience followed, after which he'd be priested.

In the narthex, waiting to greet his family, he glanced at his rector who stood with his chin lifted and hands piously folded. He prayed the events at community day would not affect where he would be sent for his next assignment.

Seventeen

Truth and Freedom

Things are not always as they seem...
~ Phaedrus by Plato

Rebecca

For no sensible reasons other than Grace enjoying playtime with Tammy's daughter and my passion for self-flagellation, I obediently walked across the street whenever the Bible study convened.

In three years, the Ladies of Magnolia Circle's prayers had not gained returns. My marriage was not resurrected. Nate didn't get saved. Now deemed as a lost cause, my problems were no longer being offered up. Wendy, a pregnant Magnolia Circle newcomer with an unsaved husband became the new victim.

Toward the end of the Bible study, Tammy made an announcement. "Wendy is getting baptized in my church on Sunday. Y'all are invited."

I set my cup on the coaster and turned toward the new convert beside me on the couch. "I thought you were baptized a few weeks ago."

"That was in my old church. The preacher only said, 'I baptize you in the name of the Father, the Son, and the Holy Spirit.'"

"What's wrong with that?"

Tammy rolled her eyes. "That's why she's getting baptized again. That one wasn't valid. The minister has to say the word, "Jesus," not just "The Son.""

"You should get baptized in my church," one mom said. "Full immersion is the only way."

"I thought Jesus was the only way." Religion made my head spin.

"Wendy, didn't you grow up Catholic?" Sarah sipped her iced tea.

"That baptism didn't count since only an infant baptism." Wendy rested her hand over her rounded stomach.

As Sarah argued with the ladies, I reached for my purse. "I need to go home before my head flies off my body and careens into outer space."

Larry Boy, the Cucumber, had just saved the day when I entered the den where the kids played. Perfect timing. I took Grace's hand, we said good-bye, and crossed the road. Grace hummed the Veggie Tales tune that never left my head. Though Harriet often called Nate to remind him that all of our souls were in jeopardy, Grace was a happy child. I was fine. Nate's soul wasn't for me to judge.

Ironically, though the Ladies of Magnolia Circle reminded me that God hates divorce, I'd come to understand that my only entry into the Catholic Church would be to divorce. Then, since Nate and I were never married in the church, I could go through the process to be received. Harriet's plan of rectifying my marriage would not come to fruition. Rectifying with intent to divorce was hypocritical and I'd spent too many years planning my freedom.

That evening, after saying prayers with Grace and tucking her into bed, I pulled the covers around me and read my Bible. I closed it at Paul's letter to the Romans, where he said *But if we hope for what we do not see, we wait for it with patience.*

I'd been waiting patiently. Finally, *Lessons of Love* was scheduled to be published into a small book in six months. In serpent mode for nearly four years, I'd patiently stayed in my marriage while stashing enough money to rent a small apartment and get by for a few months. Hopefully alimony, child support, and a job would cover the rest.

While I didn't expect to get rich from *Lessons of Love*, I'd had a few magazine articles published and some of my photography, too. I planned future writing projects. Someday my writing would support me and Grace. I'd wanted to return to college, but Nate refused.

Since he punched me after the last time I pushed for access to bank accounts, I was helplessly dependent. Grace and I lived as tenants. I cooked, cleaned, and did his laundry, but we didn't sleep together or share meals. We were pleasant enough with each other, but rarely went out in public together.

I adjusted my pillow and stared into the darkness. In the fall, Grace would start Kindergarten. Soon, she'd realize that most mommies and daddies liked each other.

I fell asleep and later, woke from an incredible dream—clips of woman's life a happy young girl, then the same person a beautiful teenager wanting to conquer the world, then I witnessed her sadness, her pain. Deeper lines etched a more hardened face. Then, like a reporter's voice in a documentary, a calm loving voice spoke. "Tell her I love her. Tell her not to lie down and go to sleep."

I stayed awake for hours thinking about the dream, certain Jesus had spoken. But who was she? Was I destined to meet her? Did she represent me?

The dream popped into my thoughts throughout the next few days, then one morning in the park, I looked up from the bench and saw her. The woman from my dreams watched Grace and the other children playing. My arms tingled.

I rose and introduced myself. She invited me to sit beside her. Her kids were grown, she said, but she lived nearby and enjoyed watching the children play. Her attitude fit her name. Joy, upbeat and inspiring.

Living in the Bible-Belt, our conversation naturally turned to matters of faith, but an appropriate moment to share my dream never presented itself and she spoke as a woman confident of God's love.

"Time for me to go to work." Joy glanced at her watch.

"Where's that?"

"A boutique not far from here." She pulled a card from her purse and scribbled her phone number on the back.

"When your book gets published, call me. I'd love a signed copy."

Later that evening, after I said prayers with Grace and tucked her in bed, she ran her finger across the wrinkles in my forehead.

"Momma, what's wrong."

I kissed the top of her head. "I didn't do something I was told to do. I'm going to do it now. Goodnight."

"Goodnight, Momma. I love you."

"Love you, too." I shut off her light, grabbed my phone, and dialed the number on the back of the card. The woman's voice didn't carry the same happy tone from the afternoon.

"Joy, this is Rebecca. I met you today in the park. This may seem odd, but I must tell you something."

"I'm listening."

"A few days ago, before I met you, I dreamt about you. You were really sad. Then I heard Jesus' voice. He told me to tell you something. He said, 'Don't lie down. Don't go to sleep.' He said to tell you that He loves you."

Silence.

"Hello? Joy?"

A gasp. A sob. She wept before speaking. "I'm holding a bottle of pills. I was going to take them all."

"Oh no! Why? You seemed so happy earlier, so sure of God's love."

"Things aren't always as they seem."

"Do you want to talk?"

A deep heaving sigh came through the phone. "I've tried to believe what I heard about Jesus' forgiveness and new life, but I can't shake the feeling that I'm not worthy." Her voice cracked. "Before I got the job at the boutique, I was in prison. My husband sold drugs, and I was implicated."

"I had no idea. I'm so sorry."

"I accepted the Lord during a prison ministry program. I repeated the lines that I'd been told in prison, but it's difficult on the outside."

"How so?"

"I can't hide from the shame of my past. And if I don't divorce my husband, who's still using, I'll end up back in prison."

"Joy, you are way more than the choices you've made. More than your mistakes. God showed me your beautiful soul and told me that He loves you. He loves you enough to die for you. Is that enough reason for you to live?" The words were coming freely, confidently, as if God whispered them in my ear.

She sobbed. "I've prayed for proof that He really loves me. Now, I know. Before the words were in my head, but now

I feel them in my heart. " A pause on the line, then, "Thank you."

"I've not done anything, but you should've told me the truth earlier."

"You seemed to have a perfect life. I didn't think you'd understand."

"Joy, things aren't always what they seem."

With our earlier façades stripped away, we spoke openly about our lives and our struggles. We talked for hours about divorce, freedom, and the Christian faith and what God would want us to do about our situations.

In the morning, I phoned a lawyer.

Sagai

Sagai exited the bus—stiflingly thick with pilgrims and sages—at Tiruvannamalai, the residence of Lord Shiva. The Hindu god chose to dwell on earth in the form of fire, and in the process, transformed himself into the mountain. In the night sky, the *deepam*—a column of dense fire on the mountaintop remained lit in the ancient Tamil month of *Karthigai,* from mid-November to mid-December.

Wading through a sea of devotees, Sagai wished he could go sightseeing and follow them to the archaic pyramid steeple towers, but he had to catch the bus connecting to Polur. No time.

Given the rector's mud bath and the scandalous thigh-showing photo at the Theologate, Deacon Sagai's assignment pleasantly surprised him. As a young seminarian, during his

college break, he'd served at Our Lady of Perpetual Succor in
Polur, helping Father Jansen, the saintly Dutch priest who
cared for the lepers. He hoped he'd still be there.

At the church gate, an hour later, Sagai met a tall,
slender young priest with wild wavy brown hair.

"*Unakku thamil theriyumada.*" The priest spoke with an
odd accent. A Spaniard? A Tamil speaking Spaniard? Asking
him if he knew Tamil?"*Theriyatti podha,*"

If you don't know Tamil, go away, the priest had said.
Sagai unleashed an onslaught of his native language proving
himself worthy of staying.

The priest laughed and reached out his hand. "I'm
Father Fortunato. You must be Sagai." The rector's zeal in
learning the language proved his heart for the people.

"Is Father Jansen here?"

"He transferred to a parish up north years ago."

"And the leper colony?"

"The Protestants care for them now. We have plenty of
work here."

Sagai followed his superior into the church, noting the
addition of a new high school beside the church. Before
attending a ringing phone, Father Fortunato gave orders in
Tamil for a worker to get the motorcycle.

In the hallway, photos on the bulletin board displayed
numerous smiling youths engaged in a variety of church
activities. Sagai gripped his suitcase. As a deacon he could
baptize, anoint the sick, and marry couples. These Sacraments
and parish youth ministry would keep him busy until
ordination in six months, when he'd hear confessions, celebrate
Mass, and officially bless people.

Down the hallway, he spotted the large wooden sanctuary doors. With the rector still engaged on the phone, Sagai entered the church and knelt before the Blessed Sacrament. With God's help, he'd come this far. "May all that I do here glorify Your Holy Name."

Amma always said when entering a church for the first time, pray three wishes. He prayed for a prosperous ministry, for financial help for his family, and for Father Jansen. He made the sign of the cross and touched his heart, one that pounded with zeal for his new ministry.

Back in the hallway, the noise of a sputtering engine sounded outside. Father Fortunato held the handlebars of a beat up motorcycle.

"This is yours." The priest turned the key off. "It works, at least today. You'll use the church as your base."

"Where is my mission?" Sagai held his hand over his eyes to block rays from the descending sun.

"Muragapadi. Twenty miles from here. It's a low caste village. Untouchables. Father Superior's orders are for you to serve them, convert them."

If Father Superior wanted to punish him, his mission had failed. Mahatma Gandhi had affectionately called the untouchables, the *Harijan*, God's Children. He'd serve them gladly.

Father Fortunato studied him.

"What is it, Father?"

"Father Superior is not fond of you, is he?"

"I'm afraid not."

The priest handed Sagai the motorcycle key. "You're not disappointed with this assignment?"

"Disappointments?" Sagai raised his hands. "I gave them up long ago." He picked up his suitcase. "But as far as conversion efforts, I won't make bulgar-Christians of them, offering handouts in exchange for souls. That would make us no better than the politicians who buy election votes. Conversions should come from a hunger for Christ, not a hungry stomach."

Father Fortunato grinned. "Ah…I see why you ruffle feathers." He placed his hand on Sagai's shoulder. "Speaking your mind, from your heart, doesn't make one popular with superiors, yet in this case, I agree. We cannot buy souls for Christ. We can only be Christ for them."

Father Fortunto showed Sagai the sleeping quarters, then offered a warning. "The caste system has left its gruesome mark. They are secluded, not even allowed to walk into a neighboring village without removing their shoes. Nevertheless, meet people, see to their needs."

After a few sputters and pops, the motorcycle started and Sagai headed down the dusty road. Bullock carts piled high with haystacks made it difficult to see oncoming traffic. He tried to pass, then veered and applied brakes, nearly crashing into the cart as a lorry barreled from the other direction.

Traffic lessened coming away from Polur. Sagai stopped at a petrol bunk near a paddy field where women, while planting saplings, sang Tamil film songs. Ahead of them, on another patch, men guided a plow drawn by two bullocks, turning fresh black mud. He breathed in the rich earthy smell. Smiling field workers waved as he passed. A gentle breeze in his hair, the joy of seeing good hardworking people, and freedom from scrutinizing eyes brought a hymn to his heart. He hummed thanks and praise to the Lord as he continued toward the *Harijans*.

The Hindu belief that humans were born from different parts of god's body—high or low—and designated for specific jobs ought to be eradicated, but Sagai doubted change would happen soon. Christianity also imbibed the caste system. Religious beliefs ingrained in the minds of people were difficult to break. Those thought to be born from the feet of god stayed on the bottom rung of society, untouchable.

At the outskirts of the village, women in ragged faded *sarees* carried heavy loads on their heads—baskets filled with grains and buckets of water.

Sagai turned where the sign read, Muragapadi—a small community of mud huts with thatched roofs. The place appeared abandoned. Animals were scarce, even stray dogs. A few scattered chickens pecked at the ground. No cows. A goat tied to a post near a larger hut watched him pass.

Parking his bike on the dusty street, he found signs of life under a water tank. A crowd had gathered, enraptured at the window of a sun-faded green building. Music came from the government owned utility building, the only concrete structure in the village.

He approached the congregation. Ah, a television set perched on a windowsill. The villagers, lost in a Tamil film song and dance sequence, didn't notice him.

He tapped a young boy on the shoulder.

"What are you watching?"

"*Oliyum Oliyum.*"

Light and Sound, a thirty minute song and dance bonanza from hit Tamil films was a rarity on Doordarshan TV, and only broadcasted once a week on the only TV channel on India's national channel.

The dancing and singing star on the government station, a familiar face, was now the people's Chief Minister. As typical, he'd promised utopian ideologies, but never delivered.

Sagai tapped the young boy on the shoulder again. "What's your name?"

"Venkat, Father."

"Why aren't you in school?"

"Quit."

The large number of children clamoring around the window, necks stretched, and swaying with the melodic song sequence proved Venkat wasn't the only one who'd quit school.

"Who is your village headman?"

"Shankar, the tailor." Another short answer and Venkat turned back to the box that captivated the entire village. Sagai would return tomorrow.

Circling the area on his motorcycle, he didn't see a school building. The children probably attended a government school outside of the village. Though they'd be accepted in the school, their village name would identify their caste and they'd suffer. He'd visit with children and their parents and teach them the importance of education.

Also, he'd talk with Father Fortunato about accepting some of the children at the new high school, boarding them, as well as placing younger kids in other local boarding schools. He'd spend time with them, inspire them to learn, as before. He smiled and turned onto the main road toward the parish, happy with his assignment.

The next day he stopped in front of the hut with the man-made sign that read in Tamil: Shankar Tailor. A sewing machine zipped as film songs blared from the radio.

"Hello! Shankar?" Sagai stepped onto the packed earth floor. I'm from the parish in Polur."

The tailor looked up casually, then, as if waking from a trance, his eyes opened wide. Perhaps the cassock surprised him. "Ohh!" Shankar ran the stitching too far through the saree blouse. He stood quickly, flustered, lifting his hands and nodding. "*Vanga. Vanga* Father. *Vanga*. Welcome." His eyes darted around his hut.

Sagai understood the unspoken dilemma. It would be customary to offer tea, but someone of a higher caste could never drink from the cup of an untouchable. The tailor wouldn't offer him a drink.

The man clapped his hands nervously. A face poked from behind a dusty pale curtain that separated the shop from their home, then retreated.

Though Shankar constantly fidgeted, Sagai spent the greater part of the day there, talking about the community and the needs of the people. Many villagers worked as coolies on neighboring farms or helped dig wells where they could find work. The highest wages might be twenty rupees a day, enough to fetch a meal in a tea shop, only they wouldn't go into tea shops outside their village.

Later, Sagai roamed the streets, talking with children. Adults emerging from their huts or returning from work crossed the other side of the road, or ducked into their huts.

At dusk, before getting onto his bike, he stopped at the entrance of a hut. A man walked toward him, carrying rice and dry goods, probably given to him at the government ration shop. Sagai offered to help.

He looked up with surprise on his face. "No, Father." The young man spoke quietly, shaking his downcast head. "Please."

"Manickam?" A woman appeared in the shadowy doorway of the hut.

"A father has come." His voice was low and serious. "This is Maragadham, my wife."

"Manickam and Maragadham." Sagai smiled. "Your names mean precious stones."

A timid smile spread on the man's face. "We are hardly gems." He set the rice bag on the ground. The couple acted like cowering beaten dogs, but Sagai remained in their doorway.

The woman stepped back, shoulders hunched, eyes cast downward, a shadow behind her husband. "We are no one to even receive you into our home, Father."

"Can I come in?"

"Father, I do not even have a chair."

"It's okay. I'll sit on the floor."

Manickam shuffled his bare foot in the dust, then motioned him to enter. The dark room smelled of cow dung, spice, and stale cooking oil. The shame in their faces made his heart ache. Did this young couple have dreams? Hopes?

"Can you give me a drink?" Sagai purposely asked.

Manickam stared at the mud floor, painted with fresh cow dung. "I have no tea, but I can give water. "Maragadham, get a cup of water for Father."

She went to a mud pot in the corner, scooped out water with a tin cup, and returned. She looked at it, then glanced from her husband to him.

Sagai reached for the water. "Thank you." He gulped it down. "I'm very thirsty."

In the dim tiny room, he noticed a glistening in the corner of the woman's eyes.

"Ayya." Her voice trembled. "A priest accepted a drink from us!" Maragadham knelt before three stones in the corner of the hut, shoved kindling between them, lit a match, and blew into a pipe to light the fire. She set a pot on the stones and flames soon licked the sides.

Her husband coughed and chased smoke. "Ambika will wake and cry."

A hurricane lamp, hanging from the roof, cast the shadows of the couple on their baby in a makeshift cradle, a saree tied to the roof by a rope. Proving Manickam correct, Ambika wailed.

Manickam thrust his hands heavenward and cried, "Not sure what will become of our baby girl. Where will I go for dowry when she grows up?"

His wife wiped tears with the edge of her *saree*. "When she was born, my friends suggested an easy way to get rid of baby girls. Some of them choked their girls to death by thrusting a rice seed in their throat. I almost considered it."

With tears forming in his eyes, Sagai offered a silent prayer for them. "Your baby is a gift from God."

"Don't think us bad, Father, but it is difficult," Manickam pinched the corner of his eyes. "We carry our baby with us while we work."

"Where do you work?"

The thin man banged his hand against on old mat and stretched it on the floor. "Please Father, sit and I will tell you of our plight."

The men sat and talked while Maragadham added rice to the pot.

"I am a bonded laborer. My father borrowed a hundred rupees from a landlord to take care of my mother when she struggled to deliver me. As I grew, the debt grew with me. I am now thirty-five. My parents are long gone. The interest has compounded over the years. Our children will suffer this debt too."

Sagai sighed, then shook his head in outrage against the landlord. Only money could free them.

Ambika, content in her mother's arms, made sweet babbling sounds.

Sagai thanked the couple for their hospitality and returned to the parish, taking the matter to Father Fortunato.

The priest listened sympathetically. "I can't promise anything, but meet the landlord and find out the amount owed."

The next day, Sagai followed the landlord's servant through the courtyard into his large, freshly painted concrete home outside the village. Inside the parlor, the man sat on a swing—a sign of opulence and authority. His feet swept the marble floor.

"I've come to work in Murugappadi." Sagai hid the anger in his voice. "I met Manickam and Maragadham. It seems they owe you a loan."

"That's true." The landlord stretched his arms around his paunch.

"Could you tell me how much, Sir?"

A large gold chain hung over his starched white shirt. He stood and the pure white *vetti* touched the top of his leather sandals. "What is it to you that these dogs work? Their grandfather and their father owe me. If I did not give them work, they die."

Sagai balled his fist, but kept his arms tight to his side instead of reaching for the man's throat. He hid his revulsion. Couldn't lose sight of the goal. "Tell me how much they owe?"

"Ten thousand rupees." His sonorous voice echoed off the high ceilings.

"Would you let them go for less?" Sagai swallowed hard, forcing down spit he wished to expel at this man.

They went back and forth as if bargaining for goods in the market.

"Two thousand rupees, final." The landlord flung his hands out. "But I own their hut. They must get out."

Sagai agreed and sped back to the parish. Father Fortunato said he'd get the money from the church accounts along with a small amount for them to begin their lives.

"Thank you, Father." Sagai pressed his hands together and bowed.

The next day, he carried Manickam on back of his motorcycle to the landlord's house. The wealthy man accepted the money with a grunt of disapproval.

Arriving back at the hut, Sagai tossed the bond into the fire. "You are free."

Tears of joy rolled down Maragadham's cheek. "Ayya!"

"Now leave this village and go where people mingle freely and where you won't be labeled." Sagai placed his hands on the man's shoulder. "You are children of God. Never doubt your worth. Your caste should not determine your future or your fate."

"Is it possible?" Manickam's voice cracked.

"It is. Stop by the church and thank God and the parish priest for making it happen. Father knows someone in Chennai who might give you work, but go where you wish, and prosper."

Sagai returned to the village every day, knocking on doors. The people, distant at first, eventually warmed to him. He spoke about the importance of education and arranged for their children's admittance in schools. If some of the young people could leave the village and shake the grip of the caste system, they'd have better lives and could help those left behind.

Six months passed quickly. Along with his work in Muragapadi, Sagai also assisted at the parish, preparing couples for marriage and performing ceremonies. At the end of his diaconate field Experience, Father Fortunato called him into his office.

"I have spoken with Father Superior and recommended you for ordination." He shook Sagai's hand. "You will make a fine priest."

Eighteen

A New Life

*You will go out in joy and be led forth in peace; the
mountains and hills will burst into song before you,
and all the trees of the field will clap their hands.*
~ Isaiah 55:12, The Bible, *NIV*

Rebecca

Six months after helping Joy pack, and saying goodbye, I loaded my minivan and left divorce papers on the kitchen table.

Finally.

I chided myself that it took so long as I buckled Grace's seat belt, then turned out of Magnolia Circle for the last time.

"Momma, are you sad?"

"I'm sad because of what your father did to you."

Grace looked down and pinched her pointer finger. "Are we leaving because of me?"

I took the first right into a parking lot, unbuckled Grace's seat belt, and pulled her close. I kissed the top of her head. "You are a sweet, beautiful girl. Daddies should never call their daughters bad names. They should never hurt their children. We are leaving because it's the right thing to do. We should have left a long time ago."

Holding Grace in a tight hug, I rubbed the fingertip bruises on her arm where Nate grabbed her. She'd woken early, peeked in the office on her way to my bedroom, and discovered her father taking money from a stash he'd hid in his gun safe. I reasoned he was hiding cash in the event of a divorce.

She had startled him and piles of cash fell to the floor. He swore at her, grabbed her arms, shook her, and threatened she'd be in big trouble if she told me about the money. Once he left the house, Grace came straight to me and shared what happened, her tears and sadness breaking my heart.

I sniffed. I could deal with him playing the same stash-cash game I'd been playing, but I could not forgive him for the abuse to Grace. I pulled my girl close. She may need therapy, but for the moment, she needed love. My love for her poured into the best smile I could muster. I lifted her chin, tilting her head toward my face.

"You have a grandma and a grandpa, aunts and uncles, and lots of cousins who already love you. We're going to have a great time. We'll drive for a while, then stop at your Aunt Michelle's house. Emma is about your age. You'll have so much fun. After that, we'll drive to Grandma and Grandpa's house."

Grace looked at me with a trust that made me turn away in shame. I'd held onto the divorce papers for six months, waffling. Why?

I buckled her in and checked the clock on the dash.

Almost three o-clock. With the minivan parked in the garage, I'd stealthily packed since morning. I should have told one of the neighborhood ladies that we were leaving, but I didn't want to deal with any God hates divorce talk. Sarah always spent three o'clock on Friday in the adoration chapel. The church was on the way out of town. I'd stop in and say goodbye if I found her there.

In the driveway outside the old stone Catholic Church, I looked up. The steeple spiked into a blue cloudless sky. Bells pealed three times. Sarah's Holy Hour. The time of Jesus' death when His divine mercy is plentiful, she'd say.

"Why are we stopped, Momma."

"I'm looking for Sarah."

"There she is!" My neighbor pulled up in her SUV and parked beside me.

"Your game is in your back-pack. I'll be right outside the car, talking to Sarah."

After explaining my circumstances to my friend, I looked at her warily. "I told you prayers wouldn't fix this."

She pulled me into a tight hug. "You're doing the right thing." Sarah nodded toward the church. "I'll sit with Grace if you want a moment. Go ahead. You'll feel better."

"I'm not Catholic."

"Jesus won't mind. He's there, like a friend, waiting."

With shaking hands, I pulled the iron handle of the large wooden door. Sarah was wrong. I didn't feel the assuring presence of Jesus, my friend, waiting for me. I shivered, blasted by a powerful rush that wasn't air conditioning. I'd stepped before God, The Father Almighty. I understood the term, Holy fear.

Like Moses, I could almost hear God saying, "You are on holy ground." I wanted to run. I backed up, reached for the door handle, then shook away my fear. This was not the time to run.

A white-haired woman, lips moving in silence, knelt and held a rosary while facing a statue of Mother Mary. A balding Spanish man remained trance-like on his knees before the monstrance, the place where God dwelt in the form of a consecrated host. My heart thumped so loud, I thought it would wake everyone from their enraptured states.

I slid into a small pew in the back. God could be everywhere, in the woods, in the church, in the midst where two or three gathered in His name, but there was something holy as well as chillingly mysterious in this place.

A middle-aged lady wiped away a tear, transfixed on God on the altar. Was He speaking to her now, filling the chapel with silent words, satiating the place with His holy breath?

Be still and know that I am God, came to mind. Did I recall that passage from Scripture, or was God, in his God-voice, talking to me?

I knelt and thanked Him for my life and for Grace. I handed everything over to His management my fears, insecurities, and my desires. I asked Him to lead me on the right path. I placed my palms forward and in complete submission to His holy will, I whispered "I am yours, completely, now and always. Take my life. Lead me."

A sense of separation pulled me from my body, as if drifting somewhere between the chapel and Heaven. Six again, I danced in the meadow, feeling His intense love. I didn't meditate myself into that state. Love just rushed in and nearly knocked me over, like a big puppy, pouncing and licking me with wet kisses.

I breathed in deeply and consciously returned to the present, feeling washed in Holy Peace.

"Thank you, Lord." I wiped away happy tears. Having committed my life, my now, and my future to God, I was ready to embrace anything.

Sagai

Sagai bounced on his toes. The church bells pealed. By the twelfth gong, he was ready to fly to the altar to be priested. In this same church, years ago, he'd handed Father Louis his alb. The priest explained that the garment represented the robe of mockery placed on the Lord before His crucifixion. Chills ran down his spine. White symbolized innocence, chastity, purity, and the joy of those who have been redeemed by the blood of the Savior.

The procession moved. Sagai's heart skipped a beat. The thurifer, a teenage altar server in a red cassock led the procession, swinging the gold thurible suspended from chains, up and around in circles. The sweet aroma of incense rolled heavenward on smoky clouds along with Sagai's prayers for God to fill him with the Holy Spirit.

Behind him, the solemn crucifer raised the heavy brass cross high above his head. The choir sang, "I bind myself to Thee today…" Sounds as majestic as thunder streamed from the pipe organ.

He folded his hands over the cincture around his waist, the knot reminding him of the rope that bound Christ to the pillar during flagellation, signifying chastity, temperance, and self-restraint.

Proceeding down the aisle, he finally reached the reserved front pew beside his family. Nearly a thousand souls packed the church to witness a bishop ordain a priest during Sunday Mass.

After opening prayers and Scripture readings, the bishop called out Sagai's name.

"Present." He raised his chin and stepped forward. Relatives smiled and nodded. Amma's eyes shone with pride and tears. Appa walked with him to the altar where he would formally give him away to the holy order of priesthood. His father held both hands in his, one hand covering, the other hand supporting, one last time, then squeezed his son's hands and let go.

Appa returned to his seat, and the bishop asked Father Superior to testify that Sagai had received proper training. Sagai held his breath. Surely the man wouldn't compromise this day, would he? No. He breathed again as the highest authority at the church, responded that Sagai had been prepared and approved for ordination. God alone had brought him to this place and time, not this man.

"We rely on the help of the Lord God and our Savior Jesus Christ, and we choose this man, our brother, for priesthood in the presbyterial order." The bishop spoke in a gonging sing-song voice.

Applause, shouts of thanks be to God, rang through the church.

The bishop's gaze cut deep. "Are you willing to serve Christ and his Church as a faithful priest?"

"I will!" He boomed wholeheartedly. Then the bishop, taking Sagai's hand in his, asked if he would willing obey the authority of the Church and his religious superiors. Sagai answered yes.

As the choir chanted the litany, invoking God's saving mercy and the intercession of all the saints to send down the Holy Spirit, he stretched flat before the altar of God. On the cool marble floor, he surrendered his body, mind, and soul to the Lord. He humbly prayed for the outpouring of the Holy Spirit, to be God's instrument.

Entranced in prayer, he drifted weightlessly somewhere between the church and heaven. A peace that could only have come from the throne of God washed over him. Bathed in an intense warm love, he lost sense of time and wanted to stay in that ethereal place forever.

"Sagai, wake up. It's time."

In a place filled with the sweet breath of the Ancient of Days claiming him as His own, and sounds of beating of angel wings, Sagai heard Appa's voice calling him to serve Mass.

Someone poked him. "Sagai, it's time!"

That voice wasn't Appa. He opened his eyes. It was Father Michael.

On shaking limbs, Sagai took Father Michael's cue and approached the altar, knelt before the bishop, then closed his eyes. This ancient ritual, done now to him had been performed since the time of the apostles to validly ordain men to the holy priesthood. The bishop placed his hands on Sagai's head and invoked the power of the Holy Spirit.

A line of priests stepped forward to lay hands on him. In total submission to God, a powerful whoosh of unending, unconditional love rolled from the top of his head and rushed through to his toes. He swooned. Father Michael's strong hands steadied him.

Opening his eyes, he blinked back tears. His favorite priest adjusted his diagonal stole, worn as a deacon. Now it fell parallel on his shoulder, signifying the yoke of Christ, reminding him of the words of Jesus. My yoke is easy; my burden is light.

Father Michael lifted the chasuble off the altar rail. Sewn for him by Carmelite nuns, the ornate gold vestment shimmering in red and gold sequins stood for the Lord's coat without seams for which soldiers at the cross cast lots. Also signifying the purple cloak Pilate ordered placed on Christ as

King of the Jews. Wearing it meant putting on charity above all things. Saint Paul had appealed to the Colossians, regarding that.

The bishop sanctified Sagai's hands with holy oil of Chrism. "May the Father who anointed Jesus through the power of the Holy Spirit preserve you to sanctify the people and to offer sacrifice to God."

With hands wrapped and bound in a linen cloth by the bishop, Sagai spread the tips of his fingers to touch the holy vessels which contained the sacred Body and Blood of Christ.

"Accept from the holy people of God the gifts to be offered to Him." The bishop held the vessels. "Know why you are doing this and imitate the mystery you celebrate. Model your life on the mystery of the Lord's cross."

And with that final admonition, Sagai was presented before the congregation as a priest!

Finally! A priest forever after the order of Melchizedek! Thank you, Jesus!

His throat tightened and a rush of excitement and relief escaped in a soft utterance of pure joy.

During the time of communion, he reverently held the Body of Christ and gently placed it onto Appa's tongue, then Amma's, then continued down the altar rail.

After the recession, he returned to the church and ceremoniously blessed the bishop, Father Superior, and the other clergy, beginning with Father Michael. His parents knelt before him. Sagai drew back. A son could never bless a parent, but now, as a priest, he could.

He made the sign of the cross. "I thank you for my life and I bless you in the name of the Father, the Son, and the Holy Spirit."

Stepping from the sanctuary, carrying the chasuble back to the sacristy, a quiet voice whispered in his head. *To become a priest is to begin to suffer.*

"I will accept it all, Lord. My now and my future are in your hands."

Nineteen

Beginnings and Endings

"New Beginnings are often disguised as painful endings."
~ Lao Tzu

Rebecca

The remaining flash of daylight disappeared below the Kentucky horizon. Cushioned by her favorite Teddy bear, a pink fleece blanket, and a Dora the Explorer pillow, Grace slept in the passenger seat. I prayed for happy little girl dreams to fill her head and soften the harsh nightmare of the day gone by.

I drove on, dodging emotional tornadoes that careened me all over the place. Uncertainty flung me into the ditches of doom. There, I shielded myself from flying shards of trash. Bad mother! Pathetic loser! Homeless! I slid into despair, burned with heat waves of anger, and shivered from chilling fear.

Then God laughed at me. That's right. I heard him. "Sorry, Lord."

How could I forget? Only a few miles behind in Tennessee, I entrusted my life to the One who knew how to create a universe, calm the wind, split a sea, bring dry bones to life, and a whole lot of other stuff.

I should be covered.

I called Michelle and explained that I'd left Nate for good. Like a good sister, in spite of the emotional and physical distance of five years, she welcomed me back. "Stay as long as you need," she said. "I've missed you." Then her voice cracked, her baby cried, and her daughter tugged on her sleeve. She agreed to catch up when I got there.

I hoped to spend a night or two with her, then head north to White Gull Bay if my parents would have us. Father Stan and Father Michael might approve of me divorcing Nate, but Mama stood a little more rigid and orthodox than Catholic priests.

Grace murmured in her sleep, then opened her eyes. "I love you, Mommy."

I stroked her cheek. "I love you too, my sweet girl."

She closed her eyes and slept off as quickly as she'd awoken. Her heartfelt, innocent expression of love caused me to raise my heart to God and repeat the same sentiments. "I love you, Lord." A whisper in my mind, a gentle "I love you, too, my sweet girl," returned to me.

After a few miles later, I dialed Eddie. Why'd I let so many years go by without touching base?

"Becca, are you okay?"

"Sorry I'm calling so late. I'm driving to Michelle's house."

"Coming home?"

"I sure want to."

In a long conversation, staring ahead at the quiet highway, I explained my circumstances and the reasons why I'd been away for so long. Eddie responded with compassionate consolation, then we got down to the essentials.

"So, where will you stay?"

"I'd like to stay in the coop."

"No one's lived there since Heather moved out."

"Where is she?"

"Green Bay."

I glanced at my little angel, sleeping peacefully. "Do you think Mama and Daddy will let us live there? I left nearly everything in Tennessee. I'm coming home with only what fit in the minivan."

"If you can't stay in the coop, stay with us. Barb won't mind."

"You sure?"

"You bet. The girls can bunk together. You can have the spare room. Grace and Amy must be about the same age."

"Thanks for the offer, but I...I...don't know."

"Let it be a back-up plan."

"Grace has dealt with so much rejection, I don't think either of us can take Mama and Daddy's rejection."

"Do you want me to talk to them?"

"Better I call Mama and talk to her. I'll call her in the morning from Michelle's house then let you know what she says."

"Everything will work out, and you'll be here for my ordination to the priesthood next month. I was just looking for your address to send you an invitation."

I smiled. "Looks like I'm collecting priests, but you're Anglican, right?"

"Right! Holy Catholic Church, Anglican Rite. Catholic-lite, as Barb likes to say. She was raised Roman Catholic."

"I assumed Barb was Anglican since she's from England."

"Because of her divorce and the difficult annulment process, she couldn't receive communion. St. James offered her an easier pathway back to her catholic roots."

"Grace and I need a church home."

"Come home, Rebecca. All around, I believe you'll find a welcoming family."

I thanked Eddie and promised to call in the morning after I spoke with Mama.

After midnight, with Grace in my arms, Michelle led me to an inviting bed. I fell asleep in moments.

Waking to giggles, I found Emma and Grace in the living room bonding over a boatload of Barbies; happy sounds medicine for my weary heart.

"In here, Becca." In the kitchen, Michelle spooned oatmeal into Ethan's mouth. "Good morning."

I sat across from her at the table.

"So what's your plan?"

"I'd like to stay for a day or two."

"One more bite!" She forced another bit in Ethan's mouth. "What then?"

"If Mama gives me the keys to the chicken coop, it'll be a good place to start our lives."

Michelle nodded. "What about your book?"

"Comes out in two weeks. I called my agent and explained my situation. She suggested I have my first book signing in my hometown. She wants me to start a new project." I shrugged. "I'll also need a job. Maybe I'll go back to college and get a degree. Not sure. Right now, I want to surround Grace with love."

Michelle took off Ethan's bib, wiped his mouth, then released him from the high chair. "Emma!" Michelle yelled. "Incoming!"

Robust, alluring smells drew me to the coffee maker. I opened the cupboard and searched for a mug.

"Take the one that says, "World's Best Mom.""

"Not sure I deserve that one."

"Don't beat yourself up. You're a good mom."

I added cream and sugar and returned to the table. "I try. It's not easy."

The girls ran in to the room, waving their Barbies and screaming, Ethan giggling and following. They circled the table and ran back to the living room. Michelle rose, instantly settled the issue, then returned.

"As good as those two are getting along, maybe we'll stay here forever."

Michelle stood at the sink, wetting a cloth. "John and I are good with you staying for a while, but I think you should go home."

"I know. That's what I really want."

She wiped the food from the highchair. "Besides, we're planning to move back to White Gull Bay. John wants to open a restaurant there."

"Maybe you can give me a job."

Michelle pointed to my phone, plugged in the charger on her counter. "You should call Mama. Don't put it off any longer."

~~~

Two days later, I stepped into my mother's kitchen after my shower in the coop. Our new home.

Daddy drummed his fingers on the table and Grace watched him intently. When he stopped, she grinned. "Play that tune again, Papa."

Daddy raised his head, waved, and laughed. "You play it back."

She grinned and drummed her fingers on the table in the same manner and looked up.

"Perfect. Smart girl." He reached over and touched the tip of her nose.

They finished their eggs, and he left the table. Grace followed him into the living room. I cleared their plates, then opened the fridge.

Mama entered the kitchen after showering. "Good morning."

"It is a good morning." I pulled out the milk and poured it into a bowl of Mama's homemade granola. "I can't believe Grace and Daddy have become such quick friends. I worried she'd hate men after what happened. She's not used to men and hasn't had a decent fatherly figure."

Mama reached across the kitchen bar and tapped my hand. "She'll have her uncles, too. Eddie just called. He and Barb are on the way with their girls. They can't wait to see you and Grace."

Everything was turning out better than I could've imagined. "When I get a job, I'll get an apartment."

"Stay as long as you like, Becca. I'm sorry I insisted you stay married. I was wrong, but now you're here and in perfect timing. Don't worry about anything." Mama peered into the living room. Daddy was teaching Grace to play solitaire.

She sighed. "I may need to lean on you now."

I set my spoon in the bowl. "What's wrong?"

"Daddy's cancer is back."

I put my hand over my mouth and tears rushed forward. Grace and I were just getting to know him. I'd hoped for new beginnings, not endings.

Sagai

"Denied!" Father Cyril didn't raise his head.

Was there a heart somewhere in the man's stone cold soul? "My father is hospitalized with breathing difficulties. My brother writes that it is serious. Please, Father."

The rector set down his pen. "I spoke with Father Superior. He is going to Sheveroy Hills for a retreat. He will personally check on your father." He smiled smugly and folded his hands, acting as if Sagai should feel privileged at this grand outpouring of love from such a high and almighty king.

Scoundrels! Both of them!

"Change? Can I at least have change to call home?" The parish phone only allowed local calls, and it'd been nearly six months since he had money to call home from an outside booth. Horrible man to turn him into a beggar.

"Come back later and talk to Father Simon."

His chest rose high and he controlled his heavy breathing. Go to the treasurer? For one rupee? Insanity! Yesterday, he had to beg for a few rupees for petrol for the motorcycle to get to college.

Before he reached across the desk and slapped the insincere smile off his superiors face and got thrown out of the congregation, he turned and walked out of the office. The TVS 50 waited outside. He hoped on the college's motorcycle and merged into the regular hustle of morning traffic. Turning toward Marine Drive, he headed to the college where he studied for his Bachelor of Arts. He weaved through the grid of rues and boulevards, past grand white washed villas climbing with purple bougainvilleas. Along Beach Road, a traffic policeman, wearing a red cap—a remnant of the French rule—smiled and nodded. In India's Little France, white cassocks drew friendly gestures. He lifted his head in a half-hearted attempt to return the sentiment.

The quiet beauty of Pondicherry—wide tree-lined streets, the beach promenade, fresh sea air, and finally, clean drinking water—did little to ease the heaviness in his heart.

The denial to go home was another stone piled upon his chest. Immediately after his ordination, he'd been sent to a forsaken place of pure poverty to serve as assistant headmaster, a slave to the domineering rector.

The village's name, *Vanam Partha Bhoomi* translated to "land that looks up to the sky." Rain was their only source of water. From the same reservoir where cows bathed, he would daily collect water, boil it, then drop a *'thethan-kottai'* seed in the pot to separate the mud from the water.

In the mission field, he drank the horrid water, repulsed, knowing that cows and people bathed, even urinated in it. The smell of it made him gag. Drinking it wrenched his gut and sabotaged his entire system. When he shaved in the morning, a face like the dying and dead he'd minister to on the streets stared back at him. He was no Mother Teresa.

Poor Appa, now in the hospital. A year ago, his father had visited him in the hospital after suffering from dehydration. "This is not the place for you." His father held his hand and comforted him. "I want to see you settled, happy, healthy and using your God-given talents."

Now, Appa needed him. He turned a sharp corner nearing the college. Sagai identified with Saint Paul and his affliction. A thorn in his flesh, the apostle had called it. The Bible didn't say specifically what that thorn was, but nothing could prick more than Father Superior. Still, offering his heart, his hands, his all to the priesthood—celebrating Mass and caring for the people this past year brought great joy and peace.

Near campus, he slammed to a stop, bumping his wheel on the Bajaj scooter that now stood perpendicular to his. A girl pulled off her helmet, an attractive young woman with a decorative *pottu* on her forehead. Her thick dark braid lay against her green *saree*.

Horns beeped and blared. Vehicles swerved around them.

"Why are you blocking me?"

"I know where you're coming from, and I know where you're going."

Was she teasing? Such an over-confident smile. "If you know so much, you should know I must get to class. Why would you block a priest like this?"

"I'll see you after class." She laughed, tugged her helmet on, and rode off.

Sagai arrived at the university, still thinking about the girl, her coy smile, thick oiled braid, and the smell of the jasmine flowers when she tossed her head and laughed.

He parked the motorcycle by the ashoka tree, alongside other two-wheelers. He walked around the garden area near the chapel and merged into the hustle of students along the walkways. Passing under the spreading crown of the acacia trees, he reached the college of education.

At the end of the day, she waited at the gate beside her Bajaj. He parked his TVS and approached her. "Who are you and what do you want from me?"

"I'm Shruti. I belong to your parish and graduated from here."

Her name meant music. Like an annoying, but familiar tune, she'd been stuck in his head all day.

She twisted her braid. "How were classes?"

He plucked a small orange flower from a branch that dropped below the high stone wall surrounding the college compound. "Statistics boggles my brain."

Though the girl annoyed him, she delighted him, too. She was like the sun peeking out between torrents of rain during monsoon season. But still drenched in a bad mood after the morning meeting, he wasn't himself. Appa wore heavy on his heart, too.

She smiled, looking from the flower to him. He tossed it nervously over his shoulder.

"I can help. I live close." She pulled on her helmet and hopped on her scooter. "Follow me." She rode away.

A visit to a parishioner's home would be fine, but she didn't treat him like a priest. She slowed, turned her head, and motioned for him.

Obediently, he followed.

She stopped after a few turns and parked her scooter inside an enclosed portico. What was he doing? Obedience to his superiors okay, but not to this girl, yet his feet were moving ahead without a thought, following behind her as she climbed the stairs to a second floor flat.

"Amma, Father Sagai is here," she announced.

"Vanga, Father," said a voice from within. A big woman grunted, eased off the sofa, and shut off the television. He slipped off his sandals outside the doorway and greeted her.

A middle-aged thin woman in a faded cotton *saree,* likely a maid, peeked from behind a curtain that separated the parlor from the other rooms.

"Simi, get Father coffee." Shruti waved the girl away.

"Please, sit, Father." The mother pressed her hands together, then gestured toward a chair.

"Amma, I must assist Father Sagai with his homework." Shruti's tone and look toward her mother had a sharp edge. She seated herself at the desk and shuffled papers to clear a work space. The computer, the tile floor, the sofa, the various knick-knacks in the glass curio revealed a middle class family.

Sweet incense swirled upward toward the enormous Sacred Heart of Jesus picture. Alongside it, thick jasmine and marigold garlands hung over large framed photos of beloved deceased family members. Two sets of grandparents and a man, not so old. Perhaps the girl's father.

Simi offered him a silver tumbler of steamy coffee.

With her arms crossed over her belly, the mother leaned toward him from the couch and whispered. "My daughter has been fooling around with her life, running around with friends. She should be settled." She wagged her head back and forth. "But her Appa, God rest his soul..." She raised her eyes toward the photo on the wall and crossed herself, "He allowed his only child to have a choice in the matter."

"Amma! Please!" Shruti scowled. A curl escaped her braid and framed her fair face. Her frown changed to an angelic smile upon meeting his eyes. "Father Sagai, come. Bring your homework."

"Your daughter will be settled." Sagai nodded to the mother.

The elder woman smiled, clasped her hands, and shook them as if he'd already arranged the marriage, a duty expected of a priest. "I'll take rest then." She heaved herself off the couch.

She left them alone and went to a back room. And uneasiness settled, but perhaps she wanted him alone with Shruti to encourage her to settle. He pulled the chair close to Shruti and breathed in the intoxicating scent from the garland pinned to her braid. His admiration increased when she quickly put sense and order to the numbers.

Glancing at the wall clock, he realized more than an hour had passed. "I must go. I am awaiting word on my father. He's in the hospital."

"I'm sorry." Shruti caressed her fingertips across his forehead. "You have a lot of worries? Hmm?"

Her touch—her soft hands like a healing balm, tempted him to yield to the comfort, to close his eyes… "No homework worries now." He cleared his throat, stood, and thanked her again.

"Any other assignments?" Shruti rose and brushed close.

"Lesson plans." He picked up his satchel.

"Leave it." Shruti opened the door. "Come in the morning before school, and I will have it ready for you."

After evening community prayers, while reclining on his cot in his small cell, a bell clanged, signaling a phone call for one of the priests. He rose and stepped onto the balcony.

"Phone for Father Sagai," the clerk yelled. "It's Father Superior."

His heart raced. He took the stairs two at time, rushed to the office, and grabbed the receiver.

"Your father is fine." Father Superior sounded happy. How odd.

"No need to come."

"But Vijay said it could be his heart."

"He's wearing an oxygen mask, but nothing critical. Stay put. Carry on with your work and studies."

The same sick, sinking feeling when Appa was injured near Little Lake blanketed him like the heavy morning mist in Sheveroy Hills. He shuddered.

The next day, after celebrating Mass and offering intentions for his father, Sagai stopped at Shruti's home on the way to college. She'd worked the lesson plans into a beautiful presentation with charts and graphs.

"Can you show me how to do this?"

"I can show you many things."

Her tone and smile intoxicated him. Was he encroaching upon dangerous territory? Probably. Nevertheless, he met her every day, her mother's desire for her to settle down never came up in their conversations. Some days the girl greeted him at the college, some days she waited outside the church compound.

He guarded his feelings. She offered kindness, homework help, and computer lessons. A true friend sent by God.

Two weeks after he'd met Shruti, he hopped on the TVS 50 to ride to college. She waited at the parish gate, grasping the white iron bars. "I need to talk with you.' Her eyes were red and swollen from crying.

Vehicles beeped their way through traffic. Hoards of walkers moved at determined paces. Ambulances wailed. "Come. We'll meet in the rectory parlor. He led her along the two block walk, past laughing children on a cricket field, past the large stone gothic church, to the rectory. She sat on the bamboo couch and Sagai pulled up a chair opposite to her and leaned in. "What is it?"

Shruti looked toward the doorway, then removed her shawl and turned her palms outward. Fresh cuts slashed through scars on her delicate arms.

A ribbon of pain seared through him as he sucked in a deep breath. "Who did this to you? Tell me!"

"I did it to myself." Her mischievous sparkle was replaced by fearful tears brimming the enlarged whites of her eyes.

"How could you do this? Why?" Such a lovely young woman, cutting herself? It made no sense.

"It helps to relieve the pain. My mother has found an alliance for me." She shrunk in the chair and tugged the edges of her shawl. "I don't want to marry him. You must help."

"Father Sagai." A clerk approached with a red folded paper, handed it to him, and left. A telegram. Maybe news of his father. He placed it in his lap and turned to Shruti, giving her all of his attention.

"My mother will come to arrange for the marriage. You must stop it. I'm begging you."

The door of the parlor opened again. A parishioner asked to see Father Cyril.

"One moment please." He held out his hand, still holding the unread telegram.

"You're busy." Looking hopeless and full of despair, she stood. "Come home after school."

Sagai told the parishioner to wait for Father Cyril. The office would open in a few minutes. He opened the telegram. *Appa. Seriously ill. Start immediately. Vijay.*

Fury and fear fueled him as he rushed to Father Cyril's room and banged on the door.

His superior cracked the door and frowned, splaying his finger and holding up his palm. "Why are you banging like this?"

Sagai shoved the telegram in his face.

The priest pulled his glasses from his pocket, read the telegraph, and frowned again. "I spoke with Father Superior less than an hour ago. He reported that your father is fine." Father Cyril handed him the telegram and dismissed him with a wave. "If there is need for you to go, Father Superior will call."

"My father has been in the hospital for more than two weeks. I must go see him."

"You cannot." Father Cyril folded his hands over his chest.

Sagai didn't have five rupees in his pocket. He couldn't make a call. Nor could he get home. His heart banged against his chest. Not possible to even go to class. He ran to his cell and shut the door. Seated on his cot, he used relaxation techniques he'd been taught at the novitiate to control his breathing.

"Lord, have mercy. Christ, have mercy."

Didn't work. Prayers didn't help.

Surrendering his will to these superiors was destroying him. Lately, he hardly slept. Had he made the wrong choice to have left Appa so young?

Oh Jesus, will I ever see him again?

His forehead felt clammy. He flexed his tingling fingers, numbness had spread to his arms.

"Oh, God! Am I having a heart attack? Help me, Lord." Sagai sobbed, resting his face in his hands. "What's happened to me since I became a priest? Jesus, it wasn't supposed to be like this!"

He grabbed the TVS 50 and rode to Shruti's flat. Perhaps her mother would give him money to go. If they kicked him out of the priesthood, so be it.

Shruti opened the door, her eyes swollen and red. "Amma and Simi have gone to shop."

He opened his mouth to tell her his troubles, but she threw herself in his arms and sobbed against his chest. A rush of protectiveness filled him and he stroked her hair.

She pulled back, wrung her hands and explained that while she was a teenager, the father of a boy she was pledged to marry had spoiled her. The father had recently passed away and her mother, knowing her daughter was no longer a virgin, considered a match with the son best for her.

"I'll speak to your mother." Hatred toward this dead man tightened his jaw and made him grind his teeth on the fury. "You should not marry him." It would be a horrible situation and would only lower her self-worth."

She stroked his cheek with her finger, then leaned in and pressed gentle lips against his. "Get me out of this marriage. I'll do anything. I'll be yours forever."

Stunned, he took a step back.

She glanced out the window. "Better go now. Amma will be home soon."

On his way back to the parish, Sagai's thoughts jumbled in his head and confused him. Trapped and knowing there was nothing he could do to get to Appa, but pray and wait, his worry swung to Shruti. Other priests had girlfriends, but it wasn't right and he didn't want that kind of a life for this girl or himself. He couldn't leave his priesthood and marry.

The next morning after Mass, Sagai found Shruti's mother in the parlor. She asked him to officiate her daughter's wedding.

"Perhaps this is not the best arrangement for your daughter."

She tilted her head and peered suspiciously.

He squirmed then cleared his throat and straightened his back against the chair. "Amma, have you spoken with your daughter about how she feels about this alliance?"

"She will protest any marriage arrangement. I cannot allow her to go on like this, forever running around. She's bringing shame to our house. She will not get a better offer." She folded her hands over her stomach and glared. "You promised she would marry and you did not find her an alliance. She WILL marry this boy."

"Shruti's father had given her a choice—"

The slap to her knee made him shut his mouth. She raised her voice. "Why are you so keen on preventing this marriage?" She cast an accusing eye his way.

Passerby's slowed and stared. He pulled a handkerchief from his pocket and wiped the sweat from his forehead. The woman's red face and open hand evidenced her rage. If not a priest, she would probably slap him. He told her that his exams would be in conflict with the wedding prep classes and referred her case to Father Cyril.

The next day he groaned and rolled out of bed to celebrate early morning Mass. Elevating the host, he prayed.

"Lord, have mercy upon Appa. Heal him. Help me. Help Shruti. Have mercy upon us all." Strength became available in the invisible grace.

As the day wore on, grace and strength spilled from Sagai like air from a leaking tire. The only thing keeping him from disobeying his superiors and going home was money. Trapped, confined, unable to be with his father and not hearing any news, he pushed through the day.

After class, he returned to his cell, faced the wall, and hammered his head against the cinder blocks. Why don't I have enough faith in Jesus to see me through this dark time? Lord, why can't I feel your presence? Oh God, take me back to the mountaintop where you took me on my ordination day. He groaned, slid to the floor, and recalled the psalms that expressed his angst. *Hear my cry, for I am very low. Rescue me from my persecutors, for they are too strong for me.*

The next day, he started the TVS 50 and rode toward the compound gate. Shruti waited there, a celestial vision in blue, standing on orange flowers that still floated from the branches.

"I'm getting married." She twisted the end of her shawl. "This is my fate."

He stared at the handlebars, unable to look her in the eye. He'd failed her.

"I came to say goodbye."

He looked up when her two-wheeler sputtered down the road, then disappeared around the corner. A sob caught in his throat. Too distraught to attend class, he returned to the rectory, parked the motorcycle, and paused at the bottom stair.

I need to draw strength from God. I am a priest. I am a priest. The mantra didn't help. "My world is crumbling," he whispered. "God help me." He climbed mid-way then stopped to slow his rapid breathing. He picked up his foot and took one more step.

A bell gonged—the phone call signal.

Father Cyril walked toward the office from the church. Sagai continued climbing, slowly. So tired. Finally, reaching the top of the stairs, he heard his name.

Color had drained from Father Cyril's face. "Sagai, your brother has phoned. It's your father."

Sagai gripped the railing.

"He's gone."

Twenty

A Time to Die and a Time to Live

The most beautiful people we have known are those who have known defeat, known suffering, known struggle, known loss, and have found their way out of those depths.
~ Elisabeth Kubler-Ross

Rebecca

Outside my parents' picture window, yellow finches and black-capped chickadees flitted about the birdfeeder, harassed by blue jays. Fresh snow weighed heavy on the pine branches. Michelle and I compared puzzle pieces to the box cover, a lovely snowy mountains scene with soft light emanating from a cabin's windows. Beside us, Daddy lay dying in a hospital bed. He would most likely be gone before we completed the puzzle.

Coughing, he hacked up something gross. Before I could rise, Mama stood at his side, wiping his face. This past year and a half, between caring for Grace and a few book signings, I tended to Daddy. Michelle and her family moved back to White Gull Bay, and we all leaned on each other.

The next day, when the hospice nurse turned Daddy to dress his bed sores, he screamed. Michelle and I grabbed our coats and ran. The wails and whimpers from our tough father was more than we could take. We fled to the farm.

Two miles down the road, trifle, cobbler, and an endless supply of yummy English dishes awaited us. To get through this, we did what we had to do. Barb, our British sister-in-law cooked and baked. We ate.

Barb pushed a rolled jam-filled desert, smoothed in cream cheese frosting toward me. "Jam roly-poly."

"I've never been one to pass up roly-poly." Michelle smiled.

"Barb! If Daddy survives another month, I'll weigh two hundred pounds." I cringed. I'd just wished Daddy dead, so I wouldn't get fat.

"No worries. The kiddos will eat them." As sweet as her desert, same for her accent.

"Bus will arrive shortly." My sister-in-law sat across from us on the new island bar they'd installed when they remodeled the kitchen. "Are you both okay?"

Michelle straightened on her stool. "Becca got interesting news today."

Barb hiked up her eyebrows.

"My old neighbor called and said Nate's new wife, Debbie, is expecting a baby next month."

"Lovely as a spider bite."

"Debbie is his high school sweetheart," Michelle added.

"Oh, how dreadful."

I heaved out a load of frustrations in my sigh. "Apparently, Debbie the bimbo prom queen was living in his cabin at the lake since we moved to Tennessee." I'd been so naïve. The only silver lining about her moving into my old house was that she'd been attending the Ladies of Magnolia Circle Bible Study and confessing her sins. I smiled, just thinking about how that would play out.

"Has Grace heard from the arse?" Barb wiped her floured hands on a dishcloth.

I shook my head. "Scumbag didn't even call on her birthday."

Barb crossed her arms. "Elizabeth's bloody father is the same way. Eddie's so wonderful, the daddy she never had."

I cut another brownie in half. "And he's a great father figure for Grace, too."

"Take the whole thing." Michelle elbowed me. "You know you want it."

"I only want half."

Barb leaned on the counter. "Eddie and Daddy spoke last night. Had a lovely conversation. For the first time, Daddy said he loved him."

Michelle set her fork down. "Ma told me she and Daddy had a long talk, and he asked for forgiveness for all the wrongs he'd done. I've had my moment with him, too."

I snatched the other half of the roly-poly-thingy. "I needed to do the same."

The next day, I told Daddy I loved him.

He nodded and said he was sorry. "In the spring. When we let the cows out for the first time. They go crazy. Kicking their legs. My favorite time of year. Watching them."

I offered Daddy a drink of water. He sipped then continued with pauses and labored breathing. "They smell spring through barn cracks. Fresh clover while chewing rotting end-of-winter corn silage. They want to run." Daddy sucked in a shallow breath. "What the hell are you waiting for?"

I jumped, spilling water on the bed.

"Quit sniffling and run!" He closed his eyes, then rallied again, but with a tired voice. "Don't wait 'til you're like this. Live. Be free."

I sat down, stunned by Daddy's word, not sure what he meant about living and being free. Leaving Nate, I freed myself from that mess of a marriage. That ought to be something noteworthy.

I leaned back on the couch and watched the birds at the feeder. Where would I go from here? Finish my degree? Teaching maybe? I'd been busy volunteering at Grace's school and taking care of her, and I enjoyed being in the classroom as a helper, but I had no real plan for my future.

Father Michel, now in Nagapattinam, Tamil Nadu sent me a recent letter. India, always in my heart, might be a dream I'd never realize. I had a child now. Responsibilities.

I set aside those thoughts, and as the beautiful scene on the puzzle came together, Daddy grew weaker, thinner, his face more sunken and gray. One day, I looked up at the sound of a rattle. Daddy's face went as white as the snow outside.

"I've heard this noise before." Mama sobbed and buried her hands in her face. "When my mother died. It's the death rattle."

Michelle called the hospice nurse and I called everyone else. Eddie said he'd call Father Frank, his mentor, and be right over. Those who could handle witnessing their father's death, agreed to come. Heather and other siblings chose to stay away.

Ma braved it all, speaking gentle releasing words of love while Daddy lifted his arms above his head. Father Frank said the final prayers.

"He's trying to get more air into his chest." The hospice nurse wrapped her hands around her stethoscope.

"Isn't it like him to try to prove he's tougher than death?" Eddie stabbed at joviality.

A few nervous laughs erupted. Daddy made a full circle with his hand, palm upward.

"I think he wants us to keep laughing." Bobby moved closer to the bed.

"Or keep living." Watching Daddy struggle cut so deep, I couldn't even cry. I shuddered. His hand dropped and soon he took his last breath.

We buried him in the nearly frozen ground alongside Kara. Two weeks after my father died, I closed my eyes before sleep and saw him walking through a lush green pasture flanked by extraordinary tall pines. He smiled and waved. Daddy was traveling to beautiful places.

Sagai

On the death anniversaries, Sagai lay prostrate in the chapel at Superior House. One year ago, he tossed handfuls of dirt onto Appa's coffin, in the name of the Father, the Son, and the Holy Spirit and prayed the Lord would receive his father into paradise. After the funeral, he returned to Pondicherry and offered prayers for Shruti, buried in a secluded corner of the cemetery for the damned. Though she took her life, Sagai had to believe God's mercy was greater than the church's judgment.

Through it all, he'd never complained against God or doubted His Holy presence, but often doubted himself. The recent blows, one after another, had crushed his spirit, bruised and afflicted his soul. Torrents of distress passed over him in waves every day since the deaths. Only God knew his pain, a Kindly Shepherd carrying him along.

Sagai rose from the cool marble of the chapel floor and walked across the courtyard. For the past year in Chennai, while earning his Master's in Education, he numbly trudged through every hour. Swells of pain and sadness sprung forth when he raised the Host at Mass, during community prayers, and even during the reading of The Word. The Lord wrested pain, sadness, and frustrations from his heart whenever he drew near Him. If not for drawing on strength from his Heavenly Father, he'd go mad.

"Sagai!" Father Michael waved from across the courtyard. "How are you?"

He met his friend at the bench under the crown of a lush green rain tree. The tree, as usual on sunny days, had spread its leaves horizontally, blocking the harsh sun. Tonight, the leaves would fold and lie sideways. This tree was kinder to him than his superiors.

"Come. Let's sit." Father Michael offered a seat with an extended arm.

Many years had passed since he stared into Father Michael's eyes in Sheveroy Hills and prayed the brother would select him for priesthood. Today, Father Michael would see his anger and frustration at a religious order that kept a son away from his dying father. Superiors wrongly assumed his involvement in Shruti's suicide when they gave heed to her mother's claims and questioned him.

"I said a Mass for your father today."

"Thank you." Sagai clenched his folded hands. "Appa had a heart problem. Father Superior was there. A word to the doctor would have gotten him from the ward into specialized care, then Appa would not have died. This community does not help me, Father." He slumped low in the bench. "I'm like a small bird now, unsteadily flying in loops, about to drop. But then the Lord urges me upward, and I go on for a little while again, before I swoon again. I can't go on much longer."

Patting Sagai's back, Father Michael said, "Son, you are destined to fly like an eagle with strong wings."

"Not if I'm continually persecuted."

"Others are jealous."

He straightened. "Of what?"

"Your depth of compassion with people, your direct honesty, your command of the English language. And when you use your honesty and well-spoken English against superiors, it doesn't work toward your advantage or advancement."

"What can I do?"

"Shall we pray?"

Sagai nodded and closed his eyes.

With folded hands, he prayed, "Lord, you have given Sagai a willing heart to work for Your Kingdom. Give him a stout heart to bear his burdens. Give him a believing heart to cast all burdens upon Thee, and in Your loving kindness, restore him with Your Holy Spirit. And may these tests of life make, not break him. Through Jesus Christ, we pray."

Encouragement and prayers eased the pain in his heart, at least for now. He thanked the priest, then wished him well in his new post in Nagapattinam.

Continuing his duties and studies, Sagai lost himself in the great classics. Lawrence's poem inspired him. "I never saw a wild thing sorry for itself. A small bird will drop frozen dead from a bough without ever having felt sorry for itself."

Siddhartha spoke to his soul. This young prince, while seeking enlightenment, overcame multitudes of obstacles. God often spoke to Sagai and encouraged through literature.

Each weekday he continued his one hour commute, each way, to his college. The Chennai sun beat down on a blazing hot congested city with ear-splitting concertos of beeps, pollutant-puking vehicles and potholes that caused the bus to lurch and bump along, often tossing him into laps of unforgiving passengers. God forbid if he landed in the lap of one of the male transvestites. If you didn't give them money, they'd put a curse on you. He didn't have money for a cup of coffee, let alone payment to avoid a curse.

On the last day of exams, he rode the Bullet—the congregation's beat up heavy two-wheeler—to college. Returning, that evening, a lorry carrying a wide load barreled too close. He lost control and headed into the ditch.

"Fool!" Flat on his back, Sagai stared at the sky. The Bullet on its side, several yards away, lay mangled. The driver hadn't bothered to stop. He writhed from pain in his leg, his ankle. He sat up. Blood seeped from a wound below his knee, through a gaping hole of the cassock, turning the white to red.

He pressed his bloody palm against the leg and held it until the bleeding slowed. He stood and stretched his arms and legs. Maybe just a sprained ankle and wounds. Ahead, he spotted a petrol station. He limped along, pushing the beat-up Bullet.

The man at the pump allowed him to make a free call to Superior House.

"I've met with an accident and landed in the ditch about two miles from the rectory."

"One moment."

Sagai touched his leg and waited for Father Thomas to return to the phone. The bleeding lessened.

"All are busy here. Are you able to get back?"

"The two-wheeler won't start."

"Can you push it back?"

"I...I..."

The phone clicked. Did the line cut or did he hang up? Sagai reached in his pocket. Beggars on the street had more pocket money than he. He couldn't beg for another free call.

Sagai limped on, pushing the two-wheeler back toward the community house.

As vehicles whizzed past, with only a hint of the sun above the horizon, the ache of loneliness hurt more than his injuries. Poor Shruti. He'd enjoyed his days with her. If he'd left the priesthood and married her, would she still be alive instead of buried in the secluded cemetery away from the faithful?

He thought about Bindu, her gentle kindness. How would it be to have her for a soul-mate now, a life partner who was always there for him? Someone to go home to at the end of the day, someone who cared. In the darkness, getting closer to the house, the words of the blind man came to him.

Had he chosen wrong paths?

Nearly every day for the last two years, when not riding the Bullet, he boarded the bus for college. A blind man always stood on the platform, quoting Isaiah 40:8 *"Grass withers and flowers fade, but the word of our God endures forever."* He was fragile, human, and perishable. Not a saint. Did God want him to continue on like this until his death? Was this living?

Back at the house, he cleaned and bandaged his cuts. Stuck in a pit of self-pity and anger, he should speak to his confessor priest and work through these unholy emotions.

With exams, superiors granted him a short leave and he returned to Sheveroy Hills. After kneeling at the threshold for Amma's blessings, he gazed toward the corner of the room. The outdoors encroached into his family home. Mud, weeds, mice and maybe even bandicoots could trespass through that entry. The right side of the wall leaned inward as if pressed by the weight of the outside world, just like him. He could not tell his woes to his family, they had enough of their own.

After dinner with his family, listening to their sorrows, he stepped outside for a walk. The stone hedge he used to climb on crumbled like ancient ruins. Scents of cedar and jasmine sweetened the crisp hill station air. Sagai walked the pebbly road.

Grandfather Balu's coffee plantation had surrendered to the domination of thick brambly brush. Fence posts rested against each other like tired defeated soldiers. An investment could return it to a prosperous estate. If he got a job teaching, they could hire workers. His brothers could help.

Sagai entered the chapel at Sacred Heart Church and knelt before the altar, praying for the soul of his father, a great man who taught him so much about life and love. "Lord, please help them. Please help me. What can I do?"

"I understand your pain."

Sagai rose and looked out into the nave. Bala, an old school chum, now the gardener at the parish, sat in the back pew. "I lost my *appa* last year, too. We are in the brotherhood where only God is our Father."

"Thank you, Bala. That is a true saying."

Sagai's friend met him near the narthex and said, "Thank God for Father Superior, so kind to visit your father. We were also blessed with his presence at home. He ate with us then gave money to buy an auto rickshaw and helped other families in the village get loans. All are still talking of what a holy man he is."

Anger, once doused by God's calming presence, rekindled. Father Superior had been to his home. He could have helped Sagai's family, but chose to help others. He could have gotten Appa better medical care, but did not. He stared at the tabernacle with a slow boil growing in his belly. His faith waned. Lord, help me to hold my tongue.

He excused himself and walked home, his jaw sore from clenching. By the time he reached Little Lake, he had new thoughts about his future. Before returning, he'd stop in Nagapattinam and meet Father Michael. Maybe he'd find him an alliance. Perhaps it was time to leave the priesthood.

Twenty-one

Final Struggles, Closure, and New Pathways

"Getting over a painful experience is much like crossing monkey bars. You have to let go at some point in order to move forward."
~ *C. S. Lewis, Anglican Philosopher and Theologian*

Rebecca

I sat at the desk in our cozy coop and re-read Father Michael's last letter and said a prayer for Sagai, who had also lost his father. On the map above the desk, I'd already pushed a pin in Nagapattinam, in the state of Tamil Nadu.

Grace spent the night at the farmhouse giving me a morning to myself to answer mail. Two years had passed since I'd written to Father Michael about Daddy's death. Since then, I'd worked through a plethora of emotions—sadness, loss, divorce settlement issues, anger that Nate never called Grace. The word from the Ladies of Magnolia Circle spoke of a Nate that I never knew, a great father who attended church each Sunday.

I tried very hard to get beyond bitter.

I picked up the pen and wrote about the good things; Grace doing great and loving school, soccer, and her social life with friends and cousins. I wrote about my work—as boring as it was—at the florist shop. I told about my excitement about the photography classes I'd been taking. I relayed that my book sales, though slow, still brought in a little income. I shared that we'd joined Eddie's church and enjoyed new bonds with family and church members.

Outside, daffodils dotted the edges of the driveway. Another spring arrived. I thought about Daddy's story about the happy cows, about freedom, and truly living. Though moving in positive directions, Kara dreams haunted me. Last night, I dreamt I stood on the hillside near the pond. My sister called my name. Sometimes I suffered disturbing dreams that confused Kara with Grace.

I set my pen down, grabbed my coat, and ran out the door.

A few minutes later, at the farmhouse, Barb set a stack of pancakes before five giggling girls.

"Mom, guess what?"

"What?" I kissed the top of Grace's head.

"Last night we slept in the cubby hole in Nicole's room. It was the bomb!"

That was the same deep cubby hole, where I'd stuffed Kara's things. Surely Mama had given everything to charity long ago or trashed it.

A short rap, then the front door opened and my brother Bobby walked in and knelt by his daughter. "Caylee, do you and your cousins want a ride home on the wagon?"

The girls smiled and nodded.

"Can I, Mom?"

"Bobby, will you drive safe?"

He punched my arm. "It's a tractor, Becca. I'm not going to be popping wheelies. Let's go, girls."

The kids bundled up and scrambled out the door. Then Barb blew the bangs from her eyes and poured me a cup of coffee. "Five girls can wear you out. I'm glad they're going to Bobby's and giving me a break."

I took a sip.

"What's on your mind, Love?" Barb asked.

"I need to relive the day Kara died, walk the same path I walked that day. All that happened that day affected everything in my life that followed, especially my bad decisions. It's like an obsession. I'll never be the person I need to be or the mom I need to be unless I can move past this—" I pressed my palms on the table and forced out my breath. "—this block to my wholeness to discover where I really need to be in life."

Barb leaned against the counter. "Shall I come along?"

"I need to go alone." I took another sip and stood. "Can I begin at the stairs?"

"Certainly." She shot me a worried look.

Stopping at the bannister, I thought about that morning. Halfway up the stairs, I remembered when I realized Kara was missing. I had yelled for Heather, asking if she'd seen Kara. She'd peeked from her doorway with a frightened look on her face, her chest heaving, then slammed her door.

That had been odd.

Back in the present, I pondered on Heather's reaction and left the stairs to go outside, the next thing I'd done that day. Zipping my coat against the cool spring breeze, I passed the barns and crossed the field where the flash of knowledge came and threw me to the ground. I knew, at that place, Kara was gone. Fresh guilt cut open deep wounds. Could I have saved her?

Continuing to the crest above the pond, my heart raced. Sweat beaded on my brow and I unzipped my coat. The huge sitting rock. Still there. The last time I'd come looking for answers beyond this spot, Kara's voice whispered in my head, telling me to listen and look. It whispered again.

Ahead, a small red patch in the tall grass to the right caught my eye. Kara's boot! Oh God! I'd put that boot on her the morning she died. The boot made everything real and brought it all to the present, again.

I sat in the brown, tall, winter grass alongside the boot, crying, wondering why it was there. She wouldn't have taken off one boot, then gone to the water. She only had one boot on when I pulled her out. A rustling of grass made my heart skip a beat. I turned, gasped and pressed my hand to my chest.

"Eddie!"

"Saw you walking past the barn and followed you."

"Look." I pointed to the boot.

Then I saw the bones.

My hand flew to my mouth, and I leapt to my feet as pieces of the puzzle fell into place, and I realized the horror of what probably had happened in this spot.

Eddie flattened the grass around the bones with his hand and quizzically shook his head. "Dog bones. And smaller ones. Cat bones maybe?"

"Buddy disappeared that day. He never left Kara's side. And she always had a kitten in her arms, remember?"

Eddie stared with a perplexed expression. "Yeah, I do."

Turning from the site, from Eddie, and still holding my hand to my mouth, my stomach lurching, I looked toward the pond. I removed my hand from my mouth and caught my breath. "Heather admitted Uncle Eugene attacked her the same day Kara died. Kara had asked me to take her for a walk in the woods that morning, but I told her I was busy. The rare times I wouldn't take her, she'd ask Heather."

Eddie put his hand on my shoulder. "What does that mean?"

"I think...Uncle Eugene followed them. I think...while that monster attempted to rape Heather—right here—Buddy likely sank his teeth into the pervert's rotten flesh. Heather probably ran. And Kara...Oh, God! Poor baby!"

My body shook. My teeth chattered. I faced my brother. "He killed Kara. Probably killed her right here along with Buddy and the kitten. Kara had a bruise on her head. Uncle Eugene probably threw her body into the pond."

I wept uncontrollably.

Eddie stood stiff as a board, as if in shock, then rubbed his large hands over the tears that rolled down his face.

"The next day that monster came to the door. Eddie, I saw evil in his eyes. He had a bandage on his arm! He said we'd all be better off without Kara, like he was trying to excuse what he'd done—killed the retarded, unwanted child. I think I knew, right then, he'd killed Kara, but I couldn't—"

"Oh, Rebecca. I...I...I don't want to believe it. I wasn't there that day, but...

"Think about it, Eddie. It makes sense." I crumpled to the ground. "Why didn't anyone else see it? We have such a big family. Why didn't anyone ever talk about this? Heather attacked, possibly raped, Kara murdered, by the hands of the same beast. All the while Mama at least knew he'd made sexual advances on us. Lisa was raped. Michelle said she had an abortion." I shuddered and sobbed. It's horrible!

Eddie took off his coat, put it around me, and knelt beside me. I was shaking, my teeth knocking together, my bones rattling.

"Let's go home." He reached out his hand, and pulled me up, and held me close.

My knees weakened, but Eddie held on tight.

I followed his gaze to the pond. The water was clear. That day, it was murky, when I saw Kara's body floating below the surface. I didn't want to tell Eddie how I froze then ran away. Didn't matter now.

A sudden gush of knowledge, a quiet voice spoke to me. *You are not guilty. I only wanted to warn you to soften the blow. I was with you, always. I stood by you at the pond, weeping too. I will never let you let go of me.*

I sobbed.

Eddie tightened his arms around me, hugging me. He was Jesus' body, hands.

I looked up into my brother's eyes. "I wasn't guilty. It wasn't my fault. I didn't kill Kara. Uncle Eugene did. God never hated me, never abandoned me."

"Of course He didn't."

Ragged sobs shook my body. "It's okay. Let's get out of here."

I slipped my arm around his waist as we walked across the field. I wanted to vomit from disgust at how that horrible man tainted our childhood and affected us all on so many levels, for so many years. "Poor Heather."

Eddie tugged me close. "Becca, what do you want to do now? The man is dead. I know it's difficult, but our faith teaches us to forgive. You can't let this destroy you. I believe it's crippled Heather."

"God has never let this destroy me."

We walked on, through the field. "I can't think of forgiveness now, but I'll deal with it."

"God will help you."

"I know." I looked up into his kind eyes. "Let's not tell anyone, other than Barb. She won't say anything. Michelle's been having difficulties with this pregnancy. I'm not sure how Mama will take it. And Heather—"

"It'll take a lot of prayers and love to help her. She may have buried those memories."

I hung my head, seeing both our footprints in the mud. Now, walking away, knowing the truth. Along with a renewed raw ache of hatred and anger toward Uncle Eugene, a sense of closure blanked me with a measure of peace.

"I remember something about a possible investigation, but seemed the consensus was that Kara had bruises from slipping on a rock before she fell into the water."

"I remember that." Fresh tears rushed from my eyes. "I know we live in a rural area with hometown cops, but wouldn't the autopsy have shown enough for them to continue the investigation?" My knees buckled. I slipped from Eddie's grip and dropped to the muddy field and wept, pounding my clenched fists through the fresh mud. "He killed a defenseless child. I hope he rots in hell."

Eddie once again pulled me to my feet and put his arm around me. We walked toward the house. "God is the ultimate healer, Becca. You're at a good place right now, here with us. Everything will be okay."

Sagai

Laughter and sea breezes drifted through Sagai's open window. He made the sign of the cross, as he did first thing, every day, then turned to a pair of deep brown eyes.

The compassionate eyes of Christ met him from the Sacred Heart picture that hung on the cinder block wall. It was an ordination gift from his father, the first thing he had unpacked before falling into bed last night.

"Lord, bless this day." He rose from his cot and stepped onto cool tiles, crossed the cell, then opened the rickety wooden door that led to a narrow balcony.

In Ennore, on the backwaters of the Bay of Bengal, fishermen disembarked from small boats and catamarans and dragged the sea's offerings to shore. Thick dark braids swayed on the women's backs as they shuffled around nets, choosing the best fish for market and tossing them into bamboo baskets.

Simple fisher-folks. Happy people. He imagined himself a husband, coming in from the sea in the morning, greeting his wife, then going home to his children.

Words from scripture came to his mind. *Come, follow me. I will make you fishers of men,* Jesus had said to his disciples.

Christ's words caused him to take a deep breath, as if he was inhaling them into his soul, sealing them onto his heart. "I will follow you always, Lord."

Gulls screeched and dove at discarded fish. Sagai returned to his room. After speaking with Father Michael, the truth remained clear. God had called him. Though he grew weary and desperate at times, he cherished his priesthood.

Peering into the tiny clouded square mirror hanging above the sink in his bathroom, he fingered strands of gray, peppered in his thick wavy hair. Father Michael promised his support through any decision. Though prepared to take a leave from his order, he changed his mind when Father Superior offered him this post.

His first day as Assistant Director of a Youth Animation Center. Anima in Latin meant breath, life, soul. His assignment to infuse spirituality into the souls of young people proved his heart's desire. Maybe Father Superior's heart was softening. Maybe the contents of his file were not such a big concern anymore.

He finished shaving and threw himself into his work, preparing for the first group of college students who would arrive in a few days for their weekend retreat.

By evening, he discovered the utopian view from his balcony was only a mirage. Trash floated in filthy water. Ammonia, puked out from a local fertilizer plant, stung his nostrils. Swirling gusts of wind rounded up the noxious fumes and deposited them into his room, the only priest's room that faced the sea.

At two in the morning, other coughs chorused with his. He went to the balcony and descended the cement steps that emptied onto the shore.

"*Ennanga Sowkiyama.*" Sagai greeted a man about to push off in his small painted wooden boat. His smile revealed warped singed teeth. Low rumbling coughs and whistling wheezes interrupted the predawn stillness.

"How do you cope with this pollution?" Sagai pressed his handkerchief to his mouth.

"We got used to it." The man frowned. "We petitioned the factory to move out, but they were here before us. Nothing we can do." He stepped into the boat. "You'll get used to it."

Sagai crossed his arms and watched the vessels push off to sea.

In spite of the recurring putrid smells, Sagai continued his work, offering an environment where Christian, Hindu, and

Muslim youth opened themselves to spiritual guidance and fine-tuned their relationship with God. Impassioned and full of energy, he facilitated sessions on group dynamics and leadership, empowering them with confidence.

Peaceful faces absorbed his meditations like flowers seeking the sun. In the evenings, guitar in hand, Sagai gathered everyone around campfires. They sang, danced, and told jokes. The director had given him free reign with the program while Father Abraham, a stout elderly fellow, assisted him.

Days were long, the work busy, but for the past year, Sagai found peace and fulfillment. His biggest problem became a shortness of breath.

One weeknight, a fresh outpouring of noxious waste left Sagai feeling like someone cranked a band tight around his chest. He couldn't breathe. He rose, choking and gasping his way to Father Abraham's cell.

~~~

"This is an excellent hospital." Father Abraham patted Sagai's shoulder. "Doctor Ramasamy, the chief doctor who ordered your tests, certified the death of former Prime Minister Rajiv Gandhi after his assassination. When he heard you were from the animation center he arranged this private room. You're in good hands. I'll take leave now."

"Thank you Father."

After he left, Dr. Ramasamy, a tall slender gentleman wearing wire-rimmed glasses and a goatee entered his room and patted Sagai's toes. "Don't worry, Father, you will recover."

The good doctor moved to a chair beside him. His dark eyes probed Sagai's, as if he were looking beyond the patient, beyond the priest. "Kumari, my elder daughter, attended one of your seminars. I had heard about your good works at the center and sent her." His eyes became glossy. "Perhaps I placed too much stress on her to follow in my footsteps. She had a difficult semester at school, a boy had jilted her, and she failed exams." His voice cracked. "She made a suicide attempt."

Sagai remembered the girl. "I'm sorry, doctor. How is she now?"

"Thanks be to God and to you, she is well. She's back in college and pursuing Clinical Psychology instead of Medicine. Your teachings helped, not only her, but our entire family."

He smiled. "They are the teachings of Christ. I am only his servant."

"I have two more daughters, and I would like to send them to the animation center under your direction." Doctor Ramasamy rubbed his goatee and paused. "But given the spots on your lungs, I must recommend you be moved from that facility."

Sagai sighed.

"Tell me your troubles." The kind doctor pulled up a chair as if Sagai were his only patient, and Saga poured out his worries about his future in the priesthood.

Each day, during the doctor's visit, personal, discussions continued. Sagai always turned to Christ for restoration, but this Hindu doctor showed love in flesh, a man who cared for his body and soul.

A week after his arrival at the hospital, Father Abraham returned. "I have news." He drew near Sagai's bed. "I returned from Superior House. Father Superior sent a replacement and has a new assignment for you."

"Where?"

"Vellore."

"I know it. Spent my Aspirantate there. A professorship?"

"Assistant teacher at an evening college."

Sagai gasped, then held his hand to thwart the pain in his chest. "That's a demotion!"

Father Abraham's voice had a touch of sadness. "You will never flourish under that man's rule. He only cares for members of his own caste. Before his term, I worked with him and watched him with his little notebook, scribbling notes, looking for faults instead of helping priests." Father Abraham sighed. "His assistant, Father Thomas is ditto, the same man. Nothing will change."

Sagai sunk lower and stared at the ceiling.

"You're qualified to be a professor or a director of an animation center. You're a capable, good-hearted priest."

The next day, when Doctor Ramasamy arrived, Sagai shared Father Abraham's news.

"Maybe God has a different path for you." The doctor removed his glasses. "I speak as a father would to his own son. Sometimes God calls us in new directions. Tell me. What do you want from life?"

Sagai laughed. "I'm not used to that question. I'm used to being told." His answer didn't require much thought. "I want to help others, especially those who feel suicide is the only answer. I'd like to earn a degree in Psychology, but I've always been denied that request." India is hard on its youth. He remembered Shruti, and the doctor's daughter, and other desperate souls he'd counseled over the years.

At Superior House, in a world map on the wall, red pins marked places members of his congregation had been. Father Superior had sent Victor to Rome to earn his degree in Biblical Theology, he now served as a professor at a prestigious college in Chennai. Others had been sent to England, Germany, and America. Savio was in New York. Sagai had passed that map many times and told himself those places didn't exist for him. He reminded himself he'd vowed, on the mountaintop, to always put people first.

The kind doctor interrupted his thoughts. "In your sacred text, there is wisdom: 'For I know the plans I have for you,' declares the Lord, 'plans to prosper you and not to harm you, plans to give you hope and future.' Anything is possible with God."

Sagai smiled. A Hindu man, with the heart of Christ, quoting his favorite Scripture passages.

Doctor Ramasamy handed him a laptop the next day. "My gift to you. Create a presentation of your vision. Share it with Father Superior. If he shares your vision, seek that path. If not, consider other options."

Sagai worked through the night preparing a presentation. He envisioned a counseling center with a crisis hotline, with satellite centers where youth could come for guidance.

He finished before Doctor Ramasamy arrived the next morning.

"What do you think?"

Doctor Ramasamy smiled. "Excellent. And today I'm releasing you. You are well enough to return to your Superior House. Keep me informed."

In a conference room the next day, Sagai revealed his presentation to Father Superior, Father Thomas, and his associates.

"No." Father Thomas pursed his lips.

One priest shook his head, another chuckled.

"I have a place for you in Vellore; Assistant Professor at an evening college." Father Superior folded his hands. Father Thomas nodded.

Sagai clenched his teeth. He could not allow anger to rule him. "Father, I request a leave from the order."

Father Superior tapped his fingertips together and pursed his lips.

"I will take two weeks to meet with spiritual advisors to determine God's will for my life."

"God has given me His will for you." Father Superior set his pen on the table and stared with hard eyes. Sagai maintained eye contact. The clock on the wall ticked loudly.

"Take leave then. It's best you go anyway." Father Superior picked up his pen and scribbled in Sagai's file. "Return when you're ready to accept this position."

Given barely enough money for travel, Sagai met with Father Antony, his old novice master from Bombay. He concurred leaving the order was best and suggested he become a diocesan priest, but agreed that given his troubles and his file, maybe he should take his leave and seek a new path.

Next, he met Father Michael at the orphanage in Nagapattinam. Sagai poured out his heart "I want freedom from this tyranny. God called me to priesthood. Man called me to obedience. It's a great attribute, but men are fallible."

"If you take this leave, you will not return. Yet, I see you flourishing and serving God outside the order. Maybe you will settle someday, get married. Maybe you will even go abroad as I have done. Pray. Seek God's will. He will open new pathways for you."

Sagai returned to Superior House and entered the chapel and prostrated himself before the altar. "Lord you know what I have been through. Show me the way."

At Superior House, two weeks later, he met an old priest mulling about the compound with his hand out. Sagai reached into his pocket and pressed his remaining traveling money into the priest's hand. "Father, you should not be begging. I'm sorry you have no pocket money. Come. It's nearing dinner time."

He led the elderly priest back to the retired priests' quarters. He opened the door and in one bed, familiar eyes blankly stared.

Father Costello!

The door opened, and a boy delivered two plates of food and set them at the small table in the corner. Sagai picked up the plate and spooned the watery curry and rice into Father Costello's mouth.

The man could not eat. He was feverish. Abject neglect! This once lively bicycling priest had mentored him years ago. Would it be like this for him when he grew old?

Sagai rushed to the refectory. At a table, Father Superior shared thick meaty curry with his cronies as a boy poured water into their glasses. One of the priests nudged Father Superior and pointed toward him, approaching the group.

"Father Costello needs medical care."

Father Superior's eyes met his. "The old priest is fine."

A surge of anger pulsated through Sagai's veins. He balled his fists. He wanted to knock Father Superior out of his chair.

This is not the way. The voice spoke quietly to his soul. He looked around. Others stared and murmured.

"He is not fine. He's feverish and struggling to breathe." Sagai's chest heaved. He lowered his voice and pressed his hand on the table, leaning close to Father Superior. "Don't let him die like you did my father."

Sagai walked away and phoned Doctor Ramasamy. The doctor arrived, diagnosed Father Costello with pneumonia and ordered him to be taken to the hospital.

The next day, Sagai visited Father Costello in a private room as the doctor tended to him. "He's improving. I will take good care of him. Don't worry." The gentle man removed his stethoscope. "Have you discerned your path?"

"I'm taking a leave from the order. I will be exclaustrated, which means I will live outside of the community while I discern a departure from my order."

"What are your plans?"

"I'll teach somewhere, maybe find employment in a private school."

Doctor Ramasamy smiled. "Father, I've waited for you to reach this point. I have a building and property outside Chennai, in Royapuram where I've built a nursing school. I've wanted to expand it to include a youth counseling center. Your vision matches mine. I have contacts with the government for building grants. I will take care of your college fees so that you can earn your Masters in Counseling Psychology. In the meantime, you can handle the English department at the nursing school. I believe God has sent you my way.

"Doctor! Your generosity." Sagai fell before him. "How can I thank you?"

Doctor Ramasamy pulled him from his knees. "That is not necessary. You're going to be very busy."

Twenty-two

Crossroad and Calamities

Each one has to find his peace from within. And peace to be real must be unaffected by outside circumstances."
~ Mahatma Gandhi

Rebecca

Driving home after Grace's confirmation, we stopped for a stroll along the beach before the party at the farm. At Evergreen Lane, Grace and I took off our shoes and walked the pathway to the shore.

"I didn't think I'd remember all of the prayers." My beautiful ten-year-old looked angelic in her white cotton dress.

"You did fantastic."

"I knew all the answers." She flashed me a bright smile. "The bishop said I should come to Saint James Cathedral in Kansas City and teach the confirmation class."

Grace stopped to pick up a flat stone.

"Uncle, I mean, Father Eddie was a good teacher." It still seemed odd to call my brother, Father.

"Yeah. It's cool having a priest uncle."

Though her uncles were all great role models, I often wondered if her father's absence worried her. "I'm sorry Nate didn't respond to your invitation."

Grace picked up a stone. "I'm sad sometimes, but he's the one with the problem, not me. Do we really care, Mom?" Grace answered the question for me. "No, we do not."

I stopped to pick up a flat stone.

Grace skipped hers. "Three skips. Lucky day."

I skipped mine. "Ha! Three times for me, too."

Grace put her arm around my waist. "Mom, our stones are on the bottom of the lake now, along with all the junk we've been through. Let it stay there."

"Good advice! I let go of her hand. Race me to the car, and we'll go back to Uncle Eddie's and eat confirmation cake!"

Weather grew colder in White Gull Bay and I rose from my bed to turn up the heat while Grace slept upstairs. I couldn't sleep, tossing and turning. For months, unsettled feelings often kept me awake at night. I ticked away possible reasons in my mind.

Grace? She was the happiest little girl, loved her small country school she attended with her cousins. She was fine.

Kara's death? No. Eddie and I never talked about what we assumed happened at the pond and committed to praying for Heather. She'd moved to San Francisco to live with my oldest sister. I was certain God remained at work in their lives. Michelle and I prayed for them daily. Kara was in Heaven. I'd given whatever happened at the pond to God. I was okay with all of that.

Mama and I were on good terms. She happily offered the coop rent free and stayed busy; Bible study, volunteering at church, and taking classes at the community college. She found her peace and I let go of past issues, chalking them up to stressful times and difficult circumstances. Forgiveness is essential in moving on. No one is perfect.

I had no financial woes. With the divorce settlement, Grace's child support, a few book sales, and my work as manager at the flower shop, I'd socked away a good amount of money.

Lonely? Though I had Grace, I did want to meet someone. I'd gone on a few dates, but no one special. After my first marriage fiasco, God would have to show me who to marry. I'd been praying, but he hadn't put anyone in my path. I felt confident that someday he would, so that wasn't keeping me up at night.

Unfulfilled dreams. I sighed. Oh, that thought struck a deep chord. I hadn't written anything since the book about Kara, but didn't feel inspired to write.

India, another unfulfilled dream. Not the right time to think about that. I had Grace to care for now. I flipped on my side. My India dreams were vicariously lived through letters from Father Michael, still in Nagapattinam. Maybe that was all God meant for me. Father Michael shared about his work in the orphanage, which always fascinated me. And as always, in his last few sentences he updated me on Sagai and asked me to continue my prayers. The younger priest had taken a leave from his order and worked at a counseling center called, the Snegam House, which Father Michael said, meant friendship in Tamil. I'd never seen a picture of the man, but for the sake of putting a face to my prayers, I imagined he had dark curly hair, a square strong jawline, and deep brown compassionate eyes like the man in my dream, from years ago.

As the months passed, I grew more bored with my job, more stuck in a rut, and encountered more sleepless nights, but looked forward to a big Christmas celebration at church and with family.

Christmas Day began with a beautiful Mass celebrated by Father Eddie and later, dinner and a celebration at Mama's house, with presents for all of the grandkids.

At the end of the day, as soon as we sat on the couch in the coop, the phone rang. Grace ran to answer it.

"Mom! It's Uncle Father Eddie. He said to turn on the TV."

I stared in horror at the news. An Indian Ocean earthquake had caused a tsunami in South Asia. The affected area included Father Michael's orphanage!

Sagai

At the Snegam House in Royapuram, Sagai spoke to a roomful of young men and women in leadership training. Kumari, Doctor Ramasamy's daughter—poised to take her father's place—sat in the front row.

"Close your eyes." He facilitated the meditation using the prayer of Saint Francis. First, he used breathing techniques to help them relax. Then, the prayer: "Lord, make me an instrument of your peace. Where there is hatred, let me sow love; breathe out hatred, breathe in God's love.

Where there is injury, pardon; breathe in forgiveness, breathe out hurts, wounds, all the pain others have caused you."

He paused, giving the trainees time to contemplate. Many times, for nearly three years, he'd done the same meditations, considering his own wounds. He'd forgiven his superiors. Here, at the Snegam House, he'd earned his master's degree in counseling psychology and lived in peace and happiness, but this was a temporary place.

His leave of absence from the order was almost up, and he'd have to make a decision. Should he leave Snegam House and return to his order? With her degree in clinical psychiatry, Kamari would make an excellent director.

"Where there is doubt, faith." He walked slowly among his students. "Think of the moments you doubted and replace being unsure with faith. Say this aloud, 'I believe'."

Lord, I believe you will show me the way. Eyes still closed, Kumari smiled, a look of pure peace and serenity on her face. Her future included this place, helping at her father's center.

What would bring Sagai true peace? What path should he take? Conflicted, he missed saying Mass every day, serving as a priest, but according to Father Michael and others nothing had changed in the order. Clergy who fit into the system thrived. He'd always floundered, but did that mean giving up his priesthood?

"Where there is despair, hope. Think of a desperate situation, a time when you felt hopeless, where other's pronounced doom and gloom on you and your life situation. Replace their wrong declarations and your hopelessness with hope."

He'd been persecuted, told he had no calling, ridiculed. Even if he left the order and served as a diocesan priest, he might fall into the same situations. Kumari had suggested a different route. Marriage.

"Where there is darkness, light. Think of those who are lost, in darkness. Visualize bringing the light of Christ to them. Where there is sadness, joy. Think of all of the sad young people, perhaps they've lost self-respect, dignity, or have no support system—think of bringing smiles to their faces. Think of the joy God has brought to you."

What gave him joy? Continuing in the priesthood? Marriage? He ached for companionship, for someone he could love and who would love him in return. Kumari, happily married, had encouraged him to find a spouse. But marriage meant giving up the priesthood. If he chose marriage, he'd ask Father Michael to find someone for him. He'd pray, and decide.

Sagai drew the meditation to close with the words, "O Divine Master, grant that I may not so much seek to be consoled as to console; to be understood as to understand; to be loved as to love. For it is in giving that we receive; it is in pardoning that we are pardoned; and it is in dying that we are born to eternal life."

At his amen, Sagai felt the earth move—literally—and opened his eyes. "What was that?"

"An earthquake?" A young man stood. Sagai, Kumari, and the students rushed outside.

A child ran past building shouting: "The sea has flooded Marina Beach, onto the road, even to the buildings! Run!"

Twenty-three

Rebecca and Sagai

And we know that all things work together for good to them that love God, to them who are the called according to his purpose.
~ St. Paul to the Romans, Romans 8:28

Two weeks after the tsunami hit, I stood at the airport and said good bye to my family. Couldn't believe I was flying to India. I'd called for three days before reaching Father Michael on his cell phone.

"Come, Rebecca. Nagapattinam is devastated. Many have died."

Within two weeks, our church had raised several thousand dollars. Mama presented me with a check; my family pooled donations for my ticket to India. Father Michael made arrangements for a driver to pick me up in Chennai and take me to Nagapattinam, where I'd stay with a group of relief volunteers from the city. My agent recommended I collect stories and write a book.

"Wish I could go with you." Eddie hugged me. He wouldn't be going anywhere. His bishop, in need of new priests, wanted to send him to another church, but given Barb's pregnancy and his desire to remain bi-vocational and farm with Bobby and Tom, he opted to stay in White Gull Bay.

Mama hugged me tightly. "Be careful."

I grabbed Grace and hugged her one more time. "Mom, you're going to smother me to death. You always wanted to go to India. I want you to go. I'll have a blast with Emma and everyone. I'll be fine. I'll see you in three weeks."

Michelle hugged me again. "Don't worry. We'll take good care of her. You take care of yourself."

~~~

Forty hours later, after a breakfast of *idli* and *sambar* at Father Michael's rectory at an orphanage, I wrapped the *dupatta* around my shoulders and followed him to his office. Upon my arrival in Nagapattinam, Father Michael outfitted me with the typical Indian garb—a long tunic shirt over draw string pants, and a matching *dupatta.*

The priest pointed to the line on his office wall where the tsunami waters reached. "It flooded the compound to nearly four feet." He shook his head. "Coffins were unearthed in the local cemetery and floated this way."

He wasn't the same man I'd met in America. Graying, older, and naturally shaken by the recent horrible events, the priest walked to his desk and sat with a heavy sigh and told how he waded through the waters to save children. He cried, described the horrifying moment when debris brushed against his side and he discovered the body of an infant.

After insisting I didn't need rest, Father Michael and I stepped into a car that would take us a few miles to the beachside village to meet the group I'd be staying with.

In spite of his sadness, he showed rock strong character in this strange land as he moved with fluid ease between languages, speaking Tamil as he counseled survivors coming in an and out of his office, speaking Hindi with the driver, and translating bits and pieces of it all into English for my ears.

En route, the driver dodged colorful wooden fishing boats, busted up in the streets—just as the tsunami left them, smashed against houses and trucks, spread across railroad tracks and broken underneath bridges.

When I pointed out the smoking piles in fields along the roadside, Father Michael's eyes grew sad. "Are you sure you can bear this?"

I nodded. "If I'm going to help, understand, and write about this experience, you need to tell me everything."

Father Michael explained that the smoking piles along the roadside were bodies being burnt. "Mass cremation is the only way to contain contamination. Some villages have run out of kerosene to burn corpses."

After a few minutes, the car stopped. "The volunteer group is working in this village."

We walked along sandy paths, littered with branches, through topless coconut tree groves. Father Michael spoke to a man who picked up a coconut from a pile, whacked off the top with a machete knife, stuck a straw in it and handed it to me.

"Tender coconut is good for digestion."

As I sipped on the semi-sweet juice from the hairy shell, in the warm tropical environment, Father pointed to a tall pipe on the beach, nearly thirty feet high in the open air. "It's their water pump. All the earth was swept from underneath it." He waved his hand in a wide swath. "Hundreds of homes were wiped out."

I snapped photos. Shards of villager's lives littered the beach and dangled from trees. We continued to walk along the beach, toward a crowd gathered around rubble, busted cinder blocks, and twisted metal.

"The fishermen's overturned damaged boats are now platforms to drink away pain and curse the sea. They said they'll never fish again with the bodies of their loved ones still out there. Fishing is their livelihood. They don't know what to do."

Young boys posed for me, dragging junk from the ocean—bits and pieces of lives offered back like consolation prizes.

On the shore, in the midst of hundreds of freshly planted coconut saplings, grieving voices wailed to a man standing before them.

"Are these new saplings to replace the tsunami damaged trees?"

Father Michael touched my arm. "Rebecca, this is a graveyard. These saplings mark the buried remains of the children."

I pressed my palm against my mouth and tears plunked onto my fingers.

Father Michael shook his head. "I should not have told you to come. This is too much for you to handle."

"Father, you know what my life has been like. I can handle this. I came to help. I'll be okay." I can do this, I told myself. I faced the sea, knelt in the midst of the tiny tree tombstones and framed a picture, capturing a small lone sandal on the shore. A wave rolled in, offering a low melancholy whoosh. I sighed and shook away the wretched despair that cut deep into my heart.

The sandal probably belonged to one of the children swept out to sea the day after Christmas, the same time I celebrated the Holy Day with my daughter. I lowered my camera and took a deep breath. I was here for a purpose and must remain strong.

A young woman with sleek black hair braided down her back approached us. I stood.

"This is Kumari." Father Michael patted her shoulder. "She's a counselor at the center and does wonderful work with the youth."

"Welcome." The pretty woman smiled a bright smile and reached for my hand. "Come, the survivors are so happy you are here. They want to tell their stories to the American."

She led me to a group of young teenagers. "They don't speak English, but I'll translate. I'll give you the names and ages of each child before they speak."

I turned my recorder on and handed it to Kumari, while I readied my camera.

Tamilarasi, a teenage girl, nervously tugged on the edge of her *dupatta* and spoke in Tamil. Kumari translated. "The darkish green cloud became a roaring giant, more than sixty feet high. Women grabbed babies and toddlers. Men dragged kids behind them as they ran. Screaming. Yelling. Crying. People fell in the street. Elders, knocked over, looked helplessly from the street, no clue of what was going on. Then the wave hit the shore, the sound like ten mountains colliding. It rolled fast, opening its mouth and devouring everyone and everything in its way. I was at the market with my little sister and tried to hang onto her, but I couldn't…"

Tamilarasi dropped her head, unable to continue. I lowered my camera, went to the girl and hugged her. Father Michael said that Indians weren't accustomed to hugs, especially from strangers, but the girl buried her head in my shoulder and wept as I stroked her hair.

Composed, she told the rest of her story of how the wave dragged her through the street and shoved her underneath a truck. She pulled her shawl from her arms, exposing scars. "My seen and unseen wounds are no longer bleeding and raw. They're healing. But still, there are threats of tsunami all the time. When I hear the word, tsunami, my wounds seem to tear open again and I feel the pain anew."

I'd write Tamilarasi's story. I understood her pain. I was Kara's record keeper, recording her words in the notebooks, her voice on tape, and finally into a book to inspire others. A wounded soul then, not now. I could write these stories.

Fueled with a peacefulness about my calling and knowing that God worked all things for the good, I met the next suffering soul.

Kumari translated the boy's story. "My name is Venu. I am seventeen, and I raced the wave at breathless speed, tore into our house and grabbed my brother. He can't walk because he has polio. Waters surged behind me, but I dragged him with all my might while running from the waters that had crossed our threshold. We ran into a nearby house that had a second floor and I dragged him up the stairs until it was over. My *appa* did not survive. I am now in charge of the family."

I approached him, held his hands, and looked into his watery eyes. "You were very brave, Venu. Stay strong now. God will help you."

Kumari translated my words, then looked up. "Here is our director. Sagai Raj. He's been looking forward to meeting you."

A man walked toward me, smiled, and pressed his hands together. "Welcome, I'm Sagai. So good to finally meet you."

I sucked in a deep, quick breath. Goosebumps ran down my arms. His brown eyes were soulful and searching. He had a strong jaw-line, a square cut face, and thick dark wavy hair. His smile sent waves of joy through me. I already knew him.

"Hello, Sagai. I'm Rebecca."

The End

Holly Michael, published in various magazines, newspapers, and in Guideposts books is releasing her debut novel, *Crooked Lines*. She and her husband, Anglican Bishop Leo Michael, regularly travel from their home in Kansas City to India. She enjoys watching her sons play football—Jake (NFL) and Nick (Rajin' Cajuns)—and visits from her daughter, Betsy.

Visit Holly at www.HollyMichael.com

Coming Soon

Goodness of America: Ten Years After Tsunami. A sample of America's goodness when tragedy strikes in other parts of the world. Reminiscing on the impact of help on the lives of the orphans, then and now. Holly Michael revisits South India.

I'll Be Seeing You: In Wyoming's Wind River Valley, **Charlie Willow** faces a future more unsettling than the one he imagined upon realizing he was dead. The plan, written into his will, ought to fix his children, but an angel asks for a little more help.

I'll Be Seeing You, her second novel, is an ACFW Genesis 2014 semi-finalist.

Devotional: Holly Michael and her son, Jake Byrne, an NFL player with type one diabetes, are writing a devotional contracted with Harvest House.